THE EARTH IS UNDER
SIEGE AS THE FORCES
OF LIGHT AND DARK...
OF GOOD AND EVIL...
OF LIFE AND [...]
BATTLE T[...]ND.

DEEPAK
CHOPRA'S

LORDS OF
LIGHT

DEEPAK CHOPRA'S

LORDS OF LIGHT

Created by Deepak Chopra
and Martin Greenberg

St. Martin's Paperbacks

This work is published with the permission of Harmony Books, a division of Crown Publishers, Inc.

DEEPAK CHOPRA'S LORDS OF LIGHT

Copyright © 1999 by Boldergate, Ltd.   LONDON FILMS

ISBN: 0-312-96892-2

Printed in the United States of America

St. Martin's Paperbacks edition / April 1999

10 9 8 7 6 5 4 3 2 1

ACKNOWLEDGMENTS

The author wishes to gratefully acknowledge the help and assistance of Rosemary Edghill, who was instrumental in preparing this manuscript for publication.

Contents

PROLOGUE: NIGHT OF QADR—
JUNE 7, 1967 1

ONE: ON THE ROAD TO DAMASCUS 11

TWO: THE GOOD SAMARITAN 60

THREE: WITH THE TONGUES OF
ANGELS AND MEN 92

FOUR: THE CITY OF GOLD 110

FIVE: TOWARD THE UNKNOWN
REGIONS 144

SIX: SMOKE AND MIRRORS 172

SEVEN: ROCK OF FAITH 202

EIGHT: THE WELL OF SOULS 236

NINE: YETZER HA-RA 254

TEN: BROADCAST NEWS 289

ELEVEN: ASCENSION 314

PROLOGUE:

"*Náhga, Náhga?*"

The shepherd stopped shouting. It was useless to fight the emptiness of the desert with one lone voice. He squinted at the sky. The sun hung sullenly, already too bright, just above the jagged horizon where a dark cloud of swirling sand was rising. Left alone at the mercy of a storm, the lost ewe and the lamb in her belly would surely die. The shepherd, whose name was Samir, slung his rifle over his shoulder. He had already packed the rest of his small flock into the truck. They shifted and complained. A warm scent of lanolin and dung rose from their wool.

Samir's face glistened with anxious sweat. To lose the ewe missing from his flock would be a great hardship. He had camped under the shade of a dead volcano jutting up from the desert floor. Perhaps the ewe had wandered up the sides in search of grazing. He set out to climb after her.

The Great Syrian Desert is a volcanic wasteland so hellish and barren that it feels like a declared enemy sworn to defeat human life. Yet the road which leads from Baghdad to Damascus was legendary as a trading route for over twenty centuries. The sands had been fragrant with spice and rich with silk since the dawn of recorded history. But that was no longer the case. Here, in the harshest part of the desert, there is a strange peace now, because there is nothing left that anyone could possibly want to steal.

Just last night the sky had been a spill of stars like diamonds on velvet. Soft as the tread of a desert wolf, the wind that raced before the dawn was still. The thin staticky wail of Radio Damascus, which sprinkled pirated American pop songs in with its tasty mix of government propaganda and fervent religion, cut through the silence. This morning it proclaimed the end of the world—the fall of Jerusalem into Israeli hands.

In the desert's total emptiness the war in Israel seemed far away. No one could hear the echo of hysteria and devastation out here. An old Bedouin shepherd could sleep by his flock, as motionless as if he were one of the rocks himself, his *kafeeyeh* pulled across his face against the cold.

There had been no war when Samir had set out with his flock the week before. Now, the most sacred places in Jerusalem were falling. Samir had his own business to attend to this morning. In a habit born of fear and caution, he rubbed his eyes and turned off the radio so that he wouldn't be distracted from counting his flock.

One, two . . . six, seven . . .

The sheep in the truck were all the wealth Samir had in this world, and he husbanded it with tenderness. Sheepherding among the Bedouin was usually left to children, women, and the old, but Samir's father had been killed last year in a land-mine explosion, and his wife had soon followed, dying in childbirth three months after that.

"Náhga?"

He couldn't help calling for her, even though his voice fell flat against the silence. The wind began blowing steadily out of the south like the draft from an open oven.

Then he heard the howling.

Samir stood stock-still, listening, his ears alert to danger. He knew he was awake, but the howling could have been from a dream, it sounded so much like a soul in anguish. A wolf? A dog owned by thieves? He prepared to turn back and head for his truck. Then common sense took hold. Samir said a soft prayer. "God protect me. There is no other god but God," he murmured to himself.

Walking automatically, one foot after the other, he continued on his way, still worried. He knew the *jinns*, the supernatural beings created by God when He made man and woman, lived in the invisible darkness. They were not friends to human beings but distorted, malicious parodies of them.

A mortal man couldn't see jinns, but he knew nothing was more tempting than the power they held out, and nothing was more sinful than to accept it. He hoped his faith protected him enough from them.

What would a jinn want with a poor shepherd?

As these strange fears were gripping Samir's mind, he whistled and called out, hoping his animal would respond. His legs began to cramp from climbing through the debris that littered the slope. He was about to turn back, his lungs straining from exhaustion, when at last he heard the anxious bleating of the ewe. He spied her a short distance up the slope, standing before a tangle of boulders with (Allah be praised) twin lambs at her side. One was as pure white as only a newborn lamb can be, and the other was as black as the tents of his ancestors. Samir's heart swelled with gratitude: The twins were a good omen.

He reached the ewe before he realized that what he had mistaken for a tangle of boulders was in fact a ridge rearing up out of the bedrock. There was a fissure he had not previously seen in its face—a fissure large enough to admit a man. As he stared into the darkness, Samir could see the flicker of fire playing over the rock walls.

"Hello?" he called. "Is anyone there?"

There was a faint sound from within the cave. Samir glanced back at his animals. They were the only living things in the landscape, but somehow that didn't reassure him. The wind was pulling the sand up into small dust devils, and Samir made the sign of the evil eye against the *shaitan* which prowled the desolate spaces. It would be ill fortune indeed to leave any man alone to die in a place such as this, if there happened to be a wayfarer marooned inside the cave.

"Is anyone there?" he called again, and took a step closer. Then he spied something amazing—two pigeon eggs at his feet and in front of his eyes a spider's web. His heart leaped into his mouth. Every one of the Faithful knew what this meant. When the Prophet was fleeing Mecca, on his escape to the holy city of Medina, his enemies had tried to pursue him and hunt him down. Muhammad took refuge in a cave, not the same one where Gabriel had visited him ten years before but one just as miraculous. He lay down, exhausted, to spend the night. If he was dead by morning, such was the divine will. His enemies scoured the mountainside, but to protect his chosen one, God placed two pigeon eggs and a spider's web at the mouth of the cave, making it seem that no one was inside. From that miracle the future of Islam was assured.

Trembling with excitement, Samir stepped inside. Now he could smell smoke, and he saw the light of a fire. The cave opened out into a space not much larger than Samir's own tent. In its center a fire burned, its bright bed of coals shining orange. A young man with pale olive skin sat cross-legged beside the fire, facing away from Samir and the entrance to the cave. He was quite naked. Long dark hair spilled over his shoulders, shining and smooth.

"*As salaam aleeikom*," Samir greeted the stranger shakily.

The young man did not reply. He reached into the fire, as unconcerned as if he reached into a basket of dates. The youth's slender fingers selected a coal and withdrew it from the flames. The shepherd froze—too astonished even to reach for his rifle—as the stranger began to rub the burning coal over his arms as if he were cleaning himself in living fire.

Samir took a step backward, terrified. At the scuffling sound the stranger turned and saw him.

Black eyes like wells on a starless night, and so cold . . . "Come here." The stranger beckoned. "You must have been sent."

His voice was low and musical; his face held the classic beauty that had graced temple frescoes in the Levant for thousands of years. As he rose to his feet the fire blazed up impossibly, towering as high as a man. The beautiful youth walked into it without hesitation and stood in the middle of the flames.

The angelic young man still beckoned. "Here," he said, smiling as he reached out of the flames. "Don't be afraid. Take my hand."

Trembling, the Bedouin did as he was told. He heard the youth say the God-sent words that he had dreamed of hearing, the fulfillment of his longing to be with his beloved wife. *Qadr*—the power of God's truth—rushed into his limbs. The anointment of the words fell over him: "A gracious and mighty messenger is come unto you, held in honor by the Lord of the Throne." In the sweet protection of those words, Samir knew that the fire could never harm him.

At that same moment, three thousand miles away, black clouds swept in from the Ohio Valley like furious Arabians hurtling across the sky. They brought thunder and lightning in crashing waves, but the baby didn't flinch.

"Look, Ted, how brave he is," the mother said with a smile. She picked up her one-year-old, who had somehow climbed on the windowsill to look out at the storm.

"Hey, Mikey." The father patted his head absentmindedly. "He's a climber. I guess I better take that chair away from next to the stove."

So they're calling me Michael this time. The words formed distinctly in the baby's head, and he looked back over his mother's shoulder at the rain. He had been a Michael many times, he remembered. And he knew Arabian horses, because one Michael had ridden with the Franks on the First Crusade.

"Ga," the baby mumbled, pointing to the sky at the next crash of thunder.

It seemed strange that he could think but not

speak. Images flashed through Michael's head. He saw himself riding a handsome black stallion, compactly built but incredibly powerful, that he had stolen at Aleppo when they stormed the fortress there. It was the holy year 1000, and he had knelt with tears in his eyes at the River Jordan along with all his brother knights. But some dark spell cursed that moment. It was the first instant when killing for God felt wrong—and his tears made him ashamed and weak. He felt a terrible remorse over the children roasted on spits in front of the mosque at Aleppo. He tried to block out the cries of the infidels thrown into pits of fire, and he knew that the other knights were crying for joy, having no idea of what he felt.

In that lifetime he had died in the assault on Jerusalem, scalded by a pot of boiling pitch flung from the old ramparts. He had been glad to escape. His only fear was that he would come back as a soldier again—and fear is a soul magnet. Over and over he had died in arms, until finally he despaired that Earth was anything but a charnel house, a field of death. He vowed never to fight again, and despite the rumbling clouds that loomed in the sky like black anvils, he sensed the peacefulness of the land and the family around him. This time would be different.

"Ga," the baby said again.

"What's the matter, sweetie?" the mother asked. She rocked him a little; he looked like he was about to cry.

Michael looked up into her large brown eyes. It was amazing how much he loved her, this mother. But another part of him didn't recognize her, didn't feel anything but the usual calm that attends a soul on its journey. He was well aware that he shouldn't be seeing himself as a soul. He was a child on a farm in southern Illinois. His soul bargain had placed him here with good people. They would love him; they would be tested by miscarriage, crop failures, the father's depression after a bank foreclosure in the mid-eighties. As much as they stumbled, they would never fall.

Michael's vision faded, the future dimmed. The mother set him down in his high chair. She walked into the living room, where the father was standing in front of the television.

"Honey," she said. "What is it?"

The father didn't look around. "Helluva thing," he grumbled. "Let 'em fight all they want, I'm not going over there." The images of Israeli commandos storming the Golan Heights flickered on the television as the thunderstorm rolled over them.

"No one's asking you to, are they?" the mother said. "Now come in and eat before the food gets cold."

A shell exploded on the television screen, scattering debris across a panicked Palestinian refugee camp. A mass of tanks rolled into Gaza, shooting at some unseen target near the horizon. The father turned off the set and entered the kitchen. He pulled up a chair as his wife set his plate down. He'd started to bless the food when the lights blew; a crack of thunder shook the china in the cabinets. The baby heard scrambling noises as the father went to fix the fuse box on the porch. The mother stroked his arm with soothing fingers. "Don't worry," she said. "It's not going to be dark long."

Dark? Michael didn't understand what she meant. Couldn't she see? It was so obvious. All around the room, forming a shining circle, were a dozen beings of light. They shimmered with radiance, faint blue-white, and their bodies, though transparent, were not ghostly but reassuringly present. Michael knew them all. He gazed at each one in turn, and their luminous eyes gazed back. It would be a safe life this time. The guardians were with him. They had never descended like this before, but now they had accompanied him. Michael relaxed, only slightly troubled that the mother couldn't see them.

At last, after suffering the long journey of his soul, he was safe.

Screams rang off the desert rocks, startling the old ewe out of a placid satisfaction with her offspring. She flung up her head and shuffled down the slope, but when nothing further happened to alarm her, she slowed and stopped.

Time passed. Samir did not return. The sun rose higher in the brassy sky.

There was movement in the mouth of the cave. The young stranger appeared, his face veiled by a kafeeyeh. He was clothed now in the familiar worn robes of a Bedouin shepherd. He carried no weapon, as if he needed none. Running lithely down the slope, he stopped at the side of the ewe and picked up one of her lambs.

"Hold still," he whispered. "Be gentle." The surrounding silence, disturbed ever so slightly, sank back into its hushed repose. The dead volcano didn't wake up; the dome of the sky didn't crack and fall. In that regard, at least, the prophecies were mistaken. The old ewe felt soothed and began to bleat for food.

"Soon," the young man said. He pushed the kafeeyeh aside. Standing in the desert with the black twin cradled in his arms, he turned his face toward the light, looking even more beautiful, and he smiled, posing for a mesmerized audience that was yet to assemble.

CHAPTER ONE

ON THE ROAD TO DAMASCUS

The Middle East, in the spring of 1999

It was the second week in April and the weather was already intolerable, though the *Lonely Planet Guide* said with chipper authority that the temperature here in Syria's Central Desert was temperate in the spring.

Temperate, Michael Aulden reflected sourly, must mean somewhere between ninety degrees and hell—and it wasn't nearly as hot as it was going to get; he knew that from experience. He lit a cigarette and leaned against the sagging wall of the tent. Two nurses flitted past, chattering in Arabic. In the chaos and noise he couldn't hear them, but only saw their lips moving.

"Vaccines shouldn't be sent in here—route them to Tent C," he called out, seeing a clutch of black-veiled tribeswomen with babes in arms. The nurses started shooing them away. More bodies filled the space they left vacant. Michael looked around, unable to shake off his mood. He could hear babies crying and vague low moaning, the elevator music of Hades. The aid station had been thrown together near what had once been the Roman city of Palmyra. It was staffed by foreigner doctors flown in by the World Health Organization, and its medical staff tried to provide some semblance of care for the thousands of refugees who passed through its chain-link gates every year.

The summer before, so everyone said, had been the worst in living memory, and Michael remembered it as hot enough to melt a plastic canteen if it was left on the hood of a jeep for more than ten minutes. Assuming, of course, nobody stole it. And assuming there was clean water to put into it in the first place, and that bandits or terrorists or somebody's invading army didn't shut down the Damascus-Aleppo road, which was their lifeline to what passed for refuge and order in this area.

Michael had come to the Middle East in 1996 as a promising surgeon, fresh out of residency in the U.S., but there was no need for promising surgeons once he arrived. Surgery, even the unpromising kind, was a luxury—the huddled people that he saw every day desperately needed food and water and antibiotics, not heart transplants. He did what he could for them, not what he'd been trained to do. Only the worst traumas got the privilege of making it to the OR. He had now been at it for three years. He was thirty-three years old, and there were times when he felt twice that.

The WHO was a subsidiary of the United Nations, with the express objective of upgrading health standards worldwide. That was policy. Reality was to bring a trickle of mercy to an "emergency" that had been going on for fifty years and looked good for fifty more. There were Kurdish rebels fighting in Turkey. There were Shiite Muslims feuding with Sunni Muslims almost everywhere (their arguments apparently trying for a Guinness record by lasting more than a thousand years). There was God knows what murderous mischief in Iraq. And between them, Michael complained to himself, every conflict, like all roads to Rome, bled refugees into Syria, the displaced hordes moving west and south toward some imagined refuge. They were turned back by the thousands at every border crossing, but still they came, a vast suffering tide that all the world's charity couldn't stem. But here charity was—in the person of the United Nations—passing around teacups on Hell's Riviera.

Michael stamped out his cigarette and got back to work.

"I need another suture kit," he called. "Check if we're down on saline bags, and you medics, listen up—give priority to war casualties, if we have any." That last bit was in the way of a grim joke. Three "bus drivers" had shown up on foot, nearly blown to bits. Someone, apparently for political motives that had exploded with him, had blown up a bus. The passengers were Iraqis, in Syria illegally; the army had simply buried the dead on the spot, then rounded up the survivors and trucked them back across the border. Those who were neither dead nor alive had wound up here: an increased strain on the mission's capacity. Michael wrapped a bandage around the scalp of the least wounded. The young man, who couldn't have been more than sixteen, whimpered. "Just a sec," Michael said, trying to be easier. He assumed this "bus driver" was probably one of the terrorists. This fact didn't make him feel angry or outraged; one gained a kind of numb acceptance.

Inside the triage tent the light was bright even through canvas, but what blazed in through the open tent flap was too intense to be called sunlight. It was a radiation so lurid that he still somehow expected it to make noise—to roar, perhaps, like a high-powered engine or one of the long-extinct desert lions. It seemed impossible that light could have such force.

Let the supply convoys make it through, Michael prayed almost absently. *Let there be enough water this year.*

The prayer was futile. He already knew there wouldn't be enough of anything. Not for the WHO medical team and not for the mad tumbledown city of cardboard huts and scavenged shelter scattered around the hospital huts. Without the bleaching desert sun, the stench of ordure, refuse, and unwashed bodies would be unbearable. As it was, the air smelled of despair.

He finished bandaging the young terrorist's head, and the boy jumped up, reaching into the cargo pocket of his fatigues. Despite himself, Michael backed off, ready to cover his face. But what came out of the pocket wasn't a grenade.

"Thanks," Michael mumbled, accepting the dirty orange held out by the boy, who smiled timidly. It wasn't nice enough to be fruit from Israel, which made Michael vaguely thankful. He didn't want to think that the orange had been snatched from a corpse after a border raid on the Golan.

Remember, you wanted to come here. The automatic reminder had become something of a mantra; Michael took what comfort he could from its familiarity.

He swallowed, tasting grit and dryness. "Next!" he shouted, raising his voice over the din.

Yousef, the young Arab who had attached himself

to Michael upon his arrival and who had quickly become indispensable (even after all this time Michael had not managed to master more than a handful of words in any of the several Arab dialects spoken here), ushered the next patient into the tent.

"Tell her to get up on the table," Michael said. Yousef translated, but nothing happened. The orderly shrugged his shoulders.

It was a tribal nomadic woman swathed in the chador, making her what the U.S. forces in the Gulf War had called BMOs—Black Moving Objects. The only parts of her body that Michael could see were her eyes and the hand that held a fold of her robe over her lower face in the presence of an unknown stranger, but he could tell from the way she walked that she was heavily pregnant.

"I'm not going to hurt you," Michael said. He ushered her toward the portable examination table, which she mounted shyly and very reluctantly. "It's all right." She looked away and wouldn't meet his eyes.

The woman's family, or so he assumed, crowded into the tent after her, a mass of dusty, merry, inquisitive people to whom the concept of personal space was blissfully unknown. Behind them, the horde still waiting to be seen pressed forward.

Michael fought to hide the weariness that grated in his voice. "Yousef! Tell them they have to line up outside the tent."

He heard Yousef begin to harangue the people in rapid, high-pitched Arabic. The crowd grumbled and shifted their feet, but didn't move.

"Midwife here!" Michael snapped.

A young Swedish woman in fatigues hurried in from the next tent, her sun-streaked hair tied up in

a kafeeyeh, whether from a concession to local custom or because of the difficulty of getting enough
water to shampoo with, no one knew. Her name
was Ingrid, but she wasn't beautiful.

"Help me palpate her, then tell Sergei I might be
needing an X-ray in a few minutes."

Ingrid's eyes widened. The X-ray equipment was
almost as notoriously unstable as its technician, but
she nodded and retreated to the meds cabinet for
gloves and a syringe. Michael fumbled in the folds
of the chador until he found his patient's hand. It
was warm and moist, the pulse beating as fast as a
sparrow's. Michael smiled his professional smile, but
he was dreading what he might find, what horrors
malnutrition and war would have worked upon the
woman's unborn child. His awareness barely registered the sudden upswing in the background noise
in the tent.

The sudden crack of a gunshot split the air. In the
doorway separating the screening tent from the supplies, Ingrid squealed like a spatter-movie starlet.

"Down!" Michael shouted, whirling around. A
young Arab male pushed through the crowd of relatives. His eyes were hidden behind dark glasses,
and his clothing was dusty to the point of anonym-
ity, but the rifle he had just fired through the roof
of the tent was gleaming and well-cared-for. It was
an AK-47, the most popular fashion accessory in the
Middle East. The man swung it down and pointed
it at Michael, screaming in Arabic and waving the
barrel to punctuate his remarks.

I thought it was enough to disarm the patients,
Michael thought resignedly. He wasn't frightened.
He was much too tired for that.

"*Bhutuhl—ah, Bhutuhl da!*" he said, rummaging

for the scraps of Arabic he had. "Cut it out!"

Yousef ran in. "The doctor tells you to stop!" he shouted uselessly in English. He seemed to realize this at the same time Michael did. The crowd behind the armed man, which had backed off at the first shot, now surged forward, apparently to offer helpful suggestions to both sides of the dispute.

Holding a bottle of Valium and one of their few precious sterile syringes, Ingrid took a hesitant step forward. The Arab wavered, torn between dealing with this new intrusion and the need to protect what was probably his wife. Seizing his chance, Yousef grabbed the barrel of the rifle, yanking it up toward the ceiling. Then Michael jerked it out of the assailant's hands.

"Are you the husband? Weapons are forbidden here! *Mamnoo-a!*" Michael shouted with as much sternness as he could muster. He handed the weapon to Yousef, who scuttled back out of reach.

The infuriated attacker wasn't listening. He advanced on his wife and jerked her off the table. She twisted a little, then gave in. He turned to Yousef, obviously demanding his rifle.

"Tell him he can have it when he gets to the gate," Michael ordered. "Relax, Ingrid; crisis over." The husband spat out an oath.

"He says he's got a bomb," Yousef translated unhappily. "He says you are a devil, and his wife will never be the same again. I think he's wanting to haggle a price with you."

"Then tell him—"

"Doctor!" It was one of the male nurses from the surgical tent, his green scrub suit spattered with fresh blood. "Doctor! We need you! Now!" The man ran out again, not waiting for a response.

Michael sprinted after him, shucking off his white coat as he ran. He hadn't heard the ambulance truck pull in. He never did find out what happened to the pitifully needy young mother.

The OR lights cast a greenish glare onto the table and flickered whenever anyone turned on a toaster in town. Michael leaned over the patient, seeing only the open space exposed in the surgical sheets. The body looked tiny on the table, like a scrawny doll. Michael hadn't looked at the clock for an hour. The operation was so tough that he didn't even feel the heat that was only made worse by the clattery fans by his feet.

"Hold that retractor for me, would you?" One of the Christian Arab nurses put her hand forward and took the instrument. All kinds of shrapnel had ripped through the patient, a little Kurdish girl who had been walking to school; off to the side Michael's boss, a Russian surgeon named Nikolai, was working on her sister, who had fallen over the seven-year-old when she heard the blast. You could learn a lot out of school in Syria.

The abdominal cavity was packed with sponges, but almost as soon as he stuck one in, it filled with blood. "Is her blood pressure still holding?" Michael asked. He looked over at the Egyptian anesthesiologist, Umar, who shook his head. They were reaching their transfusing limits. "Well, pump in another two units, okay?"

"I didn't hear that," Nikolai called from across the OR.

"Good," Michael said grimly. There were strict rules about how much blood they could expend. Nikolai was a good enough thoracic surgeon to keep one eye on Michael's procedure while tending his own. Neither operation was going any better than desperate. Michael glared at the last bloody sponge. "I've got to go in deeper," he muttered. "There's a bleeder somewhere we didn't find."

"That liver is dog meat," Umar remarked flatly. Michael ignored him and reached his hand lower toward the pelvic girdle—then he found it. "Jesus," he said.

"What?" Nikolai looked up, his eyes narrowing. "Tell me."

Michael's hand had nudged a sliver of metal— maybe a nail packed into the bomb, maybe a shard of casing—and suddenly blood was pumping hard against his fingers. "The abdominal aorta's going to blow," he said. Umar shook his head; Nikolai said nothing. "Come on," Michael muttered to empty air. His first two fingers found the vessel, and he pinched it together. The flow of blood stopped.

"Listen, Nikolai, make me a saint and come over here," he said. The Russian didn't look up and only shook his head. "Dammit, I'm holding on to this major bleeder," Michael yelled. "What do you expect me to do?"

For the first time he looked up at the girl's face. Umar had taken the mask away; she was pretty, a sleeping black-haired cherub. With a side glance Michael looked at the two nurses, who were backing away from the table. "Hey, it's not over," he exclaimed angrily. "Get me some gut and a number four—" All at once he jumped, feeling a hand on his arm. It was Nikolai. "Good, you're here," Michael said. "Take that clamp, okay?"

"Let her go," Nikolai said softly.

Michael shook his head. "No way, she's my baby."

"Not anymore."

Michael could hear his pulse thudding in his ear. He exhaled, realizing that he hadn't been breathing. Slowly he released his two fingers. After a bubbling first trickle, nothing came out. The girl's hand was extended out from one side of the table; it looked pale as plaster. With a whoosh Michael let out more air and stood back.

"Wait," he said. The nurses were about to cover her face. He tucked the little hand back in, securing it tightly with the edge of the sheet, then bowed his head. It was a natural thing, although he had never done it before. Why now? His mind didn't ask the question, but after a moment he looked up, and a shape was close to his face. It was like a shadow swimming in air or a shimmer of heat from a hot road in summer, only fainter and quite cool. If he hadn't opened his eyes, he would have thought that a faint breeze had brushed him.

My God, it's her soul. Michael wouldn't remember afterward if he'd actually thought these words, or if he'd just known, in the flash of a second, what this unknown thing was. As quickly as he had the flash, it disappeared. The shadow-shape grew even paler, fading away.

"Doctor?" The nurses looked uneasy, and Nikolai had turned his back. All they saw, apparently, was a colleague lost in a private reverie, and they were embarrassed, making an effort to be respectful.

"Okay, people, moment's over. Let's do the next one." The staff moved back into action. Michael looked back, and the shape was gone.

*   *   *

Michael staggered unsteadily from the surgical tent. It was two hours past midday, and the air was as infernal outside as in, but all at once he felt stifled and had to get out. The adrenaline that had kept his pinpoint focus was ebbing away; he was exhausted. There was only one scrub room, across the compound by the obstetrics tent. He headed for it.

The little girl's sister had also died. The other casualties, less injured by the roadside bomb blast, had been stabilized and sent to the wards. Without noticing it, Michael was rubbing his palms together with an automatic washing motion, but his hands, protected by surgical gloves, were clean—it was the rest of him that was stained with the spattering blood that had seemed to hang like a fine red mist in the humid airless atmosphere of the tent.

"Michael?" Nikolai came up beside him. The Russian surgeon had peeled off his green scrub tunic and was holding it over his head to ward off the sun. "I'm sorry to throw you into this—they should have routed the ambulances to a proper hospital in Damascus."

"No sweat." Michael continued walking, not wanting to talk, but Nikolai kept up with him.

"Listen, I noticed on your rotations sheet that you've skipped the last chance for a furlough, a little R and R."

"Yeah. I missed a couple of chances. You don't have to be diplomatic."

"Okay, but could you tell me why? I mean, there's no reason to go for the Albert Schweitzer award here. We're just sticking Band-Aids on a catastrophe, you know that. Spread a little vaccine, hope the local hakims or medicine men aren't cursing us behind our backs. In eighteen months the whole station pulls up stakes and we move on."

Michael had veered left, heading for his own quarters. He realized, as Nikolai talked, that he was too tired to wash; he had to get some sleep first. "Listen, Nikolai, I get the feeling you're talking with your administrator's hat on. I don't need to get out of here, and when I do, I'll tell you."

His tone of voice sounded rougher than he'd meant it to, but Nikolai seemed unperturbed. He nodded and headed in the other direction toward the scrub room. Over his shoulder Michael heard him say, "Remember, you wanted to be here." Gallows humor was spreading.

But it was also his boss's way of saying that the next time they talked, he would be ordered to take his vacation time. Michael reached his tent and met a blast of cool air when he threw the flaps back. A portable Italian air-conditioning unit, his one indulgence, kept his quarters bearable. He sank onto the metal army cot and started to doze. Nervous energy still ran through him; he realized that he was at that stage where the mind takes a long time to slow down and give itself some rest. The strange phenomenon he had just witnessed in the OR tried to creep back into his awareness. He pushed it away, not wanting to look.

He jumped up and went over to the basin in the corner; splashing cold water on his face, he ran his fingers through his loose brown hair and stared into the mirror. He recognized the face that stared back— it didn't belong to a stranger, a haunted twin, or a man so driven that he was aging before his time. But it wasn't a face that told its stories, either. You didn't see in it the hundred nights spent moonlighting in an ER dead center in a Philadelphia ghetto where every night he would be bent over some fourteen-year-old GSW—neutral shorthand that blunted the reality of so many gunshot wounds—his chest torn with bullets fired by other fourteen-year-olds. Those stories just got absorbed into the tissue of a working surgeon, toughening it and making it fit to face reality. But behind that face were other things Michael couldn't tell himself because a veil hung over them.

He had run out. To anyone who had known him in the States, he was another driven, ego-mad, demanding resident—in other words, a carbon copy of themselves—who would exchange his years of medical servitude for a climb up the ladder, after which he would take the money, get very good at his profession, and pass something along to the next generation at the bottom of the ladder. So when the WHO thing came through—no one knew he had even applied—and he turned down offers to go into practice, at least a few people were surprised. After a month they moved on; after all, if he wanted to get off at the station before the train left, it was his business.

The strange thing was that he himself couldn't unravel his motives. He didn't have dark, deep reasons for running to a part of the world where you had the privilege of being hated by most of the countries you helped and ignored by those you left behind. He'd broken up with a steady girlfriend just before he headed to the Middle East, a Chinese-American intern whose parents had emigrated from Shanghai. Liu had acted very hurt, had claimed that they were engaged or nearly engaged, whereas Michael had been pretty certain, from day one, that her family would put a lot of pressure on her, if marriage ever seriously came up between them, not to marry an outsider.

A busted-up relationship wasn't what was driving him, or the recent death of his mother, which had left his father forlorn (and probably starting to drink) back in the Midwest. The real problem, if he' looked deep enough, was more problems, layers of unresolved questions, ideals, dilemmas—the kind of archaeological site that everyone carries around inside but that few want to dig up. One could speak about a Michael Aulden who was composed of long-forgotten images, snapshots of his soul that he never intended to look at again. Yet sometimes they liked to take a look at him, rising up from the murk of his past: Desert pilgrims and desert fathers particularly haunted his sleep. Miracles as exotic and strange as the Syrian plain was blank and unapproachable. Lazarus hiding his eyes from the sun as he stepped in awe from his tomb. Dome of the Rock, where Muhammad's winged horse left its hoofprint as it sprang to heaven with the Prophet on its back. Young rabbi Jesus holding the devil at bay for forty days while he was being promised dominion over the world. (Weaker souls would have settled for a goatskin of fresh water after forty minutes.) It was amazing that the cheap color engravings in Sunday School books could continue to live inside a person, but as a child Michael had been deeply imprinted. He could see John the Baptist in his animal skins, surviving in the wilderness on locusts and honey. And though the infant who had remembered kneeling by the River Jordan in the First Crusade was long forgotten, wrapped in a mist of amnesia, these other images seemed to be leading him on, clue by clue, to the mystery of himself.

"In every sinner there's a saint waiting to be born," his Catholic grandmother had told him, "but in every saint there's a sinner hoping that God won't find out his secret. So you be careful." It was the kind of harsh teaching a lot of children heard on remote farms where the Bible was read, not just for redemption, but as a survival manual when the soybeans were burned out by drought or all the chickens died of virus.

Michael had had his share of fear and penance. But, though he hardly remembered this, he was strangely obsessed with harsh faith. No one had forced Jesus down his throat. He had made his way to the attic, dusted off thrown-aside books from the old hellfire days of an earlier Aulden farmer whose life had been broken by trying to turn sixty acres of rock and timber into wheat fields. In those books he found the lives of saints that were terrible to read— men roasted, spiked, flayed, torn apart by lions, hacked, and crucified, along with women treated in the same fashion, if they didn't rip their own eyes out or fall on a sword first.

His fascination with all this holy gore had made him strange. For a couple of years, when his mother was hard-pressed by having two more children in rapid succession, Michael had spent every day with his Catholic grandmother, and Gram, not being used to children, accepted his strangeness as one of the few things she did understand. So they formed their own little sect, praying long hours and singing hymns while she picked out beans at the kitchen table. Gram hated the pride of smug churchgoers; that was her own form of pride. Michael listened carefully. After a while he left her orbit, back in school and with his family, but if you dug deep enough into him, his lifelong sadness began there.

Medicine had finally channeled his suspicious zeal for God into a realistic cause—and then almost killed his spirit. The unfairness of death hit him harder than was thought healthy. He was rifled with self-doubt and bouts of depression when for hours he sat in a chair, his mind toxic with self-recrimination. His uncle, a forty-year veteran of country practice, who had made his way in the lean years by delivering as many colts and calves as he did babies, had been a big influence. "There are two kinds of doctors, Mike. One kind treats ten patients and saves nine. When he looks back on it, all he remembers are the nine he saved. The other kind of doctor also treats ten patients and saves nine. But when he looks back, all he can remember is the one he lost. I know which kind I am. Before you go off to med school and waste the time of a lot of expensive cadavers, you'd better look at yourself."

Michael thought he had, and he never got a chance to bring up the subject again. His uncle, a three-pack-a-day man and proud of it ("Believe it or not, when I was in med school they thought that tobacco might cure TB"), passed away from lung cancer when Michael was still in college. So Michael wrapped himself in the cocoon of medical studies for the better part of ten years, and when he came out, there was no more melancholy, no haunted saints, no child who dreamed of light-infused guardians around his bed. He went into the first year of medical school looking like a monk in training; he emerged knowing that doctors read hospital charts, not Bibles. As a weary resident had remarked over a bad cup of midnight coffee, "You only get to choose one priesthood at a time. There's no shame in choosing the one that pays."

Michael frowned at his face in the mirror. He splashed more water on the back of his neck, then threw himself down on the cot, taking a second stab at sleep.

Four hours later he came to without realizing that he'd been out. The edge of his tiredness was gone, so he stepped outside to go to the scrub room. There was a long dusty alley between the doctors' tents. Michael walked down it. In the distance he could see a pale flag of road dust hanging above the rocky desert. Instincts honed during years in an undeclared war zone made him quickly run down the list of possible visitors. It might be the supply convoy, currently four days late. Nothing else was expected. As a rule their clientele arrived on foot. Only soldiers had trucks.

Unconsciously, Michael squared his shoulders. As the oldest child, he had always been the one who looked under the bed to frighten away the monsters. Instinctively he still used that method to drive away the horrors. Confront them. See them for what they were.

This time they were friendly. When he reached the front gate of the compound, the UN soldiers were raising the barricade, and Michael could see a large Red Cross emblem on the sides and tops of the trucks, for what small protection that might provide. He turned away, relieved, rubbing the back of his neck, thinking of a clean uniform and maybe even a rare cup of Turkish coffee, now that the supplies were finally here. The Arab members of the mission swigged a black oversteeped tea that Michael found undrinkable. He never thought he'd long for instant coffee out of a ration can, but the last of his stash had run out a month ago, and he hadn't been able to replace it.

"*Khelee baalak!*"

He'd reached the edge of the main compound when the woman's voice rang out behind him, demanding in crude Arabic that the movers be careful. "No, no, no," she said. "Stop! Put it where I told you. *Allez*, that's right. *C'est bon*. Sonofabitch! Go on, you won't break. Allah be with you."

Recognizing this weird stream of tongues, Michael turned back. One of the drivers—a female—was standing in front of the lead truck with her foot propped up on the bumper, haranguing the men unloading the trucks in a camel-driver's argot and shouting accusations at the refugees who hung around nearby, alert for a chance to steal the precious supplies. She had a white scarf tied over her pale blond hair and was wearing a pair of designer sunglasses. Other than that, she was dressed for an expedition to King Solomon's mines, from her dust-caked riding boots to her khaki bush jacket.

"Susan!" Michael shouted, running back to where the trucks had stopped. The woman waved but barely slowed her stream of invective.

Susan McCaffrey was, like him, an American. She was also the senior field administrator for the relief camps across the whole Levant. Six refugee camps in a thousand square miles of desert relied on her, as liaison to WHO's Alexandria regional headquarters, to get them the supplies and clearances they needed to do the little they could. Susan was what passed hereabouts for an Old Arab Hand—she'd been in-country even longer than Michael had and accomplished daily miracles of supply through tact, intrigue, and blatant misdirection.

And she was supposed to be tucked into her air-conditioned office in Damascus.

"What are you doing here?" Michael demanded.

She turned and took off her sunglasses to glare at him. Her stare reminded him forcibly of why the Arabs made the sign of the evil eye against blue-eyed foreigners.

"I suppose you'd rather I stayed home?" she demanded. "What's wrong? Don't you think a blonde can drive a stick shift?"

She removed the scarf to shake out her hair. The white silk square was transparent with sweat. She shrugged and tied it around her neck—a slap at the customs of their hosts that told Michael just how much on edge she was.

"You should have stayed put or given us warning or asked for an armed escort. It's too dangerous here," he said inadequately, and he saw Susan's mouth settle into a harsh angry line. *Of course it's dangerous here,* her expression said contemptuously. *There isn't a safe square inch anywhere, and there never was. So what?*

"Don't say that you don't want me doing it." Her voice was almost a growl. "I spent two weeks sweating out a permit for this precious convoy, and I have no intention of seeing it dissolve into thin air like the last one."

"Where's your Egyptian, the one who sleeps with his Uzi?" Michael noticed that she had arrived without anyone riding shotgun or even the usual teenagers armed with semi-automatics sitting on the tailgate.

"Couldn't make it this time," Susan said casually,

waving away some itinerant boys who were trying to sneak around the back of the convoy. "I see you creeps. Get outta there, now!"

Michael was growing more exasperated. "You don't get to make all the rules, you know, or make unilateral decisions about when to blow them off. Running this shipment without armed escort is against regs, and you know it. You put everything at risk, and God knows the last thing we need around here—"

"Since when are you commanding the fort, *mon* Colonel?" she interrupted hotly. "Did you want this stuff or didn't you? And don't blame me if the manifest is a trifle short. Hard times, you know." She was good at keeping up the defiance, but he could see something behind her eyes, and she looked away.

"You got attacked on the road, didn't you?" Michael said. Try as hard as he might, the words came out like an accusation. "They probably killed your guards, or else the bastards ran off and deserted you."

Susan was impressed. "Let's say my guys felt they had a conflict of interest, and they took early retirement."

"Christ!" Michael exploded. "You shouldn't act so amused. They set you up, and you know it. How did you get away without eating plastique for breakfast?"

Susan stepped off the truck and smiled wearily. "I didn't know you cared this much."

"Susan!"

"All right, chief. It was reasonably amicable, for an ambush. They didn't want to kill anybody—I imagine it was just a minor renegade action from the get-go, nothing they wanted the big fish to find out about. So I handed over some cash, a box of hospital gowns, a hundred Hershey bars, and a chunk of white powder that looked vaguely like coke—did your mess cook order a lot of cornstarch, by any chance? Somebody's having a bum party with it right now."

He thought that anyone who acted cocky in this powder keg was asking for the last dance, but he had to admit that she came through the ordeal better than anyone outside the armed command would have—and a lot inside it.

You can tell me if you were really scared, Michael wanted to say, but he couldn't. It wasn't their code. He and Susan were too much alike, shouldering burdens unasked because somebody had to. But she bore a burden that was greater than his would ever be—she was a woman in the man's world of international aid, and she had been dealing with the additional roadblocks that Islam placed in the path of a Western woman ever since she'd been appointed to this post. Michael knew her well enough by now to be sure that nothing the world could do would make her back down. But it could make her angry, and frequently it did. Susan McCaffrey's rage was both sword and shield in her daily battles, and Michael had learned to respect that fact.

"You shouldn't be standing out here. Want to come back to the mess tent? I can set up a couple of chairs in the meat locker," he said. It was a peace offering of a sort, and both of them knew it. His exasperation with her methods had ripened long ago into a grudging and tentative love.

Susan smiled. "Sounds nice." Each faint line in her face was etched with the white dust of the desert, and she wiped a streak across her forehead. "I came prepared, you know. I've got the only Turkish roast for four hundred miles." She held up a silver Thermos. "Fresh brewed from the Syrian Grand Hotel at four this morning."

"I love you," Michael said fervently.

Susan laughed, a harsh rasp of unselfconscious triumph. "Why don't you take me back to your tent, then, and I can show you what else I brought?"

Michael shared his tent with other members of the mission who rotated through at random times, but all of them had found better, more alcoholic places to be at this hour. Michael automatically jerked the chain of the single overhead bulb. Fluttering yellow light filled the tent, a testament to the continued functioning of the mission's army-surplus generator. Susan unscrewed the Thermos cap and poured it full of brewed coffee. The scent made Michael's mouth water. He took the brew from her and gulped it down with the reckless ease he'd learned in residency, oblivious to the scalding temperature, then held out the cup for more. She refilled it instantly, then screwed the Thermos shut and set it down on the rickety card table in the center of the tent.

"Let's risk hypothermia, shall we?" Susan said. She turned the little air-conditioning unit on high, and it began pushing more sluggish air around as best it could.

"You're due for a couple of days in the big city, you know," Susan said, studying his face. "You could come back with us. We're leaving in the morning."

Morning, to her, meant an hour before dawn, so he couldn't even sneak in early rounds.

"We're shorthanded," Michael said. "I did a half-

dozen procedures today. Things are picking up."
The caffeine stimulated a part of him that he hadn't
known was numb, lending him an illusory strength.
It was amazing that a minute molecule could make
the difference between comfort and torment, as if a
cup of joe somehow dispersed all the soul's pain.

"You're always shorthanded," Susan said flatly.
Her voice softened. "Michael, I keep telling you this:
Don't set your expectations too high. We're not saving anybody out here. There will always be more of
the poor and hungry to break your heart—or break
your back first."

"Jesus, what does everybody think of me around
here?"

"Not everybody—me," she said. It was clear that
she knew he was trying an evasive maneuver.
"You're trying to make this job into more than it is.
What more, love? There isn't any more. The world
is what it is, and we play our cards until the curtain
goes down." She took the empty cup from his hand
and set it on the table. "Pardon the mixed meta-
phor." She pushed Michael to a sitting position on
his cot. Kneeling in front of him, she began to un-
button his sweat- and blood-encrusted shirt. Before
she'd finished, he had rolled over and fallen asleep.

The dream had the compelling force of reality, as if
it had been going on all along without him and he'd
only just rejoined. It had the dread familiarity of a
place, a geographical location to which he traveled
in his helpless hours of unconsciousness. It was filled
with burning, with the *crump* of falling bombs, with
the shrill wails of the disbelieving injured. It was
every war he had ever seen: old newsreel footage and
television broadcasts from his childhood and sepia-

toned photos from history books and glimpses of CNN caught over his shoulder in hospitals as he raced from crisis to crisis.

It was the last war there would ever be: Armageddon, Apocalypse, Götterdämmerung, the End Times. He was watching the last war that Man would ever fight.

And it took forever.

Michael had not told anyone about such dreams—even Susan, whom he'd told almost everything to. Everyone here had bad dreams. There was so much misery that even the innocent seemed to soak it up; it haunted sleep like an unkept promise, and Michael would have felt greedy and selfish asking for any compassion for himself. Worst of all, his dreams had seemed like some twisted prophecy—a movie trailer of things to come. Like some wanderer of old, he'd been stricken with visions by the crowded solitude of the desert.

Slowly, as the months had passed, Michael came to half-believe that his visions were more than the rebellion of a spirit under stress. In his mind, they had acquired a sort of objective reality. The End Time was now, in every second of his sleep. And that was the thing he wanted to believe least of all, for the vision-voice promised him that he would have a role to play before the dark completion.

The climax of each dream was the same.

At the center of the devastation a sword hung suspended before him in the air, thrust through a great black stone. Twisted images of doomed crusades fluttered through his mind like hurrying autumn leaves—of a great iron cross that fell from heaven, of a weapon forged in the blood of slaves and martyrs, so mighty it became a legend, a paradigm for honor and sacred death. The symbol had become the thing it symbolized, and the shimmering blade forged out of the fires of the sun became the very force of temptation. It beckoned to him: *Whosoever takes Me up shall be King, above Kings hereafter . . .*

No. Even in his dreams, where those he tried to help crumbled away to ash before he could touch them, Michael refused the warrior's role for himself. He wouldn't be the arm of some fevered revelation. The secret to staying alive was to wake up. Now. Despite himself, Michael began to reach for it—

Darkness.

Michael sat up, blinking owlishly and listening for the sound that had awakened him. He reached over for Susan, knowing that it was too late; she would be gone. Strangely, no one else had returned to the tent. Night sweat covered his face in a greasy sheen, and the thin, ratty sheet clung to him as if it had been soaked in water.

There was someone standing inside the tent.

The stranger wasn't wearing the fatigues of the mission, or the ragged clothing of the refugees who jammed the camp. His Bedouin robes were gleaming white and immaculate, and his short dark beard was neatly barbered. Without it, he might have been too beautiful, but with it he had the look of a desert eagle, as if the calm inhumanity of the wasteland had found a living face.

"Who are you?" Michael asked suspiciously.

The young man came closer. His pale olive skin seemed to glow, and his eyes were unfathomable, like the blackness behind starlight.

"For I come to heal the world of its sin," he said in pure, accentless English.

"What?" Michael said blankly. "Listen, if you're sick, I—"

"God is calling His children into battle," the young man said.

His prophetic words were too close to the sense of Michael's visions. He swung his legs over the side of the cot, grabbing for the man's arm. "I think you and God have the wrong tent," he said grimly.

The world exploded in radiance.

Michael was lying on his back, blinded by light. He groped for a switch that wasn't there and groggily realized that someone was shining a flashlight in his eyes. He'd still been asleep when he'd dreamed of the young prophet.

"What?" he said thickly, tasting sleep and rancid coffee. The bizarre coda to his nightmare was evaporating from his mind like a mirage.

"Come quickly, Doctor," Yousef said anxiously. "*Halan!*" At once.

Michael slipped into his khakis and T-shirt. He stuffed his sockless feet into a pair of Air Jordans and grabbed his white coat. He was fumbling for his stethoscope as he followed Yousef at a half-trot through the early morning darkness. What time was it? Where were the others?

Yousef took him to the gates of the compound. There was a crowd of locals gathered outside the fence, all staring at something in their midst. Michael climbed over the barrier under the incurious stares of the guards and elbowed his way into the crowd.

"Are you just going to stand there?" he shouted as he shoved through them. At the center he saw a man—a local villager?—lying on the ground. He was barefoot and bareheaded. His tunic and trousers were falling to pieces, the way fabric will when it has been rotted by a flash of intense heat and radiation.

"Yousef!" Michael called. "I need a stretcher here, stat."

The burning smell reached Michael's nose even from where he stood, and caused his stomach to clench into a knot of nausea. *Not nukes. Not here. Please, God, if You even exist—*

"Yousef, wait. Get Ingrid or somebody, now," Michael shouted. "Have her bring a Ringer's IV and some morphine—and that stretcher." Without waiting to see if Yousef obeyed, Michael knelt beside the man.

His hair had once been black; a few tufts still clung to his blistered and suppurating skull. The rest had fallen out, leaving yellowish bleeding patches of raw scalp behind. Most of his exposed skin was a soft mottled brownish-black, darker than what Michael guessed to be his normal color. Michael groped for the Arabic expletives that would warn the crowd back, and could not find them. Where was Yousef? What was taking him so long?

The stranger was dying. Michael knew that past all hope of reprieve. But on behalf of the living, Michael needed to know why.

"Ismak ay?" What is your name?

The man opened his mouth to answer. His tongue was as black as if he'd been drinking ink, and Michael felt a sickening sense of relief. This was not one of the symptoms of radiation poisoning that he'd been trained to look for. Something else was killing the stranger.

Thank You, God.

Michael cradled the man in his arms. He had kept the instinct to comfort the dying when there was nothing else he could do. The man's tongue lolled from his mouth as he tried to speak, and his eyes widened with the effort he was making. They were moon-blind, eyes white with cataract, but Michael would have been willing to bet that the man had been able to see an hour ago—or how else could he have reached the station? The stranger began croaking in Arabic, the words formed with laborious care.

"What is he saying? Does anyone here speak English?" Michael demanded desperately.

"He says he is cursed." Yousef was kneeling beside him, thrusting a plastic canteen into Michael's hand. "His people have all been cursed by the spirit of the desolation. Only he is left."

Gently Michael tipped water into that horribly blackened mouth. The man licked at the water greedily, then fell back, exhausted. Michael could feel his patient's agonized efforts to breathe as if they were his own.

"Yousef, quickly. I need to know exactly where he came from."

He hated himself for disturbing the man's last moments, but these symptoms matched no disease Michael recognized. If some unknown brushfire epidemic had hit the area, they needed to know where to look for it.

Yousef spoke to the old man in urgent, rapid-fire Arabic. He had to repeat the question twice before the man roused again, and when he answered, his voice was barely a whisper. Yousef had to lean close to hear. He sat up blankly once he had it.

"A village in the Wadi ar Ratqah," he explained,

and shrugged fatalistically as if there were nothing further to be said. "Over the border," he added slowly, seeing Michael's incomprehension.

There was a commotion as the station's stretcher-bearers came up, pushing through the crowd.

"Ask him—" Michael began, but it was too late. He felt the stranger stiffen and then go limp in his arms, the body insensibly lighter as the soul left its lodging. Michael lowered the corpse gently to the ground and got to his feet, letting the stretcher-bearers move past him.

"You'd better burn the body," Michael said, half under his breath. He turned to Yousef. "Get me a jeep. And a map—you'll need to show me how to get to this Wadi Rat Pack."

Yousef bowed, not bothering to correct Michael's pronunciation. Michael looked toward the east, where the wind that rises before dawn made a faint cool pressure on his skin.

There was something out there.

Something that burned.

"If you're going where I think you're going, you can't," Nikolai said as Michael came out of his tent. Michael held a day-pack filled with medical supplies in one hand, his empty Thermos in the other.

The chief of station had obviously been hastily roused. He had not taken time to shave, and the thick black stubble covering his cheeks and chin gave him a piratical look. He was still in his bath-robe, his feet shoved into unlaced combat boots— Nikolai had been a Red Army soldier long before he'd been a doctor. "Wadi ar Ratqah is in Iraq. We have no clearance to operate there," he added.

"I suppose bubonic plague waited for clearance?"

Michael asked, walking past Nikolai toward the mess tent.

"Plague? You mean typhus?" Nikolai asked, sounding worried. In a region without adequate sanitation or clean water, typhus was a constant threat.

He followed Michael into the mess tent, where Michael grabbed some ration cans, then began to fill his Thermos. "I almost wish it were," Michael said slowly. "We know what to do about typhus. But I don't know what that man died of—and I'd better go find out." He screwed the lid on the Thermos of hot water and slung it over his shoulder.

"Do you even know where you're going? Or what you'll find?"

"Very sick people," Michael shot back. He lifted the flap of the tent and ducked under it, heading for the motor pool.

"People who are likely to be shooting at you," Nikolai said, following him.

"If they're as sick as that man back there, they'll probably miss."

Michael could hear the sound of the convoy revving up before he reached the motor pool. The lights of the waiting trucks gave the compound a ghostly theatrical illumination like some strange opening night. Susan must not have left yet. The Syrian convoy drivers always liked to rev their engines as if they were about to drag race. It was a habit no one could break them of.

Michael glanced around, but didn't see her. A part of him had hoped Susan was already gone, though it was impossible that she wouldn't hear of this adventure. Nikolai would tell her in his daily report, if she didn't hear about it any other way.

His jeep was ready, and Yousef was situated in

the driver's seat. He grinned unabashedly at Michael.

"You'll never find the Wadi ar Ratqah without me, Doctor. And you'll need a quick-witted translator if you do."

Michael glanced back at Nikolai, and saw he'd get no support for making Yousef stay behind. Anyway, the truth of what Yousef said was undeniable. Michael bowed to the inevitable and climbed into the passenger side of the jeep, swinging his heavy medical pack into the back seat. Yousef switched on the engine and the jeep's motor roared into ragged life. The headlights cut through the predawn gloom, catching Nikolai in their glare and casting a long black shadow over the tent behind him.

"Michael!" Susan ran over to them, breathless, grabbing the jeep's passenger door as though she could keep it from moving by sheer will alone. "Just where do you think you're going with Sancho Panza here?"

She was dressed for the long trip back to Damascus, bright-eyed and alert even at this hour, with the white scarf tied over her hair and her superfluous dark glasses perched on top of her head.

"We may have some kind of new outbreak. I'm going to check a few villages," Michael said. It wasn't the whole truth, but it was true.

"In Iraq?" Susan snapped suspiciously. "Why else would you run out under cover?"

Rumor, Michael reflected, was the only thing that traveled faster than war. He shrugged, quietly defying her. What he did was officially her responsibility, but they both knew that he wouldn't allow her to dictate his conscience.

"I expect an answer," Susan said. Her knuckles

whitened as she gripped the door of the jeep. Michael could feel the sudden uprush of tension in the air, like the gathered energy of lightning about to strike.

"Like I said before, you don't get to make up the rules," said Michael firmly.

"Or decide when they're going to get broken. You said that, too." Susan's voice was low and vibrant. "You'd turn back rather than cross the Iraqi border, right? You know the kind of nasty business an illegal crossing would cause. We'd get bounced out of here."

Without giving him a chance to reply, she turned away and strode quickly back in the direction of the trucks.

"Come back in one piece," Nikolai told him, raising his hand in salute. "We're too understaffed to put you back together."

"Let's go," Michael said.

The sun rose, a dull hot spot in an overcast sky, as they drove eastward. As he always did, Michael marveled at the sheer quantity of emptiness. They were less than an hour from the Iraqi border, and they could have been roving the surface of the moon. No plant, no animal, no man-made structure disturbed the trackless void.

"His people have all been cursed by the jinn of the desolation . . ." The face of the dead man at the station filled Michael's thoughts, inextricably tangled with his dream. Not peace, but a sword . . .

They saw no one else on the road, despite the fact that they were approaching one of the more dangerous—and presumably well-patrolled—borders in the area. Iraq had so far respected Syria's sovereignty, but that might change at any moment. And if it did, what was now only a worn track through the desert would become a busy roadway choked with tanks and troop carriers. Michael found himself staring into the distance as if he could spot some material expression of a boundary that had no reality outside the minds of politicians and mapmakers.

The terrain had been slowly rising as they drove, leading them through a low saddle, after which the road dropped sharply. On the other side of the crest Michael could see that the track led through a valley; there was a village nestled at the base of one of the barren hills.

"There," Yousef said, bringing the jeep to a stop at the top of a rise. He pointed, frowning. "Perhaps we should not go there?"

Good try, but we probably crossed the border over twenty minutes ago, Michael thought. Susan had been right: Arbitrary geopolitical designation or not, if they were caught on the wrong side of the Syrian/Iraqi border, Yousef would almost certainly be shot at once, and causing an international breach of border protocol would probably be the least of Michael's worries.

He could always say they'd gotten lost. It might work—get them off with a tongue-lashing and an escort to the border. You never knew. Michael peered toward the distant village, wishing for a set of binoculars. The first thing he noticed was that the air was heavy with silence, like a thick suffocating blanket. The second thing was the kind of light he'd never seen before.

Through a hole in the gray cloud cover, a bright shaft shone down on the village like a beam of sunlight—except for the fact that it was far too high in

the sky an hour after dawn to be the morning sun.
And what sort of sunlight was blue-white like that,
seemingly as hot as a dwarf star and as cold as Arctic
ice at the same time? The light flickered faintly, as
if in time to the beating of a supernatural heart.

"I don't suppose you know what that is?" Michael asked.

Yousef was muttering something under his
breath. He broke off, as if cutting off a prayer. "The
desert here is the most treacherous. The locals have
a saying, that places such as this should be left to
God and the devil. They should have one place on
Earth where they can fight."

I wonder which one's winning right now? Michael looked again at the light. It didn't undeniably
look as if it was shining down. It could also be shining up, as if in that distant mud-walled village, unlikely as it seemed, there was an escalator to the
afterlife.

"Come on. The sooner we get down there and
find out what killed that man, the sooner we can
leave," Michael said impatiently.

Yousef made no move to start up the jeep.

Michael shook his head. "If you don't come with
me, I'm going alone. You know that," he said.

Yousef made a gesture of resignation. He took a
deep breath. "Insh'allah," he muttered, and threw
the jeep in gear.

He'd come expecting plague. But this . . .

This was not natural. He could smell death in
massive doses—the shadow of a corpse was printed
on the road ahead, but there was no body. Michael
suppressed the chill of horror he felt as they passed
through the deserted outskirts of the village. If he let

Yousef see how rattled he was, the translator would certainly bolt.

Wadi meant "river" in Arabic, and Wadi ar Ratqah was built near one of the small seasonal streams that dotted this region. The stream failed in summer, but the water was enough to irrigate a winter crop, and Michael could see carefully tended plots of vegetables scattered among the empty houses. Silence reigned.

The greenery everywhere was totally withered, lying brown and limp against the earth. The ground around it glittered darkly, as if it had been glazed.

Poison gas? Michael wondered.

"Doctor!" Yousef cried, pointing. There was a body beside the road—the first they'd seen.

"Stop!" Michael shouted. He was out of the jeep while it was still rolling.

The corpse beside the roadway lay face-down, as if what had killed him had cut him down in midflight. Gingerly, Michael turned the body over. The flesh beneath his touch was curiously mushy, as if the muscles beneath the skin were half-digested.

Other than that, the symptoms were the same as those of the man who had died at the camp; the blackened mouth, the blinded eyes. As if he had been burned from the inside out.

"Looks like we've come to the right place," Michael muttered. He went back to the jeep for his bag, detouring to get a closer look at one of the withered garden plots. What he'd thought at first were chips of glass lying on the ground were the glistening husks of locusts, lying dead among the crops they had not survived to devour. He realized what else about the scene had struck him as odd: The wandering livestock so common to such villages was nowhere to be seen. No goats, no chickens. Not even the starved feral dogs and cats commonly found in the region.

There was nothing alive in this place. The Angel of Death had scoured it clean.

Michael came back to the jeep. "You should stay here," he told Yousef. "I need to check and see if there are any survivors."

He had meant to spare Yousef the risk of contamination, but the translator seemed more rattled at the thought of remaining behind than at being exposed to some potential new pathogen. When Michael walked away, Yousef followed him, a rifle slung over his shoulder.

Wadi ar Ratqah was a sizable village by local standards, but its center was less than ten minutes' walk from where the jeep had stopped. Michael's uneasiness mounted as they traversed the streets. The door of every house stood open, as if the occupants had suddenly run away, abandoning everything they owned. They had left no clue behind, not even their bodies. On the far side of the street, Michael could see Yousef poking into the dwellings, by now as curious as Michael was. How could they all just be gone? Michael hesitated beside a doorway as Yousef continued up the street. Had there been a sound from inside the house? *If it's plague,* he thought, *some of them would have died in their beds.*

He went in. The front room smelled of garlic and tobacco. There was a television set with a gaudy color picture of Saddam Hussein above it, and a few pieces of worn furniture. Steep stairs led to the second floor. There was a curtain drawn across a doorway at the back of the house—that doorway would lead to the kitchen, and to what passed for the women's quarters in a household too poor to keep full purdah. Cautiously, Michael pushed the curtain aside.

The kitchen table was laid for the evening meal, but it had never been eaten. The stew and bread had congealed in the bowls untouched. There weren't even any flies attracted to the decaying food. Whatever had happened here happened last night, say between six and seven o'clock—the dinner hour. That would give the one fleeing survivor who reached the station enough time to make it there on foot by four in the morning.

But what was he fleeing from? Anthrax? Gas? The speed with which everyone had been taken out argued for some kind of super-toxin that the government immediately covered up, though Michael found it hard to believe that even Saddam would be crazy enough to test a chemical weapon so close to the zone patrolled by Allied spy planes. Engrossed in his speculations, Michael stepped outside without reconnoitering—and that gave his attacker the advantage.

"Ayee!" the man screamed, throwing himself bodily into Michael's left side. The blow knocked the wind out of him as he fell. Coughing dust, his throat constricting, he tried to get to his knees, but the assailant jumped on Michael's back, grabbing his head.

Michael twisted his head around to see who it was, but the effort threw him more off balance. They both fell sideways into the dust.

"Stop!" Michael tried to scream as loudly as possible, hoping to startle the man—he could see now that he was a crazed villager. He would have cried,

"American!" but had the presence of mind to know that this might madden his assailant even more. They began to roll over together; Michael could feel steely fingers, toughened from years of farming, clutching at the front of his face, his mouth, nose, and eyes.

All at once one hand loosened its grip. Before he could react, Michael realized that the man had found the army-issue knife strapped to his web belt. It would be a matter of seconds before the blade would touch his throat or be plunged into his chest. With frantic strength Michael shoved his elbow back into the attacker's ribs and at the same instant tried to lurch to his feet.

He was lucky. With a loud "Woof" the man lost his breath and fell backward. Michael lunged forward but was too shaken to run. He turned to face the assailant, who had dropped the knife in the road. The villager scrabbled for it on his hands and knees, and then Michael noticed two things. The man was crying in great, loud sobs, and he had no idea where the knife, three feet from his right hand, really was.

He was as blind as the traveler who had died back at the station.

"Doctor!" Yousef was running toward them, his rifle pointed at the attacker. Michael stepped in front and threw up his hands. "No, it's all right! I'm okay!"

Doubtfully, Yousef lowered his gun. Drawing closer, he saw the pitiful condition of the villager, his craziness spent, who now lay quietly in the dust, only faintly twitching.

"Can you do anything?" Yousef pleaded quietly.

Michael shook his head. "I'll try to make him comfortable." He went back toward the jeep to get his bag. Now that the struggle was over, the man's serious burns were evident, and obviously fatal. When Michael returned five minutes later, Yousef had already dragged the new corpse into one of the houses. His face was pale and dead-set with repressed emotions.

"There are others, Doctor. Come."

Neither of them spoke as Yousef led the way across the town square, flanked by the bazaar on one side and a mosque on the other. A crumbling fountain continued to run at what was the village's dead center. Michael stopped and splashed water on his face. When he looked up, Yousef was already disappearing into the shadows of the outer mosque. Strangely, it was the only building that looked as if it had actually been bombed. Yet miraculously, despite the shattered walls, the central dome was still standing; it was made of an extravagant bronze-aluminum that made it shine gold in the cruel sunlight.

Yousef reappeared at the doorway. "Come, come! They are waiting for you."

They? Hesitantly Michael crossed the square. His uneasiness mounted by the second, and suddenly he realized why.

This was the place he had seen in his dream. This was the place where the flaming sword had been offered to him. *Don't be ridiculous.* His sudden irritation helped to dispel the apprehension, and he quickened his stride. The entryway to the mosque was rubble-strewn, each chunk decorated with elaborate Arabic motifs and geometrics, a rain of destroyed beauty. Stepping through this, Michael looked down at his feet, and when he looked up, he was only a few yards from the central chamber under the dome. He was amazed at what he saw.

A dozen people huddled together in the middle of the floor. They stared, but not at him. Their eyes were fixed upward, and their faces were bright in the circle of light that shone in from the high windows circling the base of the dome. But this wasn't the only thing of remark here. Around the little knot of women, children, and two old men who must have been part of the *ulama*, the mosque elders, Michael saw dancers. They were all young men dressed in the floor-length robes and spindle hats of dervishes, and they performed their whirling steps, turning in ecstatic circles, as if not the slightest disturbance had affected their ritual.

Mesmerized, Michael watched as the dancers moved with the unearthly grace of mechanized angels endlessly swirling in devotion around the Throne. Their slippers made faint, smooth noises gliding over the stone floor, then the silence was broken by humming. The dancers began to sing a long, slow melody to match their gliding movement; the villagers joined in.

Michael felt incredibly moved. "What saved them?" he asked Yousef in a half-whisper, reluctant to break the spell.

"Faith."

Michael shook his head. To believe that would require him to have faith in faith itself, and he didn't. He looked over at Yousef, and noticed that he had subtly changed. His face glowed, and his words didn't come from the mouth of the mere hired translator who had driven him here. Michael felt his heart pound; a crazy paranoiac thought crossed his mind: *Yousef has set me up.*

But his gaze was drawn back to the scene in front

of him. The survivors of the terrible killing light—
for that was the only explanation, however bizarre,
for what he saw—seemed incredibly peaceful. One
young mother, however, broke free of the group
with a quick lurching step. She had a baby in her
arms, which she lifted up above her head, as if making an offering. *Giving up her firstborn?* Michael ir-
rationally wondered, feeling dazed. In some way he
must have been right, because the baby, a tiny girl
swathed in white homespun cotton, kept rising, out
of her mother's arms, up toward the dome. Her
body stopped in midair three feet above the group.
Everyone looked at her; no one stirred.

In stricken panic Michael knew he had to run
from this place. He turned and took a few steps, on
the verge of bolting, when he felt a strong hand on
his arm. Yousef, holding him back, shook his head.

"You don't have to be afraid. You were expected." His voice was firm and strong now, not
Yousef's voice. More than anything else, this small
detail made Michael feel queasy, and a veil of spotty
blackness began to descend over his eyes, prelude to
a dead faint. Michael shook himself free and kept
staggering toward the doorway. He was panting in
ragged breaths, and although he didn't faint, his
blurred vision made him stumble over the scattered
rubble.

Now Yousef was in front of him. "Please, sir. You
are safe here. This is the only place you are safe."

This time Michael stopped; he was mystified.
"How can you call this damn wasted place safe?"
he croaked, his throat parched with fear. Before
Yousef could answer, an old man walked out of the
shadows. He had a long white beard and wore a
coarse woolen robe. Michael felt his senses coming

back, and he realized that this was a wandering holy man, an old Sufi. In Arabic the word *suf* means "wool," denoting those who wore the austere robes, as the brown homespun of the Franciscan monks was adopted as a sign of their vow of poverty. Michael noticed that he had started breathing again, and he was growing calmer. But he didn't turn around to face the central hall again.

The old Sufi looked at him out of extraordinary eyes, eyes unlike any Michael had ever seen before— deep, full, dark, but at the same time lit up.

"He wishes to speak with you," Yousef said, now sounding almost timid.

"I'm anxious to hear what he has to say. Does he know what kind of attack this was?" The moment the words were out of his mouth, Michael realized their absurdity. A lifetime spent with contempt for irrationality had made him the irrational one in this setting. After all that he had witnessed, he still wanted everything to return to the madness of a reasonable explanation.

As Michael stopped speaking, the holy man smiled and talked volubly in Arabic.

"He says he knows you," Yousef translated after a moment.

"I don't think so," Michael said. "Tell him—"

The old man interrupted with an impatient gesture. "It is the nature of everything imperfect to end. Only God is eternal," Yousef translated. He smiled, as if the two shared a private joke.

"He wants you to know something—you cannot make a river go where you want. It carries you where it wants."

"Terrific." Worry and too little sleep combined to sour Michael's temper.

"He says that there is a reason for the things you have been brought here to see. You must not be afraid to have faith. You must reconcile yourself to believing." Yousef said all this without a word from the Sufi.

"Do you read minds now?" Michael snapped. He tried to brush past the two men, feeling a fresh anxiety about the danger they were probably still in. But the old man knelt in front of him, cleared some rubble away with his hand, and made a sign in the fallen dust with one finger. Michael stared at it, the number thirty-six.

As if he had accomplished some serious work, the holy man stood up and turned on his heels. The last glimpse Michael caught of him was over his shoulder as the Sufi walked back into the shadows.

"Come on," Michael said. "We're going."

The deserted houses seemed to mock him as he passed them at a quick march. He didn't understand what had just happened, and he didn't like what he couldn't understand. Michael flung his medical bag into the jeep's back seat so hard that the precious bottles of penicillin and morphine rattled, then he swung himself into the driver's seat. Yousef came running down the road toward him.

"You are angry, Dr. Aulden," the translator said. "Please, what are you thinking?"

I'm thinking I'd call for a UN inspection team to turn this place upside down, if there was any way I could admit I'd been here in the first place.

"Get in if you're coming," Michael said curtly. He gunned the engine. For a moment, the young stranger he'd seen in the dream and the old man in the mosque became the same person. "And I don't like it when anyone thinks my soul is up for rent. Whoever they are."

After Yousef climbed in, saying nothing, Michael decided to drive through the village and make a long loop back to the road. Maybe he'd see something along the way that would explain all of this. He was caught up in his anger, shutting himself off from the world in the same way his father always had, using his fury to build walls that could not be breached from either side. He was so involved with his feelings that he didn't hear the planes until Yousef tugged at his sleeve.

"Sir, listen!"

It was that drone made familiar in a hundred old war movies, unreal now by its intrusion into the real world. Michael saw a line of dust puffs stitch across the road ahead of him before he realized he was hearing the dull rattle of a machine gun.

Suddenly there was a jet fighter above them, strafing the roadway. Its shadow passed over, and the sound of its guns was like tearing fabric. Incendiary rounds and tracers were mixed in with the bullets, making streaks and blossoms of flame wherever they hit.

Michael jerked the wheel to one side, slewing the jeep across the road back toward the village. "Jump!" he shouted.

Yousef flung himself from the jeep and rolled sideways. Michael hesitated, wanting to divert the plane away from him, knowing that if the plane wasn't shooting now, it would be again in a matter of seconds. He floored the accelerator and jumped, all in one awkward unpracticed movement.

The impact with the ground hurt, and for a moment Michael's consciousness was preoccupied with that. Then he reclaimed the sound of the jeep, followed by gunfire as the warplane made a second run. The machine gun rounds seemed to shake the ground this time like heavy footsteps. There was a metallic battering sound as the bullets found the jeep, followed by the hissing of a tracer round and the sudden terrifying blast of an explosion. Heat— of a different sort entirely from a desert's—washed over his skin with deceptive softness.

Run, dammit. Michael stumbled to his feet and forced himself to run toward the nearest building. It was a field shack made of mud twenty yards away. Yousef was standing in the doorway, looking toward something Michael couldn't see and gesturing wildly.

Michael heard a pattering like rain all around him, and as if from a great distance his mind supplied the explanation: it was debris from the jeep's explosion, flung heavenward by the force of the blast and now raining back to earth. One piece of hot metal struck his shoulder a glancing blow, and the unexpected pain made him trip and sprawl full-length in the dust again. He bit his tongue when he fell, and the unfairness of that tiny mishap filled his mind with fury.

"Get up, Doctor!" Yousef had run out to get him, thinking that Michael was seriously hurt.

"No, I'm all right. Run back! Get some cover!" By now Michael was on his feet running, but the plane was coming back already. For the first time Michael had the certainty that they were going to aim at him. With a wild push he shoved Yousef into the roadside ditch and jumped after him. They landed in muddy water surrounded by reeds, but there was no real cover. Yousef and Michael were lying exposed, side by side. Michael knew he was about to die.

A cool shadow covered his body. Michael rolled onto his back and looked up to see the old Sufi from the mosque standing over him. He looked very calm.

"For God's sake, get down," Michael whispered, aghast. By the time he had finished speaking, the line of bullets had reached them.

Had reached them and passed over as if Michael and the old man occupied some other reality that had no warplanes in it. Stupefied, Michael lay back, feeling warmth under his back. It was the warm wetness of fresh blood. Maybe he had died; maybe this was the only real thing happening. He saw the Sufi kneel to touch Yousef, who wasn't moving. And then Michael knew that it was Yousef's blood he had felt.

"Get away, let me tend to him," he said. The old Sufi shook his head. With one glance at the bullet-riddled corpse, Michael knew that the young translator was dead. Not that he had time to judge. A blast ten times louder than anything before rocked the ground. Over the Sufi's shoulder Michael saw the village begin to blow up, five buildings at a time. The heavy roar of bombers filled the sky.

His mind black with panic, Michael bolted. He could make the field shack in less than a minute, running on desperation, and that was the only thing in his head. More explosions erupted behind him, seeming to come closer. Michael couldn't hear himself scream over the deafening noise, but a streak of hot pain ran up his leg before he blacked out in the middle of the road.

*   *   *

He woke up where he fell. A dark haze cleared from his sight, and he saw the sun shining through a rift in the clouds. The sound of the planes was gone. Michael struggled to sit up.

"They came for you," a voice said nearby. Michael turned his head, wincing with a stab of pain. It was the old Sufi, standing near the place where Yousef had fallen. Bright arterial blood dripped down the side of the drainage ditch in gaudy streaks, and Michael smelled the spilled blood with the instincts of a trained surgeon.

Everything seemed clear, expanded. Lingering adrenaline made all the colors bright, and Michael imagined he could hear the exact moment in which Yousef's heart stopped beating. "You're delirious. Don't move."

It took Michael a moment to realize that the Sufi was speaking English, an English as flawless and unaccented as Yousef's own.

"Yousef knew what would happen if he chose to come here," the holy man said.

"Now you decide to speak English?" Michael demanded. He tried to get to his feet but crumpled instantly and screamed. His right leg was broken, and the entire lower half of his pants leg was red.

"You must keep yourself safe—you are needed. I have come to you because now, against all custom, the holy must be seen—he leaves us no choice." The old man had walked up to Michael and was almost whispering in his ear. Michael turned and stared into his eyes. "I'm going to lift you. Remember: In solitude there is only fear."

"No, don't try to lift me," Michael protested, getting weaker from the pain and loss of blood. "I'm a doctor. You need to do what I say."

The holy man ignored him. "What has been apart must come together. He who will not seek shall not find."

"Look—" Michael said feebly, but the old man was pulling him to his feet now. Despite the pain, Michael was able to hold on as the Sufi lifted him from the side onto his shoulder, half-dragging, half-walking him to the field shack, which was somehow still standing. Michael anticipated that his right leg would create such agony that he'd soon pass out, but he found that by dragging it lightly and letting the holy man do the walking, he remained conscious.

They veered from the road to a narrow dirt track leading across the field. Suddenly Michael thought of something. "Mines," he said weakly. "This path could be mined. Watch out."

"I am." The look on the Sufi's face was like a parent warned to be careful in a children's game of war. Michael saw him bend over slightly and dust the path ahead of them with his sandal. The snub shape of a trigger was revealed; the land mine had been planted smack in the center of the dirt trail. "Is this what you mean?" the Sufi asked. Michael was about to nod when the old man planted his foot squarely on the mine trigger with a loud slap. Michael braced for the detonation, even though he couldn't possibly have reacted quickly enough—and he heard the old man laugh. They continued their dragging pace toward the deserted shack.

He must have blacked out then, because the next thing Michael knew, he was lying on his back on a rough wooden table, part of the threshing gear he could see around him. The Sufi was looking down at him patiently. "My leg, how bad is it?" Michael asked. The pain was sharper now, and when he gently wiggled his calf, he could feel the jostle of protruding bone. It was the kind of wound that could kill him if left untreated, and cripple him unless he got back to the aid station in a few hours.

The Sufi turned his gaze curiously down to the wound. "Not so bad," he murmured. "You'll be surprised." He wrapped his hand in a fold of his robe. "Hold still." Michael felt a warm grip around his calf, preparing to faint from the shooting pain that never came. After a few seconds the grip loosened, and the holy man held his hand back up again, with a "See, nothing up my sleeve" expression. Without looking, Michael knew that the bone was completely healed.

"What did you do?" Michael demanded, but before he could sit up, the Sufi was pushing his chest. He felt groggy and lay back with a soft groan. Slowly he began to realize how much trouble he was still in: weak from blood loss, alone, on foot, somewhere on the Iraqi side of the border, and without any idea of how he was going to get back to the safety of the mission.

"Take care of yourself, and remember," the Sufi said very close to Michael's ear.

Michael heard a weak voice—his own?—saying, "God be with you." Then a rough hand covered his eyes, and he slept.

CHAPTER TWO

THE GOOD SAMARITAN

Michael had been walking for about two hours, as nearly as he could estimate. His watch was a casualty of the strafing, so he couldn't really be sure, but the clouds had burned off, and the sun hung suspended in a flawless sky.

Spring in the Syrian Desert is a temperate season, Michael quoted mockingly to himself. The air shimmered eighteen inches above the ground, a glistening river as hot as a furnace mouth. Michael's skin was already encrusted with the salt of his sweat. He'd tied his shirt around his head, but it provided precious little protection from the vindictive scorch overhead.

He knew that he should have waited till dark to try this trek, but he had been afraid that if he lingered in the village, something worse would happen, hard as that was to imagine. Most of Wadi ar Ratqah had been set on fire by the incendiary bombs, the flames devouring everything but mud and stone.

"You must keep yourself safe—you are needed." The old man's words throbbed through Michael's brain. Even in memory he could feel the force of holiness that had radiated from the white-robed imam; a demanding goodness. He had challenged Michael to join the battle forecast in his unquiet dreams, the war of absolutes in which an uncompromising joy threw down the gauntlet to an unconditional despair.

And in which a pillar of fire challenged him to lead it. Michael looked up, and to his eyes, it was a pillar of fire rising somewhere near the horizon. Yousef had said that this was where God and the devil fought. Had God been at Wadi ar Ratqah? Had an angel preserved those people Michael had seen in the mosque and kept him from being cut down by the same attack that had killed Yousef? Why should he deserve to be spared?

You're nobody's candidate for sainthood, Michael told himself. He drew a deep breath, feeling light-headed. The desert air seared his throat all the way into his lungs. He shaded his eyes. The pillar of fire was still there, and the bright plume, visible even in the full sun, was coming closer.

By the pricking of my thumbs, something wicked this way comes.

Michael glanced around, just as if he hadn't seen everything there was to see within fifteen seconds of setting out. Though it tilted slightly, the landscape was flat and littered with small rocks. There was nowhere to hide, even if he'd thought hiding would do him any good. He couldn't last much longer out here anyway.

But as the plume zoomed straight toward him, Michael saw that it was not fire, and he had enough clarity left to be thrilled by what it was—road dust; coming from neither a jeep nor one of the ubiquitous canvas-roofed trucks, but, incredibly, from a shiny black limousine.

The limo slowed as it neared him, and then stopped in a rolling cloud. One of the rear passenger windows rolled down with a smooth electric hum. A man leaned out. He was dyed-blond and immaculately barbered, wearing a khaki bush jacket with a camera strap over one shoulder. When he spoke, it was in a reworked British accent that had started somewhere in the Midlands and made its way south toward London.

"Stranded, chappie?" he asked, as if there was any other possible reason for Michael to be here. "A bit toasty for the odd stroll."

"I should have thought of that," Michael answered. His mouth was dry and swollen with thirst.

"Hop in, then," the man said, raising the window and opening the door of the limo. "We'll get you back safe to wherever you should be. Got a mad dog with you?"

The interior of the limousine was air-conditioned to an Arctic temperature and blindingly dark after the desert. Michael sat back gratefully into the seat and began untying the shirt wrapped around his head. His rescuer leaned forward and rapped on the partition that separated them from the driver. They started off again.

"Lovely beast," his host said happily, sitting back. "Used to belong to a local oil sheik and armored like a bloody tank. No, better than that—tanks don't come with a/c and a wet bar." He opened the refrigerator and handed Michael a bottle of water.

"Nigel Stricker, by the way," he added. "Temporarily pampered member of the fourth estate in search of a story." He indicated the clutch of 35mm cameras on the seat beside him. "And you?"

Michael unscrewed the cap and swigged, careful not to drain the bottle all at once. The icy water seemed to etch his throat with silver; he almost thought it might make him drunk. "Michael Aulden. Temporarily lost Yank doctor. I don't suppose you know where we are?"

Nigel shuddered theatrically. "The wrong side of a ticklish situation. So you figure to be WHO, yes? Rather off your pitch, though." The Englishman smiled crookedly, looking meditatively out the tinted side window.

"My jeep exploded," Michael offered without elaboration. "Look, there's an aid station set up a couple of miles outside Palmyra. Do you think you could circle back there?"

Nigel spread his hands in a gesture of apology. "I would if I could, dearie, but at the moment I'm off to see the wizard. And my boss wouldn't appreciate it if I missed what might just be the story of the millennium. I can at least see you back to my hotel in Damascus. Will that do?"

"That'd be great," Michael said with a sigh of relief. He wasn't staring disaster in the face after all, though the loss of the jeep and supplies would hurt. He could check in with Susan at the Grand, and maybe she could get things straightened out.

"What's this story, anyway, Mr. Stricker?"

The photojournalist held up his hand. "Please. Nigel. What friends I have do call me that. And I shall call you Michael, after the captain of the armies of God. As for our destination, it seems that the sacred sands have once more brought forth a prophet . . ."

Michael lay back exhausted as the man babbled. He wondered what kind of journalist wouldn't notice his bloody trouser leg or even ask about the exploded jeep. But now he had his answer—a journalist tracking the story of the millennium.

The tiny village was near the Sea of Galilee, which despite its name was more of a large lake as well as an important source of fresh water. The Israeli border was only a few miles away, but while Galilee and Nazareth were popular tourist spots, lush and picturesque, the landscape through which Nigel and Michael drove was the same barren poverty-stricken expanse of scrubland that characterized the Occupied Territories.

Save for one thing: straight ahead, it was filled with people—two hundred, three hundred. Maybe more. The crowd blocked the road, slowing the limo's progress to a crawl. Its destination, so far as one could be seen, was an olive grove atop a hill at the edge of some nearby village. There were already almost a hundred people clustered at the bottom of the hill, looking up the slope with expectation written largely across their faces.

To Michael's eye, the crowd had the restless look of refugees, but many of them were too clean and well-dressed to qualify. Bright Western-style sports clothes intermingled with traditional dress, and there were a surprising number of automobiles scattered around—even a couple of buses parked haphazardly beside the road. Whatever event the people had gathered for had something of the air of a holiday, and Michael was not surprised to see that the crowd had drawn the inevitable collection of falafel and lemonade sellers, who added to the carnival atmosphere with their shrill cries. The jabbering of so many people was enough to penetrate the sealed cabin of the limo.

Nigel rapped sharply on the glass divider. "Amir? Is this supposed to be the place?"

The partition slid back. The driver was a young local man, his olive skin deeply pitted with acne scars. He could have been Greek or Turkish or Egyptian, a member of any of several races stewing together in this melting pot of war.

"If we are here, I am sure it is, sir," Amir said carefully in heavily accented English.

One thing odd about the crowd, Michael realized, was the large number of the sick or injured mixed into it. He spotted half a dozen nearby making their way along on crutches, and others with bandaged faces or missing limbs. Nigel followed his glance. "Poor buggers. You'll never kill superstition. They'll wait around for another half-crazed messiah to touch them rather than go to a proper doctor. But that could hardly be news to you, eh?" He rapped harder on the divider. "Why are we stopped, Amir? Fuck it, I've got to get closer."

"What can I do, sir?" Amir protested, obviously balking at plowing into the crowd.

"For God's sake, man, they'll get out of the way," Nigel grumbled. "Just do it."

The car began to inch forward, and the sea of people parted around them, but not without pounding fists on the hood and giving dirty looks through the tinted windows. "That's better," Nigel said, beginning to fumble with his equipment. "Once the show starts, we need a bloody front-row seat, or what's the use, right?"

"You still haven't told me what the story is, remember?" Michael prompted.

"Right. Well, seeing is better than believing in this instance, but here goes: These folk are all loping up toward that hill up ahead, atop which sits that semi-crazed messiah I just mentioned, and they're not likely to grab lunch until he produces a credible miracle—or reaps the consequences if he doesn't. Such consequences, if they include ripping off limbs or stoning, would make a better story than what we've come all this way to see, or not see, as the case may be."

Michael added in a few rumors he'd heard at the WHO outpost and interpreted this stream of self-satisfied verbiage as the following: for the last couple of weeks rumors had come out of the desert about a holy man with the power to heal the sick and raise the dead. Unusually for this part of the world, he did not claim ties to any established religion. At least he hadn't so far.

"The car will go no further, sir," Amir announced, as if the fact had nothing to do with him.

"Bloody fanatics having a picnic—I guess the world's never seen that before," Nigel snarled. "Look here, Michael, d'you want to stay in the car? Amir can keep the engine running for the a/c."

"No," Michael said slowly. "If this guy's an actual miracle worker, he might put all of us out of business." He thought of the old Sufi in the devastated village, though trying to get his mind to accept those experiences was turning actively painful. The mundane world was burning out the print of the supernatural. "There might be something peculiar here," he added lamely.

"No doubt," Nigel replied sourly. He sighed and began looping cameras around his neck. "C'mon, then." He opened the door of the limousine. "Time to feed the lions."

It was a little past two, the inferno of the day. The heat rolled over the two men like a soft implacable wall, and Michael felt his skin prickle as sweat sprang out through every pore. Before him was a scene no different from others he had witnessed a hundred times since coming to the Middle East, but now the spectacle was infused with a mystery it had never held before. Questions that Michael realized he had totally dismissed were pushing again to the forefront of his consciousness, demanding immediate attention.

He couldn't break the habit of thinking like an agnostic—this is the irony of miracles, that they confound the mind but rarely dissolve old beliefs. The agnostic in Michael was a failed idealist. Only when he was a child had the battle between Good and Evil seemed anything but a tired cliché. When he was ten or eleven, the drama had seemed new and worth winning. Myths sometimes have more flesh and blood than reality. Michael could remember when Eve tempting Adam with the apple actually felt like a cold but thrilling betrayal. When he'd first heard the stories, Noah might have drowned in the flood, Job might have suffered until he died, and the Ark of the Covenant had been the only guarantee against future annihilation. "Not with a flood but with the fire next time. . . ." Michael could barely reach back that far into innocence (who could?), to when his experience of the stories from Genesis had been as real to him as his own life, when it had seemed just and right that the world's first time filled his young heart with wonder.

He knew that spiritual apathy was like dry rot to

the soul, but even he, whom others might see as suspiciously inclined to believe, was often sick with
doubt and had no name for the hole he felt in the
pit of his stomach when he saw suffering win out
over healing. He secretly admired the bedraggled,
ignorant Muslim villagers—the self-named Faithful—
for their fierceness of belief. It was fanatical, it was
a sword lopping off the head of tolerance, refusing
debate. Theology meant one thing: Fear God. Redemption meant one thing: Obey this fearsome God
and He would save a place for you in heaven, forever. The very word *Islam* meant surrender, and for
those who refused this step, a hell awaited just as
cruel as paradise was delightful, a hell where fire
burned off your skin until the pain made you beg
for death, and then by some black miracle, as you
were about to die, a new skin appeared, and torture
blossomed in a new season of pain.

God and the Devil. Print the words in lurid cap-
itals, scream them from a televised pulpit, degrade
them with hellfire sermons pitched to the lowest
level of hatred and fear, mock the whole childishly
horrific setup, and it all might be true anyway, cos-
mically speaking. Who really knew?

Perhaps, if he could be honest with himself, Michael had come to this part of the world hoping to
soak up some of the simple fierceness, the spiritual
steel he saw outside the car. That hadn't happened,
but now something certainly was happening in its
place—no doubt about that. Not after today. Michael shook his head, trying to banish these
thoughts. He followed Nigel and Amir as they
pushed through the surging throng.

*   *   *   *

The press of bodies became denser as they neared the small hill. At the summit there was a shaded cluster of olive trees—this area was famed for its olives—and a young man with dark hair, barefoot and dressed in a spotless caftan, just as the old Sufi had been. He stood with a small group of disciples surrounding him. The crowd stopped at the foot of the hill, as if they'd run into an invisible wall.

"Shit! Amir, move these buggers out of my way— I can't get a shot," Nigel complained. His voice rang with the pure self-absorption of the Western journalist, who believes that the world was created so that he could record its gossip and neighborhood feuds.

The reluctant driver did what he could, pushing and shoving and haranguing the crowd in threatening-sounding Arabic, but the three of them were able to move forward only a few feet. Several hundred yards still separated them from the edge of the invisible cordon that the miracle worker seemed to maintain. Even though Nigel couldn't get a clear shot, Michael could tell well enough what was going on.

The young bearded Isaiah or Elijah on the hill— Michael found it hard to think of him as anything other than a prophet, though Nigel had said during the car ride that he'd made no speeches of any sort yet—gestured to the disciples who moved down into the throng, selecting individuals to be brought into the prophet's presence. One by one they crept up, then screamed and fell to their knees.

Michael stared into the sun-dazzle, trying to be sure of what he was seeing. The young prophet seemed to be healing people by laying on of hands. His acolytes would drag the healed ones away, semi-

conscious or sobbing fitfully. Faith healing, Michael
thought with disgust. He could see the same thing
in any revivalist meeting back home. A combination
of mass hysteria and the power of suggestion, the
effects of such so-called miracles faded within hours
or days.

Were you expecting something else? Michael felt
oddly disappointed, as if he now deserved wonders
on command, a sign that the whole day hadn't been
a hallucination. Beside him Nigel was getting what
shots he could over the heads of the crowd. At each
healing, the mob became more excited, until it was
egging the young miracle-worker on with shouts and
cheers. Suddenly the whole scene—the anxiety, the
adulation—filled Michael with a deep feeling of re-
pugnance.

"Give me the keys," he said. "I'm going back to
the car."

Nigel waved over the din: refusal, acquiescence,
or simply a request to wait, Michael wasn't sure
which. Around them, the crowd parted slightly.
They were bringing another sufferer, this one on a
tarp, up the hill to be touched. Michael hesitated,
about to turn away. Something held him back. Two
of the disciples got the supplicant to his feet, holding
him upright between them a hundred feet from the
summit. Without the tarp, the man was helpless, unable to move. Seeing this, the prophet started coming
down toward him. Michael couldn't tell for certain,
but he thought the afflicted man was missing a leg.

Ambitious, he thought sarcastically. But he kept
watching. The crowd blocked a clear view. They
roared, and he realized that if a miracle had been
performed, he had missed it. Beside him he heard
Nigel give a profane howl of triumph, and the crush

of bodies that surrounded them pushed forward, shouting, pleading for attention. Michael blinked, trying to focus on what he was seeing. The cripple that the prophet had touched was standing. He was standing on his own two feet.

Michael felt the hair stand up on the back of his neck. Had he been mistaken in what he originally saw? Tricked? Hypnotized? If he was baffled, the crowd had no doubts about what it had seen, and it was seconds away from rioting. People surged in every direction, pinning Michael against Amir, squeezing them both as if in a giant fist.

"*Estanna!*" the prophet cried. It was a word Michael knew. Wait.

The prophet continued to shout at the crowd.

Amir, seeing Michael's confusion, translated into Michael's ear. "He says, 'I proclaim unto you that those who find favor with the Father shall be healed. And those who do not find favor—' "

Amir's last words were obliterated by screams, for the prophet had gestured, and one of the olive trees on the slope burst into flame, the living wood being consumed impossibly fast until nothing but cinders were left. Michael's skin crawled with undifferentiated awe. Because now that the prophet was nearing the place where he was standing, Michael recognized him as the stranger who had entered his dream. It was the same beautiful head and piercing eyes, but he seemed to have put on a new persona of power as he toyed with the crowd. Despite the healing, Michael thought the whole show was just a means to an end, not a good deed performed in service. The bearded young man hid deep motives, and not necessarily charitable ones, behind the mask of miracles.

But none of this cool analysis was coming to Michael except through the seismic activity of his brain, which was shaking after the trauma of the day, coupled with the stress of the last three years. The disorder would have to sort itself out a bit before he could really think and absorb anything else. Pure instinct had taken over. *Beware the saint who fits your picture of a saint.* Michael needed that warning as much as the crazed pilgrims around him. But what about the harsher warning? *Beware the miracle that takes away your power to do miracles.* God, would he ever stop worrying about temptation?

The young prophet began walking down the hill even as the olive tree was still burning. The crowd backed away and pushed forward at the same time, those who had come for healing frantically reaching out to touch him. "Master, master!" What could have become a riot was instead a kind of communion, the violence of the crowd held at bay purely through the young prophet's desire that this should be so.

And the fact that he can do to any of them what he did to that tree—they all know that, too.

Nigel pushed forward ruthlessly, until he stood directly in front of the prophet. "Press corps," he said, as if that were a magic talisman. He held up one of his cameras. "Do you speak English? I want to take your picture. Do you understand? Picture? Amir!" But the chauffeur wouldn't move from Michael's side. Michael could feel him trembling in terror, shaking his head as Nigel shouted for him.

I ought to be just as frightened, Michael reflected. Wasn't terror the appropriate response to the irrational? But that wasn't what he felt. He felt as if he'd discovered a new order of reality, a set of truths that went beyond the ones he'd known. These new truths contained their own structure and logic—something he could, with time, understand. Invisibly, the supposed prophet of his dream had turned into the Prophet before him—actual, undeniable—yet this raised more doubts than it settled. Would miracles make the spirit stronger or only the flesh weaker? Did this amazing apparition appear from the world of angels or demons? Did such worlds even exist, and if they did, would the whole fabric of modern rationality be ripped apart? In one day, Michael saw, the cosmic drama that had haunted his dreams for as long as he could remember had acquired a face.

Nigel and the young miracle-worker were several yards away, but there were not many people between them and Michael, and he could clearly see the sweet smile upon the Prophet's face as he shook his head in response to Nigel's barked questions. The young man placed both hands upon the camera that Nigel held out and touched it gently for a moment, then stepped back.

"Wait!" Nigel said. "I'm from London! You need someone to tell your story!"

He was talking to empty air. The Prophet was moving through the crowd again, and Nigel was unable to get near him. After a few moments Michael lost sight of the figure in the gleaming white caftan.

"C'mon," he said to Amir. "Let's get somewhere where we can breathe."

The limo's air-conditioning was beginning to take hold by the time Nigel rejoined them. He was as manic as if he'd done coke—his eyes glittering, his body twitching in its effort to rush off in all directions at once.

"Vanished!" he cried bitterly, flinging himself into the seat opposite Michael. "Into thin air like a bloody magician's bunny." Nigel didn't seem to be able to understand how anyone could voluntarily turn away from publicity. He shook his head. "Amir! Get this heap back to the hotel. Chop-chop! I've got to develop these negs. Did you see him?" he demanded of Michael.

"I saw something," Michael said cautiously. He wasn't entirely certain of what he mistrusted about the performance he'd witnessed. *Performance* implied that it was all staged. But for whom?

"That was so fantastic, freaking unbelievable," Nigel burbled as the car swung back onto the main road. "The Second Coming, right here on CNN—"

"You don't believe that, do you?" Michael asked, almost horrified. "That you've just seen the Messiah?"

"Who cares?" Nigel said brutally. "He's young, charismatic, he'll photograph better than ten Spice Girls dressed in cellophane. And he can do miracles. Water into wine, right here on the six o'clock news—it's bloody bombproof." He began to unload his cameras, kissing each roll of film as he stowed it in his vest.

Michael didn't bother to argue, staring out the window. Nigel was right. The mysterious young man could perform true miracles. He'd explode into the news and ignite a tinderbox. The orthodox Muslims couldn't accept the appearance of a new prophet under any circumstances, but in the Muslim underground, there was wild desire for a supernatural Imam to lead the faith. Christian fundamentalists on the eve of the millennium hungered for signs and wonders. Rightist Jews in Israel were feverish with the possibility that a messianic age was dawning. And as for the oil-and-water mix of the secular and the sacred across the Holy Land, if this phenomenon tried to position himself as the declared Christ or Antichrist, Michael couldn't even begin to imagine the backlash.

Once they were away from the town, the road quickly became deserted once more. In the heat of the afternoon—it was nearly four o'clock now—there was not even local traffic to break the monotony. Long-haul drivers did their best not to travel in the middle of the day, and when Michael spotted a truck pulled over to the side of the road, he entertained the notion that the driver had simply decided to wait out the heat as one might wait out a hailstorm.

But that was a ridiculous notion. No one would stay out in the desert sun a moment longer than he had to. And besides, the hood was up.

"Look over there," Michael said, pointing. There was someone inside the truck's cabin, slumping behind the wheel.

It didn't even occur to him that Nigel wouldn't order Amir to stop, so the truck had flashed by before Michael realized they weren't even slowing down.

"Wait! There's somebody back there."

"You're joking! There's no time. We've got to get this—"

"Stop the car!"

Suddenly furious with Nigel's self-obsession, Michael struck the partition with his fist. "No, you don't!" He shoved Nigel back in the seat as the photojournalist leaned forward to countermand Michael's order. The limousine stopped. Amir rolled down the partition.

"Sir?" he said, carefully not looking at either of his passengers.

"Go back to that truck we just passed," Michael ordered.

He turned to Nigel, who was glaring at him sulkily. "I walked for two hours this morning before you came along. If someone needs help, we're going to respond."

"I'm not Mother-bloody-Teresa," Nigel snarled. "I've got the biggest story since Jesus invented the light bulb to file."

"For God's sake!" Michael snapped.

Amir retraced the limousine's path by the simple expedient of backing up at full speed.

"And don't even think about driving off and leaving me here," Michael warned. For an instant pure fury washed away every other emotion.

"Don't take precious long," Nigel whined as Michael got out. The driver, realizing rescue was at hand, was climbing out of the cabin. As Michael had suspected, it was Susan. He ran over to her. She was grimy and bedraggled, but she wasn't bleeding. Michael hurried her to the limo, unsure of how long Nigel would remain safely cowed. He breathed an inward sigh of relief when both of them were safely inside the car.

"*Ándale! Ándale!* Chop-chop!" Nigel shouted the moment the door was closed.

Michael reached into the refrigerator and pulled out a bottle of water. Susan tilted it back in one go. "Careful! What are you doing here?" he asked. The lone convoy truck had been over a hundred miles south of where it was supposed to be. Susan lowered the bottle from her lips, panting from the long swigs she'd taken.

"There was a roadblock on the Damascus highway, so we had to circle around to the south. When my truck broke down, the other two went on. I thought I'd be out there until the next bandido needed new wheels."

"You're lucky to be alive," Michael said. Susan shrugged with a fatalism born from the wellspring of experience.

"Thank you, kind gentleman, for rescuing me," she said to Nigel, turning on a few volts of charm, all that she could manage at the moment. "I don't know what I would have done if you hadn't stopped." She pulled off her scarf and ran her hand through her hair with a sigh. Antique clichés though they were, her words had the desired effect. Nigel's face lost its pettish look, and he smiled back.

"Always happy to be of service to a lady," he said. "Nigel Stricker, journalist at large."

"A journalist, well!" Susan assumed a look of impressed interest.

"I take it you two know each other?" Nigel added.

"Michael's one of the doctors at our Palmyra mission, and I can't wait to find out how you ran into him," Susan said. "What happened to the jeep? Where's Yousef?"

"Dead," Michael said somberly. Susan's eyes widened. "The jeep was blown up, and a whole damned village burned out. The bright side is that we probably aren't looking at a plague outbreak."

Susan, her genial mask gone, glanced from Michael to Nigel, trying to decide whether he was joking for the other man's benefit. She shook her head slightly, cautioning Michael not to say more, but he knew that Nigel was too preoccupied with what they had seen near Galilee to take much notice of anyone else.

For the next several minutes Susan focused entirely on Nigel, charming and soothing him. Michael had occasionally seen her in action, and once more he marveled at the unfailing social radar that allowed her to zoom in on the most important person in any situation and concentrate all her energies on him. Just as a scant few doctors had the ability to heal outside the confines of normal medical procedures, Susan possessed something Michael would have had to call "combat-strength empathy," the ability to radiate approval at her target until she had her subject entirely on her side, anxious to help. Nigel warmed up even more when he discovered who Susan was; journalists always needed informed sources, and the WHO mission was privy to a great deal of information about the inner workings of the region.

Michael kept quiet as Nigel told her the story of the phenomenal apparition that they had gone to see. Apparently the Prophet had surfaced only a couple of weeks before, walking out of the desert and beginning to minister in all directions, to all comers. No one knew anything about him for sure, even something as basic as his name. Islam rejected the authenticity of any competition with Muhammad, yet his inner circle seemed to be Muslim at this point, or at least Arab.

"He appears to be heading toward Jerusalem. They'll stop him at the border, of course, but what a day to corner the market on palm branches," Nigel said.

"What a potential bloodbath, you mean," Michael commented. "You saw those people today, man. They were the next thing to a rabid mob. And he may not always be so lucky, Messiah or not."

Susan looked startled, wanting to hear more from Michael, but Nigel smirked and waved away discussion. "That's the sixty-four-thousand-dollar question, isn't it? Messiah? Or . . . not."

To Michael's surprise, Nigel wasn't staying at the Sheraton Damascus as most foreign journalists did. Amir drove them through the crowded cosmopolitan city streets toward a familiar destination: the Syrian Grand Hotel on the edge of the Old City. The Grand was a relic of French colonial days and looked as if a sweating Sydney Greenstreet might stride through the doorway with a suspicious native boy in tow at any moment.

"This is where I hang my rumpled hat," Nigel said cheerfully as the car slowed. "Not fancy, but oodles of atmosphere, and a good deal kinder to the expense account than somewhere plusher. Shall I have Amir drop you somewhere?"

"You don't have to," Susan said. "I live here, too." Most people who found themselves in the Middle East for an extended period of time found it easier and cheaper simply to rent an apartment, but circumstances were slightly different for a woman living alone.

Nigel beamed. "Then you must come up and have a drink while I develop my snaps, after which we can all pop out to dinner somewhere before I think of some inspiring words to go along with them."

"I'd be interested in a peek at those snaps, after everything you've told me," Susan said.

She and Michael followed Nigel through the tattered-genteel lobby and up to his room. Like most of the hotel's long-term residents, Nigel preferred the stairs to the possibly lethal uncertainty of the hotel's ancient elevator.

"Welcome to Chez Stricker," he announced grandly as the door swung inward. The room was dimly musty, the stale, oxygenless air immobile like the glories of vanished empire. "Make yourselves at home." Nigel hurried off through another doorway; he'd apparently secured one of the prized rooms with private bath, which he had converted into a darkroom.

Michael threw himself into a sagging armchair covered in stained silk. Susan started nervously pacing. "What's really going on?" she asked abruptly. Michael shook his head, overtaken by a wave of fatigue.

"I don't even know where to start," he mumbled, wishing that he could sink into a numbing sleep. "If you want, we can go back to your room and—"

Susan noticed his weariness, and her impatience softened. "I'd rather stay here, if you don't mind. Let's see what he brings out."

Michael nodded, but he wished for the strength or wits to get her out of this. The first steps had happened too quickly and automatically; he'd let Nigel babble on, and now Susan felt herself a part of something that actually she was quite outside of— safe outside. The momentum would gather, and something as fragile as Michael's feelings for her could easily get smashed in the chaos. Susan sat down on the edge of the bed. "If you feel like it, tell me what happened in that village. I liked Yousef."

"I'll have to pay for that jeep," Michael muttered ironically, wanting it to sound like a joke. From the way Susan stared at him, it must have come out wrong. "Okay," he said. "As you know, I thought there was plague in a village across the border, and I decided it was worth the risk investigating, as long as we didn't make ourselves conspicuous—wait." He could see the disapproval in her face. "We've already had that fight. We're way past official sanctions now or arguing over judgment calls. I didn't find the plague."

"What did you find?"

He looked away. "Christ, I don't know. We got caught in an air raid, some kind of cover-up. The village we were in was bombed out of existence around us, and Yousef died in one of the strafing runs."

"Who was covering up what?"

"That I really don't know. God, if I could only get back there." *Get back to where?* he asked himself. *The village or the time before this madness broke out?* Maybe neither. He needed to get back to a state of confidence in himself, a time when he knew who he was. More than that, he needed to be able to trust again and to love without question. He needed to pluck the fire from his chest.

"You'll never get back there," Susan remarked dryly. Michael wondered for an instant if she had read his mind. But she had taken him literally. "No one's going back there, not if someone went to all that trouble to get rid of one isolated village. The whole area will be crawling with security forces."

Michael nodded. "Can I just think for a while?" Susan backed off, delaying her intense curiosity.

There was a look in her eyes that he wished he could interpret. Their relationship was being propelled beyond the boundaries previously fixed by both of them; in a way this strange situation had made them like new lovers, or else strangers, two unknowns who couldn't rely on their past history to tell them where they were headed.

Susan looked around Nigel's room without interest. It seemed to have been furnished for the hotel's opening a century ago and never redecorated since. The furnishings consisted of a bureau with a greenish, flaking oval mirror, an enormous wardrobe, the bed (unmade) swathed in mosquito netting, and its night table and a couple of kitchen chairs scavenged from God knew where.

The gas fixtures that still stuck out of the walls— Nigel treated them as coat hooks—no longer provided light to the room; that function had been taken up by kerosene lanterns and cheap dime-store lamps. The Tabriz rug on the floor had been worn away until it was little more than a pattern on a burlap backing.

"What kind of friends do you suppose Nigel has?" Susan mused. "I mean, besides other pigs." Piles of dirty laundry were heaped in the corners of the room next to crisp brown-paper parcels from the hotel laundry—those in the know rarely used the dressers the hotel provided, as scorpions and centipedes liked them, too. Photo equipment—cameras, lenses, tripods, a camcorder—was stacked in another corner and strewn across the bed. There was a row of liquor bottles ranked in front of the splotched greenish mirror atop the bureau. "Nice smell, too," Susan added. "Fetid precolonial." It was the same basic room she herself had taken and transformed into a rather Graham Greenish expat fantasy, but Nigel had made no similar effort.

"Never mind," Michael said dully. With the familiarity of residence, Susan pushed the mosquito netting out of the way, climbed over the bed to pull back the shutters and open the window, then stood on the mattress to start the ceiling fan in motion. In a few moments slow-moving outside air was brushing across Michael's skin.

"You meet such interesting people here," Susan said ironically, too restless to lie down. "I don't know what Nigel's going to show up with out of his darkroom. He seems excitable." Her voice became more tentative. "I'd heard the Second Coming was supposed to have a little more in the way of bells and whistles. On the other hand—"

Michael rose from the battered chair, his face grave. "We're next door to Jerusalem here, where a couple of hundred tourists every year decide they're Jesus Christ Himself and have to be sent home buckled into a canvas shirt. There's even a clinical name for it: Jerusalem syndrome. And after what happened at Wadi ar Ratqah. . . ."

He paused, thinking of Yousef's blood in the ditch, the mind-shattering convocation at the mosque. "Right now I don't know what to expect. As for Nigel's phenom, I think that I believe what I saw." He laughed dryly at his equivocation. "But the timing makes me suspicious. Why should God tip His hand now, when He's got us all used to mucking through on our own? Changes of rules in the fourth quarter don't make any sense. I always thought religious fantasies were something infantile you grew out of, like training wheels on a bike or a potty seat. Wait, strike that. This isn't trivial, but could you really believe that next week everyone is going to wake up and see a crack in the cosmic egg? It'll make a hell of an omelet."

Susan shrugged. "Connection hazy, try again."

He looked over and found her studying his face; in her eyes was an understanding, and a pity, that frightened him.

"Sweet Jesus in nappy drawers!" Inside the cramped darkroom, his face reflected red in the baths of developing solution, Nigel couldn't believe his luck. "Where's the damn cell phone? Denby's going to have a cow when he hears about this." In his haste, Nigel had forgotten to take a phone in with him, so he couldn't crow to London just yet, couldn't rub the regional editor's nose in the unbelievable story that would raise Nigel above all their sneers about social jump-ups and he-used-to-have-so-much-promise.

"Careful, that's my baby," he cooed as he swished the wet paper around in the last bath of fixative. He gingerly lifted out another print and examined it. The sequence of pictures centered on the one-legged cripple was going to be a knockout. Once Nigel had forced Amir to bend over so he could stand on his back, the angle over the crowd had been perfect. The Prophet's face, as caught by the camera, almost looked illuminated from within (funny that it hadn't been that way in real life. Or had it?). Nigel's heart pumped like a racehorse's from the adrenaline rush of seeing everything all over again. He wondered if being healed was like the best orgasm of your life, then laughed at the idle blasphemy behind the thought. *Wham, bam, here's your new limb.*

Nigel Stricker liked to think of himself as an uncomplicated man. He'd been born in Hull, a Yorkshireman who voted Labour when he bothered to vote at all, and he knew without sorrow that he would die a member of the British working classes, no matter what knighthoods and manors he might acquire along the way.

It was his plan to acquire both, by fair means or foul, for the fact that Nigel Stricker had been dealt a losing hand at the day of his birth didn't mean that he was without ambition. He was as cheerfully honest about that as he was about anything else that didn't matter. He wanted to snatch money and power, in approximately that order, which gave him a taste for sensationalism, his keys to the Kingdom.

He defined money as wealth so extensive that not only did one never again have to ask how much something cost, but one could spend money as a recreational activity, for the sheer joy of manipulating others through expenditure. Money led inevitably to power, though Nigel was willing to agree that the two were very different things. There were any number of powerful people who didn't have quite the amount of cash that figured in Nigel's fever dreams, but had power nonetheless: power to bully, to force compliance, to end careers or make them, to move through life with an oblivious ruthlessness that forced the weak to look on admiringly and the lesser predators to draw back. The truly powerful could do things that the impotent were arrested for attempting.

Nigel hung the last of the prints from a drying clip. He didn't feel that he had either power or wealth yet, though he had more of both now than he'd ever dreamed possible as a child. The car, the fashionable London flat, the gold cuff links, the occasional Turnbull & Asser shirt . . . he had all these things, and they had been the furthest limits of his childhood dreams.

Everything he had was worthless in his eyes, however, because it was not the one thing he really craved: the invincible armor of deference received. He knew that fame was the first rung on the ladder of lights which led from the muck of earth to the crown of glory. And this unknown Prophet would gain it for him.

Heal the sick, raise the dead, blast the unbelievers, and make them cower—it was all one to Nigel, so long as it involved the stunningly miraculous and a fresh photogenic young face. The combination would prove irresistible to the jaded public, and he, Nigel, would be the man to provide them with their bread and circuses.

The bathroom which Nigel had converted had a tiny window that looked out over the street. He had spray-painted it black the first day he'd moved in. With the ease of long practice he mixed a harsh batch of chemicals in the weak scarlet glare of the safelight. First the developer—he mixed it fresh every few days because it tended to go off quickly at temperatures over eighty—then the fixative. He'd shot parts of four rolls, and he had only developed two.

The next one was coming out black-fogged or overexposed or something else in this damned climate that God had invented as a photographer's nightmare. Next time he'd shoot color, but color required something better than a makeshift darkroom, and that meant imposing on whichever friend could be induced to loan him time on an embassy setup.

Maybe the blonde with the gunsight eyes he'd rescued today could be of service there. He'd plucked
her off the side of the road and saved her from the
proverbial Fate Worse Than, so she ought to be
grateful, though in Nigel's experience attractive
women seldom were. And Susan McCaffrey was still
very much a looker; she was a good ten or fifteen
years away from that twilight hinterland where a
woman became obsequiously grateful for any romantic attention at all, especially from a younger
male.

Nigel snapped back and returned the majority of
his attention to the task at hand. It looked like he'd
shot the whole of the fourth roll, though he didn't
remember having done so, and as soon as the neg-
atives were dry he pulled a contact sheet using the
portable enlarger that balanced precariously on the
lid of the toilet. "It's not like I need more, but at ten
thousand—no, a hundred thousand—pounds sterling per sale . . ." With honed instinct Nigel picked
the most promising images in the series to enlarge.
They were mostly head shots. He splashed water
everywhere as he rinsed the prints, cursing the tepid
trickle from the sink, and soon there was another
line of eight-by-tens strung along the cord he'd run
between the walls, dripping languidly to the tile floor
as they pretended to dry.

Only then, in the ennui that is the aftermath of
great excitement, did Nigel really register the dis-
comforts of his surroundings. It was over a hundred
degrees in the cramped bathroom—the enlarger
threw off heat like a furnace—and as humid as mon-
soon season in Delhi. The fixer made a sharp acrid
stink, like burned cordite, that mingled with the

sweet fleshy scent of mildew and the blandly penetrating scent of developer.

"Shit, I need to get out of here." Nigel's dyed-
blond hair lay plastered to his skull. He'd sweated
so much that the sweat no longer had any apprecia-
ble salt content and hardly stung at all as it ran into
his eyes. His Nikes—his leather chukka boots had
survived approximately one week here before beginning to rot—squished each time he shifted his
weight.

He badly craved a cigarette and a drink.

Nigel pushed open the door to the bedroom and
peered around to see if his guests were still there.
Satisfied that they were—Susan sitting on the bed,
Michael in the chair—he turned back to the damp
sheaf of prints that he held, taking a look at them
for the first time under normal light. "Wanna see?"
he asked like someone used to showing off the most
precious gold gathered from the bottom of the sea.

Susan had used Nigel's phone to make a brief check-
in with the Damascus office, and now she and Michael were talking in a desultory way about what
would happen next. The office would radio the mission to let them know that Michael was all right,
and Susan would be able to put in a call to Alexandria tomorrow to report the whole story.

"But what exactly am I going to report, Michael?" she asked, just as the bathroom door opened
and Nigel emerged. Both of them stopped and
stared. Nigel looked puffy and soaked to the skin,
as if he'd spent the last half-hour in a sauna. He was
mesmerized by several still-damp prints he was holding in his hands, and the expression he had on his
face made Michael get to his feet.

"Holy bleeding Jesus buggering Christ," Nigel said, his voice low and triumphant. He held out the prints, then pulled them back suspiciously.

"You were there, Mikey. You saw all of it, right?" he demanded.

"Yes." Michael nodded.

Nigel thrust the prints under his nose. "Prepare to be amazed."

Michael took the pictures in hand. The glossy wet paper had the resilient rubberiness of an orchid petal, feeling fragile and unpleasant all at once. Carefully, trying to keep them from sticking together, Michael leafed through the images.

The first one was a close-up of the young healer. His face filled the frame. Michael supposed Nigel could have gotten that with a telephoto lens, but the angle was subtly wrong. Nigel had been shooting up the hill into the olive grove, while the angle of the portrait suggested that the Prophet was kneeling before him.

The second picture was even stranger. The Prophet once more, this time floating suspended in midair, a nimbus of light around his body, his arms outstretched. There didn't seem to be any background—no trees, no other people, nothing that would tie this picture to any particular time or place. It was the same oversweet image of Jesus made familiar by a thousand dime-store pictures, and only the young man's dark beauty rescued the picture from insipidity.

"These aren't the photos you took," Michael said, confused. Susan had come to stand beside him, reaching out for a look.

Nigel's eyes narrowed. "Don't spoil perfection,"

he said. "I don't need your corroboration, you know."

The next image was another close-up. It showed the Prophet kneeling, blood running in black rivulets down his arms. A chaplet made from thornbush branches had been jammed on his head, and his scalp and brow were covered with deep bloody scratches. Across his shoulders lay a squared-off piece of wood, a little longer than a railroad tie.

"Well, I'll say this," Susan remarked. "He's not one to shun the obvious. This is spiritual eye candy, or it would be if it didn't look so creepy."

"Are these supposed to be a joke?" Michael asked in disgust, thrusting the photos back at Nigel. Alarmed, Nigel looked again. Many of the images were totally new to him. He was baffled.

Susan plucked more out of his hand, leafing quickly through the rest of the batch. "How did you fake these?" Michael asked.

"I didn't, matey," Nigel said defensively, hiding his nerves. "You saw me pop off four rolls of film today. Well, the pictures you're seeing are from the roll that was in the camera when he touched it— that's what came out."

"Looks like you've got most of Holy Week here," Susan commented, holding up a photo that was an image of a brightly glowing figure standing in the mouth of a cave. "Including the Resurrection."

Nigel picked up one of the glasses from the tray and went over to the bureau, where he grabbed a bottle of gin and poured sloppily. "Better days," he said with feigned indifference.

"You're not going to use these, are you?" Michael demanded.

Nigel shrugged. "I'm a realist. Since I don't report

to you, I don't have to satisfy your doubts. This is going to push the Queen's sex change off the front pages of every sheet in the UK, and after that—"

"After that, the world," Michael mocked.

Susan was looking again at the photos. "Back in the sixties there was this American psychic named Ted Serios," she said slowly. "He was supposed to be able to make images appear on film just by touching the camera. I don't know whether he was ever exposed as a fraud or not. Maybe your Messiah's a psychic."

"As far as I'm concerned, that's just as good—the more powers, the better," Nigel said calmly. He rummaged through the bureau drawers until he found a pack of cigarettes and lit one, turning half its length to ash with the first drag.

"Some of these images do match what I saw," Michael admitted reluctantly.

"Well, it doesn't bloody matter, does it, dearie?" Nigel said around the cigarette in his mouth. "I think I've made that clear enough. I need the true gen—and that boy's it."

"But why did he make bogus pictures in your camera to go with the authentic ones?" Michael insisted. "Propaganda? Spiritual seduction?"

"How do I know?" Nigel shrugged. "Do you expect me to read the mind of God?"

Actually, it was the best question anyone had asked so far.

CHAPTER THREE

WITH THE TONGUES OF ANGELS AND MEN

Nigel was in a foul mood after that, and they had to get away from him. Michael and Susan went up to her room to take turns in the shower—the private showers were cold water only, but cold water in the Grand Hotel was around room temperature, a welcome respite from the still-simmering heat in the streets outside.

Michael sat on the edge of Susan's bed, wrapped in a sheet and eating Huntley & Palmer biscuits out of a tin as he listened to her shower. A bamboo fan turned slowly overhead, stirring the sluggish air. His clothes had been sent out to be cleaned: one of the few luxuries of the Middle East was the enormous amount of personal service that could be commanded with a handful of Syrian lira. At an exchange rate of fifty lira to the American dollar—and many prices held low by the Assad regime—it was easy enough to feel wealthy here.

Like Nigel's two floors below, Susan's room was a mirror held up to her personality. Care and attention had turned squalor to charm; there were pictures hung on the fresh-scrubbed walls and painted floor mats bought in the bazaar took the place of the ancient rug. From somewhere the hotel staff had unearthed a couple of enormous Victorian wing chairs which flanked an octagonal cedar table inlaid with sandalwood, ebony, and mother-of-pearl. Michael tried to imagine Susan practicing the tactful and submissive indirection that in the local custom was the only way for women to thrive here, and failed. She confronted life on her own terms, and did it as she did everything else: uncompromisingly.

Though he'd only gotten about three hours' sleep in the last twenty-four, and it was already early evening, Michael was too keyed up to rest. The more he tried to push away the things that had happened to him, the more they crowded into his consciousness, gathering weight and gravity.

The undeniable fact was that none of the events he'd witnessed in the last twenty-four hours were random—they all focused ultimately around his fuzzy concept of God. It wasn't as if the bleak landscape of the Middle East was foreign territory to the so-called Almighty. He had taken an early lease on Palestine and its periphery, from the days when the Euphrates River ran east out of Eden. The landlord was sometimes absent, sometimes frighteningly present, but he always cast a spell over the mind of any tribe who wandered across the spiritual flypaper of these hills. God was stuck here, so henceforth everyone here would be stuck on God.

"The desert is fertile in only two crops—fanatics and mystics. The one thinks he's found God, the other thinks he's found the only God." Nikolai liked to say that whenever he wanted to unsettle Michael. "Every thousand years or so, a new crop is harvested and shipped overseas in crates marked *Imperishable Truth: Handle With No Care*. And people tend to believe labels." Raised in the former Soviet Union as a cheerful, guiltless atheist, Nikolai regarded the desert's Seven Pillars of Wisdom, along with the Ten Commandments and the Five Duties of Islam, as something between hypnosis and mass hallucination, brought on by "too many nights alone with flocks of sheep, camels, goats, whatever. That's who they have to talk to, and the hoofed species are easy to convince."

Michael appreciated the recreational cynicism, but to him it was still a cause for wonder how the most barren land on earth, steeped in violence and privation, gave birth to mysteries that the modern age still couldn't unlock. The sacred masters, who were supposed to be explainers of mystery, somehow wound up making it deeper: "I tell you this: if anyone says to this mountain, 'Be lifted from your place and hurled into the sea,' and he has no inward doubts, but what he says is happening, it will be done for him."

This promise by Jesus went far beyond anything understood in the rational, Einsteinian, three-dimensional world. Jesus had hesitated to perform the very miracles that proved his point. Even so, the New Testament chronicles thirty-four of them, including three instances of raising someone from the dead. These acts of faith sent waves of awe radiating out from the desert for the next two thousand years. But a miracle happens only once, while the potential for miracles is timeless; the one is local, the other is eternal. That was the reality Jesus couldn't show, but could only teach and exemplify. Reality, unlike the painted pictures of God, doesn't sit on a throne levitating in the sky, doesn't have a beard or hands or feet. It is faceless and stark. Like the desert.

Which is undoubtedly why the world's most abstract faiths emerged from this part of the world.

All three desert religions—Judaism, Christianity, and Islam—taught one to love the Word. "In the beginning was the Word, and the Word was God, and the Word was with God." In Michael's opinion, the hypnotic rhythm of those sacred words failed to disguise an obvious question: what word? Every few centuries since they were written, many millennia ago, a blindingly bright soul has come along to cast light on the Word, but for every one prophet who unriddled the Word, millions of ordinary people died for it. All this death, century upon century, had seemingly thrown God into a permanently sullen mood. Michael had an image of God brooding while the dogmas hacked away at each other here on Earth. And for long epochs, the common man was told that if he didn't volunteer to die for his faith, he was damned.

If all the scriptures from the Holy Land were condensed to one practical bit of wisdom, Michael knew what it ought to be: *Fear the Lord thy God with all thy might and all thy strength and all thy heart.*

No, he thought, *you don't even need to examine scriptures.* The admonition to worship in fear was inscribed in the desert rocks. It was indigenous. Mothers raised their children to believe that other faiths were hateful because they didn't fear God *enough.* Or they didn't suffer enough, hadn't been punished, scourged, tortured, dispossessed, bound into captivity, and decimated to the satisfaction of the truly holy. How, he wondered, did fear get so wrapped up in what was supposed to be joyful worship?

All at once, Michael realized that he knew exactly

why the Prophet had arrived—to give those who craved Armageddon what they really, really wanted. And that frightened him more than anything else.

Susan's mind had wandered in a different direction. She stood in the shower and let the lukewarm water wash away the sand and grit she'd accumulated in one of the strangest days of her life. She hadn't seen any of the apparitions and marvels that had so affected Michael, but she sensed that he was troubled by the events of the past day. She, too, was feeling unsettled, and not only because of what he had told her he'd seen. He was clearly still keeping a good portion of his ordeal to himself. She had been through quite a bit herself in the last few days—she recognized the symptoms. And she knew that nothing would ever be the same between them again. Whatever happened next, the bond that they'd been tentatively weaving between them was about to be tested. They stood on the riverbank of a new relationship to each other. The prospect of being dragged under by the current made her tense and wary.

Who is Michael, really? she wondered. It wasn't that she needed to know everything, but part of her demanded to know more than she did. They'd spent three years snatching time together in the middle of a war zone, they'd talked about everything under the sun, but in some ways, Michael was still a stranger to her. And the wild events of the last twenty-four hours had merely served to cast that fact into bright relief. Who was this man who'd seen miracles and madness in the desert? Could she trust him?

She supposed her caution was excessive—after all, in the times and places she'd spent with Michael, surrounded by the harsh landscape and the terrible traumas they'd tried, in some small way, to alleviate, a person's true nature became evident very quickly. Michael was a good man. But still she worried. She supposed it was only natural after Christian.

Christian. He'd been her brief attempt at false adulthood in her late twenties. If she'd been honest with herself at the time, she would have admitted that who she married didn't matter as much as the perfect wedding, the perfect accessories, the chance to decorate a "real" apartment and toss the words "my husband" casually into the conversation. Two careers, one apartment, a glossy lifestyle tailored out of magazines, and a role for her to play that was supported by everyone she met.

None of her friends had questioned her choices, or even suggested that they weren't the only possible choices to make.

Five bitter years of what could best be described as trench warfare had taught her the folly of a false union. Christian felt that she'd lied to him, promised to be someone she wasn't, and then had hated her when she refused to keep up the bargain. By the time she realized he was serious about this, he'd wounded her pride and frayed her temper—then all she wanted was revenge. In the end, she dragged herself from the smoking ruins of her marriage with the same feeling as a pilot walking away from a crash.

Any landing you can walk away from, as they say . . .

She wasn't sure anymore about what she expected from others, and so she had shied away from any intimate contact. Sick to death of hypocrisy in any form, she'd developed a reputation as a take-no-prisoners administrator, someone who could stand up under pressure. By the time she'd realized what she was doing to her emotional life, it was an entrenched habit—refighting old battles in a venue where she could win.

She had always searched for the meaning that underlay events, but she realized she couldn't find enough meaning in other people, or even in service to others; therefore she accepted that her journey was to be a solitary one. If there was an original sin in Susan's book, it was that most people gave themselves too cheaply, rejecting the happiness of self-discovery with both hands.

She wasn't going to sin again, not if it was in her power to prevent it.

The sound of the shower stopped, and a few moments later Susan came out, wrapped in a white terrycloth bathrobe that had SHEPHERD'S HOTEL, CAIRO embroidered on the breast. She finished rubbing her shoulder-length hair dry and tossed the towel over the door.

"My, aren't you a toothsome sight," she said, finger-combing her wet hair. "The sheet gives you a nice Roman Imperial look."

Michael smiled. "Enjoy me while you can. I won't be here forever."

"You have to stay in Damascus at least for a few days," Susan said. "Look at you. Whatever's been eating at you for the last few months has just gotten worse, hasn't it? I don't think it's something you can carry by yourself any longer, Michael." Her voice held the dispassionate judgment of the surgeon, without malice or fear. "I'm ready to listen."

"Have you ever seen angels?" Michael asked, startling her. His voice came out harsh, strained, as if someone strange to him were speaking. Susan shook her head. She went back to the open wardrobe to get some clothes.

"Go ahead," she said.

"I've thought about this for a long time. The word *angel* means 'messenger,' and they don't have to come with robes and wings. In the Bible, the stories always say that the people confronted by the angels don't recognize them at first. I imagine that also holds for those who see angels at their death—the messages could be terrifying or wonderful."

"So do you think you've seen an angel?" Susan asked, returning to sit beside him. "Is that what's happened?"

"Not exactly," Michael replied. "But I just keep thinking: How would you know if you did meet an angel—or let's say a messenger? Most people, because they've been exposed to wings and haloes and harps, imagine that angels are oversized devotional candles, a larger-than-regulation fairy approved by God, or else a guardian to make sure the demons don't bite. Not that they've ever seen a demon, either."

"I'm getting lost here. I have no problem with angels being decorative or useless. They can go the way of the leprechaun if they like—what's wrong with letting the imagination have its own playground?"

"What if the shape doesn't mean anything, though? What if we've spent centuries painting the messenger and missing the message?"

"Go on."

Michael's face became as grave as a boy's at first communion. "We're hypnotized by images of winged beings because that's what we're conditioned to look for. We see with the eyes of the body. But all the while, messages are pouring down on us, trying to open a different pair of eyes. The angelic message is always the same: *Look, look, look*—and we don't. We keep repeating the same mistakes because we're so hypnotized by our old way of seeing."

Michael paused, catching himself up short. "Does this make any sense to you?"

"I'm not bothered, if that's what you mean," Susan said coolly. She saw the look of disappointment that came over his face. He expected more from her. "Listen, when I was growing up, they fed me a lot of stories about this other world that was supposedly as close as anything I could see or touch. Your angels were there, keeping watch with Jesus and Mary and Holy Father. But man doesn't live by stories alone. As far as I know, you can spend a lifetime praying, sending messages in a bottle to this other world, hoping they will land on some shore you'll never actually see until you die, and the messages don't arrive—at least mine didn't. So I take care of myself, and I don't worry about that other world anymore."

"Susan, many of those pictures were real," Michael said with intensity.

"Is that what you were building up to? I'm sorry, but you're being awfully cryptic this evening. But what you're trying to say is coming through. The curtain has parted for you, the veil has lifted, and now you see the other shore. Great. I'm glad for you. Only remember, I'm on the outside of this experience. For all I can tell, you're receiving radio signals from Mars through your wisdom teeth. Don't expect me to validate what I can't honestly see."

He was surprised that she picked that moment to

lean over and kiss him. It was a loving gesture, a softening of her words. Yet Michael felt that a hand had pushed him back. In fear? In blind disbelief? She had no intention of revealing herself until she found her own good time.

Susan walked back into the bathroom with an armful of clothes, and emerged a few minutes later, crisply professional in a calf-length khaki skirt and a long-sleeved white blouse. "So," she said. "Where do you want to have dinner?"

"Like this?" Michael asked, indicating his make-shift toga.

"I'll sneak downstairs and steal some of Nigel's clothes, and that brings us back to Topic A. Those pictures, Michael. If he didn't fake them up himself—and I don't think he did—where do you suppose they came from?"

"You mentioned this guy Serios," Michael said. "Some of the images jumped into the camera on their own, but I can vouch for most of the rest. That's where we have to start."

"You mean you're taking this on as a mission? What about your work?"

Michael shook his head. "It's not going to be my choice. Events are pursuing me."

"Of course it's your choice. Walk away, or at least wait. When you come right down to it, is there that much difference between a psychic and a wizard?"

"*Wizard*'s the wrong word," Michael protested.

"You mean semantics is going to resolve this thing?" Susan smiled ironically. "Choose your own terminology. I'm hungry."

A moment later there was a soft knock at the door. A porter held out Michael's clothes, cleaned

and pressed. Michael took them gratefully, and retired to the bathroom to change. He felt better once
he was dressed again, though having his clothing
back intensified his regret for the things he'd lost in
the desert—most especially his black bag and its precious medical supplies.

"Ready," he said.

"Well, we don't look upscale enough to venture
on Sindiana," Susan said, naming a popular expa-
triate hangout on the Mahdi Ben Baraki. Sindiana
was one of the few French restaurants worth the
name in all of Syria, and the prices were correspond-
ingly high. "But they'd let us into one of the good
cafés."

"Just as long as it serves coffee," Michael said,
pulling his belt on and tucking his passport and bill-
fold into an inside shirt pocket. He was lucky that
both had survived his adventures; the routine security measures meant to deter pickpockets had also
been enough to keep his documents safe through a
bombing and an apparition.

The late afternoon sun gilded the rooftops of Damascus as Susan and Michael walked out into the
street in search of *kibbeh* and *bourak*. They found
an empty table at one of Susan's favorite places. It
was hours before the usual Damascene dinnertime,
and from all sides men were hurrying to the mosque
in preparation for evening prayer. Over meat pies and
cheese pastries and tall, cool glasses of *laban*, the
salty yogurt drink universally relished by Syrians, Michael returned to the subject that disturbed him.

"I guess you're right, the veil is lifting, as you put
it," he said reluctantly. "Only I'm not sure what I
see behind it. Given what you said back there, we'll

agree that you want to protect your skeptical rights. Fair enough, only I've seen things that assault skepticism without creating faith. What do you call the state in between?"

He felt awkward as soon as he'd said this, but he didn't know any other way to put his situation into words. For the first time, he thought, Susan smiled at him sympathetically.

"I can see this isn't a game with you."

"Not at all."

"I almost have to laugh at myself, you know. Here I've spent twenty years making sure that I wasn't just a pillar standing around to support some man's ego, and now you expect me to support your soul. How do I do that? Show me what you want, show me something."

"I don't expect anything from you," he said, flushing red. "If you think I'm trying to use you in some—"

"No," she replied calmly. "Maybe you're regressing to something in your past or in your subconscious, and maybe it's just too hard for me to see you do that, much less to buy a ticket and come along. I'll offer up a little confession of my own, okay? When I was seven I ran away from home for some reason that I can't remotely remember anymore. I think my father spanked me with a belt for something I did. That wasn't the significant event. The significant event was that I felt hatred for the first time.

"It was a terrible feeling, but it really had hold of me. I ran off into the woods behind our house. I deliberately avoided any trail because I didn't want them to find me, and after a while I'd gotten into some thick brush, crawling under brambles and wild blackberries so tangled that even the birds couldn't nest there. After a few hours it started to get dark, and I realized that I didn't know the way back, so I started crying. That lasted a while, by which time it was pitch-black, without a moon under an overcast sky.

"By then I could hear creeping things in the underbrush; a big barn owl swooped down from a tree and snatched up a mouse ten feet from me. I was so scared I crawled under a pile of leaves and covered myself up. I was shivering too hard to fall asleep, when suddenly a flashlight was shining in at me, right through the leaves. A man's voice said, "Susie?" I didn't know who it was, but I sat up, and he turned off his light so it wouldn't hurt my eyes."

"You knew who he was then?" asked Michael.

Susan shook her head. "That's the thing. I didn't, but for some reason he didn't scare me. He picked me up in his arms, and I fell asleep. The next thing I knew, I was in bed waking up a few hours after dawn. My parents never talked about it. They acted like I'd never run away."

"Some stranger just found you in the dark? Maybe he was following you all along."

"Or maybe he was a dream or a presexual projection—believe me, I've tried on all the plausible explanations. Let's give it the benefit of the doubt, the way we are with Nigel's snaps and your experience. He was an angel, sent by God to rescue me, and he appeared in a form I could accept. I mean, that's what your Prophet is about, isn't it?"

"Except that we don't know if he's here to rescue anybody."

"Granted. But in my case, one supernatural experience as a little girl didn't change my life. I met an angel. Okay, but then I grew up—in all senses of the word—and I found out that it didn't really matter whether the experience was real or not, because people would always find a way to ruin things, divine intervention or no."

"That's a pretty defeatist attitude," Michael said. Strange words, coming from him. Until today, he'd thought the same: Humans will find some way to make anything worse without needing to resort to the supernatural.

"You know me, Michael. I prefer to call it realistic." Susan said. "And I still keep hoping, I guess. If it weren't for my angel, I'd have given up a long time ago and said it was all nonsense. I suppose, down deep inside, everyone wants to believe that there's a power to turn water into wine, or pain into joy. Because God knows we need something to make the world bearable."

Michael still couldn't express what had happened to him directly, not quite yet. But he couldn't talk around it anymore.

Susan studied his face intently for a moment.

"I'd question my judgment, if I were you—very thoroughly," he said. "Especially in this part of the world. Sometimes I think that reality is spread a little thinner here." It had gotten dark, and now the call to evening prayer wailed out over the city, carried into each home and shop by loudspeakers and radio. Michael and Susan waited without speaking until the moment had passed. Then he told her the last details about the killing light that had shone down over Wadi ar Ratqah. About the dervishes in the mosque whose prayers were the only thing holding back the desolation. About the old Sufi who had seemed to be able to see into Michael's soul as if he were made of glass. Susan listened gravely, offering no protest. He ended with the strafing from the jets that had killed Yousef.

"And it should have killed me, too, Susan. I was right in the path of the bullets. They just seemed to skip me—because the Sufi was there. His shadow protected me; and then he spoke to me in English. I don't know why or how. Yousef had to translate for him before. . . .

" '*You must keep yourself safe,*' he said. '*I have come to you because now, against all custom, the holy must be seen—he leaves us no choice. Remember: In solitude there is only fear. What has been apart must come together. He who will not seek shall not find.*'

"And I wasn't surprised by any of it," Michael admitted reluctantly. "Because I'd been dreaming about him—about that village—for months." It was only as he said the words that he realized they were true.

"What did you dream?" Susan asked.

"I dreamed that the world was burning, dissolving in fire." But somehow that was wrong. It was as if creation were being sucked backward and that made the light of creation bad instead of good. Michael shook his head. Words could not contain the deep understanding that had vibrated within him in his dream. "But the worst part isn't the pain. It's the unnaturalness of everything, the perversity of it. A light that kills but doesn't save."

He became aware of Susan holding his hand. How long had she been doing that? He said, "I'm a doctor, but M.D. isn't a credential you want when it stands for manic and delusional."

"It's not as bad as that," Susan said. "I know someone who can help you."

"I don't like that word *help*," Michael said, disappointed at her implication.

She shook her head. "Not a psychiatrist. Just a friend. He helped me once, when I needed it very badly."

"Is he here? Or in Alexandria?" Michael began calculating in his head, trying to decide how long in conscience he could be away from the mission.

"Neither," Susan said. "He's in Jerusalem."

"But that's a long way from here," Michael said blankly. For years, ever since Israel and Syria had been feuding over the Golan Heights, travel across the border was strictly militarized.

Susan grinned at him, almost laughing. "Don't worry. I can get us across and back safely. We can do it in less than a day."

"Your friend, what does he know about this that I don't?"

"Hard to say," Susan replied, obviously relieved that he was at least considering a rational solution. "He's only had three thousand years to think about it."

There was a curfew over Damascus, and only a madman or someone far more desperate than Michael would attempt to cross the border into Israel at night. In the morning they'd make their attempt, when sunrise had caught the Sultan's turret in a noose of light. Susan woke an hour before dawn and shook him, lying next to her. Michael started awake out of a black and dreamless sleep that was somehow as frightening as the visions had been. They

were so much a part of him now that to be cut off
was like an amputation.

Susan was in an efficient mood. "C'mon. I got the
hotel kitchen to pack a picnic for us and there's a
car waiting downstairs." Michael sat up, running a
hand through his hair. He got to his feet and groped
around for his shirt while Susan handed him his
pants. He took the cup of coffee she held out and
gulped at it while trying to button his shirt one-
handed. His Nikes were still blood-spattered from
the surgery he'd done two days ago, despite the
ground-in dust from his trek across the desert.

"I hope this friend of yours doesn't have a dress
code," Michael said, getting to his feet.

"He does, actually," Susan remarked, holding the
door.

By the time the sun was a sliver on the horizon
they were heading east on Highway Two. The car
was allowed across the border into Lebanon as soon
as the gates opened for the morning, and less than
half an hour later they were heading south toward
the Israeli-Lebanon border. It, too, was closed to all
of its neighbors except possibly the Sinai Peninsula.
Michael would have offered to drive, but he had no
taste for driving in an area where it was considered
a blood sport, and Susan did. She moved off the
crown of the road exactly far enough to allow a
truck heading for Beirut to scrape by without tearing
off their side mirror, then swerved back to the middle.

*Does she intend to run the border with false doc-
uments or lies? She is capable of both,* Michael wondered, staring out the window. Otherwise, there was
no way they would enter Jerusalem. Susan had explained things somewhat: The man they were going

to see was named Solomon Kellner, a retired rabbi living in the Old City. She stopped there, withholding how Kellner could help, and Michael hadn't wanted to press her. *You've got to have some faith*, he told himself, wishing there was another choice. Altogether, faith seemed to be one thing the world had too little and too much of, at one and the same time. It was ever thus east of Eden.

CHAPTER FOUR

THE CITY OF GOLD

For over three thousand years there has been a city in this place. It has suffered destruction, total or in part, at least forty times. As it rose and fell, the Jews were always drawn back to rebuild from the ruins, and they variously called it Ariel, Zion, Salem, the City of David, the City of Judah, Jebus, the City of the Great Kings, the City of Truth, the City of Gold—or, most often, simply the Holy City. It went without saying that under every name it was the city of tears.

David marched in triumph through its gates with the Ark of the Covenant, a gold-covered chest that contained the most precious relics of their history, including the tablets on which Moses received God's commandments. David's son Solomon built the First Temple in order to enshrine the Ark, replacing in stone the nomadic tents, known as tabernacles, that had been the traditional places of worship for the wandering twelve tribes. On the day of consecration, the Temple was filled with white-robed priests blowing trumpets, sounding cymbals and drums, when a wonder occurred. God entered the chamber as a cloud swelling everywhere, giving His presence and blessing to the overawed worshipers. Solomon's First Temple in Jerusalem was consecrated 418 years after Moses had led the Israelites out of slavery in Egypt.

Solomon's work was meant to be eternal, but the tide of destruction seems to be set in its rhythms here. The Babylonians reduced the Temple to rubble and scattered the Ark and its relics to oblivion. Centuries passed. Ten of the twelve tribes were lost, but the Jews never lost the attraction of their sacred magnet. A Second Temple rose on a grander scale, enlarged by King Herod to great magnificence. When the Romans quelled the rebels of Palestine, who had been a minor nuisance off and on ever since the whole region became a colony of the Empire, they razed Herod's structure. All that remains of the Temples are layers of lower foundation stone along the Western Wall of the city. This wall is not the center of the world to devout Jews, but it is the closest they can come, because the actual center, the Temple Mount, is forbidden ground to walk on. This for two reasons: After centuries without their holy place, no one has been able to be purified of the touch of death with the proper rituals, making the people too impure to step on the place that is the holy of holies. Second, and more practically, the Mount is occupied by the sumptuous golden Dome of the Rock, said to be the most beautiful Islamic building in the world.

Like a mistress who becomes coveted because so many other men want her, the city has attracted greedy attention since the beginning. The last conquerors to come and depart were the British. From 1948 to 1967 Jerusalem was a city divided against itself, with the Mandelbaum Gate standing as the crossroads of this sacred Berlin. Even after reunification in the Six-Day War, the city remains what it is content to be, despite all the suffering: a battleground. The City of Gold keeps rising on the backs of its old corpses, and it has remained the most renowned prize in the East, too tempting for any conqueror to pass up, whether they were Persian, Assyrian, Babylonian, or—to name the newest landgrabbers from abroad—Greeks, Christian crusaders, Mamelukes, and Ottoman Turks. Perhaps too much conquest eventually made the city want to return to the ordinary unholy status of other places, because she cannot help but kill her prophets and stone those whom God has sent to her, to paraphrase Jesus.

This is Jerusalem the Bride.

It was late in the morning when Solomon Kellner left the tiny synagogue where he prayed morning and evening. Adjusting his coat over his prayer shawl, he began walking slowly in the direction of the Wall. The spring sunshine was like a benediction, and as he walked he meditated upon everything he had to give thanks for in the seventieth year of his life.

Solomon Kellner had been born in the other Berlin in 1929, into a family of scholars and professors whose name had been an ornament to the university since his great-grandfather's time. The family had not considered itself wealthy, but there had been comfort and happiness, books, music, and fearless laughter. He didn't remember when his parents had begun to speak in whispers when they thought he and his sisters might hear. But a child lives in the present, in the bright times between the uncertain moments.

November 1938. He was nine years old on the

Night of Broken Glass. He remembered walking the streets the following morning, seeing the fragments from the shop windows lying in sparkling drifts on the sidewalk like a strange early snow. The sound of trumpets seemed to echo in his ears. He could hear the shouts of battle, and had pressed closer against his nurse. He could feel her fear, and for a moment he thought she had heard what he had, but she had not. The trumpets had sounded for him alone, and Solomon knew in that moment, young as he was, that all the certainties of his life were gone, and that his future would be consecrated to war.

Two years passed. The time that his family could have used to flee, to emigrate to America or Canada or even Palestine, had gone, squandered by his father's belief in the power of reason, his mother's trust in the permanence of friendship. Neither foresaw that things would go so far. They had always believed that something could be salvaged, that the Chancellor's new laws were a temporary measure that would be overturned by the ridicule of sane men.

But there were no sane men left.

In the spring of 1941, when Solomon was twelve, the Kellners received their orders to report for resettlement. His mother wept, and his father looked grim, but they steadfastly believed—or pretended to—the proffered story that they would receive farmland in the East. Each of them packed one suitcase, as they had been told to, and left the bright and airy apartment on the Thielstrausse behind.

He never saw the apartment again, nor did he see the suitcase his mother had packed for him, filled with warm clothes and favorite books. In later years, that small cruelty had tormented him more than anything else: Why did the Nazis demand that they pack suitcases, give them a list of approved contents, when they never meant them to be used? By then Solomon knew, without having concrete concepts to cloak his knowledge in, what was to happen. Each new outrage was no surprise, only the manifestation of something that was already real to his inner eye. The boxcars in which they were transported without food or water, the long journey away from everything familiar, the whispered tales passed among the strangers herded together as if they were livestock intended for sale in some far-off, grim market stall.

The train stopped in a place where the walls were made of barbed wire and the sky was made of ash. His mother and three older sisters were harried in one direction, he and his father in another. It was a mistake—Solomon was young enough that he should have been sent with the women and children—and it saved his life. An hour later an angry-looking man with a clipboard pulled the eleven-year-old boy from the processing line where the new intake was being routed to the showers. Before this man and his superior could decide whether it would be too much trouble to send one little internee over to the women's side, the workday had ended.

His life continued to be spared from day to day. He understood implicitly that there was no need to search for his father. Solomon was young and strong and determined to live. He survived four years in that place of wire and ashes, and it was there that he began to study Torah. His family had not been deeply religious—all the scholars produced from the Kellners had been secular, not sacred. Solomon was called to be a warrior, and here in hell he discovered the spiritual tools for his battle, in the hearts and minds of men who passed them to him as they died.

On June 10, 1943, Berlin was declared Juden-rein—cleansed of Jews. Two years later the camps were opened, liberated by the Allies. Solomon Kell-ner was sixteen when the Russian army arrived. The war was over. He was still alive. Some went home to places they had known before the war, but Sol-omon could not bear to. The Berlin of his childhood memories was gone, and to return to what she had become would be a bitter mockery of those memo-ries. Like so many of the war's disenfranchised, his gaze turned to America. The treasure he carried within his heart waited patiently.

For the next twenty years, ten square blocks of New York City were home. He attended Columbia and gained a degree in psychology. He studied To-rah more intently, married, fathered his children, but always he understood that the war to which he had been born was not over. In 1967 he and his family emigrated to Israel, to gain citizenship under the Law of Return. In Jerusalem his practice prospered. When he turned forty, he sought out a teacher from among his colleagues in the Old City and began his study of the *Sephir Yetzirah*, the *Book of Creation*, and delved into the endless mystery of Intention transformed into Manifestation.

Years passed, quietly, filled with the small tri-umphs and tragedies of domestic life bounded around by prayer. When he reached an age that made him impatient with the intractable neuroses of lives lived in spiritual oblivion, Solomon put aside his secular life entirely. He became Rebbe Solomon the teacher. There were times when he wondered if he had chosen the right path. Every man and woman had a star-self within them; the holy fingerprint of the Most High's fashioning. Yet people seemed almost automatically to turn away from the knowledge of that inward spark, to spend their days wrapped in the pain of manufactured confusion. They prayed to God in shrines and rarely set foot in the shrine of their own heart. He knew this so well, but somehow God had not gifted him with the eloquence to awaken those who slept to the simple power of Innocence Regained. And so he spoke to those who were already stirring in their sleep. Young men who had known no other way of life than the yeshiva looked to Solomon to guide their studies. Because Solomon comprehended that there was one among the tribes of men whom he must find, one to whom he must say the word that would fully awaken him to mindfulness.

Emerging from a narrow cobbled alley, he reached the square near the Western Wall—a plaza he saw cleared from a ramshackle Muslim neighborhood a few days after the victory of the Six-Day War—and as he crossed it he paused now and again to speak to acquaintances: "Yes, how are you?" "It was a lovely birthday you had last Adar." "Of course the rabbinical court is open to you." "Why shouldn't you be heard if that's the kind of girl your Shmuel has given his money to?" This was how the length of a man's life was measured out: in prayers and friendships through the streets of a sacred city nestled within a secular one.

As he approached the Wall he saw a young man standing before it, staring as if he had never seen its ancient stones before. On the day that Moshe Dayan first entered the Old City to reclaim the Jewish right to pray at the Western Wall, he had followed tradition and inserted a folded piece of paper between the stones, on which he offered this prayer: "May peace descend on the whole house of Israel." Dayan was not famous for being religious—rather the opposite—but his prayer made as much sense politically as religiously. To date, God had not granted it on either ground.

The young man Solomon had spotted now caught sight of him. Like Solomon, he was dressed in the plain dark clothing of the Orthodox, his wide black hat and long coat looking both strange and proper beneath the radiant Mediterranean sun.

"Simon, what's wrong?" the rabbi asked, greeting his pupil. "We missed you at prayers this morning."

"I could not pray," Simon said, his voice low. "I had a dream, and you must advise me what it means."

"A dream means that you didn't die in your sleep," Solomon replied. The student didn't smile but only lowered his eyes respectfully. "So what was this dream, that you could not pray after you had it?"

"I saw the end of the world. I saw the doors of the houses marked in blood as the Angel of Death passed over, and this time not even the firstborn of Israel were spared. I saw the face of the sun covered in blood, and I saw the Ten Plagues released once more to cut the People down. And the Lord hid His face—and did nothing."

That God should seem to do nothing while good men suffered was a worldly truth that had broken many hearts and spirits before Simon's. Solomon thought of the Passover that was to begin at sundown on Friday. It was the symbol of the Jews' deliverance from bondage in Egypt, and of the promise that God had made to them, but there were moments lately when Solomon wondered if the Passover would be eaten this year. A report came in from one of the kibbutzes near Galilee that overnight all the fruit had withered on the trees—one of those portents that sends a wave of panic and fervor through the religious right—and a family was burned alive in their home nearby, even though the neighbors swore that no more than ten minutes passed between the first sign of smoke and total destruction of the dwelling.

And then there were Solomon's own terrible dreams of the Final Days. It was bad enough that he should have seen such visions himself. But how much worse that Simon, with his untroubled boyish face, should see them as well. What did it mean? *No doubt You will make this clear in Your own good time*, Solomon thought.

"After your dream, how did you feel when you woke up?" he asked.

Simon hung his head. "I felt I could not love the Lord, Rebbe, if this was to be my portion. I was too afraid."

"Love?" Solomon manufactured a snort. "Ey-eh-h, what are we, Gentiles? God asks our obedience, not the impossible." He patted the younger man on the shoulder. "It's like marriage, Simon. Love comes later, first you do right. Now go home. Ask God to remove your fear. And if you dream again, come to me. We'll talk."

"Yes, Rebbe." Simon squared his shoulders and strode off.

When he had walked a little farther, the rabbi whirled around. "You, Simon!" The troubled student turned. "It's not always wise to know everything. When God created the world, do you know what He said? 'Let's hope it works!' Understand?"

"No, Rebbe."

With a shake of his head, Solomon turned away and muttered to himself, "Maybe you need to die in your sleep after all." A pang of remorse struck him, and he looked up at the sky. "You should forgive an old man—thank You."

Simon's troubled words didn't leave him, though. Solomon spent his day in the usual holy places, but as his steps turned toward home that evening, he realized that the moment he had fitfully awaited for sixty years was about to overtake him.

Susan had flirted with the guards on both sides of the border, chattering to the clean-cut Israeli soldiers in English as she handed over her documents. It was a diversion to keep them from perusing the ink too closely. The car was searched thoroughly, first by the Lebanese, though this was a relatively quiet crossing, away from the turmoil of the Green Line that separated Israel from the Occupied Territories. The sentries had not let Michael get back into the car after the first search, and so he walked beside it as Susan drove slowly across the frontier to the Israeli checkpoint, where the entire search was repeated.

"Y'all have a good time now, y'hear?" the young Israel Defense Force lieutenant told them in a pure Dixie accent as they drove off—one last bizarre note. Dazed by the press of recent events, Michael hardly even reacted to the incongruity. The drive south and east took them most of the rest of the day. The landscape near the coast was typically Mediterranean—with the car's windows down, they could smell the sea and the biting fragrance of herbs harvested for their aromatic resins. The air was soft here, soft with moistness and the aroma of cultivated ground. It was a place as unlike the desert as possible, yet somehow it carried the memory of the desert with it, as if desolation were the foundation and this lush beauty an ephemeral overtone. The knowledge that to escape the desert was a privilege that could easily be revoked seemed to inform everyone who lived here that their garden could be taken away at whim by God or Nature. There isn't much difference between them when you're a farmer. Except that you can hazard a bargain with God, perhaps. . . .

Once they were a few miles away from the border the area began to look more like normal settled countryside to Michael's American eyes. For a moment he was oblivious to his surroundings. The images of one last firestorm rose behind his eyes as they had in his dreams, but he rejected them as proof of nothing but fear. Because if they were not dreams, the role they urged on him might not be, either.

And that couldn't be.

"A drachma for your thoughts?" Susan intruded, drawing him back to the present.

Michael shook his head. "I was just thinking that I'm out of my depth."

"You never know that for sure until you drown," Susan said cheerfully.

The outskirts of Jerusalem in the distance gave Michael an unexpected rush. When he saw the tangle of buildings from many kingdoms glowing golden in the rays of the late-afternoon sun, he tingled as if he had found a loved one safe after all hope was dead. Was this awe? The release of grief? None of the familiar labels seemed to fit—he was still left with a powerful sense of ambiguity, like a man about to make a leap that could be redemption or suicide.

They entered the environs a little before sunset; since today was not the Sabbath, this normally mattered little in terms of being able to find lodging. Susan followed the Jaffa Road. They passed the usual roadblocks and entered Jerusalem proper, which was divided into New City, Old City, and the predominantly Palestinian East Jerusalem, driving up David Street in the direction of the tourist souk.

"Where do we go now?" Michael asked, distracted by the surge of people on all sides. It was the beginning of Holy Week, and the city was jammed with visitors on bicycles, foot, and car, from the deeply religious to the deeply oblivious.

"The Jewish Quarter," she said. "We might as well go straight to the house—there's no way we're going to get a hotel room, and it's useless to waste time asking."

They inched their way through the crowded souk and reached the Cardo Maximus, the reconstructed High Street that would bring them into the Jewish Quarter of the Old City. In Michael's eyes it was the Hollywood version of Bible Land, where low dun-colored buildings opened onto narrow cobbled streets, and signs in mixed Hebrew and English exhorted visiting women to be modest in their dress. He saw one old man in gabardines leading a laden donkey down a narrow street, flanked by three soldiers with Uzis. It all felt faintly surrogate somehow, as if this was a sanitized re-creation of antiquity doing its best to nullify one world by glorifying the world that should be. *No wonder hundreds of people come to Jerusalem every year and go crazy,* Michael thought, staring out the window. *It's unreal and too real at the same time.*

"This is about as close as we're going to get," Susan said, slowing the car and stopping in front of a limestone doorway.

"What about the car?" Michael asked, sliding out through the narrow space between the car and the wall.

Susan shrugged, slinging her tote bag over her shoulder. "It will either be here when we get back, or it won't."

"Does fatalism somehow make you feel safe?" Michael asked.

"Something like that." She grinned.

Elizabeth Kellner, called Bella by everyone, had known that her husband was increasingly troubled these last several weeks. He kept a gloomy silence, even with her, but after half a century of marriage it would be surprising if she didn't know what went on in her husband's mind. When he came home from prayers early that evening, he had pushed away her greeting with a wave of his hand. "Are you telling me you don't want dinner?" Bella asked.

"Maybe some soup," Solomon replied absently. This was his shorthand formula for *Don't bother me about food. I have important things to think.* She ladled out a tureen of matzo soup and set it on the table between them. She sometimes wondered, when her strangely inward husband got into these moods, if she could give him a bowl of hot dishwater without him even noticing as he ate it.

Their marriage, from its birth in Brooklyn, had taken them to many strange places, finally to live in Israel. Some had said that only the Messiah could create the kingdom of Israel over which he would reign, and any attempt to hasten that day was impious. How could the Jews found a nation on the site of their ancient homeland and call it Israel before the Messiah gave them the right and power to do so?

It was a question for scholars, not for her. Bella Kellner, born and raised in Borough Park, New York, had followed her husband to this intimidating land without complaint—at least not much complaint, once she'd realized he was serious about his studies. She had patiently learned Hebrew; strangers on the street sometimes mocked the Yiddish that she spoke as her *mamaloschen,* though then as now it was understood through most of the country. She had adjusted to living in a state of unending war alert, learned bomb drills and gas-mask drills, and how to smile when her daughters, along with her sons, were called up for compulsory military service. Through it all she had made a home and known the lives of all who lived within it, so how should she not know now that her husband was deeply troubled?

There was nothing he wouldn't tell her, except this. Even the arcana that religious conservatives felt were unfit for a woman's ears—the study of Creation and the mystical nature of God through his holy Kabbalah—were common currency at their dinner table, for (so Solomon said) if God had made woman, and God had made Kabbalah, how could it be wrong for one to know about the other? She couldn't recall a time in the last twenty-five years when there had not been at least six people disputing around the table, eating, laughing, filling her kitchen with argumentative joy.

But now they dined alone, and Solomon was silent. Bella didn't know what words to use to break the silence.

"Are you sure this is the place?" Michael asked.

"The last time I checked," replied Susan, consulting a page ripped from her address book. Michael looked down the street, which was so narrow that he could stretch his arms and almost touch the walls on either side. Sickly yellow illumination came from two distant street lamps and the feeble light shining through curtained windows. The upper stories of the houses were built out over the first, narrowing the space above until it was almost as if he and Susan were walking through a tunnel or slot canyon. The worn stones beneath his feet sloped slowly into the center like an old mattress, shaped by the tread of centuries.

Susan rapped the knocker at Number 27. It opened, and Michael found himself staring over Susan's shoulder at a short, plump woman who looked to be in her sixties, her blond hair the traditional wig required of a married Orthodox Jewish woman. She was wearing a long-sleeved blouse with a sleeveless vest and calf-length shirt.

"Can I help you?" she asked.

"Bella! *Vos tut zich?*" a man called from inside the house.

"*Los mich tzu ru!*" she replied, and then, switching to English again, "That man gives me no peace." She shrugged, smiling, and looked more closely at Susan.

"Do I know you, dear?"

Susan nodded. "We met at a human rights conference in Switzerland. We've come to see Dr. Kellner."

"You know he does not practice anymore?" Bella said; then, before they could answer, "But come in! Where are my manners? We were just sitting down to dinner, but I'm prepared for guests; there's plenty of food. Come, come—"

Without giving them a chance to refuse, Bella led them upstairs to the second floor, where the dining room table was set with two places. An old man, wearing the *kipput* and *payess* of the Orthodox Jewish man, was seated at the head of the table. He got to his feet as they entered.

"Susan, welcome!" he said, smiling, and then looked past her to Michael.

Michael, inspecting the man's face, saw it take on a look of watchfulness, as though the old rabbi awaited the outcome of events. That alone would have been enough to fan the fires of Michael's disquiet. But the rabbi's eyes were the same eyes as the Sufi's at the bombed-out mosque.

"It took you long enough," Solomon said.

"I didn't know we had a date," Michael shot back. "I don't even know why I'm here."

"No," Solomon contradicted. "You know exactly why you're here. What you don't know is whether I know why you're here."

Susan looked confused. "Did I miss something?" Neither man answered her. After a tense pause, Solomon said, "Let's not make small talk, *nu*? There is no time for that." He pointed to the window. "Jerusalem is such a holy city, one more miracle and maybe we'll all get killed. Do you want to die?"

"Nobody wants to die," Michael answered, almost by reflex.

"Then a lot of people do what they don't want to," Solomon said. Outside, a screeching street preacher's voice rose and fell; even if Michael could not understand the words, the message was universal—fanaticism, hate, and exclusion.

"All right. Sit down, have dinner. Then I'll explain, and you'll call me a crazy old man. You have a place to stay in Jerusalem? No? My son-in-law runs a hotel in the New City. He'll have two rooms for you and the lady. She's a good girl."

Despite himself, this description of Susan amused Michael. Solomon saw the faint smile and snorted. "I'm a frail old man; I'm safe from anything women can do to me, except revenge." He took Michael's arm. "Come. Savor these last moments of peace before I tear a hole in your head."

Bella returned from the kitchen, where she had silently retreated. The meal was simple yet bountiful: cabbage and matzo soup, lamb with new potatoes, and an enormous salad. Regardless, Michael wolfed it down impatiently. At last, after an ending of honeyed oranges and strong mint tea, Bella rose, bowed, and left Solomon alone with his guests.

Despite what Solomon had said earlier about there being no time, the table talk had been light and social, studiously so. "God told me you were coming," Solomon abruptly announced. "I admit I wasn't overjoyed, but He told me I was a fool."

"God told you?" Michael repeated. The words were flat and uninflected. Any meaning could be read into them.

"This is Jerusalem; God runs a talk show here. My neighbor's boy David decided last month the Messiah was coming if only we all showed sufficient sincerity. He's out at the Wall now telling a bunch of *kasniks* that murder of unbelievers is a sacrament. He'll be arrested before the week is out, and then what will his parents do?" Solomon sighed. "But come with me. It's time I talk to you seriously." The rabbi got to his feet and began to walk from the room.

Michael glanced at Susan, but she had been husbanding her silence since the meal began. Shrugging, he followed Solomon. They went to his study, downstairs at the back of the house. It was a well-appointed room, with recessed lighting and thick Oriental carpets. The walls were lined with shelves of books in a dozen languages, a treasure-house of learning. The bookshelves were strewn with other treasures as well: a polished shofar; a worn silver kiddush cup; an ancient terra-cotta representation of the Babylonian goddess Anatha, who had once been the bride of Yahweh, seated upon her totemic lioness. There was a lectern desk in one corner, and in the center a long wooden table surrounded by chairs. More books were piled upon the table, as though those who studied here had only a moment ago departed. A long-necked halogen lamp hung over the table; when Solomon switched it on, it cast a pool of stark white light. He shook his head, and switched it off again.

"This is better, yes?" Solomon had gone to a cabinet and returned with an old bronze oil lamp, its base ringed with Hebrew letters. He took out a wooden kitchen match and held it to the spout. A small white flame leaped up. Though it was small, its illumination seemed almost as penetrating as that of the harsh overhead light.

"Do you know Talmud? The oil lamp is a symbol for the human spirit. If the lamp should go out, the world will end. So we Jews believe. And like all beliefs, it is partly true and partly false. Sit down and tell me what has happened to you."

Michael seated himself on a long narrow bench. He hardly noticed when it was that Susan later crept in and joined them. The old rabbi took his place across the table. For a moment there was silence, as Michael struggled to find the words with which to begin.

"Yesterday," he said awkwardly, "I saw something funny."

"Funny ha-ha," Solomon asked calmly, "or funny peculiar?"

This time, Michael's telling shaped events into a coherent whole—he'd had the time now to think it all through. He left nothing out of his narrative, since Solomon seemed to have some inexplicable foreknowledge.

"And?" the old rabbi said when Michael finished.

"Isn't that enough? I'd like to think I'm just crazy—"

"But in your heart you know you're not," Solomon finished. "That young man with his miracles, it's too bad you saw him. You'll meet again. God has marked you for his."

Michael winced.

"You don't like the sound of that?" Solomon remarked. "You are in a strange situation now, neither here nor there. Have you ever heard the saying, 'Don't go to sea with a foot in two boats'? That's how I see you."

"I don't understand."

"It means that you were born an ignorant person, and if you stayed ignorant, you would be happy and perhaps safe. In time you will become a wise person, and in that case you would also be happy and probably safe. As it is, you are in between, and your responses are therefore not to be trusted."

"What do you expect me to trust—you?"

Solomon got to his feet, pacing back and forth as if he were in a classroom. "Let me explain a few things about the world you live in—but first I must explain about the world I live in: the world of Kabbalah. You have heard of this?"

Michael nodded. "But I know very little about it."

"The Kabbalah is the ancient book of mysticism of the Jews. It was first made known to history in fifteenth century Spain, but tradition teaches us that the Lord gave this knowledge first to Moses. Do you believe in the Lord?"

"Do I have to?"

Solomon smiled. "We'll see. What is hard to believe, when it's plastered on billboards all over Jerusalem selling Coca-Cola, is that Hebrew is a language of magic. Each letter has a meaning— *aleph*, 'ox'; *bet*, 'chair'—and each letter has a numerical value as well. When a word is written in Hebrew, the language in which the Lord created the world, so we believe, it automatically has a numerical value. And each word whose numerical value adds up to the same number is the same word. This is a mystical concept. It is only in the mind of God that a dog and a thornbush can be one and the same, but the fact remains that numbers are spiritual entities. Mathematical angels, if you will. The number forty is the number of completion. When God caused it to rain for forty days and forty nights, He was saying: This is it, this is enough, already, this is my final word on the subject. And so it was.

"In the numerology of Kabbalah, the number for Life—*L'chaim*—is eighteen. Twice eighteen, or thirty-six, is the number of Creation, because from two lives, man and woman, all the world sprang. In Hebrew, the number thirty-six is *Lamed Vov*.

"The Bible tells us the tale of Sodom and Gomorrah. For their disobedience and depravity, God proposes to destroy the cities of the plain by hurling fire and brimstone from the sky. But Abraham challenged him, saying, 'How can you destroy the just along with the unjust if you are a just God?' This is a good debating point, and God is coaxed into a promise: If even one pure soul can be found, He will withhold His wrath."

"That pure soul was Lot," Michael interrupted, "who wasn't even a Jew, as I recall."

Solomon nodded, pleased but unwilling to be interrupted. "But Lot did not save Sodom and Gomorrah. God destroyed the cities, only sparing Lot's family if they left without looking back. We will skip the pillar of salt and the disobedient wife. This fable of the pure soul isn't a fable at all but another mystical symbol. Ever since the Fall, man has been defiled by the touch of death, but God spares the impure—which means all of us—by allowing a pure soul to exist. It is this pure soul, you understand, who alone permits the world to continue, because of the covenant that Abraham made with God. The pure soul, like the Kabbalist, would have perfect knowledge of God."

"You're saying such a person exists—has to exist—to keep Apocalypse from happening?"

"I hate to disillusion you, my son, but there is not just one pure soul," the rabbi said, lowering his voice conspiratorially. "There are thirty-six, the number of Creation. Always this has been, always this will be. And I'll tell you another secret: They are half men and half women, and, usually, none of them knows that the others exist.

He threw up his hands, as if to ward off Michael's questions. "Didn't God create everything that is, blessed be He? It is true that the Jews are His chosen people—such an honor, I can't tell you—but this doesn't mean that it is left to us alone to make up the numbers of the pure souls. Whoever they are, they do not meet—they know themselves in their hearts—and I like to imagine them: a Russian nun and an Australian shaman, Brazilian Candomblé priestesses, a Catholic cardinal, Pentecostal faith healers, Tibetan Buddhists, Shinto priests, and, if God wills, perhaps a Jew."

"Have you ever met one of these people yourself?"

"People? I have pored over the texts for months. How do we know they aren't animals? Maybe God finds a stray cat more pure than anyone among us?" Solomon said. "No, I have never met a Lamed Vovnik, but perhaps you'd like the pleasure."

"Maybe he's already had it," Susan said.

Solomon raised his white eyebrows. "This is so?"

"Can the thirty-six heal and perform miracles?" Michael said.

"You are asking the wrong question," Solomon replied, shaking his head. "Nothing can limit the thirty-six, and nothing can make them perform any act that is not completely of their will."

"Then you might meet one and never know it, because he—or she—chooses not to reveal his identity," Michael said. "On the other hand, the next

Messiah could walk out of this group, right?"

"That, as you know, is the only part of my little lecture that really interests you. Am I right? Good. One truth Kabbalah never abandons: God is willing to be known. Therefore His Messiah must also be willing to be known. But would he be of the thirty-six?" The old rabbi stopped with a sense of drama that was the product of much rehearsal. "I can't tell you."

The two Americans looked deflated. "Maybe it takes one to know one," Susan said, breaking their disappointed silence. "I mean, maybe only a member of the Lamed Vov can recognize another."

Solomon shot a finger into the air. "At last, you have raised a new possibility. We have been talking too long. Come!"

"Hear, O Israel, the last warning Yahweh has granted you! Don't you know your sin? You do, you cannot escape it. Your heifers are spotted and barren, you walk on the ground where maggots eat the dead under your feet, and therefore you will die. Where is the red cow that will nurse your soul with burnt offerings? How long can you jog in Nikes over the graves of your fathers? The Lord hath no Adidas!"

Among the hawkers and the idly curious who roamed the outskirts of Ha-Kotel this night, the boy that Solomon had worried about, his neighbor's son David, took his place. His eyes were glazed with fervor, and as he raised his voice, reciting cracked prophecies and bleak warnings, people laughed or circled around him.

The crowds gathered at Ha-Kotel, the Western Wall, were still heavy after sunset. Passover is al-

ways a time when both the men's side and the
women's bustle from dawn to dusk. Hundreds of
prayers are folded in paper and stuck between the
cracks every hour, then gathered up and buried so
that the direct line to God will not become clogged
with callers. The hyssop herbs gathering dew in
these same cracks are badly crowded out. Inside the
barrier separating the worshipers from the sight-
seers, prayers were being mumbled or whispered.
Outside this area, though, there were street hawkers,
vendors, religious beggars who harass anyone in
sight for a "donation" to the holy cause of themselves. Even the most Orthodox Hasidim, dressed in
their wide hats and thick black leggings, smoke and
snack, despite the official rules against such desecra-
tion of this sacred place.

David's diatribe was not totally insane, because
to many ultra-Orthodox Jews, the coming of the
Messiah depended upon a strange portent: the birth
of a pure red heifer in the state of Israel. Some men
on the outskirts of David's harangue listened intently
and nodded. How mad could he be if he devoted his
whole heart to the red cow? It was a mystery that
wise brains had never seen to the bottom, so why
not let a cracked brain try?

The curiosity is that, strictly speaking, this site,
the most holy place in Judaism, is not sacred in itself,
nor is the Wailing Wall even its right name. This
massive rise of golden limestone, some sixty feet
high, is the last remains of the Temple destroyed by
the Romans. It is therefore correctly called the Western Wall, but it is the Temple itself, not this retaining
wall deep inside its foundations, that is sacred.
When Jews face here to pray, the Holy of Holies that
is near the Western Wall—a chamber that only the

high priest could enter one day a year—is the invisible object of devotion. After the cruelty of razing the Temple to the ground, the Romans made the bereaved Jews pay for permission to visit the ruins, and when they saw the men and women weeping with grief as they entered this devastated place, once crowned with marble pillars and gates of silver and gold, onlookers gave it the name of Wailing Wall. If you are Jewish you do not use this semi-offensive term today.

Prayers are said here out of hope and remembrance, but the two thousand years of lamentation also continues. The rabbi intones, "Because of our walls, which are fallen," and the worshipers respond, "We sit alone and we weep." The most important day of lament is in the month of Av, in midsummer, the month when the Temple fell, but tears have no calendar. In Israeli Jerusalem, unlike the Jerusalem of the crusaders and later the Arabs, who often restricted Jewish access to one day a year, the Western Wall is open to everyone throughout the year.

As is the case with many schizophrenics, the look in David's eyes was hard to distinguish from a prophet's, suggesting how close saintly visions come to paranoid illuminations. The great difference, perhaps, is that David was illuminated with terror that could only break the surface of his mind as holy babble: "I speak with the tongues of angels and men, you hypocritical bags of pus, you filth whom God loves so much that He will burn you alive before He sees you lose your way."

No one paid serious attention to this latest example of Jerusalem syndrome. Mostly David was an object of mild suspicion, because the police knew that the tunnels underneath the Wall, which went a thousand feet along the deep foundations, were tempting targets for zealots. The mosque of al-Aqsa stood above these tunnels, and although the surface of the Temple Mount was tightly patrolled by Arab and Israeli police, the rumor never died that Solomon's treasure or the tablets of Moses or even the Ark itself lay buried somewhere in the tunnels. Some night a crazy David could somehow get a bomb in there, with the intent of blowing up the mosque, while his cheerleaders from the sidelines longed to foment a mass movement to dig for the sacred objects sullied by Muslim presence.

Counting the ancient ones, ten religions have some claim, mostly of the bloody and painful kind, to this place. No outsider could grasp the intricate warring beliefs hidden in the holiday crowd as Solomon approached with Michael and Susan. They stopped a hundred feet from the area where women would have to cover their heads with a scarf and Jewish men donned the *tefillin* and learned from volunteers how to say the blessings.

"Why are we here?" asked Michael.

Solomon raised his hand. "Wait."

For a moment nothing happened in the quickly ebbing twilight. Then there was a peculiar hum that seemed to come from nowhere in particular. One of the Hasidim, a small boy still in shorts and black leggings to denote that he hadn't been bar mitzvahed yet, began to do a little dance by himself. His uncut sidelocks swung as he whirled around. People began to notice him, it wasn't clear why, because there were other noisy children running through the crowd. Solomon frowned and pointed his way.

The boy threw a few handstands into his dance,

then his eyes began to glaze over and he looked upward. Michael heard the tootling of a clarinet to his left as a strolling klezmer band piped in. Now the boy became a little frenzied, throwing his arms out wide. Was he imploring God or inviting the other Hasidim to join in the communal dance that was their custom at weddings or on the Sabbath?

Solomon's face had darkened and he shook his head. People started to clap, and suddenly, as the humming in the air increased, the boy gathered a crowd. "What's going on?" Susan asked, but the old rabbi had turned away, grabbing at the arms of men who were attracted by the dance. "No, stay back. Don't go," he said. Some heeded him; most stared and jerked away.

The sky had been clear, and Michael could see the first stars appearing, but his attention wasn't on them—a shaft of pale blue-white light had appeared, at first very faintly, shining down on the dancing boy. His gaze became more ecstatic, and he began to leap and tumble like one of the inflicted medieval dancers throwing off a spider's poison with a frenzied tarantella. Seeing the shaft of light grow brighter, Michael pulled Susan away. "It's amazing," she murmured, resisting him.

"Please, this is what I saw with Yousef," Michael warned, but the crowd had begun shouting so loud, swaying by the hundreds around the boy, that he didn't know if she heard him.

"Don't, come back!" Solomon exhorted anyone who would listen, but the shaft of light was growing much wider now, and its color became luminous, hypnotic, the air creating its own music of humming, now freshened with a cool breeze that lifted the women's scarves and ruffled the hair of the few bare-

headed men. The communal dance embraced everyone, and the klezmer band, encouraged to pick up
the beat, switched from the old shtetl tunes of Po-
land and Russia to the jazzier pop of "Hasidic rock"
that you could hear in taxis up and down the Via
Dolorosa.

"This is going to be a disaster!" Michael shouted
at Solomon. It was weird to be the only two spoilers
in the midst of a party that now engulfed the whole
enclosure, including even the old men, who ceased
nodding their ritual prayers at the Wall and clapped
along with the crowd.

"We have to stay!" Solomon shouted back. "But
we need cover." He pointed toward the two arched
openings to the left of the men's section and started
pulling Michael with him.

"What about Susan?" Michael protested. She
would never be allowed past the barrier. Solomon,
suddenly reminded, pointed toward another escape
route, through the tunnels. The three of them began
pushing their way through the crowd, which wasn't
crushed on the edges; they made quick time and
ducked into a dark opening next to the Wall where
some steep steps led down to the tunnels themselves.

"Stop here," Solomon said calmly, able to be
heard at normal volume for the first time. When Susan and Michael turned around to face the plaza,
they were dumbstruck. The dancing boy could no
longer be seen, because the core of the mob, perhaps
five hundred people, had jammed in a knot around
him, holding tightly to each other until they formed
one swaying, hysterical organism. Women, men
shouted out in garbled Hebrew, and the organism
began to revolve in the shaft of light, totally envel-
oped in its radiance.

From a distance it looked like a strange community of joy, except that not everyone could keep up with the circle as it revolved. First an old woman, then two toddlers, tripped and fell. The massed bodies didn't pause but trampled over their bodies, and the Hasidic rock drowned out their cries. Michael shuddered and grabbed Susan close to him. "I should have gotten you out of here," he whispered.

"There was no time," she said, unable to remove her eyes from the spectacle. Like a many-headed monster, the crowd now began to howl. More people fell under the tramping feet of the dancers, yet the mesmerizing light drew in even more. Michael felt his heart pound, not just from the terrible sight but from the fear that he would be drawn in. For the shaft of light was like everyone's vision of God's light, and as it grew ever more brilliant, he understood why in near-death people feel anguish if they cannot go into the light and drop the burden of earthly life. Here was a light they didn't have to reject—couldn't reject—and the mass of bodies danced on despite the blood under their feet.

Solomon seemed to read Michael's mind. "You won't run in," he said.

Why not? What's holding me back? thought Michael, but there was no time for speculation. He caught a glimpse of the boy David, hoisted on the shoulders of another dancer, screaming at heaven with wild ravings that were drowned out in the deafening hysteria.

"There has to be another way out of here," Michael shouted; the light was expanding closer to their protected spot.

Solomon shook his head. "We aren't here by

choice. This is the beginning of the world, not the end."

"What do you mean?"

"This is their savior, the one who's going to change history." Before Solomon could explain any further, a change occurred in the dance. The sweaty faces of the dancers, red and inflamed with emotion, began to break out with some kind of weird epidermal eruption. In a few people, then more every minute, sores appeared on their arms and hands. The afflicted tried to ignore these portents and kept dancing—perhaps they thought that God was testing them like Job, or purifying them. But this stage passed quickly. Now Michael saw the sores swell; and panicky cries were mixed in with the ecstatic shouts. Quickly, too quickly for escape, the light was starting to burn.

No, no, he thought, knowing that this was how it must have been in the village. He held Susan tighter, not looking at her but only wanting to keep her from any wild temptation to run toward the monster. The heavenly light was now so bright that from outside it you could not see what was going on—only every few seconds another victim would run out, burned with flesh hanging off in bleeding, lurid strips, or more often with hands pressed over his or her eyes. The blinding had begun, and there was no way to prevent the massacre as the knot of dancers stamped on each other, slipped in their own blood, and died or inflicted death with nothing to see but blackness.

Horrified as he was, part of Michael's mind stood aside from this spectacle and wanted to—*laugh*. The preposterousness of what he was seeing, the whole bloody melodrama, had either deranged his reason, releasing the tension of such an incredible sight by insane laughter, or the urge to laugh was something else. Michael didn't feel crazy, and the laughter was not the catharsis that explodes at a wake, when grief is too painful and the immediacy of death can only be survived by a merry dance in the presence of the corpse. Mirth and death have always been bedfellows, but he knew that if he actually broke out laughing, it wouldn't be a species of grim hilarity. What it would be, he couldn't imagine.

At that moment there was no time to think about his peculiar reaction. The killing light was changing—one could see tiny flickers in it and then a gradual fading. The force that held people helplessly inside it also must have faded, because suddenly dozens of victims staggered out, some half-blinded and able to see their way to safety, others staggering piteously in random zigzags, screaming for someone to take their hand and guide them.

"Come on!" Susan shouted, bolting from the cover of the stone arcade at the mouth of the tunnel. She plunged into the throng, taking one blinded child by the hand and folding her in her dress; the little girl's clothes had been almost completely burned off. "No!" Solomon warned as Michael started immediately to run after her, but the need to tend the desperately wounded overrode the danger. Michael shouted for doctors and nurses to gather around him if they could hear his voice. Several came forward, those who had been on the edge of the light or who had managed for some unknown reason to escape its withering power.

"Where's the nearest hospital?" Michael demanded. "We have to keep all these people from dying of shock, and we need to start triage on the

worst of the burn victims." Although half of them
were on the verge of collapsing from shock themselves, a few of the survivors pointed behind his
back, toward the Jaffa Gate and the Tower of David
hulking over it. "West," someone gasped nearby,
meaning that the modern part of West Jerusalem
had the necessary hospitals and ambulances. Michael felt helpless; he couldn't put his hand on supplies or equipment, not even blankets. "We've got
to do something. Can we get them into houses on
the side streets?"

At this point, realizing that the tragedy was far
beyond anything he and this small band of survivors
could handle, Michael looked around to make sure
he could find the others. Susan was crouched on the
women's side of the enclosure, helping the worst
wounded to a safe place by the Wall where they
could lie down. The ground was littered with prayer-
books singed and in flames; the rolls of Torah stored
on shelves on the men's side were scattered here and
there, also burning. Michael couldn't see Solomon
in the melee of victims, who were now randomly
milling and crying out for their relatives and friends.
Then by chance an opening appeared, and through
it he spotted Solomon holding up the insane boy David, who had somehow survived with only small
burns on his face and arms.

"Bring him here," Michael shouted. "He may be
in shock. I can have someone walk him home." But
Solomon, if he heard him, didn't pay attention. He
wasn't tending the boy for trauma at all, Michael
noticed, but kept shaking him by the shoulders. David looked dazed; the rabbi started shouting at him
and then slapped him hard across the face. This
caused a dramatic change in the boy, who shook his

head as if waking up from a drugged sleep and immediately tore himself from Solomon's grasp. A second later he was running away down Al Wad Road, back into the heart of the Jewish Quarter.

Michael was baffled by this silently played out scene; he felt that he was watching a drama with a hidden plot. The gap in the crowd closed up again, and he lost sight of Solomon. To the right, where the Wall bordered Islamic land beneath the Al-Aqsa mosque, the commotion suddenly intensified. He saw people beginning to clump around a figure coming their way.

"Susan!" Michael called out, but before she could turn and answer him, the shaft of light, which had been steadily fading, began to crackle as if filled with lightning. He knew that it was time to run, but the mob didn't seem to be magnetized by the light anymore. A path opened, and through the mass of people Michael saw the Prophet. He was dressed in the same white robe as before, his face raised upward as he addressed the light in a commanding voice.

"This . . . shall . . . not . . . BE!"

The words were almost supernaturally loud; people backed away, covering their ears. The Prophet's face was grim as he advanced directly into the light, which seemed imperceptibly to tremble. He spread his arms out, and tears appeared as if he were beseeching a God whose presence was floating directly overhead.

"Jerusalem, who kills your prophets and stones those who are sent to you, be not shaken! Come to my mercy."

He had changed from English to Hebrew, and Michael could see that many onlookers were shaken and others deeply moved—he wondered if the quotation from the words of Jesus was a gratuitous jibe thrown in by the Prophet. There was no quibbling with his staging, however. The killing light faded quickly, its ominous humming with it, and the shaft was now so narrow that it functioned as a spotlight for the Prophet's performance.

Michael was not surprised at what happened next, a repeat of the miraculous healings under the olive trees at Galilee. Blinded and burned victims rushed to be touched, and as the young miracle-worker obliged, flicking his power with no more than the brush of a finger here, dramatically seizing someone's face between his two hands there, the crowd responded with ecstatic cries and shrieks. The mob almost got into a second trampling frenzy in their eagerness to get close; only Solomon and his small group hung back.

"So that's him," Susan said. She couldn't help sounding impressed despite the suspiciousness of such a perfect last-minute entry. "I see why Nigel is crazed to bring him to the world."

"There will be lots of Nigels now, it's only a matter of days," Michael muttered. Turning to his right, he saw Solomon shake his head in disgust before beginning to walk off toward one of the narrow side streets. "Wait, Rebbe, do you know what's going on here?"

"Yes, I'm that lucky," Solomon said over his shoulder, and disappeared into the shadows of the Jewish Quarter.

CHAPTER FIVE

TOWARD THE UNKNOWN REGIONS

It was only ten o'clock, but Bella was asleep in the upstairs bedroom when she heard the door bang and the sound of disturbed voices.

"Quick, get out of sight."

"Why, we're safe inside, aren't we?"

"No, do as I say. He is a wolf, he has a good sense of smell, and I don't want to tempt him."

She recognized her husband's voice and those of the two Americans. Troubled and curious, she put on her robe and wig, slipping out to the top of the stairs. She hadn't decided whether to speak up when her husband saw her there. "Please, go back to bed," he said seriously. But by then she could hear a loud noise that seemed to be from the street. She opened a lattice window and saw a crowd squeezing its way down the narrow passage; the sounds of cheers and excited babble reached her. She decided to run downstairs.

"Have you locked the door?" she asked, bursting into the parlor. "I've never been in a pogrom, God be thanked, but I have the worst feeling about this."

Solomon looked impatient. "These aren't Cossacks, woman, and they're not going to smash the door with axes." But the old rabbi looked troubled and intent as he turned to the Americans. "There's something you can't be here for, do you understand? Bella, take them upstairs."

"I'm totally confused. This surrogate Messiah has already seen me, and I've seen him. What kind of danger are we in?" Michael asked.

But the crowd noises were much louder now, and they could hear the grumbles and shouts of neighbors coming to their windows after being awakened. Susan had a strangely grim look on her face. Shaking her head for Michael to stop protesting, she took his hand and led him upstairs with the rabbi's wife.

When he was alone, Solomon threw the door open. He stepped outside, but almost immediately his back was pressed against the wall by the first ranks of the crowd. They had come from the Wall, waving shirts as banners, brandishing makeshift torches. It would only be a moment before he appeared. Solomon waited tensely. "So this is what you expected of me?" he muttered under his breath. "I spend fifty years trying to understand what happened to my people, and now you ask for what I cannot give, even to you?"

The crowd was more packed around the Prophet, as knotted and squashed as they had been around the dancing boy in the light. Solomon couldn't move, but he shouted, "Impostor! Stop this wickedness and show yourself!" The people nearest to him stared; some laughed and tried to push him aside. But Solomon's timing had been impeccable—the Prophet, though surrounded, was almost in front of his door.

"There is nothing pure here. He is trying to deceive you, all of you!" Thinking the old man must be out of his mind, a few people backed away, and now Solomon had a direct line of sight to the Prophet, who had stopped in the street, a quizzical look on his face. The old rabbi took two steps forward, his face fierce and set.

"I am Rabbi Solomon Kellner, an old man. I have lived with my secrets for too long, but now I have no choice. Face me."

Amid the jeers and catcalls of the mob, the Prophet seemed confused. He turned his head from side to side, as if deaf in one ear and trying to find the source of a mysterious sound.

"Who are you?" he called out; he seemed to be addressing a ghost.

"I am much more than you and much less," Solomon replied, a note of derision in his voice. "I would rather be killed by Sameel, the devil consort of Lilith, than healed from leprosy by your hand."

This bizarre defiance made the Prophet laugh. He raised a hand as he saw two angry men heading for the old rabbi. "Leave him alone."

"But, master, he isn't fit to be in your sight," said one of the men, a red-faced lout who still bore faint burn marks up and down his arms.

"Are they calling you 'master' already?" jeered Solomon. More elements in the mob were growing incensed, and he opened his door and backed inside, leaving it open. The Prophet, though still looking confused, moved toward the house.

Inside the parlor, Solomon stood his ground, staring intently as the Prophet stood in the doorway. The miracle-worker didn't step inside but only smelled the air curiously. "There's more of you here, eh?" he said.

Silently Solomon stood his ground. He heard a

faint shriek behind him, and Bella's voice said, "*Der Teufel!*"

"Be quiet and don't be afraid," Solomon whispered without turning around. "The devil's not in your living room." But the next moment, the Prophet took one cautious step inside. Although Solomon was apparently invisible to him, he saw Bella, who was standing with a soup tureen and ladle in her hand. Nervous and unable to stay put, she had run downstairs to wash dishes after dinner, running out of the kitchen when she heard her husband return.

"Is this your house, and are you alone?" he asked.

"I was making soup," Bella replied, flustered and unable to hide her fear. "Please take all those people away from here."

If he had taken two more steps, the miracle-worker would have run into Solomon, but he stopped short. "I smell deception here," he said. "And once I smell it, I never lose the scent. Live in peace." He turned and left swiftly. Solomon closed the door as Bella collapsed onto a chintz-covered sofa.

"I told you to stay out of sight," Solomon chided gently.

Bella could not stop shaking her head. "*Der Teufel*, in my own house. What will we do? What if he comes back?" She seemed on the verge of tears, frightened by a sensation that had nothing to do with the harmless, even benign presence others saw in the handsome healer.

"If he comes back," Solomon replied calmly, "try not to offer him any soup."

*   *   *

Solomon was in a talkative mood; his eagerness to open all his knowledge to them was suddenly irresistible to him. Before letting them go to the hotel room he had promised them, he insisted on enlarging on his theme of the thirty-six pure souls.

"I had to take you to the Western Wall—the Ha-Kotel—to see for myself, to assess if we are entering an emergency. Now I know that we are."

Michael was too wrung out even to be curious, much less diverted by the old rabbi's lecture style. "No lead-ins, please," he said. "Tell me what's happening. Be as straight and plain as you can."

Solomon looked annoyed but decided to comply. "I told you several hours ago that I would tell you something about your world, but first I had to tell you about my world. Now you've seen a very small piece of what I meant."

"You mean the scene at the Wall—that's something you're used to?" Michael asked incredulously.

"Yes and no. Perhaps it would help if I explained it this way. 'Pure soul' means much more than someone who polishes an apple and leaves it on God's desk, and more than someone who is sticky with virtue. *Pure* also means 'clear,' and the thirty-six are totally clear."

"About what?"

"About everything. They cannot be deceived, which means that they live in the truth. This is what the holy texts mean when they say that someone sees the light. They are not asleep or blinded like the rest of us. God needs such clarity in order to maintain the world. Do you think that the stars and mountains and seas exist on their own? They are as faint and shadowy as dreams. To keep this world intact, God needs someone to dream it, century after century. Without a dreamer, everything you see would disappear. This is the secret meaning behind the Torah's tales of God destroying the earth."

They were talking in the parlor, all of them together. Susan sat on the carpet near Michael's feet. Bella, who had been allowed the best armchair, had fallen asleep in it. When Susan kept absorbing the old rabbi's speech without comment, Michael wondered if she had fallen asleep, too.

Solomon continued, "Think of the thirty-six as the glue by which God maintains creation: The Kabbalah teaches that the Lamed Vov are the switching mechanism through which all human consciousness moves. Normally the thirty-six simply are—what you would call a passive system. But the power of Creation flows through them, and if they choose to take control of this power, they can literally change reality. It is at this point that we approach the crux of our problem."

Michael didn't even dare look at Susan now. It was too complicated, too vast, too confusing, and utterly surreal. He was being asked to believe in a God who meddled in His own creation through a network of anonymous secret agents.

"Okay," Michael said cautiously. "There are thirty-six pure souls. I don't see how they relate to this evening's disaster."

The rabbi smiled sourly. "You will, my son. The Kabbalah teaches that each of the pure souls has his counterpart, so that everything should balance, as Chokmah balances Binah and Kether balances Malkuth. Eighteen pairs. Think of it as God's chromosomes. It is said that if all the rest of creation were to perish, it could be rebuilt from the bones of the thirty-six."

The rabbi settled himself in the chair opposite Michael and gazed somberly into the flame of a candle on the center of the windowsill. "So long as there are thirty-six, the Covenant is kept, but if they fall out of balance, Creation becomes vulnerable, as now, when the ancient enemy from the shadow side of the thirty-six appears."

"Then that is who this is?" Susan asked abruptly, unable to keep still any longer.

Solomon nodded. "Because he is as far away from the light as the thirty-six are close to it, I call him the Liar or the Dark Soul. He is not Satan or a demon but a human being who has seen into the light and then chosen to back away. You recall my mention that the pure souls have certain powers? Well, here's a mystery: They're not meant to be used. Their power is a by-product of their knowledge of God, nothing more."

Convenient, Michael thought, watching the old man's face. He could feel Susan's warmth as she sat beside him—even if she and Solomon Kellner were friends, he could not believe she'd ever heard this from him before.

"So. With their power, the thirty-six could do many things. They could set aside death. But nothing in all of Creation is meant to be eternal, save the mind of God. Instead, each Lamed Vov dies in his or her time, and another pure soul is born to take his place. Now I bring up a problem. There are not thirty-six anymore, and yet thirty-six remain."

"That's a pretty riddle," Susan said. "If one of them is gone, how can there still be thirty-six?" She sounded faintly indignant.

"One betrayed the rest. He didn't die." The old man was gravely serious now. "There was this young man—call him Ishmail, the Dark Soul, he who lies to God. He was one of the Lamed Vov. His time came to die, but he didn't. He used the power he had acquired to step outside of Creation, outside of time. To mock God in the worst way, by refusing to listen.

"You see our problem now? The Liar was not dead, so his replacement couldn't be born. But he was no longer a pure soul, so the Covenant with God could not be kept: The thirty-six were no longer thirty-six. What to do? They had to improvise— bring someone up from the promising candidates, so that the framework of Creation could remain whole. Of course, if they chose the wrong one, he would be destroyed by the Glory of God instead of coming into his power, and Ishmail would gain valuable time to work his will, perhaps even to suborn others of the Lamed Vov.

"He knows this, and for many centuries, every time there is a chance that he will be replaced, he comes back into this world to create unbearable disaster and chaos. And now he's come back again. No one knows his plans. But you've seen the young miracle-worker gathering his following. He pretends to be good, but to do what he does at all is to insult God. He wields his transformative powers openly, heedless of the effects they have on the souls of the Unawakened. And he is out to destroy everyone who might complete the sacred number. As David is being destroyed."

"David?" Michael asked, startled.

"Yes," Solomon said heavily. "A good boy, a scholar—he could have purified himself to an extreme, given time. And Ishmail knew this: He came to David, sent him visions of the Apocalypse."

Just like he sent them to me, Michael thought. But the comparison was too monstrous, too egotistical, and he thrust it aside.

"Now David has fallen. And Ishmail is confident enough to take possession of man's world as he sees fit."

"I'm sorry," Michael said quickly, getting to his feet. His heart beat very fast. "It's—I'm sure you're sincere. . . ." He stopped, not completely sure what he was going to say. "I'm not one of them," he finally managed. "I'm not pure. I don't even believe in God. I may even hate Him."

"Why not?" Solomon asked, puzzled without seeming offended. "Do you think I have never cursed God? In America you preach that God's love is easy, that it comes raining out of the sky like soup, and all you have to do is hold out a bowl and fill it. Then you hold out your bowl, and surprise! there's nothing there. So you weep big crocodile tears. You think that anything that isn't easy is impossible. You're wrong. Love is like gold, not soup: You must dig hard for it, but it's there.

"The holy books declare that each of the Lamed Vov sees so much suffering that his heart freezes solid and becomes a block of ice. After death God must warm it between His hands for a thousand years; only then can the soul enter Paradise. When you have suffered that much, come to me and tell me about hating God."

Michael shook his head despairingly. "This Prophet whom you call Ishmail, you're basically saying he's the Antichrist, but somehow you want me to stand up and fight him. You don't exactly say how. I'm an ordinary man, not a 'promising candidate.' "

Susan was regarding him with alarm. "What's gotten into you? No one said anything about you or what you had to do. Calm down."

The old rabbi shook his head. "Look to your own heart for answers; God does not gossip about His intentions. I'm going to go call my son-in-law at the hotel."

When Solomon had left the room, Michael turned and looked at Susan. "But what am I supposed to do?" he demanded angrily. "Everybody keeps telling me to follow my heart: Well, I've got a bulletin for everyone. My heart isn't saying a damned thing other than thump-a-thump, at racehorse speed."

Susan twisted a smile. "Either you'll figure out what to do, or this Ishmail will find you and settle it for you."

"This is your idea of comfort?" Michael asked.

Solomon came back into the room, holding a small piece of paper in his hands. "You know the city?" he asked, and Susan nodded. "Fine. I called Yacov; he's saving you a room. Here's the address. God go with you—and do not stay more than one night here, Michael. You may not believe you are one of the chosen, but he may. And he fears you."

"Great," Michael said. "Maybe that's an apprentice power—I've got him shaking in his boots for fear he'll die laughing when he sees me again. Paralysis affects some people that way."

The New Jerusalem Hotel was at the edge of the Christian Quarter of the Old City, near the Jaffa Gate. A hundred years old, it had the same worn look of faded grandeur as the Syrian Grand in Damascus. Each was the high-water mark of a fallen empire, each a relic of a world incomprehensible in modern terms, as unattainable as lost Atlantis.

In a night that seemed overstuffed with portent, it had been another miracle that the car was still where Susan had left it. They reclaimed it, and it was now parked in an alley a few blocks away. Susan's overnight bag had still been inside the trunk, but Michael's possessions had been reduced to the clothes he stood up in before they'd even started on this quest. He leaned against a massive faux-marble pillar as Susan, whose polyglot of tongues was extensive, proceeded to the desk to see about their room. Even at midnight the lobby of the New Jerusalem was jammed with a cosmopolitan mélange of travelers, hotel porters, vendors, and guides, and Michael marveled at Solomon Kellner's ability to have secured them a room at this most crowded of tourist seasons, son-in-law or no son-in-law. All around him, in the worn Oriental splendor of the lobby, diverse foreigners huddled with their battered piles of luggage, squabbling with one another and remonstrating the hotel staff. Vendors hawked meat pies and warm sodas, palm-leaf crosses and olive-wood rosaries—along with pieces of the True Cross on demand, Michael thought sourly.

He heard some American voices in the babble—after a long time without hearing it, English sounded rather loud, flat, and uninflected, like barking dogs. But he was not tempted to introduce himself to any fellow countrymen. His eyes were scratchy and dry with lack of sleep, and he felt an indefinable hollowness in his midsection that did not come from hunger.

It was a relief when Susan returned from the front desk, dangling an old-fashioned key with a brass key-tag between her fingers.

"Our room is ready. Annihilation will have to wait, at least until I get a bath."

The room was on the fifth floor, overlooking a quiet backstreet. Michael supposed it was the holdout room that every busy hotel saves for dire emergency; it was too good to be left unoccupied during Holy Week for any other reason.

The place smelled clean and close with heat, like sheets fresh from the dryer. The furniture was Danish modern dating from the sixties, its low sleek lines an odd counterpoint to the Victorian proportions of the room. A half-open door led to a bathroom with an old-fashioned iron clawfoot tub.

Susan walked over to the window and opened it. The night air was cool and smelled of oranges and spices wafting through engine exhaust.

"Do you believe him?" Michael asked her.

"Who, Solomon? I suppose I have to. The real question is what that means. I'm sure we're going to wind up alone in this. Your miracle-worker is going to sweep through the world like a bonfire, you know that."

Michael nodded. He brushed her hands away, getting to his feet and walking over to the window. "People don't just smuggle themselves across the Green Line for fun, especially middle-level WHO administrators. You knew what he'd tell me, didn't you?"

"I was pretty sure," Susan admitted in a low voice. "I knew he was a scholar of these things; they're not foreign to Solomon's reality."

"The word *reality* is coming up too often in our conversations," Michael remarked, staring at an Arab tenement across the way. He could see a family arguing around a table set with dirty dishes and wine bottles. "The thing is, when used properly, the word *reality* refers to things that are real."

"It doesn't always work that way," Susan said. "The human mind has a tendency to equate the unknown with the impossible. What makes something real? Ultimately, just the fact that we know it exists. But tons of things could be just hiding, ready to spring out at us."

"I can't help resenting Solomon for what he told us."

"Why?"

"He said he was going to tell me something about my world, but really he started tearing it apart. What kind of a world is it when thirty-six people, assuming this isn't all a fantasy, could simply lift a finger and solve everything?"

"Is that what you'd want?"

"My brain's not exactly steel-honed right this minute, but wouldn't you?"

"I don't know. These Lamed Vov, what would be the effect on ordinary people if they came waltzing through our lives, making everything perfect? A lot of other things that make us human—the striving, the hope, the heroism—would all be gone, wouldn't they?"

"You wouldn't sacrifice them for ending misery and sickness and war?"

"That's the peculiar thing. Human beings most of the time aren't defined by good and noble things. We make messes to clean up, devise enemies and dark forms of ignorance to fight against. Maybe the thirty-six would strip us down to a skeleton of ourselves, because there'd be nothing left for us to fight against. Our lives would be sublimely tedious and outside any will of our own."

"So you're saying that all the wars are worth it?" Michael said. "All the people who starve, who still die every day of diseases we've known how to cure for almost a century, who are kicked to death by soldiers just for being in the middle of a dusty road running from destruction—that's okay?"

"Absolutely," Susan said sarcastically, her voice cutting through the dark. "Give me your version. Once you've got your paradise on Earth, what then?"

"What do you mean? You've got paradise on Earth. What more could there be?"

"People are still going to die," Susan said. "Even if they only die of old age. And the new Lamed Vov who are born—they're the ones who have to keep paradise rolling, right? Maybe they can't do that unless they're born into a world that needs them, and there goes your paradise in one generation, just about the time people will have started to forget. Or say the first pure souls who create paradise decide to use their powers to end death? What happens then?"

"Everybody lives forever?"

"Wouldn't that just lead to a senile world for eternity? And if you solve that, overpopulation turns into the greatest evil. Eventually there are no choices left for anyone to make but our pure-soul dictators. Even if the Lamed Vov worked miracles to feed every hungry mouth with manna from heaven, how long until there were only soulless robots to tend to?"

"Okay," Michael relented slowly. "But why can't

they do something? Cure cancer or AIDS or save the Amazon?"

"And how could they stop there? How much interference is okay, and how much is too much? Do you know?" Susan demanded.

Michael shook his head in frustration. "But it doesn't make sense. They're perfect, aren't they?"

"Perfect enough to know their limits, apparently."

"You've given this a lot of thought," Michael conceded, slumping deeper in his chair and not at all reassured by her conclusion.

"Not as much as you're going to have to," Susan said.

After waiting so long, making love had had a special intensity that seemed to sweep away all minor concerns and bind the two of them together in an understanding. Whatever might happen in their lives, there had been a moment of intimate honesty and communion that would become the foundation of their future together.

"Why do you like me so much?" he had asked her afterward. "Because you found out I'm a god?"

"No." Susan laughed. "Because I figured out we're both probably going to be dead tomorrow."

A veteran of many late shifts and sleepless nights, Michael had become a connoisseur of the hours before dawn. Each one had its own texture, its own peculiar taste. Even in a windowless room you could feel the night pass, each phase slipping away, followed by the next, like a parade of shadow creatures beneath a lightless sky.

In the bed, Susan's even breathing attested to her

peaceful and untroubled sleep. He envied her that, even though for one night the visions hadn't haunted him.

Maybe there won't be any more premonitions, Michael thought. *There don't have to be. He's here.*

Michael smoothed the sheet around Susan as he rose and walked over to the window. Most of modern Jerusalem lay to the north and west of the hotel, and its lights cast a faint burnished glow over the horizon. Jerusalem the Golden had transformed itself into an electric aura, modernized, secular. Before yesterday, if someone had performed miracles here, people would just have laughed and turned away.

"You hope," Michael whispered, very softly, but down deep he knew that people were never that rational. It was so much more likely that a miracle-worker would touch off riots the like of which the city had never seen. Especially here, especially now. With that spark, war and chaos might soon spread, because the faithful hate nothing more than a miracle owned by a competing faith.

Was that what Ishmail wanted? Michael didn't think that Solomon had told him everything he knew. He had claimed that the Lamed Vov had no contact with each other or with outsiders, but in that case, how did he know that Ishmail had fallen and refused to accept death?

Michael leaned his forehead against the cool window glass. Despite his argument in front of Susan, he didn't know if he wanted to meet any of the pure souls. Michael was the child of a mechanistic cosmos that ran by itself, of a blind watchmaker who didn't play at dice. What room was there in this philosophy for men and women who held the power of transformation in their mortal, finite hands?

As a doctor, he only had a faint echo of such power, and doctors, notorious for playing God, more often played at suicide and drug addiction. *We are not meant to have complete power. No one has the wisdom to use it wisely. No one.*

This, then, was his position: He rejected the Lamed Vov and wanted to deny their validity. As soon as he told himself this, the hell of the visions he carried within him faded a little. He knew what the sword was, now. It was choice, it was mastery, it was the freedom to let the darkness be.

Now he wouldn't draw power from the stone. Temptation had lost. In the final analysis, it really didn't matter whether Solomon Kellner's words were true, whether the Lamed Vov were real, whether a master of lies was afoot in the world with apocalypse in his hands. None of that mattered in the face of the single salient fact that Solomon had offered Michael the chance to wield the same force that the thirty-six had already renounced.

I won't play their games.

He thought of the young Prophet doing such spectacular good with such devious and terrible ulterior motives. What else was new? Hadn't Pontius Pilate said there was always a new prophet out of Jerusalem?

He'd tell Susan in the morning, and the two of them could make their way back to Damascus, then he could return to work. And he could try to forget the visions entirely, now that he knew what they represented.

Ishmail might hunt him down and kill him at Palmyra, but if the Dark Soul had the power that Solomon claimed for him, he'd realize that Michael was no threat to him and his plans. The old rabbi had implied that there were many who shared Michael's potential to become a pure soul. Let him and Ishmail chase after another one of them, and let their candidate not be a doctor who already had too many memories and too many hostages to fortune. He crawled back into bed once more.

He was alone in an empty bed when the late morning light finally dragged him back to consciousness. Michael rolled over extravagantly, then scrambled to avoid the edge of his narrow army cot before he realized that he wasn't in his tent at the aid station.

A hotel in Jerusalem. That was where he was. But where was Susan?

Splashing sounds behind the bathroom door gave him his answer. Reaching for his clothes, he began to dress. His life had been nearly wrenched out of its tracks in the last few days, but now he'd found his equilibrium again. There were things he could not be asked to do, that he was probably incapable and unworthy even to attempt. He had mapped the edges of his world, and that was the way things were.

Susan tested the water in the steaming tub gingerly. Maybe she'd gone a little overboard with the hot water, but at the Syrian Grand the choices were a tepid shower in your room or a problematic tub bath under semi-public circumstances in the basement.

She wished they were going to be staying longer in Jerusalem, but she knew it wouldn't be safe. The man Rabbi Kellner had called Ishmail would be searching for Michael, to destroy him before he could become one of the Lamed Vov. Whatever choice Michael made, Ishmail would see him as a threat and move to attack him. According to the Rabbi, his tactic was to eliminate all those who might be elected to the thirty-six before he moved against the group itself.

Susan had only suspected about the Lamed Vov when she had risked bringing Michael here, but she had known that Kellner was a doctor for diseases of the spirit, and the same capacity for healing was in Michael. As the daughter of a doctor, she knew they weren't saints. But Michael had shown unsuspected depths. He had tolerated her obsessive wariness. When he'd passed through Alexandria on his way to Palmyra, she had immediately classified him as too good to be true, the sort of gilded WASP prince who wouldn't last three months in the primitive conditions of a refugee camp or a medical aid station. She'd been wrong. He had lasted and come back for more. She became curious enough to dig deeper; he became a riddle that Susan had to solve.

She found out that underneath his surgeon's confidence he could be shy, frugal, caffeine-addicted. He lived to work, like her. Somewhere along the way she stopped seeing him as a riddle and began to see him as a person: kind, vulnerable, but also dedicated, if he was driven by demons, to keep them from her. Michael had healed her of scars she thought she would carry forever, and she knew that he had a similar effect on others around him. The only one who didn't see this was Michael himself.

In the last half-year they'd fought more than ever, brawling with the kindred savagery Susan had learned in her own family. Michael started working insanely long hours without rest and throwing himself carelessly into harm's way. When he was determined to backtrack the plague victim into Iraq, she feared that she would never see him again, that he would finally greet the annihilation that he seemed to have been courting so ardently. Then he'd shown up at the side of the road like a white knight in a black limousine, and when he explained about the terrible visions, his self-destructive behavior had finally made sense.

The water in the tub had cooled while she daydreamed. Susan climbed out and wrapped a towel around herself. The bathroom was filled with steam. She walked over to the mirror and used a corner of the towel to wipe it clear.

Something that was not her own face stared back at her from the mirror's surface.

A face. Young and olive-skinned, the face of a beautiful youth just crossing the border into manhood. Then she recognized it from Nigel's photographs. Ishmail. He smiled at her, a radiant smile, filled with joy.

Then he reached through the mirror as if it were a window frame and touched her face.

Susan screamed.

There was a desperate, unbelieving quality to the sound of the scream that galvanized Mi... action before he could think. Th... of a spider that had crawl... on and on, ripped fr... mortal terror.

"Susan!"

He flung him... opened inward... have sprung ba... like hitting a... shocked breathles...

"Don't go in there."

Michael scrambled to see who had spoken.

An old woman stood in front of the closed door that led out into the hallway. Her age could have been anywhere from sixty to eighty. She was an archetypal little old lady in tennis shoes. She appeared to be only five feet tall and stooped with the calcium deficiency of age. Her warm brown eyes were bright and alert in a face seamed with living, and she wore a flowered scarf tied over her mouse-gray hair. She was dressed in a pink cardigan and a short flowered skirt. She was carrying a shopping bag from a local department store and was wearing tennis shoes that looked more like running shoes.

Michael took all of this in at the same moment that he was still reacting to the fact of her presence. She looked so completely harmless, like anyone's grandmother, but there was no way she could have gotten into the hotel room through that locked—and bolted—door.

Even while he turned this over in one part of his mind, Michael was clambering to his feet and preparing to assault the door again. The screaming ʳoke off abruptly, and the silence that followed was ᶠᵉʳ worse.

ˡ shouted. He flung himself at ᵉpared for resistance.

ᵃn cried. "I'm warning

ʰe bathroom door ᵃel hit it one last

ᵉl was gone. The ᵒrway where the

bathroom had once been was a sheer drop onto the floor of a desert canyon a thousand feet below. The door, knocked from its hinges, was falling into space, spiraling downward into the void, leaf-small already with distance. Its fall made the absurdly impossible grimly real. Soft parching wind blew at him as though someone had opened an oven. Michael teetered off-balance, feeling his momentum carry him forward, leading him through the door into empty space.

Where he would die.

Strong fingers, sharp as claws, gouged into his arm and dragged him back. Michael fell backward onto the worn dusty carpet of the New Jerusalem. He scrabbled crabwise away from the doorway until his back was pressed against the side of the bed.

"Who are you?" he demanded, still staring at the hole in the world that had suddenly opened. The mystery woman was kneeling beside him, still holding his arm. This close, he could smell a faint old-lady smell of scented talc and fresh laundry. She was real beyond dispute.

"Your friend," she said.

He turned his head to glance at the bedroom window, and felt a pang of sickening nausea as he saw that it still reflected the rooftops of Jerusalem. Window and door—one of them was a lie.

The walls of the room all at once burst into flame.

One moment they were the genteelly faded striped wallpaper that had become familiar through a night's residence. The next, they were covered in sheets of fire, behind which the pictures on the walls hung unconsumed. Fire gave the room the brightness of the desert sun at noon, and Michael could hear the sound that a firestorm makes, the rushing, roaring sound of incandescent motion. With tremendous will, he could have ignored the flames as a species of visual hallucination, except for the heat pressing against his skin as if the walls themselves had moved inward. It was the deadly heat of a firestorm, sucking the oxygen out of the air and killing within seconds.

He was dying. There was no escape from the ring of fire. Even the open doorway was filled with it.

There was not even time to judge his own sanity, to think and reflect and decide what was real or how these things could be. Instinctive as an animal, Michael reacted to the irresistible evidence of his senses. He gasped and struggled for air, but breathed only searing heat, terrifying heat. Sweat erupted on his skin and dried instantly, coating him in his own body's salt.

"Be calm," the woman said beside him. "Focus. He can't see you. He lost the Light, and now he can't see it. He's guessing that you're here."

He'd forgotten she was there. He stared into her eyes. There was no fear in them—no fear and no fire. She held out her hand again. Michael took it. Her clasp was strong and dry and warm.

The flames went out. The absence of heat was like a cold shock. Michael bent forward, leaning his head on his knees, gasping.

"I'm Rakhel Teitelbaum," the old woman said, in American-accented English. "Is this your first visit to Jerusalem?" The question struck Michael as bizarre. He didn't want to look toward the bathroom door again, but he forced himself to look.

The door was there, closed and innocent. He felt his ability to remember the last few moments slacken, as though what had happened possessed the vivid perilous immediacy of a dream, and like a dream could find no place for itself in the world of wakefulness. Soon it would be gone, and his life would knit itself together around the gap. He got to his feet, realizing with a pang of surprise that Rakhel was still there. She grimaced.

"Now you say: Hello, Rakhel, I'm Michael. Shalom. Next time let me save your life," the old woman said, answering herself.

Shock. I'm in shock. He felt light-headed and wanted to weep. The symptoms were familiar: the disorientation, disorganization of thought, inability to associate with his surroundings. Something very bad had happened, and with growing dismay Michael realized that he didn't know what it was and had no way to find out.

"Susan?" he said weakly. For a moment he entertained the very real possibility that there was no Susan at all—or if there was, that she had not come to Jerusalem with him. *No. She was here. Or she had been. What had happened to her?*

"I don't want to rush you, but we should leave," Rakhel said.

Michael stared blankly at her.

"Leave? But we've got to get Susan." He took a hesitant step toward the bathroom door and turned.

"Who are you?" he asked at last.

"Rakhel—" she repeated, but he cut her off with a sharp gesture.

"Who are you really?" His voice low and dangerous. "You're one of them, aren't you? What have you done with her?"

As he spoke, out of the corner of his eye he saw a ripple of motion.

"Guess," Rakhel said sarcastically. "We don't

have time for this now. Trust me. It's time to go. Past time, in fact."

Michael turned toward the movement. The mirror over the dresser was melting.

That wasn't quite right. It was shimmering, like a pool of quicksilver that someone had blown on, like a pool of water that had been tipped up on its side and hung there in defiance of gravity. As he watched, the surface stretched and broke, the silver flowing back from human fingers. Hands . . . arms . . . a face.

The face of the Prophet. Ishmail turned his head this way and that, looking around the room as he climbed through the mirror like an open window. He was dressed as he had been when Michael had seen him near Nazareth, in the robes of a desert wanderer. For a moment his gaze crossed Michael's, but Ishmail's expression didn't change. He couldn't see either of them.

Is he blind? Michael wondered, in a moment of automatic assessment. But his movements were those of a sighted man. *He can't see us because he can't see the Light.*

Rakhel's fingers were plucking at his sleeve, urging him silently toward the door.

"Where's Susan?" Michael shouted. Behind him, he heard Rakhel hiss.

Ishmail's head whipped around, focusing on Michael's voice. He stared, his perfect face calm.

"She's with me," he said. "Why don't you come with me, too?"

There was humor in the voice that chilled to the bone. It made one think of the mindless, selfish hunger of a grinning shark.

There was nothing he could do for Susan here,

Michael realized. His best hope was to escape and go back to Rabbi Kellner's. He was the one who knew how to fight Ishmail.

"You don't want me for an enemy, Michael. I can be really petty."

Armageddon. The bar where everybody knows your name, Michael thought, with a desperate flippancy. He took a step backward, but Ishmail's gaze didn't follow the movement. *He still can't see me.* Rakhel's hand was guiding him back toward the door.

"Don't punk out on me, now. I imagine that you've got a lot of questions. I can answer them, you know. Michael? Are you there?"

His tone was so seductively reasonable. Now Michael's back was pressed against Rakhel's side; he could almost feel the sensation in his own hands as she grasped the doorknob and slowly began to turn it.

"Don't leave me!" Ishmail cried loudly, stepping forward.

Rakhel opened the door, and suddenly she was knocked backward into the room again, staggering Michael so that he stepped forward, almost into Ishmail's arms. Behind him he heard an indescribable clamor. A pack of wild dogs—coal-black and larger than any Michael had seen in his time here—boiled into the room.

If he touches me, it's all over, Michael was thinking with a preternatural clarity. He threw himself sideways, across the bed.

Rakhel was pressed up against the wall, unmoving. The wild dogs had found her shopping bag and were fighting over it, worrying it to bits, but they didn't seem to see its owner. Carefully, Michael rolled across the bed and began to let himself down on the far side. He glanced up and caught Rakhel watching him with an approving expression.

Ishmail rushed forward, throwing the dogs out of his way as though he hoped to find Michael underneath them. And though apparently he could hear human voices, the noise of the dogs quarreling effectively masked all sound, giving Michael and Rakhel some breathing space.

But the room isn't that large. He'll find us eventually, unless we can get out of here.

Suddenly the barking of the fighting dogs ceased. Michael slid under the bed and looked across the carpet. Only Ishmail's bare feet on the carpet. He looked around for Rakhel's feet but couldn't see them anywhere. He squirmed farther under the bed.

"Michael? Why are you doing this? Join me. Help me. We're the same, you and I."

"Don't you believe him, *bobbeleh*," Rakhel breathed in his ear. He twitched spasmodically, but didn't utter a sound.

Most hotel bed frames are bolted to the floor, so that enterprising guests cannot steal them. But either the New Jerusalem attracted a better quality of guest or their beds weren't good enough to steal. Looking up, Michael could see that the mattress was on casters, able to move freely.

Wired on adrenaline and sheer terror, Michael tipped the bed up and over. "Go!" he shouted, pushing Rakhel ahead of him.

Michael heard Ishmail's start of surprise. "Go, I said!" he yelled again. The bed was teetering on end; he gave it an extra shove.

Through the open door he could see the hall beyond. He flung himself through it, unable to see the old woman, and as he turned to find her he felt the floor dissolve under his feet, leaving him sliding down as through phantom sand—

Into darkness.

CHAPTER SIX

SMOKE AND MIRRORS

Susan screamed, recoiling from the man in the mirror. She slipped on the tiles and would have fallen, but Ishmail reached out of the mirror and grabbed her left arm just below the elbow. His touch terrified her with an atavistic, irrational fear. She scrambled for her balance. All her weight was hanging from one arm as Ishmail pulled her toward him. She could see his arm thrusting through the mirror: the sleeve of his rough cotton, worn with many washings, and his smooth perfect skin, only faintly sun-kissed.

"Don't resist," he said in an eerily calm voice, without anger or urgency. His face behind the mirror glass was serene, uninvolved in her fate, concentrating wholly on the task at hand. But his fingers dug cruelly into her flesh.

"Let me go!" Susan whispered fiercely. After her first scream, she realized that, close as Michael was on the other side of the door, there was no use calling out for him.

Then Ishmail pulled, and her fingers met the surface of the cold wet glass, hard and resistant beneath her touch. She clutched her other hand around the edge of the sink to brace herself. But no matter how hard she pulled away, his grip didn't slacken. Needles of pain shot up her arm as the heel of her hand pressed hard against the mirror glass. In another moment it would break.

And then she felt the fingers begin to sink in as if they were sinking into a plate of aspic: cool, closing around her skin with a slick remorseless pressure. Her arm slid in quickly now, allowing Ishmail to retreat completely to his side of the reflection. She could no longer feel the separate pressure of his grip on her arm; it was like being caught on some demonic conveyor belt sucking her into the unknown.

Oh, God, no—don't let it get me. I won't fit. I won't fit. He's trying to tear me apart.

Her other hand slipped off the edge of the sink, and she was jerked into the mirror as far as her shoulder. Her cheek slapped stingingly against the glass, and she felt sudden new terrors of asphyxiation, of blindness, of being buried alive in an unknown grave.

There was nothing she could do about it. The supernatural traction was lifting her off her feet. Susan thrashed wildly, turning this way and that, fighting for a few more seconds of life. Her chin was pressed against her chest, but almost immediately she felt the cool kiss of the glass against the nape of her neck as the back of her head began to sink into the mirror. She tried to pull her head forward and couldn't. The cool insistence began to creep over her scalp, over her ears—and there was silence. She was breathing in great gasping lungfuls of air now, her staring eyes fixed upon the window only a few feet away.

Outside that window was morning, and the city, and all the details of a normal life in a normal world.

Tears spilled out of her eyes and ran down the glass. She shut her eyelids tight as she felt a tickling pressure at the corners, and when she changed her mind a moment later she found she could not open them again. She had time for one last openmouthed gasp before the coolness filled her mouth, and she was gagging and choking trying to spit it out, fighting helplessly as the glass meridian moved down over her body.

"He's using her," Rakhel said calmly. "That was always the danger. Love makes us vulnerable—but without love, we aren't human. It's a paradox, *nu*? God loves paradoxes, you may have noticed. Like crossword puzzles."

"I never had time for crossword puzzles," Michael said with supreme irrelevance. He was in pitch-black darkness, sitting on something firm, though he had no memory of landing, only of beginning to fall as he passed through the doorway of his hotel room. He reached out, and his fingers encountered a smooth surface, neither hot nor cold, faintly yielding like hard rubber.

"Where are we?" he asked, trying to control his fear and the strong nausea in his stomach.

"Nowhere. I thought that would be the safest place to take you," said Rakhel.

It looked like nowhere. When he inhaled deeply, he could smell nothing, not even dampness. He could not tell whether the space surrounding him was large or small. In the absolute blackness, it came as a relief when he touched his face and could feel that his eyes were open.

"What can you see?" Rakhel asked.

"Not a blessed thing," Michael said.

"Good. Now maybe you'll stop all this nonsense and we can talk."

"Me?" Michael asked, indignant. "All I was doing was trying to stay alive." Rakhel snorted eloquently. He felt a surge of irritation but pushed it down again as a useless emotion. He tried to recall exactly what had happened, only to meet a disturbing blank wall in his mind.

"Do you like movies?" Rakhel asked, apparently sitting to his left about two feet away. "I understand that when they hire extras to flee from a disaster, it doesn't look convincing if they all look completely terrified. People are different, even in a catastrophe. So some are told to show grade-one panic, another group is assigned grade-two, grade-three, and so on. It's much more realistic that way."

Ignoring her, Michael got to his feet, but the darkness disoriented him. He tried to cling to a nonexistent wall for support.

"Careful," Rakhel warned.

"You can see me?" Michael asked, barely catching his balance.

"This is your private darkness," Rakhel said calmly. "Naturally, everyone's darkness is private in one way or another, but that's not really the point here, is it?" He decided not to answer but to concentrate instead on regaining a grip on his mental faculties. "The point here is panic," Rakhel went on. "If you were fleeing the giant lizard that ate Detroit, I'd assign you grade-two panic. I mean, you're actually at about grade-six, but you don't show it well."

"Maybe I just hide it well." Hearing her laugh, Michael was sorry she had baited him into answering. "Look," he said, voice tight. "Could we get out of here or could you turn on the lights or something?"

"I don't know. I'd have to trust you a little more. Try breathing."

"What?" Then he noticed that in fact he wasn't breathing. This insight didn't cause him to suddenly inhale, however. He felt dizzy and with a conscious effort tried to draw air into his lungs—it didn't work. The air all around him, tepid and unscented, was a plausible fiction, nothing more. He was drifting through a void, and suddenly his mental image of his location changed, and he stood on an infinite plain in a lightless universe.

"It's not your choice to live or die," Rakhel said, her voice reaching him faintly from a distance. "If you don't breathe, you'll just pass out."

He wasn't listening. The oxygen deprivation in his body was starting to reach his brain, heading for the four-minute limit that would cause cerebral damage. Michael accessed this bit of medical minutiae quite clearly. Suddenly there was a spark of light in the darkness, and at the moment of its appearance the cosmos developed three dimensions, orienting itself with relation to the spark. *And God said, "Let there be Light."*

He wondered if he was dying, and if so, when it began. Probably Ishmail had gotten him after all, and this was some kind of death struggle. Michael stopped resisting as the light increased; he wasn't even afraid that it would blister his skin and blind him, as he knew it could if Ishmail was tricking him. Or perhaps he would be floating above his body soon, watching it expire in the hotel room. The prospect made him curious. *Experimental results in double-blind trials, although on a strictly limited scale, suggest that increased neuronal activity in the right temporal lobe, consistent with the phenomenon of near-death experiences, can be induced artificially by—*

"Thank you, very good, you can leave now," Rakhel said, speaking close to his ear.

Suddenly he sucked in a deep breath, and the light disappeared.

"Who are you thanking?" Michael asked, realizing that he was lying on the same hard surface where he had landed. He gulped in more air.

"Your brain," Rakhel said. "We're going to have to turn it off for a while. It was putting on a good show. Who can blame it? It wanted you to have a story, an explanation."

"Why are you doing this?" Michael asked weakly. He sat up, realizing that his panicky hallucination was clearing and his dizziness fading away.

"I'm not doing anything," Rakhel said. "I already told you, this is your nonsense."

He had the feeling that they were back where they'd begun. He allowed himself to give in to exhaustion and the numbness of feeling which follows tremendous excitement. Dully, he heard himself say, "Susan. She's in trouble, and you say—"

"That he's using her. Right," Rakhel replied. "Let's leave her aside for the moment. What about you? I'd say you've actually returned to some version of normal."

"As normal as you can be without a brain. Can I have it back?"

Rakhel snorted again. "Don't be so literal. I just meant that you have to detach yourself from the wild things running through your head. You're like everybody else. You pretend to have fear or terror or rage when in fact they have you—in their control, I mean."

She was musing quietly, and as she did, a small soft candlelight appeared in her cupped hands. Its glow cast her face into sharp definition, and a rosy brightness radiated through her skin. In the light Michael could see himself, though he could still see nothing around them. Rakhel was sitting on the same dark featureless surface he was standing on, about six feet away.

"There," she said. "Better?"

"Sanity would be better. An explanation would be better. I still feel like I'm losing my mind," Michael said.

"Good," Rakhel said forcefully. "If your mind is as confused as most people's, it was worth losing." Michael sat still. He had to admit, given that he knew nothing about this bizarre old woman, that he should stop debating with her. In the chaos of events back at the hotel, he had registered an immediate impression of an old lady in faintly absurd costume, but he'd been wrong. No first impression could possibly catch her, whoever she turned out to be.

All at once her face, which had betrayed only an eaglelike alertness so far, softened. "I haven't given you credit for making it this far," Rakhel said. "You thought about escaping, but that was only your ego, your shell. The better part of you has decided to stay. That's probably what *he* sensed, which is why he pounced so fast."

"Did he kill Susan?" Michael asked grimly. His brain was sending him coherent images now, and he saw her struggling behind the bathroom door, first screaming, then going quiet.

Rakhel shook her head. "I don't think so. She's too clever for that."

"Clever? You mean she's outwitted him? Then we've got to go find her. Which way is out?" Michael felt his exhaustion washed away with hopeful excitement. He was on his feet, gazing around at the outer darkness beyond the candlelight. He felt Rakhel's small but tight hand on his arm.

"You're a good boy," the old lady murmured. "Good but conventional. I told you where we are—nowhere. This isn't a *real* place, not in the way you understand that word. He would get to you in most of the real places I could whisk you off to."

He felt deflated, but he was stubborn—there was no other admissible feeling at that moment. "Let's go now and talk later," he said. "I've gotten used to some of this mystification, and I can tell that you're his equal. Let's get Susan back, and then we'll worry about me."

Rakhel smiled, completely without mockery, and suddenly Michael could see the young girl she had been beneath the ruined mask of age. In that flash of intuition he caught just the most tantalizing glimpse of himself and the life he might have had with the girl she once had been. The moment spread like ripples in a pond, and then it faded without a trace.

"Look, Rakhel—have I got that right?—while we're dinking around here, he's getting away. Doesn't that mean anything to you? He's supposed to be your enemy."

"We're the thirty-six," Rakhel said, as if that were an answer.

"Exactly," Michael retorted impatiently. "You've got the same powers he does, right? So use them."

Rakhel shook her head. "You should have listened better when Rebbe was giving you his lesson, *mein gaon kinder*. We're witnesses, nothing more. We watch. You think God needs hired guns? Bang-bang, just like a Rambo? You want the Liar stopped, you figure out how to stop him."

Michael shook his head, hating his helplessness. "I can't."

The old woman was getting up, grunting a little from the exertion. "You want to die for a cause? Sensible enough if you love her. But you can't make a decision without all the facts. Look here." The glowing light dipped and wobbled until she was on her feet, holding it steady once more. Michael realized with remote absurdity that one of her shoelaces was untied.

Rakhel held her cupped hands out to him. The steady white light slowly expanded, as if pure white could gain another dimension. It seemed to gather new qualities within itself: of sound, of texture, until Rakhel was holding forth an exquisite blue-white lotus, nesting within its petals a captivating story. What the story communicated was wordless—it was about lives and times, each life a petal that shot up from the center of the lotus, almost instantly replaced with a new one. Michael thought he detected voices that blended old and young, each birth linked so swiftly to death that he couldn't tell the difference between them. The flower kept growing from within itself, and although petals were born, rose, and fell away, none of this change harmed the glowing blossom, which was ever sweet and alive.

"Beautiful, isn't it, the human soul?" Rakhel said at his back. "You ask why we don't fight—once we have seen this, not just in good people but in everyone, why should we fight? It's there, you know. In every single one of us. Didn't I tell you God loves a paradox?"

The need to see it again tore at Michael like homesickness that couldn't name the home it had lost, as if he had been cast out of a perfect unknown place. But if he looked, if he listened, if he believed . . . it would change him.

"This isn't going to work," Michael said hoarsely. "You tell me you're not going to do anything about Ishmail—you tell me I'm supposed to stop him—and now I'm supposed to forgive him instead? Maybe you'd like to explain to me how that is going to do me or Susan any good."

"Forgiveness," Rakhel said simply, "is never wasted. Think of it as God's eraser. Without it, all you've got is another level of blame and violence."

Michael closed his eyes, concentrating on Susan's face, rebuilding it in his memory. Her danger was his responsibility—Ishmail was only using her to get to him. Even Rakhel had said that. Death stops being a surprise to a doctor fairly quickly, but he couldn't bear the thought of Susan dying from some random act of terrorism that was within his power to avert.

"I'm not one of you." His voice was loud and tight, his hands clenched. He was trying to control his emotions, but he found himself shaking with a cold distant anger.

Rakhel made a *tsk*ing sound. "It's amazing how much people are willing to suffer, so long as they can remain the same. All right, we'll do this your way. We'll go rescue your *shayna maidel*."

*   *   *

Susan had fallen through the bathroom mirror head first, but Ishmail was there to cradle her and set her upright as if he'd done nothing more spectacular than pull her through a small hole in the wall. He smiled. She stared at him through tears of shock— naked, panting, unable to orient herself after this terrible violation of the laws of nature.

Ishmail was looking at her, his face as impossible to read as when he had first reached out for her. He wasn't touching her, and he made no move to get closer. "Why did you fight me?" he asked.

"What?" Although she felt deeply shaken, Susan realized that she wasn't terrified. "I—"

"If you thought it was a kidnapping, look around."

Susan wiped her face with both hands, childishly. She took a step forward and stopped—she was still in the bathroom at the New Jerusalem. Her toothbrush was on the sink, her towel on the floor where she dropped it. But the mirror was on the wrong side. "Michael?" she whispered, in a voice made husky with screaming. Where was he?

"You see? No harm," Ishmail said. "You've simply been . . . reoriented." She examined closer. If she stood facing the window, the mirror should be on her right and the tub on her left. But somehow he had turned the room inside out.

Susan picked up the towel and wrapped it around herself, pulling it tight. Through the open door she could see the hotel room just as she'd left it, only in reverse. Michael wasn't there. She walked through the door, just to make sure she wasn't missing him somehow. A bottle of vodka was still on the dresser, just as the two of them had left it the night before, only now the letters on the label were all reversed.

She thought Ishmail might grab her and pull her back, but he was unperturbed.

"Why?" she asked.

The Prophet shrugged and for the first time faintly smiled. "I wanted to be considerate. This is a version you'd recognize, as close to the original as we need for now. There could be other versions, of course. Remember that. In fact, remember everything."

His voice was calm and unthreatening, but Susan hardly noticed that, or the words he spoke. She was shaking, cold and nauseated from the excess of adrenaline. She barely managed to make it to the bed before her legs collapsed under her and she lay there, trembling and sick.

"Take your time. Move around," Ishmail said. He stood over her, but not with any overt intention to touch or attack.

With the dream slowness of nightmare Susan forced herself to act. She staggered to her feet and grabbed her clothes, wadding them into a bundle, lurching like a drunk. She only grabbed what she needed to cover herself, abandoning everything else. She'd finish dressing in the hall, in the lobby, in the middle of the street, only she had to get out of here before the Dark Soul could toy with her any more.

Her hands shook as she twisted open the locks on the hall door. She broke a nail, tearing it across the cuticle and leaving a faint smear of blood on the lock, but the door opened at last. She ran out without interference and hurried down the hall. The fact that she couldn't hear footsteps behind her created a worse dread than before—she could understand how someone might literally die of fear.

The hall was empty. Terror made it seem cathedral-wide. Susan ran to the end, down the stairs, and into the lobby, drawing breath to scream for help. The lobby was also empty. Empty and silent as a small-town funeral parlor. The midmorning sun slanted in through the windows. She skidded to a stop, bouncing from one bare foot to the other as she took in this fresh impossibility, then she ran for the door to the street. The towel slipped, and she clutched it tighter. She'd feel safe if she could only get out of the hotel—she knew she would.

She pushed open the door—and found herself staring at the front desk, with the door leading out of the hotel at her back. Susan shook her head, whimpering, unable to understand how she could have managed to make such a stupid, dangerous mistake.

She tried again.

And the same thing happened, and then again, until she realized it would happen every time. The door only led one way: back inside. Slowly she walked back toward the desk.

"Hello?" she whispered, very softly. No one was there.

She dropped the bundle she was carrying and began to pick through it as though getting dressed were the only important thing in the world. To keep some vestige of control, she dressed herself with meticulous care: white blouse and khaki skirt, professional armor, symbol of normal life being carried on even under trying circumstances. Her hair was still wet; she combed it out of her face as best she could and sat down on the carpet to put on her shoes. She still had both of them, a small victory.

"Ah, there you are." The voice was light, arch, cheerful. She flinched and wouldn't look.

"Susan." The voice was full of good humor,

drawing out her name, chiding gently. She bit her lip until she tasted blood, staring at her hands on the shoelaces.

"If you won't even look at me, I'm going to be very hurt." Susan had had enough experience with the aftermath of wounded male pride to know that this was a threat. She looked up. Ishmail was standing at the foot of the stairs, leaning on the newel post looking at her. He was still dressed as he had been in the mirror, like any of the nomads and displaced tribesmen that filled the refugee camps, but there was something alert shining out from his eyes. His expression was as knowing, his smile as mocking, as that of any high-priced defense attorney out to sell justice without a qualm. The guise of the Prophet had slipped away, even though it was outwardly the same person.

They say the devil's a lawyer. . . .

A despairing humor welled up inside her. "You must have missed the 'Do Not Disturb' sign," she said, getting to her feet. "We'll let it pass this time."

Ishmail threw back his head and laughed. "Will we? Come on—we've got a lot of ground to cover and a lot of places to be."

He came the rest of the way down the stairs. She stood her ground, twitching once when he threw his arm over her shoulders, but otherwise making no move to stop him.

There was a sudden spark, brighter than a thousand suns.

Michael was staring at a rock wall, the side of a dark tunnel. Sunlight was faintly spilling in through an opening a few yards away, exposing the colors in the pale limestone along the passageway. From the texture of the rock, he could tell that the stone had been worked, probably by ancient hands.

"Rakhel?" he called. He had lost track of her footsteps in the dark, although he couldn't remember exactly when, just as he couldn't remember when the undefined blackness had turned into a cave. Shepherds took refuge in these places all throughout the Middle East, so he had no idea if he was in Syria or Israel or even Saudi Arabia. Different things are romantic to different cultures. In Islam, a dark hole in a rock cliff was tinged with the romance of spirit, because the prophet Muhammad had met the archangel Gabriel in one, on the Night of Qadr, in the year 610. It was described in sura 97 of the Koran. Michael wondered if he could be transported back to that time as easily as he had been transported "nowhere."

"Don't dawdle," Rakhel said behind him.

"Is this the right way?" he asked.

"If you don't know where you're going, what does it matter where you start?" Rakhel replied.

"Thanks."

Beyond the opening, Michael could see the dazzle of glints on a rocky hillside. He groped toward the entrance, impatient to search his surroundings for clues. "Would it hurt you to give me an idea where we're coming out?" he grumbled.

"No, it wouldn't, but thanks for asking."

Rakhel was clearly amused at having him lead the way. They had been traveling, sometimes on foot, sometimes on hands and knees, through passages that would unexpectedly turn wet with drip from the cave roof. The hard conditions didn't seem to bother her—only once did she comment that they would have had an easier time if he wasn't caught up in rebirthing myths. Michael had ignored that one.

Now the tunnel led out into what looked like an old quarry. Michael stood in the opening for a moment, staring out at a vast panorama of nothing. Heat shimmered on the pale stones, radiating from the terraced walls and streaming upward into an empty blue sky.

"Here you go," he muttered, turning to help Rakhel over the piled-up rubble at the cave's mouth. She wasn't behind him, though, and he tried not to grimace when he heard her voice some ten yards off.

"Be careful of the snakes." She was under the shade of a tamarisk tree that Michael was certain hadn't existed the first time he'd looked. He trudged toward her, making a show of not being careful of the snakes at all. He was stuck between pride and the realization that his heroic efforts, if they began this ludicrously, were not likely to improve with time.

Rakhel dusted off a flat stone beside her. "Thirsty?" she asked. She produced a canteen and metal cup from her skirt pockets. He stared and was about to say something, but Rakhel cut him off. "You know enough not to ask," she said. "We've gotten that far, haven't we?" Michael wouldn't answer. He accepted the cup and drank, then collapsed to the ground, staring up at the sky through the lacy pale green shade.

"You're really going to let me do this on my own, aren't you?" he said. "Why?"

"Everyone does everything on their own."

"Really? You think babies are born with driver's licenses, for instance? Or maybe bringing up children doesn't fit your notion of help?"

"Don't waste energy. We can argue when you

have more confidence that you might win." Rakhel's calm assurance wasn't that exasperating, now that he was used to it. But Michael looked away. He was worried that her voice, with its light irony, its adult amusement at his efforts, would make him forget the real danger facing him and Susan.

"All right, how do we get to a road?" Michael asked, taking refuge in practicalities. He stood up. They were still halfway down the quarry, blocking any view toward the horizon. "I'll go reconnoiter," he said.

"Is that the word for getting more lost?" Rakhel asked. He grunted. There was a narrow footpath that led to the top. Michael inched out along it, his back pressed flat to the hot pale stone, and tried not to look down. Reaching the lip, he balanced on the edge, breathing hard. His hair and shirt were wet with sweat, and his trousers clung to him clammily. He shaded his eyes with his hand, scanning the horizon. The terrain was cut with gullies where no rain had recently fallen—the baked skeleton of wadis that only ran in the early spring. The sparse desert vegetation witnessed that water would one day return. There was a dirt-track road carved into the desert, and, parked in the shade of a large boulder, Michael saw a jeep.

He glanced behind him and saw Rakhel toiling up the narrow path. Loose rock cascaded from beneath her tennis shoes, skittering down the slope toward the bottom of the pit, but she paid no attention, seemingly careless of her personal safety. He waited until she neared the top, then pointed at the vehicle.

"Much obliged," he muttered.

"What have I got to do with it?" Rakhel said innocently. She was almost believable. "You need to put your *goyischer kopf* to better use than figuring out what you'll never figure out."

"I don't know what that means, but it doesn't sound complimentary," Michael said. "Come on. Maybe we can find the people that jeep belongs to."

Fifteen minutes later, after a futile attempt to attract anyone's attention in the vicinity—Michael knew very well there was no one to begin with—they were on the road. The back seat of the commandeered jeep had yielded another canteen, two bush hats, and a rifle. Michael should have been pleased; he felt silently mocked instead.

His mood wasn't helped when Rakhel insisted, as a condition of getting into the jeep, that she was going to drive. Unlike his experience of Susan's reckless approach behind the wheel, Michael didn't have any impression that he was likely to survive this journey. Rakhel seemed to aim the jeep like a weapon, picking a point on the horizon and heading for it at top speed. She seemed determined to hit every stone and rut along the way.

"What are you doing?" Michael demanded, after a stone flung up by the jeep's wheels starred the windshield with a nest of ugly cracks.

"I'm trying to get us killed," Rakhel explained. "Battle, murder, sudden death—we might as well get into the mood."

"Slow down!" Michael shouted as they bounded abruptly, flying through the air for a short moment, then coming back to earth with a crash. He grabbed for the steering wheel and wrestled them to a halt.

"Let me," he said, when he could trust himself to

speak. "If I have to risk death, it doesn't need to be this way."

"Suit yourself."

Rakhel climbed out as Michael clambered from the passenger seat into the driver's. For a moment he thought wistfully of racing off and leaving her there, but he knew he wouldn't do it. He waited as she climbed back in and settled herself, then flipped the ignition. Gingerly, he steered back onto the dirt track, hoping nothing was broken.

"Sulking isn't 'the only alternative," Rakhel shouted over the wind rolling past their heads as Michael gunned the engine through clouds of dust.

"I'm not sulking, I'm planning," he said.

"Have it your way."

"Will you stop saying that? The goddamn problem is that I'm having it my way. Isn't that what you've been trying to tell me?"

"*Mein kind*, whether you call it sulking or not, there is another approach, I'm telling you."

He realized that this was the closest to placating him that she would ever come, and if he wanted to step down from the tower of pride, she had put one foot on the ladder for him. "All right," he said. He threw the wheel sharply to one side, braking as the jeep stopped on the wide bare shoulder of the road. But whatever she was about to say never got said. Rakhel's eyes were narrowed, and she stood up in her seat.

"Hmmm. This doesn't look good," she murmured.

"What are you looking at?" Michael asked.

"That." Rakhel was pointing now. On the horizon, towering up into the dimming sky, greenish black clouds billowed like the smoke from a roaring fire. "Take us there."

As they approached the storm, things started to look more familiar. The road signs were once again in Hebrew. As they passed the first one, Michael realized he was driving on a paved road. He glanced over his shoulder, but all he saw behind him was asphalt, stretching back as far as the eye could see. *I couldn't have just blanked on that.*

"I didn't notice where the dirt track ended," he said suspiciously. "Is this country real?"

"As real as anything unreal can be," she said, without smiling. Rakhel's mood had darkened with the gray mass swirling up from the horizon. She looked straight ahead, her eyes sharp as if she could see through heavy smoke. The storm filled all the sky now, and Michael could feel its electricity on his skin, making the fine hairs stand up. It seemed to feed the sense of urgency he felt. The last road signs had been pointing the way toward Har Megiddo, a prominent hill in the distance. Michael remembered vaguely seeing the name on a map of northern Israel, on the road to the Sea of Galilee.

"So we're back in his favorite territory again," Michael shouted, slowing down to be heard better. "This is roughly where I first saw the Prophet."

Rakhel nodded. "He likes symbols."

Michael glanced over at her. "Are you going to explain that?"

She pointed toward the storm, which was now centered directly over the hill. The jeep was rising over a winding pass, and Michael knew that beyond it lay the fertile fields of the Jezreel Valley. "And there were voices, and thunders, and lightnings," Rakhel recited. "And there was a great earthquake, such as there was not since men had been upon the earth, so mighty an earthquake and so great."

She broke off, and her voice regained its light irony. "You wouldn't think the world could come to an end, not with a bang or a whimper, but with a mispronunciation." Michael knew to let her go on. "Say 'Har Megiddo' as fast as you can," Rakhel demanded.

He tried it several times, running the syllables together. "Harmegiddo, Harmegiddo."

"You're almost there. Drop the *h* and you've got it."

Armageddon.

She seemed pleased when the word hit him. "Strange, yes? People think it's an event when it's really a place. The famous Hill of Battles where forty centuries of armies have spilled blood to capture— what?" She pointed all around. "If you didn't know that you were in a legendary place, would you even notice? But the odd thing is not to notice. You're driving over bones and chariots this minute, older than any culture you can remember or even record. This was Canaan for a little while, a mere two thousand years, before the Assyrians, Egyptians, and Israelites couldn't live without it."

"You think he wants it now?" Michael asked.

Rakhel shook her head. "Of course not. He can see, can't he? It's a hill."

The skies were so dark now that it was nearly impossible to tell day from night. Rakhel was right: Armageddon was just a hill, a mound, really. It had been piled up from buried towns, twenty in all, that extended back some four thousand years. Every army had vanquished an enemy here, built a fortress town, and then been vanquished in turn. The Hill of

Battles counted as a site engraved on the ancient mind, and the world was small enough then that when Saint John's own mind turned for a place suitable for ending the world, Har Megiddo loomed larger than Normandy, Moscow, or Vietnam would today if you lumped them into one bloody ground. Har Megiddo was where the seventh angel gathered all the survivors of the first wars of the Apocalypse, to make a last stand for God against ultimate Evil.

"You don't think—?" Before he could finish his question, Rakhel rapped sharply on the windshield.

"Think that the world is coming to an end? I told you, you're conventional," she snapped. "I won't say you've caused this particular scene, but I'm beginning to know you better, and you may be infected with a taste for cheap melodrama. Hurry."

The winding road had taken them past the local kibbutz to a graded parking area at the base of the mound.

"What now?" Michael asked. Rakhel looked at him as if he alone contained the answer. Just then, when he wanted to tell her to stop mystifying him, the storm exploded.

It was like a detonation, and Michael flung himself from the jeep, reflexively hugging the ground as if a bomb had gone off. A moment later the first drenching raindrops hit his face, and he relaxed fractionally. But the storm light flickered around him, and his sense of wrongness grew. He got to his feet, already soaked to the skin. The dirt parking lot was fast turning into mud soup; his shirt and pants were filthy.

Rakhel was standing on the other side of the jeep, waiting patiently. She'd put her pink cardigan on and retied her scarf over her frizzled hair, but other than that, she made no concession to the tempest. Soaking wet, her flowered skirt plastered to her body, she looked like a shipwrecked nanny.

"I hope you didn't read the Bible carefully," she said. Michael couldn't quite read her tone of voice.

"Let's hope he hasn't," he said.

"Don't worry, you don't have to read it if you're in it."

With a faint "Humph," Rakhel marched off. Michael was looking up toward the top of the hill. A corona of lightning, blue-green in its intensity, wreathed the old stone ramparts and gates up there, lending them a distinctly eldritch cast. An office-bungalow was the only shelter in sight, but he had a feeling Ishmail was there.

As he started running up the path, with Rakhel well ahead of him, Michael realized that her mocking assurance had given him false courage. He felt that would drain out of him like crankcase oil if he didn't stick close to her, and a sense of shame overwhelmed him. What was her phrase? This is only as real as anything unreal can be. In the midst of a deafening crack of thunder, he lost the wits to hope that she was right.

The top of Har Megiddo was only a few hundred yards up. The instant he reached the crest, the storm stopped. Michael shook his head, adjusting to the sudden silence. The place was peculiarly deserted. Hesitantly, he started toward the larger of the two buildings, the archaeological museum. But that didn't feel like the right choice somehow, and when he saw that the door to the bungalow was lying on the ground as if it had been torn from its hinges, he headed toward that instead.

"Rakhel?" he called in a low voice.

"Here."

It was gloomy inside from the small aluminum windows and the storm clouds. But he instantly saw Susan. She was lying on the floor in the hallway, sprawled on her back. The front of her blouse was red with blood. Michael dropped to his knees and ripped open the sodden shirting, recoiling from what he saw.

There was a hole in the middle of her chest about the size of a dime. It was impossibly neat, as if a surgical knife had been used. The cavity welled with blood; a lot had wicked into her shirt, but most of her blood was still inside. Michael lifted Susan in his arms, cradling her gently. More blood spilled down over his hands. Still warm—she must have died only minutes before.

"See? We could have done it my way," Rakhel said calmly.

"Goddamn you," Michael cried, not looking up. "You tried to keep me away. You treated it like a joke."

"Rule number one," Rakhel said. Her voice was hard enough to make Michael look up. "Never bow to his power, because when you do, you feed it. To play against Ishmail, you must have no fear, no doubt, no weakness."

"Play?" Although he felt numb, Michael was overcome by a rush of bitter rage.

Rakhel paid no attention. "And you need to know his plans. Susan's been with him. She knows more about now than you or me. Ask her."

"What?" Michael couldn't believe he was hearing this. "She's dead. Can't you see that?"

Rakhel made a dubious sound. "She was alive five minutes ago, and what's five minutes? A twelfth of an hour, that's what. So try. See what you can do. You've had enough proof already. Try."

It was the first time he'd ever heard her speak in such a peculiar coaxing rhythm. He looked down at Susan's face. It was relaxed, the eyes closed, as if she would wake up unless he kept quiet.

"You want me to raise the dead?" Michael asked in a toneless voice. He didn't know whether to laugh or cry. Tenderly, he folded the bloodied white blouse over the wound in Susan's chest.

"It could hurt to try?" Rakhel asked. "You can't make things worse, can you? I believe she can live. Maybe I'm right."

And they said to him: Master, can these bones live? Michael felt obscurely frightened deep in a part of himself that had not so far been touched by what had happened. What if he tried it—and it worked? What sort of a world would his world become then?

"Susan," he said, feeling like a cursed fool. "Susan, wake up. I need to ask you some questions."

Nothing happened.

"So convincing!" Rakhel mocked. "You must love her a lot to want her back this much."

"Shut up!" Michael cried, his nerves as taut as a garroting wire. Then, without warning, all of the anger, all the fear, all the frustration and need of this day coalesced into one bright bolt of will. "Susan, wake up!"

The air froze in time. Susan's head lolled limply against his arm—or did it turn of its own accord? No. It hadn't worked.

Something deep inside of him was relieved.

Michael set her down and got to his feet. "I can't participate in your fantasy. If this is how you want me to be, how would I be any better than this Ishmail of yours? I just can't—" He choked and stepped back.

"Oh, you can," Rakhel said, shaking her head. "But you're afraid you won't be able to stand it if my rules are right." She stepped forward and knelt beside Susan, placing her hands on either side of her head. "Dear, it's Rakhel," she said gently. "It's time to wake up."

As his throat tightened, Michael realized that there would be no more miracles, no more breaking natural laws, not today. Then Susan's chest rose and fell, and he saw with awe that she was breathing.

"Yaaah!" Susan shouted a wordless sound of fear and flung herself away from Rakhel's hands. "No! Don't touch me!"

"It's all right," Rakhel whispered. "It's not him."

But Susan couldn't understand. She thrashed, pushing herself along the floor. "No, no!" she moaned. Michael was like stone, wanting to reach out to her but frozen in place. Her eyes looked at him without recognition.

With a hard slap Rakhel hit Michael across the face, and at the moment when he came to, so did Susan. She rose to her knees, still dazed, but taking only seconds to realize where she was and who she was with. "Michael!" She started to fling herself onto him, then saw the blood. "Oh, my God—are you hurt?"

It was so far from the truth that he laughed helplessly. "No. That's . . . something else."

You're alive! You're alive! Joy stunned him as much as terror had earlier.

"Am I hurt?" Susan stared down at her bloody shirt. "The last thing I remember is Ishmail pointing his finger at me, and then . . ." She pressed her hand against her chest, over her heart, eyes wide with memory.

"Don't think about that," Rakhel said firmly. "He didn't hurt you. How could he hurt you, a clever girl like you?"

"No," Susan said, sounding puzzled. "I guess he . . . he wanted me to love him. That was what he said."

"So now he's a comic," Rakhel muttered. She held out her hand. "I'm called Rakhel—*shalom*."

Súsan automatically shook the proffered hand. "Pleased to meet you."

"You won't be later," Rakhel said.

"Where did he go?" Michael interrupted. His clothes were covered with mud and blood, and he couldn't escape the doom of what the Prophet had just done. It was his way of throwing down the gauntlet. But Susan was alive, and that was a miracle beyond comprehension—even though Michael knew with certainty that the miracle came with strings attached.

Susan shook her head wordlessly. Outside, there was a crack of thunder. The storm seemed to be gathering again, like a play resumed after intermission.

"We'd better get out of here," Michael said. "I think he might be coming back." As if to underscore his words, the building shimmied. There was a low rumble punctuated by the crash of things falling off shelves as the flimsy bungalow shuddered. He stared out the window. Armageddon, the mispronunciation that three religions awaited as impatiently as an amorous bridegroom.

"Earthquake?" Susan asked, bewildered.

"Michael," Rakhel said urgently, "it's you now.

He's got you convinced. I didn't see it happening, but that doesn't matter. You've got to stop doing this."

"Doing what?" Susan looked frightened and baffled.

Rakhel grabbed Michael by the shoulders, not letting him look away. "Accept what you are. Nothing's going to work right until you do."

"I know what I am," Michael said distantly. Without waiting for Rakhel's reply, he led Susan out through the door and into the rain.

"Michael, who is that?" Susan asked. She seemed to be glad for the downpour, using it to wash her face and hands clean and rinse away as much of the blood from her shirt as possible. "Where did you find her?"

"She's one of them, and she found me. She's trying to get me to do something. Now let's not talk anymore, all right? Just go." He calculated how long it would take them to cover the two hundred yards back to the jeep. It was a moment before he realized that Susan had stopped and was standing in the rain staring at him. At that moment another tremor struck. The rain-slick mud rocked beneath them; Michael staggered, and Susan was knocked off her feet.

"What are you doing? You can't let go of me," Michael shouted, but she had already scrambled back up and was slogging determinedly back to where Rakhel was standing in the doorway.

"Susan!" he howled in frustration. Lightning flashed overhead, blindingly, underscoring the need to flee. "Don't you think I know better than they do what I am and what I'm not? Come on!" The storm was building, gaining intensity. There was a hair-raising crack as a bolt of lightning struck the building itself. Ishmail was coming back. Michael was sure of it.

Rakhel said something to Susan—her words were covered by another roll of thunder—and gave her a little push. Susan took a hesitant step toward Michael, still angry, shaking her head and looking back at Rakhel.

The ground shook again, and Michael fell, but the shaking didn't stop. He lay sprawled full-length on the ground. There was a ripping sound. He felt the vibration of it through the earth, a separate thing from the shaking of the quake. He raised his head, floundering upright in the mud. Susan was lying on her stomach, thrashing as if she were trying to swim across the ground to him. Behind her, the office building was canted up at an angle like a sinking ocean liner. Michael could see Rakhel still standing in the doorway, clinging to the frame with a hand on each side. A gaping fissure opened in the earth, slowly gulping down the building, foundation and all. Michael was shouting over the grinding roar that filled the air, as if they were all inside a giant cement mixer.

"Take my hand!" he shouted to Susan. She had been thrown down running toward him; now she was crawling, trying to close the distance between them. Michael saw with a thrill of horror that she was flailing uphill, swimming desperately against the tilting earth that threatened to sweep her into the ground along with the building.

But now the mud was his ally. It made the ground slippery enough that he could yank Susan toward him without resistance.

"Run—run!" he screamed as she clawed her way

past him. He got to his knees. "Rakhel—jump!" He held out his arms.

The old woman shook her head. The doorway was high above him now, nearly vertical. "Believe!" Rakhel shouted. "Trust! Nothing will work right until you do!"

With a sudden plunge, the building sank into the earth and was gone. Michael jumped to his feet and ran after Susan.

CHAPTER SEVEN

ROCK OF FAITH

It took them about four hours to drive from Megiddo back to Jerusalem. Michael had lost all track of time, and he wasn't surprised to find that the sun was setting as they arrived. Neither of them talked much about Rakhel. It wasn't clear whether she had sacrificed herself or had died to teach Michael some obscure lesson he needed to learn—maybe it was her way of giving up on him.

Was it only this morning that Ishmail had appeared in their hotel room? So much had happened since then that it was too exhausting even to think about all of it. Michael had lost any certainty he might have had about doing the right thing. Right and wrong were lost, wandering in a fog; he hadn't had time to think about anything subtler than how to survive.

But Ishmail was not their only source of danger. Both Michael and Susan were now traveling without identity papers or money. Without these things, they couldn't be safe anywhere but Israel, and even there they might attract police suspicion. They had to get their identities back. The best place to find them— if they were lucky—was in New Jerusalem.

Michael still had the room key in his pocket, though he didn't remember putting it there. It saved him from trying to get the desk clerk to let them back in, which, considering their bedraggled condition, might have been none too easy.

"I don't know about this," Susan said as Michael opened the door. "It's a big risk coming back here. Your jeep's unregistered. What if it belongs to some army somewhere? What if the local police spot it and put surveillance on us when we go back to get it?" These were real things to be nervous about, but talking about them was really her way of disguising a deeper fear: Their hotel room was the last place where Ishmail had been.

"You can stay out here while I look around," Michael offered. She shook her head and followed him in. Both of them gazed at the empty room, as spooked as children in a haunted house. It looked completely innocuous. Even the bed was made up.

"I guess the maid's been here," Michael said inanely.

He felt Susan brace herself to walk around the room. Moving quickly and methodically, she seized her knapsack and began stuffing things into it: her passport, her wallet, the keys to their rental car. A moment later she had everything and stood poised to run, the bag clutched in her arms like a football.

Michael thrust his wallet and passport into the pocket of his pants. He felt battered and grungy: sun-burned, wind-burned, dirty, and bruised. He longed for a bath, a bed, clean clothes. *Is the human mind constructed to want creature comforts before it can think of anything higher?* He didn't know the answer, but he knew he could only go on if he disciplined himself to never think about ordinary life again.

"Want your toothbrush?" he asked, reaching for the bathroom doorknob.

"Don't go in there," Susan said quickly, and Michael drew back. A sudden fierce memory of a bottomless drop where the bathroom floor should have been filled his consciousness. How could he have forgotten about that, even for a moment?

He shook his head, backing away from the door. "You're right. Come on."

Michael had considered going to the U.S. Embassy— a logical enough destination for travelers in trouble. But after they'd picked up the car, he found himself driving deeper into the Old City. He didn't have heroic motivations or the insatiable curiosity of a sleuth. Of the few things Susan had said about their adventure at Armageddon, there was one sentence that Michael couldn't escape: "He's lost the Light. He can't see it anymore."

It turned out that when Rakhel had whispered her last words to Susan, just before the earthquake engulfed the bungalow, this cryptic message, surely meant for him, was what she had spoken. For several hours Michael had pondered who Rakhel was referring to, Ishmail or himself. There was only one person left to ask.

The traffic was even worse than usual, and it was half an hour before they were standing in front of a familiar door. Susan knocked. No one came.

"Rabbi! It's us! Please answer," Susan called.

It took several minutes before the door was opened by a young man whose *payess* and full beard marked a member of some Orthodox sect, one of the many hidden away in every nook of the Jewish Quarter. He stared at Susan, standing there bareheaded, in a torn and muddy blouse, with barely concealed distaste.

"Solomon Kellner? Is he here?" Michael asked.

"No." The young man began to close the door.

"We have to see him," Michael insisted, pushing forward and leaning into the door. "Can we wait?"

"I told you, he is not here," the man repeated in heavily accented English. "This is *bait kn'ne'set*—a house of prayer! *L'ha'veen?* Do you understand?"

"But this is his house!" Susan protested from behind Michael.

"Not unless he's God," the man snapped. "Now leave us alone." A moment later the door shut in their faces, and they walked away.

"Can that be true?" Susan asked blankly.

"That it's a synagogue? I don't think Solomon would lie to us, or ask someone else to," Michael said, slowly feeling his way through the possibilities. "I don't think he's in there. The question is, did he go voluntarily? It's strange—everyone wants me to see certain things and not others. They force me to have a peek, then they draw the curtain back again. I don't get it. Who's on whose side here?"

"We don't have enough information yet," Susan said warily. "Ishmail could have changed things. It can't be that much for him to move an address."

Michael shook his head. "It's not the details we should be looking at. So far, what do we know for sure? We've been party to some incredible events, but those are just for show. It's the invisible events, the hidden motives, the unspoken alliances that everyone is hiding from us. Face it, all kinds of realities exist that we have to understand just from a few clues. It's like trying to learn a foreign language from scraps of newspaper picked up on the street."

"Meaning what? That someone, presumably this group of thirty-six, is trying to teach you little by little? Maybe they're just as reluctant to get you in deeper as you are."

Michael nodded. It was all but impossible to speculate about a secret society whose members didn't know each other, and moreover who were pledged simply to watch, not to interfere. The bald truth was simple: He might be at the end of the trail. Either he had played his part or he hadn't. Only "they" knew.

The few passersby on the streets at this hour were giving them curious glances, and Michael was again made aware of how disreputable they both looked. They needed to clean up before they were arrested as vagrants, sufferers from Jerusalem syndrome, or worse. A trip to the tourists' souk a few blocks away provided caps, jackets, T-shirts, a pair of Levi's for Michael and a wrap-skirt for Susan, and sandals to replace their ruined shoes. They found a Chinese restaurant nearby, and took turns washing and changing in the tiny bathroom at the back until they both looked reasonably presentable again.

While they were waiting for the waiter to bring a dish of hacked chicken, Susan kept wrestling with their dilemma. "Michael, there's something not right here. I'm not sure what it is, or how to put it into words, but any of these weird characters could have hurt you a lot worse than they have—and me, too."

"Yeah." Michael closed his eyes for a long moment. "Do you want to go back to the hotel?" he asked reluctantly.

"Absolutely not," Susan said immediately. "I

don't really know what to do, but going back isn't the answer, and neither is stopping." They both knew that she was saying something concrete, but her underlying message was extremely significant— she had recovered enough from the trauma of Har Megiddo to want to go on.

Above their heads a cheap battered television was playing constantly. Suddenly the flashing blue lights and eerie wail of a police car whipped by the front of the restaurant, followed by three more. Michael glanced at Susan, then up at the screen behind her shoulder. It was after eight, and the programming had switched from Arabic to Hebrew, but suddenly a familiar voice in English cut into Michael's thoughts.

". . . here at the Dome of the Rock. It seems to be the figure of a man literally walking on air. As authorities rush to the scene, observers speculate that this might be the same man who has been preaching and even allegedly working miracles to increasing crowds along the West Bank and the Occupied Territories . . ."

On the screen a flickering image showed the floodlit facade of the Dome of the Rock mosque. In telephoto one could see, incredibly, a floating figure. The figure was wearing black jeans and a white T-shirt, and, though the image was tiny and distant, Michael thought he was wearing sunglasses. Only his feet were bare.

"My God," Susan said, turning to look. "It's him."

"And our friend Nigel doing the feed," Michael said, jumping to his feet. He had to get out of there, but his eyes remained glued on the set.

". . . city poised for religious celebration as well

as war, is his appearance the sign that millions have been waiting for, both in this crossroads of three faiths and across the world?" Nigel's electronic voice sounded excited but controlled, preserving an objectivity that was meaningless at that moment.

Suddenly, as if the station had suddenly realized what it was showing, the screen went blank and a moment later switched to the pale blue background with the menorah-and-palm-branch logo of Television Israel, along with a crawl in Hebrew that probably said "Technical difficulties."

In the distance, more sirens wailed.

Michael threw money on the table and dragged Susan back onto the streets. "That's what he was wearing at Megiddo," she said as they pushed their way through the market. Her eyes sparkled with tears, though of fear or fury she herself didn't know. "He went looking around the offices for something to wear, and that's what he found. No shoes, though. The barefoot Messiah. Oh, my God."

Normally they could have walked to the Dome in ten minutes, but the crowds were swelling and agitated. Michael heard more sirens and what sounded like gunfire. Ishmail's appearance at the Dome of the Rock would tear the city apart. There'd be rioting by morning, if there wasn't already.

"If Solomon got his family out of here ahead of time, he was smart," Michael said, having to raise his voice over the mounting din. "I also have a feeling he could shift addresses as easily as the Prophet. They're all playing a deep game, every one of them."

The narrow streets were clogged with humanity the closer they got to the Dome, like gullies overfilled by a flash flood. Michael pulled Susan into a butcher's shop with a television above the counter.

Several dozen people were crammed in to watch it, some with packets of wrapped sausage in their hands.

The image on screen was, if anything, more electrifying than before. The night sky over the Temple Mount was crisscrossed with searchlights, and one could hear the whir of helicopters flying low overhead. At any time the gold-sheathed Dome was a spectacular sight, the emblem of multifaith Jerusalem and the inescapable symbol of its conflict. All three faiths claimed it, and to reinforce their claim, they placed a dozen miraculous events there and all but a few turning points in history. This was the exact spot where Abraham offered Isaac on the altar to Jehovah, where King David erected his own altar, after buying the whole place and some sacrificial oxen for fifty shekels of silver. Here was the spot Solomon chose for his temple, and where the second temple was after the Jews returned from exile in Babylon.

According to the Talmud, the holy rock also covers the entrance to the Abyss, where if you are devout enough, you can hear the roar of the waters of Noah's flood. It has also been called the Center of the World, since Abraham started two religions, Judaism and Islam, here. And the Stone of the Foundation, upon which the Ark of the Covenant rested. And beneath which the Ark still lies buried, hidden ever since the destruction of Jerusalem that razed the first Temple. On the holy rock is written the great, unspeakable name of God—*shem*—which was deciphered by Jesus; it was this act that gave him the power to perform miracles.

Here, centuries later, Muhammad was brought by the archangel Gabriel and ascended to heaven on a winged horse. The Dome of the Rock is called the

Haram Ash-Sherif in Arabic, and *haram* means "forbidden." But since there are no remains of any temple aboveground, the place is forbidden to Orthodox Jews as well as devout Muslims, a ground tainted by death until the tenth in a line of pure red heifers—the ninth was offered up by David—can be sacrificed to purify the worshipers.

In Muslim belief, the Rock itself stands on no foundation. It is supported only on a palm tree watered by the River of Paradise, and the palm itself is suspended over Bir el-Arwah, the Well of Souls, where every week, if you listen devoutly, you can hear the dead assemble to pray, waiting for the final Day of Judgment.

But now, as Michael watched the scene over the heads of the butcher's customers, he thought it was appropriate to give the place its other legendary name, the Mouth of Hell. The apparition of Ishmail had disappeared—he was lost somewhere in the mob—but since the networks were replaying it every ten seconds, the levitation might as well have been permanent. Looking around, Michael could see armored trucks moving down the side street toward the Dome.

"She said he likes symbols," Michael muttered.

"Who?" Susan asked.

"Rakhel." They were out of the shop now, trying again to force their way through the crowd a foot at a time. "She only dropped hints about him—that was one."

"Who needs hints? Isn't he the devil's advance man, or something a lot like that?" Susan said.

"We'll see."

When the dry river of humanity came to a dead stop, Michael realized it was a bad idea to have come here, but it was too late to retreat—he and Susan were squeezed into the middle of a mob composed of pilgrims, natives, and edgy soldiers with automatic rifles, all shoving and yelling at the top of their lungs. The din made it impossible to talk, impossible to think; the sound rose and fell like the gabble of the ocean.

Michael remembered what Solomon had said to him the previous night, half in jest: *One more miracle and maybe we'll all get killed.*

"We've got to get out of here!" he shouted in Susan's ear. He saw her nod, saw her lips move, but that was all. They both knew there was going to be a riot.

Pushing and shoving, they somehow managed to get their backs against a wall. If they could find a side street to slip down, there was a chance that they could work their way back toward one of the main thoroughfares and retreat westward. There was no chance of getting anywhere near Ishmail—or near Nigel Stricker, either. He wondered what sort of a partnership Ishmail had formed with Nigel, and if it was too late to put an end to it.

The searchlights had given a glow to the sky over the Dome, but now it grew brighter, as if the Dome itself had caught fire. The mob noticed and grew quiet for a moment. Even from that distance, which Michael estimated at no more than a quarter mile, a crackling sound could be heard. A dull, ominous ache hit him in the chest. As much as he liked symbols, maybe Ishmail liked destroying them even better.

"Can you climb?" he said to Susan. The silence had lasted only a few seconds, and the mob was poised for pandemonium. She nodded rapidly. Michael stooped over, making a stirrup of his hands, and when she put her foot there, he boosted her as high as he could. The medieval architecture of the Old City came to their rescue now: Susan was able to find a foothold five feet up the crumbling wall, then another. There was a tinkle of glass as she broke a window with her bag. Michael did his best to duck the falling glass. When he looked back, she was leaning out the open window, holding the strap out to him as a lifeline. He heard a rattle of machine-gun fire in the distance, and screams that sounded like the far-off calls of sea birds.

There were more screams in the direction of the Gate of the Tribes. Suddenly the unruly crowd became terrified, everyone desperately trying to flee the heavenly calamity. In moments sheer panic would spread even this far away.

Michael managed to scramble up onto the tiny balcony outside Susan's window. Its wooden railing tore loose beneath his weight, but she dragged him inside just as the balcony fell into the seething mass of bodies below.

The noise from the street was indescribable now, sending atavistic chills along Michael's spine. He heard a loud booming that might have been mortar fire, but from the angle of the window he could see nothing of what was going on closer to the Dome.

"How did you know that was going to happen?" Susan asked in a low voice.

"There was a light in the sky—Ishmail's doing."

"He's not shooting death rays at them, though, not like before."

"No," Michael said. "They'll turn on him if he does something like that again."

"Not if he promises to save them from it," Susan

pointed out grimly. "I think that after tonight, he's going to look like their only hope."

"Yes," said Michael. "He's trying a lot of things, but there's one theme running through all of it. He's going to save the world—from himself."

Jerusalem, and with it the whole of the religious world, went into shock when the image of the Dome, destroyed by fire in a matter of hours, spread globally. Holed up in what appeared to be an abandoned apartment, probably owned by rich foreigners who only came in for vacation, Michael and Susan sat in the dark and watched the television.

The chaos was magnified because everything happened at night. The pillars supporting the gilded Dome had buckled early from the intense heat of the fire, sending down tons of metal and stone and completely burying the holy sites. Besides the ruin of the most beautiful sacred building in Islam, Jerusalem faced the specter of sacrilege on someone's part or punishment from above. Either choice inflamed thousands of people in the city. Vengeance fires broke out at the Church of the Holy Sepulchre (the second place designated by the faithful as possibly the Center of the World), and mobs poured down the Via Dolorosa—the street down which Christ marched to his crucifixion—looting and smashing windows. The Arabs had already destroyed most of the ancient synagogues of the Old City before they lost it in the 1948 war that made Israel a state, but now even the standing relics of archways and columns were thrown down. It was the visible acting-out of hatred that had never really left the minds of a great many people—all but the ones who had given up the religious life, it seemed.

It was three A.M. before Michael thought they could venture out safely. The nearby streets were angry and swollen but no longer maddened. Police were everywhere, using bullhorns to impose a city-wide curfew. Wednesday turned into Thursday. Sunset tomorrow was the beginning of Passover.

When they finally made their way back to the jeep, they discovered it was gone, a casualty of the riots. Though their papers would give them some immunity from arrest, neither wanted to take the chance of being shot by extremists roaming the city. Jerusalem was under martial law, with roadblocks on nearly every corner. Not all of these were manned by the IDF, and the most they could manage was to stay out of the way of everyone who might possibly want to kill them.

"The Red Cross will have a medical station set up around here," Michael ventured.

"In Israel you're talking Magen David Adom—David's Red Star—but I hope so. Near the Jaffa Gate's the best bet; they'll probably have turned the New Jerusalem into a refugee center, and we should at least be able to call the embassy from there."

Michael nodded and led the way. His eyes stung from the smoke; it hung low over the city, reflecting the numerous random fires until every holy place was swathed in a red pall. Armed patrols of a hundred different warring factions were out, roaring through surreal devastation. Bodies lay heaped in the gutters. Old scores had been settled with bombs and torches, and half the city might have been burning. After Ishmail's trial run, Armageddon had come in time for Easter.

It took Michael and Susan an hour of backtracking and circling to reach the hotel, and when they got there, they found that the New Jerusalem was in flames. Tanks were parked along the wide street in front, guarding the fire trucks. One jeep had a howitzer bolted to the back. Soldiers were everywhere, stacking bodies in the street, trying to avoid the puddles of water running off from the hoses. As Michael and Susan watched, two firefighters ran from the burning building, dragging a third between them. His head lolled limply. Michael elbowed his way through the crowd and ran over to them.

"I'm a doctor!" he shouted.

The firefighters relinquished their burden into his arms, and Michael lay the man down on the pavement. His face was black with soot, the uniform charred on the arms and legs.

"You're going to be all right," Michael said. "Do you think you're in shock?" The fireman shook his head, but his staring eyes said something different. Michael pulled open the heavy coat. His hand came away bloody. He stared at it in bewilderment. Someone had shot this man. He ripped open the shirt beneath. A gunshot wound, high on the left shoulder.

"Can you save him?" someone behind him asked.

"Get me some morphine," Michael ordered. He had thought to carry a makeshift kit of medical supplies in a knapsack from the vacant apartment. He found a wad of toweling and began applying direct pressure on the wound. "Hold that—push hard!" he said to a bystander. "We can keep him stable until the ambulance gets here."

Susan appeared. The wounded fireman began to thrash weakly, groaning with pain. "Snipers are setting fires and then waiting for someone to respond," she said.

Michael felt for a pulse with one hand, rummaging through the knapsack for scissors with the other.

"My men tell me you're a doctor?" someone said above his head.

"Yes, did you bring that morphine?" Michael said. An unseen hand slapped a charged hypodermic into his grasp. Michael ripped the patient's sleeve open and probed roughly for a vein; the skin beneath his fingers crackled. He rammed the plunger home and pulled another wad of toweling out of his bag. "I need a stretcher here!"

Dawn found them at a makeshift medical station nearby; casualties had been piled on blankets in the absence of beds. Michael had followed his patient there and stabilized him as best he could before he was loaded into the back of a pickup pressed into service as an ambulance.

The night had blurred into an endless stream of the injured. Susan worked beside him seamlessly, moving like a second pair of hands as Michael treated burns, broken bones, stab wounds, bullet wounds. A truckload of medical supplies and two corpsmen appeared, and he commandeered them all. They ran out of surgical gloves early and he was reduced to washing his hands in vodka, hitting everything he could with a shot of antibiotics and praying to the god of asepsis that this would be enough to stave off infection.

He and Susan were evacuated a few hours later to a Magen David Adom station on the Mamilla Road. He showed his papers and told them that Susan was his nurse. No one questioned the story. As he worked, someone brought him endless cups of vile coffee, but the tide of suffering came almost as a relief—or at least a reprieve—from the other world that hung around him, where he had no power or competency, and shadow figures played dice with his future.

In all the confusion, the only hard information anyone seemed to have about the Prophet was that he had disappeared when the riots began. Perhaps he would reappear on Sunday, three days from now, if they had proven themselves worthy. But in the wildfire of rumor, Ishmail was already Jesus resurrected. Or he was the true Mahdi, the Imam returning from "occultation" to reign over a perfect world, an angel of Satan, a space alien, or a CIA plot. He'd come to save them. He'd come to kill them. He was their only hope.

Just before sunrise Michael had sat by a line of stretchers, unable to sleep but needing to get off his feet for a few minutes. An Israeli army major, who looked African since he was ethnically Moroccan but culturally Jewish, joined him. They chatted in idle, exhausted voices, exchanging half a cigarette. When Michael mumbled a few things about his encounter with the Prophet, the major was most interested in his name.

"Ishmail? You know what that's about, don't you?" he asked. Michael shook his head. "It's a very powerful name, the one given to the Hidden Imam," the major explained. When he saw the baffled look on Michael's face, he backed up the tale. "I don't know if your fellow is really named Ishmail or whether he adopted it for dramatic effect, but this is how it goes. In Islam, the line of prophets, beginning with Abraham, must end with Muhammad. Muslims are officially very skeptical about saints. But among the folk, and particularly among the Shiite Muslims, who are a powerful minority in the faith, there has always been a belief that a sort of messiah, called the Mahdi, will one day appear. Millions of the faithful believe in the seventh Imam, a supernatural being who has been hidden since the year 757, when the sixth Imam's son was passed over in favor of his undeserving brother. The undeserving brother was named Musa; the passed-over one was Ishmail.

"So you can see that this is a time bomb. Until the Imam returns from hiding, the whole world is impure, fallen, and bereft of spiritual greatness. But on the day Ishmail reveals himself again, God has signaled the triumph of one religion in the name of Allah over all others—a bloody triumph, I might add. And it doesn't hurt that Islam is derived, as far back as they can look, from a son of Abraham also named Ishmael."

The major, it turned out, was actually a professor from Hebrew University drafted into the reserves. His thumbnail sketch of the religious strife in the Mideast made Michael realize that he was getting closer and closer to what the Prophet was about. He went to Susan and filled her in.

"Maybe he really is the Hidden Imam," she speculated, taking the last stub of the cigarette from his fingers. "Solomon would know. I mean, even with his story of the thirty-six, he made a point that the pure souls didn't have to be Jewish; they could come from any faith."

"I don't think purity is the hallmark of this particular Ishmail," Michael said. "Conceivably he could be inciting some kind of Jihad or holy war on behalf of one religion, but my guess is that he's into equal-opportunity mischief. He's a manipulator, magnetized by anyone who succumbs to manipulation."

They ended their ten-minute break and went back to work until the Red Star provided a shift of professionals from Tel Aviv around ten in the morning. Then they surrendered to the exhaustion that had been held at bay and slept, curled up on cots behind an ammunitions locker, until six that night. When Michael woke up, Maundy Thursday was ending. He didn't know what the term meant, only that yesterday had been Ash Wednesday and tomorrow therefore Good Friday. The significance of Holy Week might have meant something if it hadn't been the backdrop for five times the casualties that would have occurred during a normal week.

His skin felt greasy, crusted with sweat and soot. He wondered if any amount of soap and water could manage to clean him of what had happened last night. Was this, too, his fault—a consequence of his refusal to fight? Or would it have happened no matter what he'd done?

"Press! I'm a journalist, damn you! *Capisce?*" There was someone shouting over on the other side of the tent, a hoarse, strident English voice. Nigel. Michael rushed toward the sound, tripping over tent wires, until he could see the front gate. At the opening in a hastily erected barricade of sandbags and barbed wire, Nigel was standing in a safari vest over a striped Rugby pullover, a battered Tilley cap on his head. Behind him was a crewman with a minicam on his shoulder.

"You don't bloody understand." Nigel was talking to a stolid Israeli guard blocking his access to the aid station. "I want to do some interviews with people who've seen him. Look, who's your commanding officer? Do you even speak English?"

"Almost everyone here does," Michael said,

walking over to the gate. "We like to think of it as the language of friendship among the diverse peoples of the Middle East." Across the street Michael could see a white van with the BBC logo on it. The van had several fresh dents and holes, as if it had been shot at during the night.

Nigel's face went from shock to calculated delight.

"Michael, old son! You are a sight for the proverbial. Could you tell these apes to let me in? We're seven hours ahead of New York. I've just got time to scarf a few more sweeteners before we put last night's footage together."

"You seem to think I'm kindly disposed to you," Michael replied.

"Why shouldn't you be?"

"I don't know—guilt by association? You seem to be consorting with types that start riots and stir up religious zeal, all before breakfast."

Nigel's eyes widened. "Listen, I didn't have to look for him, he found me. Just walked into my hotel room in Damascus and told me he might go to Jerusalem. Coming here wasn't my idea, you know."

"I bet. And you don't think his presence here is the least bit unhealthy?" Michael swept a speaking glance around the horizon at the charred buildings, the evidence of night-long rioting. "Be sure you get on your knees for the broadcast, Nigel. You need to give people a hint of what kind of work you do."

Nigel appraised him shrewdly, wondering how much of this was sincere and how much a blow-off of tension. "I don't wear knee pads except for the bitch goddess Success, you know that. It's not my job to hide a phenomenon, or to judge it."

Michael said angrily, "For God's sake, man, look

around. Your pet has started a war, all by himself. Thousands of people are dead."

"That isn't his fault," Nigel said quickly. "Extremists have distorted his message. He had nothing to do with any—"

"He started all of it, deliberately," Michael said.

"You're being irrational. He'll make his position perfectly clear when he addresses the Knesset at noon today. Carried live, of course, though they'll want to rerun it at a decent hour for the States."

"Christ! Listen to you."

Nigel paused. Seeing that he had nothing to gain, he shook his head with contempt. "Let me give you some advice. Your opinions are going to make this city very unsafe for yourself. This Prophet, if I may use the term without having my head bitten off, will do more to unite three warring religions than anyone in the past two thousand years."

"And in exchange for bringing this blessing to our notice, what's your cut—thirty thousand pieces of silver?"

Michael knew that he sounded as stupidly zealous as Nigel, without the benefit of being on the winning side. He had no illusions about that. "Look," he said, "I don't have time for this. I've been up too many hours trying to stitch up everyone your two-bit Prince of Peace put through the wringer last night. If we're all still alive by sundown, I expect I'm going to be doing the same again tonight. Do what you have to, but don't ask me for any more photo ops with the bodies."

The back door of the satellite van opened, and Michael caught sight of black jeans and a white T-shirt out of the corner of his eye before he had the first flash of recognition. The guards recognized him, too. They moved back nervously from the gateway, then one of them—Michael thought he might be an Arab Christian rather than an Israeli—dropped to his knees as the Prophet approached.

"Rise, my son, and walk in peace," Ishmail murmured, placing a hand on the man's head. The overwhelmed soldier clutched at it, kissing it fervently. Michael wanted to turn away, but he was fascinated by this new persona—he couldn't connect it with the mocking tormentor who'd taken Susan just the day before.

Ishmail's eyes swept the surroundings behind his dark glasses, ignoring Michael. "I could help many people here," he said. "But I sense that my help would be rejected. Do you know the scriptures? 'O Jerusalem, who kills your prophets—'"

"And stones those who are sent to you," Michael finished. "That's turning into kind of a worn-out sound bite, don't you think?" He was amazed at himself for daring to confront this creature whose powers were proving limitless, but it wasn't just bravado. There was no doubt that Ishmail could have killed him a dozen times already. And he imagined it was no coincidence that had led Nigel to pick this particular outpost to look for his interviews.

"Nigel? Who are you talking to?" The Prophet spoke a perfect, cultured English now, though Michael would have bet he hadn't known a word of it three days ago. His voice was sweet and gentle, a loving kindly voice, the sort that children hoped to hear tucking them in at night or that lovers yearned for across the pillow.

"Nobody important," Nigel said sulkily. "C'mon, we can do without the local color. I've got a lot of work to do."

The note of casual familiarity in Nigel's voice bordered on impudence, and Michael was sure that Ishmail noted it. If the mouse was safe living between the paws of the lion, that might not last for long. Before turning back toward the van, the Prophet scrutinized the soldiers and the tents curiously, but his gaze didn't stop on Michael.

He lost the Light. He can't see it anymore. Rakhel's words surfaced, plucked out of memory along with the skirmish in the hotel room yesterday morning. Now, as then, Michael could see Ishmail, but Ishmail, he was sure, could not see him.

Michael held his breath, praying that Nigel would say nothing to give his presence away. But Nigel simply stamped angrily across the road, his cameraman following.

"If the wicked will turn from all the sins that he hath committed, and keep all my statutes, and do that which is lawful and just, he shall surely live," Ishmail said, turning away. Michael thought it was a rehearsal for an audience that hadn't updated its religious entertainments for several centuries, but he also knew, watching the Prophet disappear into the van, that the act would suffice very well.

He should have told Susan about the encounter, given their deepening intimacy and the bond of war that drew them ever closer together. But he didn't, judging that it was even more intimate to keep her unaware for a while, out of respect for the fear he knew she was still harboring. It was an act of gentleness not to intrude on that.

When he told her that he was going into West Jerusalem to see about medical supplies and maybe some breakfast food, if the stalls hadn't been raided bare, Susan seemed content to stay behind. He left her washing up in the women's facility and walked first toward a market street in the Christian Quarter for some bread and cheese, perhaps some fruit if he could find it. The need to eat had been wrung out of him by the grim excitement of the night's violence, but he could get down a little simple food. The curfew would be lowered after dusk, so he had to hurry.

The crowds were still very troubled, despite the strong military presence. Michael watched where he was going, and therefore he was on the alert when he saw the boy. His slim figure, dressed in black, was just slipping through a group of soldiers next to a grocery.

"Hey!" Michael shouted. Despite the packed crowd, the boy somehow knew that this was for him. He turned a startled pale face toward Michael. "David, stop!" Michael called, but when he heard his name, Solomon's mad neighbor turned and ran. Within five seconds Michael was in pursuit.

He saw the boy drop his paper sack of groceries. A quart of milk smashed on the cobblestones. David wasn't near home, but he seemed to know the streets and alleys. Chasing him, Michael jostled angry pedestrians, dodged a screeching Vespa, and nearly knocked over a street vendor. The crowd didn't part or stare curiously; they were all still enclosed in their own bubbles of shock and dismay.

After three blocks, Michael felt his wind giving out; he had sharp stitches in his ribs and his knees ached from pounding the stone pavement. David seemed to speed up, energized by panic. Michael didn't think he could catch him, but it wasn't so hard to keep him in sight, and maybe he would head back to the people who had sent him out for food—that was Michael's best hope.

A couple of times the boy veered toward a major street, and when he neared one of the big barricades, Michael almost shouted, "Stop him!" But he knew that the military weren't likely to believe him over a frightened Hasid boy. Fright didn't steal David's wits, it turned out. When his shoes trampled broken glass from a milk bottle, Michael realized that he was being led in a circle. He stopped, wheezing and panting, and let the boy get away.

"The quality of mercy is not strained—good." Whirling around, he saw an amused Solomon Kellner looking at him from across the street. The rabbi was juggling two cabbages in either hand, trying to pick one from a vendor's stall. "It was merciful to let him go. The poor boy's done nothing wrong beside lose his wits somewhere in the Talmud."

"I didn't want him anyway," Michael gasped, his breath slowly returning.

"You wanted me, *nu?*" said Solomon, paying the vendor and starting to walk away. Michael kept up.

"Something like that," he said. "Assuming you can tell me what I need to know."

"Better I tell you what you shouldn't know." Michael waited for a clarification. "You shouldn't know who I am, where I live, what I am going to do next," Solomon continued. "You have a sense of the melodramatic, and this is about something totally different."

"Your friend Rakhel told me I liked melodrama as well," said Michael.

"What do you call that—baiting me, drawing me out?" the old rabbi grumbled. Michael grabbed him by the sleeve.

"I'm not bantering. I'm seeking you out because I know, for certain, that you weren't totally honest with me. You're one of the Lamed Vov." He didn't stop to let Solomon protest. "Look, it's fine with me if you want to preserve your own confidences, but you left an awful lot of clues. At least Rakhel did for you, because she said he cannot see the Light. That means Ishmail. And when we were hiding in your house that night, you deliberately stood in the front room to see if he could see you. Who else would do that?"

"You were spying?" Solomon said accusingly.

"I happened to come downstairs. I wanted to see if you were in trouble," replied Michael. "In any case, this isn't exactly the time for more evasions, is it? Because the fact is, he can't see me, either. So what do we do about that?"

Without answering, Solomon pointed up ahead. "Come with me. Curfew has already fallen. We're not safe here, and your pretty girlfriend will just have to wait and worry. It can't be helped."

Five minutes later, after a few diversions around some patrolling soldiers, they were in front of the rabbi's old house. Solomon opened the door and stood aside for Michael.

"But I was already here," Michael protested. "And it wasn't your home anymore."

"Don't blame me. I've gotten used to cheap tricks." Saying nothing more to elaborate, Solomon pushed him into the front parlor. It was dimly lit by a single candle, and the curtains were drawn. "I'll take this food upstairs to Bella. You meet me in my study, yes?"

While he sat in one of the old leather chairs staring at the rows of old leather-bound books, Michael realized that his awareness had changed. No single event had caused this, maybe no single thought or decision on his part. But somehow he had gotten into a boat and sailed away from normal life, which appeared only distantly to him now, as if sighted on a far horizon. Is that what made him invisible to Ishmail, or was someone shielding him?

In his mind's eye, he could imagine the escalating violence spreading out from the Prophet's appearance. This wasn't a dream anymore. He had only to close his eyes and find himself walking through a city in flames, only this time the buildings that burned were tall and modern. The Prophet was there, and his words were fire. The more he preached, the higher the flames rose, and Michael looked on without fear. If this was the essence of how he had changed, he wasn't sure it was good. Being fearless struck him as a dangerous stance when you really didn't know anything.

He broke out of his reverie to find Solomon standing in front of him with a gun pointed at his head. Michael jumped up. "What are you doing? Put that thing down."

Solomon pointed the gun away. "We've come to a critical point. Just because Ishmail can't see you doesn't mean he will ignore you. Quite the opposite. The invisible is the only threat to him, and he realizes how dangerous we are. The question is, do we agree to be a danger, or do we continue to watch and trust?"

"I don't see how we can just stand by. If the thirty-six have any power—"

"You are tripping over words, mere words. What do you think power is?" asked Solomon.

"I don't see how that matters. This is one of your

own, maybe a renegade but still someone like you and unlike anybody else. You said the thirty-six had unlimited power."

Solomon shook his head. "Ishmail is like us, true, but what makes him so is free will. We are people who have tasted the temptation to alter reality, only to renounce it. He has not renounced, yet that doesn't mean we can control him."

Michael felt his heart sink. "So you're just going to be fatalistic while thousands die, while chaos breaks out on a mass scale? I see." He looked around the room, wondering glumly if three thousand years of wisdom amounted to this. His head was turned when he felt a blow to his left side. It hit his whole body, almost throwing him off his feet, while at the same time there was a massive crashing sound.

He followed me. The one thought was all he had time for. Whirling around and catching himself from falling, Michael saw the entire wall of the study that fronted the street suddenly collapse. Brick and mortar dust filled the room in a matter of seconds. The wall was reduced to a pile of rubble, and he could see the street outside, quiet and dark except for a distant streetlight.

"Stay where you are!" Solomon ordered. He stared at the opening in the wall with hard eyes. At that moment a figure climbed over the brick rubble, and despite the heavy clouds of dust, Michael knew instantly who it was. He knew that being invisible was no protection now. Ishmail could cause the whole house to collapse on top of them. With a desperate lunge, Michael threw himself toward the dark figure, while at the same time a sharp explosion went off near his ear.

His head ringing with pain, Michael landed on top of Ishmail's body. They rolled over twice before he realized that his opponent was inert. There was no struggle in him, nothing at all. Solomon was standing over them with his gun.

"You can quit fighting now," he said dryly. Michael sat up, letting the body go. Ishmail crumpled onto the piled bricks, his arms splayed out.

"Is that satisfactory?" Solomon asked. In the background Michael saw that Bella, dressed in her flannel nightgown, had rushed in from upstairs. She stood with her hand over her mouth in shock.

"How could you kill him?" Michael asked in a daze.

Solomon coolly put the revolver back into his desk and locked the drawer. "You mean, how was it possible? Everyone is mortal. I never said that he couldn't die. You shouldn't make assumptions."

Michael stood up after feeling for a pulse in the arm that lay closest to him. Blood oozed from a clean wound that the small-caliber round had made in Ishmail's forehead. A sick dizziness blended with the wave of incredible relief Michael felt. "It's still unbelievable," he said.

"Seeing is believing. Isn't that the general rule?" By now Solomon had joined Bella and was holding her in his arms. "Please, go back to your room. Pack a bag," he told her quietly. "This young man has helped attract this to us. Now we will have a visit from the soldiers. I want to get you out of here."

The rabbi's words came true almost as soon as they were spoken. An armed jeep appeared on the dark street, and two Israeli MPs, guns drawn, walked over the rubble. "Stand back, put your hands in the air," the lead one barked. Bella began to cry, and Michael went white. Between hallucination and violence, he felt that he wasn't even real anymore. Things moved swiftly over the next two hours. The police cordoned off the house and made them stand outside while the coroner's team was notified.

Michael never saw them wrap up Ishmail's body and cart it away. He and the Kellners were all taken in a truck to the Kishle station near the Jaffa Gate. Normally this was the tourist police, dealing with purse snatchers and lost traveler's checks. After dark the place was nearly deserted, except for a few stray visitors deprived of their passports who needed police clearance before they could return to their hotels. These visitors gawked as the desk sergeant booked the three, handcuffed and silent. Michael never knew what happened to the Kellners. Before dawn Susan showed up to bail him out; in any event the police notified him, as he was signing for his wallet and belt at the desk, that he wouldn't be charged with a crime. They had a confession from the rabbi, and if he pleaded guilty at his arraignment, Michael wouldn't even be called as a material witness.

The ordeal of the Prophet was over.

Perhaps because his advance man had been killed, the devil never showed up. The disappearance of Ishmail was not enough to stop the rioting in Jerusalem, not right away. Hatred and spilled blood continued for three months, steadily declining or at least going back into its old secret chambers until the next eruption. Despite the spectacular outbreaks of isolated terrorism that create headlines, Israel lays claim to being one of the most secure states in the world. The police and army forces were in place and had experience; before the month was out they had cleared Jerusalem of foreign visitors, secured the borders with the West Bank, and put every effort into restoring civil order. Even the Dome of the Rock was repaired—the process of the reconstruction a sign of the healing city.

Michael and Susan were among the first sent back home, which in their case meant back to their work. They had talked about relocating her immediately to Palmyra, but when they touched on the topic of marriage, something cautious and cool had arisen between them. They were both surprised by this. It wasn't like returning to their old relationship, but the momentum to move forward had disappeared. In a way Ishmail had changed them, and now he was gone. They were like soldiers who had been brothers in the trenches but knew that they would not be brothers once the war was over—it gave a strange feeling of true but provisional intimacy.

Therefore in the end Susan took the next flight back to Alexandria. Michael saw her off at Ben Gurion Airport the day after Easter Sunday. "You're sure about this?" he said. She gave him a searching look, almost accusing him of laying the decision on her shoulders, but they were long past emotional games that disguised real motives. No one was being sabotaged here. They both knew that simply readjusting to the normal world would be difficult enough without trying to add complications. She left quietly.

Michael drove himself back in a new jeep to replace the one lost with Yousef. He took care to cross the worst part of the desert at night, spending the torrid middle of the day in wayside inns or napping under palm trees if he happened to spot an inviting wadi. For all its hostility, the desert seemed a comforting place to him now—he needed to be refreshed by absolute stillness. For its part, the desert seemed to have no reaction to everything that had occurred. It accepted and kept its counsel.

He debriefed Nikolai the night he returned, adding some few details to the news stories that had filtered into the camp. The more incredible parts of his story were glossed over; considering the fantastic events that had to be absorbed by the whole world, Michael's small portion became almost irrelevant. The immediate task was to pull up stakes and move the medical team to their next assignment near Aleppo. Lost in the overload of work, plunged again into the routine of treating hundreds of patients a day, Michael could block out his phantoms. Lying awake at night in his tent, he listened to the radio, at first expecting some kind of spiritual tidal wave to sweep over the world. After all, Ishmail's miracles and his apparition over the Dome had kindled apocalyptic fever almost immediately. But when nothing else followed, humanity sank back into its old ways, and whatever the zealots would make of all this, the ordinary person went back to sleep.

Within nine months Michael was handed transfer papers sending him back to the U.S. Since his new job was nonsurgical (they were assigning him to an administrative desk out of Washington), he took the option of resigning. With two months' severance pay in his pocket, he flew to Damascus, but the connecting flight to Rome was canceled.

"You'll have to stay over until tomorrow," the airlines clerk said, punching her keyboard. She shook her head. "I don't think you'll want this, but there is a later flight through Cyprus with change of planes in Jerusalem and Cairo. Not likely, huh?" Knowing that he was making a serious mistake, Michael took the flight. He brooded in the air, spending the hours looking down over the blue sea and then the brown blank land below him. Hypnotically he deplaned in Jerusalem and hailed a cab.

Solomon opened the door almost as soon as Michael knocked. Michael stared in shock; he'd expected to see Bella. "You're out of jail?" he blurted. Solomon said nothing but stood aside to let him in. "I-I'm here to apologize to you," Michael stuttered. "I can't stop thinking about what happened that night. You shot him for me, didn't you? I goaded you into it, with all that fantastic talk about how you had the power to stop him. I can't express how much—"

He had rehearsed the speech a hundred times, thinking that he would be saying it to Bella, but one thing he never could have anticipated was Solomon's reaction. The old rabbi turned on his heels and marched into his study. Michael stopped and waited, wondering if he would reappear. He did, a few seconds later, and he was carrying the same gun he had used to kill Ishmail. It was pointed at Michael.

"This is insane," Michael protested. "Just let me go."

Solomon shook his head and waved Michael toward him with the gun. "Just come in here and sit down," he said.

Michael obeyed, feeling sick to his stomach. It was the nausea of fear, but something much eerier as well. "What are you doing?" he demanded once he had taken a seat in the leather chair facing the desk. He knew that Solomon was re-enacting the scene when they'd last met. "If this gives you some kind of twisted satisfaction . . ."

At that moment his face was not turned, as before, to look at the bookshelves. He was facing the wall instead, the one that Ishmail had broken down that night. A rumbling sound began, coming from that direction. Michael sat bolt upright, wanting to flee but unable to.

"This isn't about satisfaction," Solomon said calmly, pointing the gun away from him. "It's about learning. Do you think you've learned anything?"

Before Michael could reply, the low rumbling turned into a crash as the wall collapsed in a flurry of bricks and mortar. A choking cloud of dust filled the room, and a dark figure appeared outside. It was the same figure, silhouetted against the same black street lit from a distance by a lone street lamp. This time Michael wasn't frozen with fear, and no furious rage impelled him to leap on their assailant. He watched with weird detached interest as Ishmail climbed over the pile of brick rubble and entered the room.

Solomon turned and pointed the gun at the Prophet, who swiveled his head from side to side, unable to see them. "Quit meddling," he shouted. "Do you understand?"

"I think he might," Solomon said quietly. Ishmail's eyes whipped in the direction the voice was coming from. Michael stood up, taking in the scene.

"Shall I shoot?" Solomon asked. "We can still do it your way."

"You've made your point, Rebbe. There's a lot more to learn than I thought," Michael said—or he might have said. At that moment the whole house was plunged into darkness, and the last sound he remembered was the clatter of Solomon's gun as he threw it against the wall with a grunt of total disgust.

CHAPTER EIGHT

THE WELL OF SOULS

When the light didn't return, Michael assumed that he'd taken another trip to nowhere. The blackness was just as absolute, only this time he was much calmer—breathing without needing a coach—and the air had no cavelike dankness. Then he realized that there was noise around him, traffic noise coming in from a closed window.

"Solomon?" he said.

There was no response, but almost immediately Michael realized that he couldn't move. He arms were tied behind his back, and although he couldn't see them, he knew that his feet were also bound—he was tied to a chair in a cheap room somewhere, in the classic movie pose of a kidnap victim.

"Be quiet," Solomon's voice ordered from behind him. Michael tried to wrench his head around, but there was nothing to see and no light to see it by.

"Hey, get me out of this," he protested.

"Be quiet. Are you going to learn or aren't you?" Solomon sounded stern and serious. Whatever the game was turning into, Michael decided to follow orders. Outside he could hear distant sirens and honking of horns. Even without a trained ear, he knew he was in America, even though there was no memory of being transported from place to place.

"What you call ordinary reality is kept in place by thoughts," Solomon began. "The more orderly the thoughts, the more orderly the reality. Can you begin to see this?"

Michael could hear the rabbi walking, circling his chair as he spoke. "I am talking about everyday thoughts, nothing exceptional or magical. In other words, your own thoughts."

Michael nodded.

"Your mind is incredibly disordered, although this is nothing special by normal standards. We have watched the chaos created by everyone like you, and we haven't interfered. It isn't possible for us to step into your minds and clear them. How could we? An ordinary mind is like a steel chamber with a million bullets ricocheting around inside. At best, if you let me enter your mind, I could only catch a handful."

Michael was listening, but he couldn't help twisting in his seat. Being tied up was uncomfortable, and a subconscious animal rage resisted this kind of forced captivity.

"Even now," Solomon said, "you want to struggle. You still don't believe that I am your ally in all this."

"Ally?" Michael burst out. "You've twisted my life out of recognition."

"No, you've twisted it, only because you're not aware of what you're doing, everything moves slowly; therefore you are always ready to blame things on someone or something outside yourself. All we did was bring your attention back where it belongs."

"All right." Michael stopped short, overwhelmed

by the futility of arguing with any of them. After a
few seconds he felt a broad sticky band of tape being
drawn over his mouth. It happened quickly; he
barely had time to let out a muffled shout of rage.
Wildly he rocked his chair, trying to strike up
against Solomon, perhaps grab him with one of his
bound hands.

"There's something in you that needs to be pulled
out." Solomon's voice was close to his ear now.
"And only you can pull it. You talk about power?
You'll never understand the meaning of the word as
long as you hide behind a shield of fear and resistance. You understand?"

Bastard! Coward! Michael was screaming behind
his gag. With the clarity of terror he knew that Solomon was going to abandon him here.

"You'll understand your power when you stop
struggling," Solomon said. "It's the struggle that has
kept you in fear, but you think just the opposite. So
now let's see how far fear can take you."

Michael heard no footsteps leaving, but the room
went quiet except for the distant traffic. He
wrenched his chair violently, trying to rip the rope
from his wrists, and then he toppled over, crashing
to the floor on his side. He screamed for Solomon;
his muffled screech died in the room. He decided to
stop.

Hours passed, and he might even have fallen
asleep despite his racing mind. The next thing he
noticed was blotched yellow light coming in through
the drawn paper shades. He turned his head in the
direction, raising it up a few inches from the filthy
carpet. Every detail confirmed that he was in a flophouse. He was staring at peeling wallpaper with
brown streaks running down it. There was one win-

dow, filthy and cracked, to let in the wan midday light. The room stank of poverty—urine and rancid fat and industrial disinfectant.

This was where he was supposed to be, according to everyone but himself.

He shook his head groggily, trying to change the picture he saw. His whole body, forced into one position, ached with dull pain. Almost by reflex he thrashed a little, letting panic have its way. But he wasn't going to get out of there by force or, he imagined, by a supernatural act of will. Next to the iron bedstead he saw a dingy clock that read ten A.M.

It took a long time for anything to change. The room started to get cold. He could hear the toilet flushing down the hall in a communal bathroom, and once or twice heavy footsteps passed by the door. Michael tried thumping his legs on the floor to attract someone's attention. This was likely to be the kind of hotel, he knew, where the policy was to pay no attention to anything, up to and including a spare corpse.

He wasted the next hour running through all the revenge scenarios he could imagine. His hatred was easily channeled toward Ishmail, less toward Solomon. He wouldn't mind seeing either of them pay for what they'd done to him—but before what court? And would he be alive to see it? The vindictiveness ran out of steam; it had only succeeded in making him more exhausted. He lay still and dozed off again.

When he woke up he wasted no time or energy on anything stupid. He made his mind turn to the topic Solomon had been teaching him about: power. What had he been a witness to, ever since he left the medical station, but a daunting display of power?

Solomon had told him—and Rakhel, too—about the extent of what was available to them. The power of transformation, the power to make and unmake creation itself, on a whim. To transcend time and space, if not death; to reshape reality ... all the powers that myth, legend, and pulp fiction had essentially ascribed to the gods.

Now, Michael thought, *I'm finding out what it's like to have a god mad at you. We are to the gods as flies to wanton boys. They kill us for their sport.* But that was the hang-up, wasn't it? No one had killed him, and Solomon had even obliged and killed his enemy before his very eyes. Why didn't it stick? What were they trying to show him?

He realized that he was getting very hungry and thirsty. Now that he was calmer, he wondered if he could scoot the toppled chair near enough to the door so that he could pound on it with his feet. It wasn't worth a try, but he had to prove that. After expending massive effort to clump forward half an inch, Michael went back to thinking.

He took a new tack, forgetting about gods. *Let's assume that the thirty-six are just human beings, as they portray themselves,* he told himself. It was impossible to imagine how they made it from ordinary waking reality to the dreamlike reality they lived in, but Michael had been dragged along. So he had to assume that he was still inside a human dimension. Never mind how or why this had happened. It was a given. Therefore, struggling to go back across the border was pointless, as pointless as wanting to regress back to childhood. If that was true, then the only way to go now was straight ahead.

The clarity of his reasoning shocked Michael. He had the strange sensation that these thoughts were almost thinking themselves, like transmissions from outside his brain, but the voice in his head was his own, not an alien's. Wait—he'd lost his focus. He took a deep breath and went back to where the thoughts had left off.

The only way to go was ahead. What did that mean? He'd tried to remain uninvolved, but events had pursued him with relentless precision. He'd tried to fight the enemy, to outwit him, even in his weak moments to give in and let catastrophe sweep over his head. No alternatives mattered, not in the slightest. So either everything was equally dangerous, or everything was equally safe. In some way the thirty-six felt safe. It was this last possibility, completely new to his mind, that riveted Michael's attention.

In what imaginable way was the world safe with Ishmail in it? That was like saying that the world was safe with evil in it. Had the thirty six managed to solve evil?

There was a knock at the door. The knob rattled as someone tried it.

"Hey—it's locked. Who's in there?" a muffled voice demanded suspiciously. Michael moaned, but whoever was at the door stopped turning the knob. *Try it again*, Michael thought. He willed himself to be calm and not to struggle. *It isn't locked. It's open.*

He saw the doorknob rattle again, and this time it turned. A stooped, bedraggled man came in, then stopped in surprise. He wore thrift-store sneakers without socks—that was all Michael could see without craning his head.

"What are you doin' in my room? Why are you lyin' there like that? I bet the cops don't know you're here."

Michael resisted the urge to protest or squirm. *You're not afraid. It's okay.* After a long pause, the sneakers came closer. Raising his head, Michael looked into dull bloodshot eyes. Bristly grayish stubble covered the jaw, longer in some places than others, artifact of a halfhearted shave too many days ago. The man looked homeless, one of the lepers for a new millennium—addicted, ill, making the rounds of soup kitchens and hot-air grates. But he spoke with a New York accent, giving Michael his first bearings in a long while.

Michael closed his eyes and went quiet inside. After a moment, he felt the tape being peeled carefully from his mouth.

"Geez, Mikey, didja hurt yourself? I just went down ta the corner ta buy some . . . some soup, that was it. I toldja you shouldn't try ta go cold turkey like that, man, you coulda got hurt. . . ." The derelict's voice trailed off.

"Untie me, will you, buddy?" Michael said.

The man's fingers fumbled with the knots, slowly releasing Michael's wrists.

"How'd ya fall over like that?" the derelict mumbled.

"That's why you tied me up, remember? I told you it wasn't just going to be twitches. I come down hard." Unshaven and in his cheap dirty clothes, Michael looked like he fit the story, wherever it came from. As soon as his hands were free, he untied his own feet and stood, rubbing the shoulder he'd fallen on, stretching the kinks from his cramped limbs.

"Thanks a lot, man," Michael said. "I appreciate it, I really do."

"Hey, no problem, Mikey," the man said. He had lost interest in Mikey, however. He just made it to the iron bedstead before he blacked out. Michael stared down at him. It cost him a pang of guilt, but he couldn't afford to call the desk. He'd have to contact EMS when he got to a pay phone. Over on the battered dresser, he spied a familiar object—his wallet. He picked it up. It was full of American money. He pulled out a couple of twenties and laid them on the bed. "Here, and godspeed," he whispered.

The hallway reeked of mildew and disinfectant, a stronger version of the smell inside the room. There was a staircase at the end of the hall; Michael took it. He was only one flight up. He walked across the lobby without attracting the notice of a clerk watching TV behind a grilled window. On the street he spied parked cars with New York plates. His best guess was that he had landed in Alphabet City on Manhattan's Lower East Side. The wind was icy. He shivered in his T-shirt and missed the light jacket he'd bought in the bazaar, when he and Susan had shopped there.

Susan?

He had a sudden, crazy thought that if he walked uptown, he'd run into her on some corner, stepping out of Saks, breaking into a smile when she caught sight of him. But this time the magic that was half-wishing didn't work, and Michael continued up the street, chafing his arms to keep warm.

Winter. Why is it winter? He wasn't thinking "how" anymore. The ability to toss him somewhere strange in time, or even to alter the climate, was now a given in his mind. Maybe this was a way of throwing him out of danger. No, more likely it was a test or challenge. They had sped up time, or skipped over a lot of it, to get him to the crisis point, like flipping the pages to get to the chase. *Now is the winter of our discontent.* It would fit Ishmail's fondness for symbols to choose this time of year when people are reminded, however briefly, of holiness. Twenty minutes later, after wandering aimlessly, he crossed the Bowery and found himself on Broadway, just above Houston. The manager of a sporting goods store on the corner didn't much like the look of Michael, but he sold him a down parka, a watch cap, and boots to replace his sandals. On impulse Michael tried his credit card and found that it still worked. Curious.

He got back on the streets and wondered why it held no surprises. Ordinariness seemed threatening under these circumstances: ads for *Cats* and the Marlboro Man on the sides of buses, city workers rushing by with ski masks over their faces to repair a steaming vent in the street, taxis playing chicken with pedestrians at the stop lights, nobody minding if a fender came half an inch from knocking them to the asphalt. Michael picked his way, staring at his feet, wondering what to do.

Tiny snowflakes drifted down out of a leaden sky, though nothing was sticking. He saw a newsstand across the street. *Might as well get the bad news all at once,* he thought. But when he asked the bundled Indian freezing at the counter for a *Times,* there was nothing startling in any of the headlines, not even a mention of the Middle East. Fumbling for change, his eyes fell on the *Post,* and he started. The headline read, RUDY GRATEFUL, DENIES TAKEOVER CHARGES. The rest of the page was filled with a picture of Ishmail shaking hands with the mayor on the steps of city hall.

"It's not a library. You want that one, too?" the freezing Indian grumbled.

"I'll take one of everything," said Michael.

*   *   *

Michael read one newspaper after another. According to the mastheads, it was November 14. He'd lost six months out of his life, and in that six months, the Prophet had made his mark. Michael unfolded each page carefully, laying them out like a jigsaw puzzle. He had walked to a nearby greasy spoon on Avenue B. Paying for a blue-plate special that he had no appetite for, he tried to piece together what had happened. The *Times* still looked like the *Times,* but when he read closer, the content was surreal.

The Middle East created no headlines, because four months earlier, with the threat of war hanging over the region, the weapons of all combatants had refused to fire. Apocalypse blew a fuse. The three faiths called a truce by holding hands around the Temple Mount, dividing it into equal portions for a new Dome, a basilica to the Virgin Mother, and the fourth Temple. A dozen red heifers were born in Israel, causing great rejoicing.

In Texas the leading fundamentalist churches held a barbecue convocation; the next day they voted to take a wait-and-see attitude toward the coming of the Antichrist. Since it was widely held, by those who deplored anything but a strict reading of Saint John, that the Antichrist would have to be Jewish, and his battle plans consisted of starting a war that would wipe out all but 144,000 of the Jews on earth, the decision to hold off was greeted with relief. "Any reprieve from genocide is always welcome," a source in Tel Aviv was quoted as saying—he refused to be identified.

Ishmail was in the thick of this. His apparition above the dome was seen as (a) an attempt to save it; (b) the thing that destroyed it, giving the world's religions a much-needed wake-up call; or (c) a total hoax. Those who held the last opinion didn't get invited back on camera again, and some actually disappeared from view altogether.

A week after the disaster Ishmail had reappeared, demanding that the warring fanatical factions make peace. Those who refused had been struck by devastating plagues that slaughtered half the populace overnight. (A UN resolution was introduced deploring this retaliation, should it have come from the Prophet. Caution being the better part of diplomacy, the resolution failed to pass.) Now everything from Turkey to Egypt had become the "Eastern Economic Community," and all borders were gone. Official joy reigned while they were still burying the dead and rebuilding what had been destroyed.

The Prophet had not declared himself king; he declared that he had come to bring love and to destroy forever anyone who resisted. It was not a message that countries were equipped to fight—he asked for nothing, ordered nothing, merely told people that he was an instrument of their own power. The more powerful they became, through purging the darkness inside themselves, the closer they would come to paradise on Earth.

Somewhere in the shadows of the Vatican, it was felt that the Muslims had stolen the spotlight with the return of the Mahdi, added to which there was a certain nervousness—after all, St. Peter's had its own dome. It looked awfully vulnerable until the assembled cardinals dredged up the doctrine of papal chair-warming. Since the Pope was merely a temporary office, a vicar awaiting the return of the Church's true owner, the seat of Rome could be vacated on a moment's notice. Perhaps the Prophet would like to occupy it? With the coyness of a movie star turning down a golden deal, Ishmail refused to be coaxed into the Second Coming. A sigh of relief swept through Christendom, however, when he publicly announced that he was not the Imam, either. And just to prove that he wanted to be an equal-opportunity messiah, he flicked a finger and wiped out every secret stronghold of Hamas and Black September in the Occupied Territories (now cannily renamed "expanded Jerusalem" so that everyone had a piece of the pie).

Michael flipped the pages devoted to Ishmail's triumphant world tour. All the stories had a monotonous similarity, as though they'd all been written by the same hack and dictated by the same invisible watcher. Like the old Russian joke about *Pravda* and *Izvestia*: "There's no news in the *Truth* and no truth in the *News*."

Ishmail was greeted joyously at every stop, perhaps out of love, perhaps because national leaders had had a good view of what would happen if they withheld their welcome. Nobody likes a plague. If there had been assassination attempts, they had all failed, and should any government oppose Ishmail, they risked riots from their own citizens. The Prophet went wherever he chose, preaching his message of the Eden to come. The humble of the world bowed down, the not so humble waited their chance, afraid that it might never come.

The *Times* reported worldwide prosperity, deserts turning into gardens, the end of deprivation and hunger. No new AIDS cases had been reported since the Prophet's appearance, and those who had suffered from the disease were quickly healed. An inability to change from HIV positive to HIV negative was seen as stubbornness. Cancer, polio, typhoid, cholera, meningitis . . . gone without comment once the first months of openmouthed incredulity faded from memory.

It was, Michael reflected, a perfect world.

"One Yankee pot roast with mash. You need a refill, doll?" When the waitress noticed what he was reading, she smiled with genuine affection. "I wouldn't mind reading that after you. Have a nice day," she said. If having Ishmail in the world was a danger, Michael thought, the illusion was too seamless to show any cracks.

He had to decide what to do. He still had a profession, if not a life. As one of the early resisters, he could have been denied his condo in Eden, but that didn't happen. After wandering the streets for several more hours, he stepped into the emergency room of New York Hospital. He walked up to the reception desk, where three nurses were leaning on the file cabinets having coffee.

"Sorry, I know this is the wrong area, but could you tell me where the chief of staff's office is? I'd like to apply for a job," Michael said.

The nurses stared at each other. "Good joke," one of them said. "I guess."

There was an embarrassed snicker, then the most prim of the nurses said, "They're waiting for you in trauma two, Doctor." Michael must have looked completely confused, because she quickly added, "I'm sorry, I'm Rebecca. We haven't met since they sent me over from Mount Sinai." She smiled tentatively, just in case he was the difficult type. Michael turned on his heels and walked away.

When he got to the cubicle marked "2" at the end of the hallway, Michael pushed open the swinging metal doors. A young resident was bent over a man on a table; the man's shirt was open, all his clothes bloodied. "Just hold still for me, I know it hurts," the resident was saying. The man groaned. Noticing Michael, the resident nodded but continued giving orders to his nurse. "Cross and type for five more units, and tell the OR to be ready."

Michael knew it was the moment of truth, but he felt no doubt or alarm. "Sorry," he said. "I got paged by Bellevue just when you called." He reached out for rubber gloves and a gown. The nurse handed them over quickly, without hesitation—or had her eyes flicked over to the resident for just a second?

Michael felt confident that he was going to fit in, and he was right. The resident held up some X-rays. "No problem. I think we've got him pretty much stabilized. Here are his pictures."

"Let me just check for a second here," Michael said. "Nasty splinter fracture of that fourth rib."

The resident nodded. "I noticed that right away. There's a fragment very close to the kidney." He pointed to a section of the X-ray as Michael, seamlessly flowing into the scene as if it were written for him, knew that in a way it had been. Someone had dropped him into a world that had always had a place for him. He only wished whoever it was had thought to drop Susan into the landscape while they were at it. He knew without thinking that this patient, the victim of a hit-and-run in Midtown Manhattan, was like a prop in a cosmic drama. All Michael had to do was figure out if this was a comedy or a tragedy.

"I don't think that splinter is as close as you think," Michael heard himself say.

"Really?" The resident took back the X-ray and stared at it with a puzzled expression.

"You thought it might have nicked the renal artery?" Michael asked.

"Yeah. I mean, the guy's quite a bleeder, and—"

"I think it's generalized." He turned to the patient, who was groggy but coherent. "Did anyone ever tell you that your blood doesn't coagulate very fast?" he asked. The man nodded. "I think we should try a little more clotting factor, and see if that solves the problem," Michael said.

Still baffled, the resident gave the orders, and the nurse turned to the meds cabinet. "I could have sworn—" the resident started to say, but Michael was already snapping off his gloves.

"Don't worry about it," he said. "Make sure the OR knows you're not sending anybody up. I'll catch you on rounds later."

Slipping into a parallel universe was one of the easier things he'd ever done, Michael thought as he walked down the hall back to the chart rack. He had a ready-made identity, a professional position, and everyone already knew his name.

"You're April, right?" he said to the youngest nurse at the desk. "Sorry I didn't catch it at first. We keep being on different rotations." She smiled, pleased to have been noticed. Michael took the next chart, a rare gunshot wound resulting from a domestic disturbance, and went back to work.

The rest of the day flowed with the boring ease of a long-running mediocre Broadway revival. As he walked through his part, Michael wondered if there would be any real decisions for him to make, or whether every day would pass with this kind of detachment. He knew in advance what was wrong with every patient, and without fail he saved them from danger. Someone had decided to fulfill his fantasies or else to mock him from behind the curtain. The super-doctor as puppet. At least it gave him time to consider where he really was, and decide what he had to do next.

By the time he waved good night and left the building, it was seven o'clock and dark. The light snow had stopped; the streets were clear. He could have returned to wandering, but he knew where his car was in the parking garage—he'd already found the keys in his pocket. Just as certainly he would be able to drive to the brownstone on the Upper East Side that had been his for the past six years. When he actually got there, his home was comfortably but not luxuriously furnished. Michael slumped in his favorite leather chair in the study, the one that had followed him, like a faithful brown tick hound, from medical school to every job he'd had on the East Coast.

If he was in a mood to be astonished—which he definitely wasn't—it was remarkable how every detail had been thought out. The rooms were set up to match his taste. He liked all the food in the refrigerator, and his brand of scotch stood on the sideboard. Every book on the shelf, every photo on the mantel had a story to tell; his life was littered with reassuring memories. He only glanced around at the memorabilia for a second, however. The realism of a faked existence meant nothing except that the prop manager, whoever he was, knew his job. With the fate of the world hanging by a thread, and Susan still missing, Michael expected that the joke would turn progressively more sour the more days he was forced to live it.

Was *forced* the right word? Solomon, like Rakhel, had kept referring to doing it his way or another way. Resistance to Ishmail had failed; he saw with his own eyes that the thirty-six existed on a plane where time could move in circles—and no doubt backward or sideways—and events were as easy to manipulate as dreams.

That was what real power was all about, then. Crossing the line between dream and reality, even though those terms were totally inadequate. A dream feels like a dream, and when you wake up, you can spot the transition to real life. Here, things didn't work that way. Every time Michael looked around, he was moving from one unreal state to the next, like waking up from a dream to find yourself in a new dream. The hallucination was seamless.

All right, so that was a given. Now what? Michael decided it wouldn't hurt to pour a little scotch for himself, maybe more than a little. He turned on the television, which was predictably filled with good news. One could tell that some of the news anchors hadn't quite adjusted to reporting the newest peace accord or miracle cure. Behind the mask of smiling confidence was a hint of panic. Michael understood. *Whoever giveth can taketh away.* Actually, any hint of discomfort was subtle and hard to detect. Wheeling through the channels, he detected very little disturbance. Why should people kick when you give them everything they want? It was just a matter of transition and adjustment.

He caught the tail end of one tragedy, a man who had jumped on the tracks in front of the IRT subway. If this was someone who had had a little adjustment problem, maybe too much guilt to feel comfy in paradise, it was a small price to pay. You could even look on the bright side: No one was being forced to accept the new world. No one could be accused of falling for mass hypnosis. As Solomon had said, reality is formed from ordinary thoughts and wishes, nothing magical.

After an hour Michael had no more doubts. He was in a place where the worst problem was an inability to accept perfect happiness. The thought made him decide to get totally drunk. He spent the evening waiting for the alcohol to work, and he passed out in his old chair about midnight. The last thing he heard—and he wasn't even sure he heard it—was the sound of moaning, like souls crying out from the bottom of a deep well.

CHAPTER NINE

YETZER HA-RA

There had to be a catch somewhere. Michael went through his days trying to find it. The detachment of fitting into a prewritten scenario continued. He was never fully engaged, even in the most complicated surgical procedure. Not that many came his way. Medicine had been reduced, for the most part, to ER trauma care—Ishmail couldn't keep drunk drivers from getting into crashes—and warehousing the chronically ill and dying.

Michael took to not going home much; the perfect setting for his new self made his skin crawl after a while. Its false coziness, and its real emptiness, just reminded him of everything he'd lost—especially Susan. His rotations were sometimes thirty-six hours long. The staff was perplexed, given that the other senior attendings came in less than twenty hours a week. But Michael passed it off as the habits of a workaholic who needed to get up to speed in trauma surgery. Everyone bought the story, as everyone bought every story. Peace and harmony was the new conformism.

There was no conceivable way that he could poke a stick in Ishmail's eye. Pointless rebellion seemed like a reasonable alternative for a while. He took up chain-smoking and staying up all night in the residents' lounge, idly flipping channels and throwing back scotch. After a week, however, the pointlessness outweighed the rebellion, and he stopped. But he took comfort roaming the parts of the city where squalor and crime kept a last toehold.

On one of these rambles he saw a derelict prowling a Dumpster. He rushed up, imagining for a moment that this was the flophouse denizen who'd freed him that first night. He was dressed in layers of worn, stinking clothes, grayed by too many washings over the years.

"Hey, man, remember me?" Michael said hopefully, but he didn't need to look into the derelict's confused, blank-eyed stare to know that this was wishful thinking.

"I'm not hurtin' nobody," the man mumbled, brushing Michael's hand from his shoulder. "I'm just goin' my own way."

"Right, sorry," Michael said. He would have backed out of the grimy alley, but these few harmless words struck him.

"Do you just go your own way?" he asked. "I've forgotten how."

"Huh?" the derelict mumbled.

"You've given me a clue," Michael said. "Do you know that? I bet you don't." He looked around at the broken glass and scraps of paper littering the ground. He was so energized that the stench of the alley didn't even fill his nose anymore. "Someone told me that if you don't know where you're going, it doesn't matter where you start. So I'm going to start here." He could see that the derelict wanted to get out of there, but Michael grabbed his arm.

"No one's going to hurt you. I just want you to give somebody a message for me," he said. His eye caught sight of a Three Musketeers wrapper; he picked it up.

"What kinda message? I can't read no addresses," the derelict mumbled.

"Doesn't matter," Michael said. He was feeling not just happy now but jubilant with the first taste of power. He knew that the next stroke would tell the tale. "Here's twenty dollars. You just have to do what I say, okay?"

He pressed the candy bar wrapper into the man's hands, closing his fingers around them like a magician asking someone to hold on to a card from the deck. His eyes met the derelict's. Nothing passed between them, no hypnotic stare, but when he opened his hand, the man was staring at a twenty-dollar bill. He smiled a gapped smile. Michael smiled back, his heart almost jumping out of his chest. Yes!

"Do I have to remember anything?" the derelict said doubtfully, afraid to pocket the money. He had been set up for police harassment too many times.

"Just listen," Michael said urgently. He gave his message in the careful voice of someone leaving it on an answering machine. "I know what you want me to do. I'm going to take responsibility, starting now. No fear, no doubt, no illusion. Thanks for giving me this chance." He paused, wondering if he should add anything specific. "I don't exactly know who this is going to reach, but I'm sure it's going to the right ones. This is the first man I've met who's going his own way, so he must be heading toward you somehow. Be good to him, and—" He realized that he was rambling, that even the need to speak out his message wasn't all that sure. "Okay, that's it," he said.

He expected the derelict to look baffled, perhaps even frightened about running into a well-dressed lunatic. If that was his assumption, it couldn't have been more wrong. The derelict's face wore the smile of a coconspirator. He nodded slightly. Michael almost thought he would throw off his disguise and turn into an angel or one of the pure souls, who would congratulate him on his cleverness. Instead, the knowing look faded instantly, and the man turned to walk away.

"Good luck," Michael called after him. The derelict mumbled a last phrase without turning around. Michael didn't catch it, but it might have been, "God bless you."

When he got home, Michael threw the scotch and the cigarettes down the garbage chute. It was a symbolic gesture, just as the message to the thirty-six, assuming they would ever hear it, was also symbolic. But the excitement was still real. He knew without a doubt that this cardboard paradise was a stage setting, not for the Prophet's power, but for his own—if he had any. Or rather, if he wanted any. Lying in bed, Michael remembered his last thoughts in the flophouse before the knock on the door. Either Ishmail was completely dangerous or completely safe. The choice wasn't fixed in advance; it was open. Beyond this, nothing could be known in advance. Michael was at the base of Everest, not knowing if he would collapse with fear at the summit or die from a fall or even get beyond the first base camp. He only knew—and this was the first time he knew—that he wanted to climb.

*   *   *

Someone had been listening. Michael was certain of that the minute he walked through the doors to the ER. It was six in the morning, and usually the graveyard shift had cleared away the three or four cases brought in by ambulance. The waiting room served as shelter for a few vagrants that the security guards were ordered to let in. But this morning the room was a teeming cauldron of the sick and maimed.

He stood at the door transfixed. Crying mothers with babies, a gunshot victim collapsed on the floor with orderlies shouting for him to hold on, an overdosed diabetic being fixed with an emergency IV as a nurse injected him with insulin—with a sweep of his eyes Michael recognized the scene. He'd confronted it a hundred times during his residency, when an inner-city ER was a world of urban suffering compressed into one chaotic room.

"Doctor!" One of the young nurses had run up, not even waiting for him to get to the chart rack. "GSW in trauma four, they need you immediately. And we've got more lining the halls. It's like gang warfare broke out."

Michael immediately left off his reveries and jumped into the fray. The gunshot wound was a fourteen-year-old Hispanic caught between rounds of street firing on his way home from school. His chest was nearly ripped open, and Michael saw, from the moment he stepped in, that shrapnel might have impacted the heart. Within five minutes he was running beside the gurney as they prepped the boy in the hall on the way to the emergency operating room. He was barking orders all the way from the trauma room to the elevator. The swirl of events was something he knew how to deal with. Over the next hour he learned that there were two things he didn't know how to deal with, though. The first was that the boy died on the table from a ruptured left ventricle. The other was that there was no sense of detachment about it. The prewritten comedy was over.

Someone had been listening for sure.

He was on call for fifteen grueling hours of nonstop surgery before he could grab a break in the second-floor lounge. Too exhausted even to take the stairs down a flight to the doctors' lounge, he collapsed in front of the TV in the alcove reserved for families awaiting the outcome of surgery. An older black woman with two young kids stared at him—presumably they were her grandchildren. Michael nodded and grabbed the remote. He was curious if things had totally changed in the outside world.

There were two hours of prime time devoted to the Prophet every night of the week: All the networks carried the show simultaneously, since there was no point in programming anything against it. One hour was devoted to a review of miracles he had performed in the previous twenty-four hours; the other was a worship service led by Ishmail himself. He appeared from varying undisclosed locations around the world, during which he gave advice and healed those in attendance as well as those watching at home.

"Dr. Jesus doesn't want you to be sick anymore. He wants you to have a personal miracle," Ishmail was saying, his voice as unctuous as any televangelist. The woman at his feet, who had walked onstage totally deaf, shrieked loudly. "I hear you!" she cried. The Prophet smiled, none too genuinely. His little joke of sounding like a redneck preacher hadn't made anybody laugh. He was taken too seriously and feared too deeply. Michael leaned forward to look closer. The face was unchanged, only perhaps there was a hint of boredom in the eyes.

"I have commanded the darkness to rise and the suffering to cease," Ishmail was saying. "Thou hast wandered in the valley of blind misgiving and sorrow, but now the wine of faith has been harvested, and your cup shall be full." The camera swept across a mesmerized audience, and again no one reacted. Apparently the shift into biblical malarkey made no impression. Michael sat back. He knew he wasn't afraid of Ishmail anymore, but that didn't mean he knew him. The Prophet had nothing to prove anymore, and he was lapsing into riffs that were a parody of his original healing act. Did that prove anything or nothing?

And who would know? Michael clicked the remote to change the channel, but nothing changed. He laid his head in his hands. It was all he could do not to fall asleep, but there was to much to consider. He had no evidence that anyone was playing the game but himself alone, or possibly Ishmail. Yet what was the game? It wasn't viable to think of it as warfare. The Prophet had saved the world—at least this version of it—and he'd allotted Michael a perfect place in it. The sudden increase of suffering people in the ER had come about because Michael wanted it so. No, that wasn't right, either. This could be another test, a mocking hallucination, a challenge thrown down by his enemy—or none of the above.

It wasn't going to be simple, and he would have to figure it out by himself.

He must have dozed off then. When he looked up the black woman was gone, and the television was hissing with white noise over the test pattern. Four in the morning. He got up, his back aching from the chair, and took the elevator downstairs. The charts were now piled up at the nurses' station. The swollen number of people waiting to be seen hadn't decreased at all. He signed out, yawning and not speaking to anyone, then began to weave past the stricken who were waiting on their feet, spilling out from the limited seating.

"Excuse me, Doctor. Wait."

When he turned, a nurse was thrusting a clipboard into his face. "I'm sorry, but if you could take this last one." He nodded, rubbing the sleep from his eyes. "Okay, coming through." People reluctantly parted as he half-pushed a path between them. He glanced at the chart, assuming that his patient, another gunshot wound, would be stacked up somewhere down the hall. She wasn't, and he was surprised to see a light off over the door of trauma two, indicating that it was empty. He pushed open the door.

The victim was an old woman, though he could barely see her. Two nurses were struggling to hold her down in her wheelchair, their bent-over backs blocking her from view. She was screaming very loudly, for someone with a bullet inside her. "Let me go! You don't know who you're dealing with!"

"No, you calm down. Just calm down or we're going to have to call somebody," one nurse said, obviously tired and exasperated.

"Try calling a real doctor, just for a change," the woman shouted. "You don't know *bupkis*, girlie."

The other nurses caught sight of Michael. "Doctor, we're a little overwhelmed here."

"I can see that," Michael said. He walked over to the old lady's wheelchair. "Ma'am, we're going to

have to use restraints unless you let us care for you."
He wondered why he was saying these words when
all he wanted to do was burst out laughing.

A wizened gray face was tilted up at him in rage.
"You think three of you can tie me down? Just try."

"We can call for a psych consult, Doctor. I know
they're swamped, but—"

Michael, who was looking at the chart, shook his
head. "I don't think that's what Mrs.—Teitelbaum,
is it?—wants." In reply, the old lady ripped the IV
needle out of her arm and pushed the stand over.
The saline pack smacked on the floor as the tubes
snaked out of reach. The nurses were about to
pounce again, but Michael raised his hand.

"Go ahead and get those restraints, and a gun
while you're at it," he said. "I'm sorry, Mrs. Teitelbaum, but we're going to have to put you down."
The nurses looked paralyzed, their jaws open. It
took a good deal of coaxing before he could per-
suade them to leave. Once they had, he leaned
against the wall and crossed his arms. "How long
did you intend to keep up the show?" he asked
wryly.

"Hah!" Rakhel snapped before she gave an indif-
ferent shrug. "An old lady can't walk out for some
whitefish and a bialy without a punk shooting her?"

"Don't tell me you're actually hurt?" said Michael.

"Only that you're not so glad to see me." Rakhel
tried on a woebegone face, then yawned and
stretched as she got up from the wheelchair. "My
mother said I had talent, I should have gone on the
stage. But nice girls didn't do that, not back then."

"There was a time when you were a nice girl?"

"Don't be smart with me." It took only a moment, but all traces of the irascible—and badly acted—Mrs. Teitelbaum had vanished. "So, *mein kind*, where did we leave off?"

"As I remember it, we left off with the tasty scene of you being swallowed up by the Earth," Michael said. Despite his calm, which was in imitation of her, he felt much more astonished than he was showing.

"Right, that was a death scene, let me tell you," Rakhel said with some satisfaction. "The things you put me through."

He knew enough not to object. "All part of my melodrama, huh?"

"We aim to please. Compared to some, you're not so bad. You should see me as an angel. I've had to kiss some real types on their deathbed. Makes them feel they're loved."

"Meaning they aren't?" Michael asked.

"No, of course not, but low self-esteem tends to prolong the agony. What can you do?" By this point they were seated side by side on the examining table in the center of the room.

"How much time do we have?" Michael asked. "I mean, before they come back with your strait-jacket."

"Time is the least of our worries." Despite her flippancy, Michael found himself going tense. "Stop that," Rakhel said, noticing him. "The next thing you know, I'll have to hemorrhage. Better yet, I'll have a baby."

Michael couldn't help laughing. "So, somebody got my message?" he said.

"Everybody got your message," Rakhel corrected. "That's all right, you couldn't help it." After all the banter, she seemed to grow pensive. "How do you like this place you've landed in, eh?" she asked.

"What's not to like?"

"Don't make fun. I'm asking a serious question."

Michael shook his head. "At first it was incredibly confusing. I'd gotten used to thinking of Ishmail as an enemy. But you can't blame him for tearing down a parking lot and putting up paradise."

"Of course you can. You're not happy here, are you?" Rakhel asked sharply. Michael didn't have to answer. "Exactly," she said with a note of triumph. "What is this place? It's nice and good and clean and so what? Not that I'd rather be in Philadelphia." She couldn't resist staying a little bit in character. Neither of them said anything for a moment. "Do you really want to know what's wrong?" she asked almost somberly. Michael nodded.

"The basic mistake you made," Rakhel began, "is wanting to be good. Not that I blame you; most people are at least tempted. Of all the temptations, good is the worst." She put up a hand. "Don't interrupt, please. I like talking this way. You want to ask what is so bad about being good? It's not human. That is the answer. I could give you a longer answer, I could send you to the seventh heaven and back, but why bother? It's a long trip and when you got back, this would still be the answer."

Michael couldn't help himself. "Not human?"

"Of course not. Human is what it is. It's dirty thoughts and overeating on Passover and pinching the altar boy. Excuse me, but you're so shocked? I'll use another example. Human is stealing from the collection plate and sleeping with the organist.

"Who cares that any of this goes on? Not God, at least not so you can tell. But you imagine that He is very angry. Original sin, the Fall, Adam and Eve forced to locate to a not-so-nice neighborhood.

What a scandal! Only, if you ask me, it doesn't make sense."

Michael couldn't tell when she was being serious and when she was popping back behind the mask of Mrs. Teitelbaum, the half-cracked Brooklyn yenta. He waited and listened.

"Naturally, your mistake was picked up by this other character," she said.

"Ishmail?"

"Let's call him that. He has the same ridiculous idealism that you do. He worships goodness; he can't stand to see pain. So what happens? He runs amuck like a crazy person, and no matter how hard he tries to do good, nothing but good, it turns into a mess."

Michael was amazed. "He's trying to do good? But—"

"I told you, he's just like you. How many times have I said that you're responsible for all this? Thank God you've begun to listen. That was your message, wasn't it? You don't have to answer. He's stuck to you now, and you have to get rid of him. I think you know that."

"No, I was just coming to terms with that."

"So come already. You've got a plague of goodness on your hands, and you caused it."

"I couldn't have caused it. I'd have to cause a whole world."

She threw up her hands. "Right. You see a problem here? Believe me, there are enough worlds to go around. This happens to be the one revolving around you."

"But that can't be true. What did I do to deserve—"

"Nothing, that's the point. Everyone is stuck in a

personal world. They just don't see it. They can't admit it to themselves because taking responsibility for a whole world seems crushing when you can barely run your life."

"You're saying that in reality—"

"In reality you create the world just by living a life. You think it's a separate job you have to apply for?"

He was listening with complete attention now. The setting for this discussion was far from anything he'd ever imagined it would be, yet with certainty he realized that he had been waiting to hear this for many, many lifetimes.

"You should see your face," Rakhel said lightly. "You're so serious. I think I liked you better when you swung an axe and chopped heads off laughing."

"Don't."

"You think I'm kidding? You practically drank blood for breakfast, and you wore a string of skulls around your—"

"Stop it!"

"—neck. Or was it your waist? My son, it is fated for anyone who loves good with your stubborn intensity to wind up, every so often, being very bad. How long can you expect to hold it in?"

Michael stood up and began to pace. "So that's basically what's happening to Ishmail? He's about to burst?"

"He's a saint so enraged with the evil of the world that he's about to explode with it. That's why you got the job. Two of a kind." Rakhel was staring at him now with more than casual interest. "The problem is, you don't really want to stop him."

Michael realized he wasn't beyond surprises yet. "Really? Why not?"

"I'm no mind-reader. This is your assignment. But I have one word for you. In fact, that's why I've come. You've been wasting a lot of time, and although this is all a game, it's the most serious game there is."

"You mean something real is at stake. So what's the word?"

"*Yetzer ha-ra.* You don't have to memorize it. In Hebrew it means 'evil impulse,' the itch to do bad."

"All right. What's this supposed to teach me?"

"Not to tamper with God. That seems to be the lesson of the day. When humans were created, they received a double nature. One side good, the other evil. On each side there was an impulse of life. The good impulse is known in Hebrew as *Yetzer ha-tov* and the evil as *Yetzer ha-ra.* So far as anyone knows, this is part of the deal, creation-wise. There's no getting out of it, except . . ."

"Except?"

"Except that no one forces you to accept yourself. Choice is always up to you, and some people—I'm too polite to mention names—are not comfortable simply being human. They want to go places. They sit around figuring out what is so terrible that all they can expect from life is to remain a human being. Somewhere, somebody went, 'Aha! I have it— the problem is evil.' "

"And you're saying it isn't?"

"Let's pray that this realization didn't just strike you. Of course that's what I'm saying. If you try to wipe out evil, you can only do it by attacking human nature. You look inside and there it is—Yetzer ha-ra—the impulse to eat and make money and cheat and screw around. How terrible! Where did it come from? That's all it took. Kablooey."

"The war between good and evil."

"Bright lad. Satan was born when everyone bought the absurd notion that being good would get them closer to God."

The logic was so simple that Michael wanted to laugh and cry at the same time. He had realized, halfway through her talk, that Rakhel was some sort of master spirit, a being he couldn't recognize in pure form who had assumed the semi-amusing shape of an old, rather crabby Jewish woman. If so, the disguise worked. He still felt comfortable. He wasn't going to jump out of his skin, and he didn't tremble with the vision that a flaming sword was about to pierce him.

"Knights Templar," Rakhel remarked casually.

"What?"

"The image of the flaming sword was put into your head when you came to Palestine with the Knights Templar. I don't mean to butt in, but you're drifting." In the time it took her to say the words, Michael had seen it all—the assault on Jerusalem where he had been killed, and the anguish in his heart that he had not been alive when the crusaders captured the Temple Mount. It was that event, the defeat of the infidel Jews for all time, that had inspired the soldiers to call themselves Templars—and now he knew why the symbol of the Temple Mount had kept drawing him back time after time. The loss of the Holy of Holies had torn his soul apart, and the knowledge of his deep sin, the stain of evil that had prevented him from ever entering the Temple again, had goaded him on, seemingly never to end.

"It ends," Rakhel said calmly. "Everything does, eventually."

*   *   *

He was too dejected even to notice how bad the coffee was. The counterman kept refilling the cracked white china mug, and Michael kept drinking, lost in thought. Ishmail, who had started out as a pure symbol of evil in his mind, had somehow become his shadow brother. Rakhel had said many things, but she didn't let him off the hook on that point. It seemed incredibly unfair.

"You sure like coffee," the counterman said. "Wouldn't surprise me if you jumped out of your chair."

"Yeah." Michael's time with Rakhel had ended when the nurses ran back in with restraints and a psychiatrist in tow. It took some doing, but Mrs. Teitelbaum was released with a caregiver to walk her home. God only knows what happened on that little trip. Images drifted through Michael's mind. He saw the impish dancing boy who had started the mob scene at the Western Wall. In the midst of the mayhem and panic, when the light was burning the flesh from people's bones, Michael had seen him run away, not simply unhurt but with a mischievous grin.

What would Rakhel say to that? Did she even care if evil went unpunished? Was it simply enough to wave your hands and pass it all off as being human? (The only clue she had dropped on this subject was that to some Hasidim, children are not innocent at all. Given to lying, playing tricks, and disobedience, small children are perfect examples of Yetzer ha-ra, and therefore, in a peculiar way, they are more to be feared than adults.) In a short hour Rakhel had finished the job of turning Michael's whole world upside down and stamping on it, just for good measure, while never losing that knowing, ironic smile for more than a minute.

The phone by the cash register rang, and the counterman picked it up. A beatific smile broke over his face. "Hey-y-y-y . . . Manny, that's great! Great! Thanks for spreading the word. I owe you." He hung up the phone, scraped down the grill, and began turning out the lights.

"Come on!" Michael said, startled.

"Oh, sorry, buddy, I thought you stepped out," the counterman said, throwing on his coat. "Listen, food's on the house, okay? I gotta boogie."

"Where to?"

"Prophet's broadcasting from New York tonight. Times Square, an hour from now." The man grabbed his hat and rushed out of the darkened diner, leaving the front door unlocked.

Michael got to his feet and shrugged into his parka. If he wanted to know what was going to happen next, there was no better way than to confront his spiritual double face-to-face. If it wouldn't help him figure out how to stop what the Prophet was doing, it might give him a clue how to escape the horrible world goodness had created.

Michael laid a ten on the register to pay for his meal. The owner's willingness to abandon his business just to go and hear a word from Ishmail's mouth disturbed Michael. He found a ring of keys next to the door and locked it behind him, then shoved the keys back through the mail slot so that they lay on the shabby cream-and-green linoleum floor. It was the best he could manage.

The air was damply cold, though without snow. Michael headed toward Broadway, looking for a cab. Times Square was more than forty blocks south and six west; he didn't want to walk the whole way in gathering darkness.

The streets around Central Park were as deserted as Wall Street on Sunday, and all of the shops he passed seemed to be closed. Word must have spread about the Prophet's impending appearance. After half an hour Michael finally gave up hope of finding a cab—none seemed to be on the streets—and hiked over to the subway. But when he reached the nearest station and walked down the stairs, he found the gates at the bottom chained shut. Even the subway was closed.

"Subways aren't running, bub. You from outta town?"

The voice came from behind him. Michael turned, squinting into the fading light at the figure standing at the top of the stairs.

"I've been away awhile," Michael said. He started back up the steps. Maybe it would be easier to get a cab on Sixth Avenue. The man, who had greasy Rasputin hair and was dressed in a red plaid jacket over a sweatshirt, laughed harshly.

"Changed? More than you know, Aulden." Michael froze on the top step. Some instinct made him look down and he saw the broken bottle in the man's hand.

"What are you doing?" Michael said slowly, tensing to dodge the first thrust. The man came in swinging, his face twisted with a desperate sort of yearning. "Purge the urge!" he shouted. "Purge the urge, Aulden! Let the darkness out!"

It was the same slogan Michael had been seeing posted all over the city, and it didn't take a leap of imagination to know that it had originated with the Prophet. Michael had guessed right and sidestepped the first swipe of the bottle; he punched his attacker in the stomach and plowed into him as he doubled over, knocking the bottle from his hand. It went spinning in pieces into the street.

Michael hunched over defensively, waiting for the next move.

"You're not worth it," the attacker spat, backing away.

" 'Purge the urge,' " Michael said, panting. "What does that mean, exactly?"

"Figure it out, man." In a moment the attacker was gone, stumbling across the street through the thin traffic.

If this was the sort of gospel Ishmail was preaching now, Michael had a feeling that he was turning into the figure described by Rakhel, a driven soul caught in the manic-depressive swing between light and dark. His unpredictability made him all that much more dangerous. To deny your inner demons and yet act out their desires was a recipe for annihilation. The greedy and the shortsighted would seize on his every mood as a shortcut to their own ends, but in the final analysis, what it meant was death and destruction for everyone and everything.

Was that what it took for Michael to get out of here? He took a deep breath. He could only hope that he was right.

The closer Michael got to Times Square, the more people he saw. Wary from the attack, he stayed clear of them as much as he could. It became harder and harder in the vicinity of 42nd Street. The Teleboard that dominated Times Square had been converted into a giant stopwatch, ticking down the minutes till the Prophet's arrival. There were no cars; Broadway and the side streets were swollen with the waiting masses—a vast, yearning, needy crowd, all coming to see their savior. Their desperation was as palpable as the electricity of an oncoming storm.

So the sudden influx of patients in the ER had just been a taste. Ishmail's perfect world was fraying around the edges.

The Prophet's hold over people was going to change face into a primeval thing, elemental as love or hatred. It would be up to him how it moved. Michael felt certain that the multitude assembled around him would kill themselves—or each other—or tear the city down brick by brick if Ishmail played on their passion to do it.

He's here. The flash came to Michael an instant before he heard the roar from uptown—a frenzied sound, somehow hopeless and fulfilled at once. Moments later Ishmail appeared standing on the back of a flatbed truck draped in gold fringe like a parade float. Acolytes in long black topcoats, wearing sunglasses despite the evening gloom and looking eerily like cartoon Mafiosi, walked beside the vehicle, surrounding it and keeping the crowd from coming too near. Despite their presence, the mob surged forward with a roar, and Michael saw the black-coated roadies wielding short truncheons that sent everyone they touched flying back into the crowd spasming like stunned fish.

As the flatbed inched downtown at a stately two miles an hour, never stopping, the Prophet began to speak.

"My friends, each day I come to you hoping that today will be the day—but it never is. I do my best. I do it all for you. Everything has been for you—I've healed the sick, raised the dead, fed the hungry, amused the languid and lost. I do this because you have given me the power. You understand that?"

The people in the street looked confused; they had grown suddenly quiet as the float made its way. This wasn't the speech they'd expected or were prepared for. Michael saw fear around him. The unspoken wrath of their savior, so far held in check, was showing its teeth.

"We could have had a perfect world, a second Eden. That's what I wanted for you, each and every one. And you have the power! I have the power! Then why is there still darkness?" The Prophet pointed toward the sky, which was dark with more than the falling night—a low leaden cloud cover had descended almost to the tops of the skyscrapers. Strangely, it didn't reflect the bright lights of the city but absorbed them into its gloom.

"Why don't we have the ultimate perfect light we're entitled to? I'll tell you why. It's you—and you—and you." Ishmail pointed randomly into the crowd. "You're still holding yourself full of darkness. Now, that's just selfish. Isn't that selfish?"

The float was near enough that Michael could see the sweaty, pious satisfaction on Ishmail's face. It was a perfect mask for the laughter that no doubt was hidden behind the cheap demagoguery.

No longer stunned, some in the crowd groaned and swayed, taking the cue that they were in a backwoods revival tent. Others roared, "Yes!" as if obedience were the Prophet's demand, even when he was demeaning them.

"And what do we do about selfishness?" Ishmail asked, squeezing the microphone to his lips as if he would chew it off.

"*Purge it!*"

"What do we do?"

"*Purge it!*"

"How will we destroy everything that's holding us back, keeping us out of heaven's embrace?"

"*PURGE IT!*"

"I can't hear you," he taunted them, and the crowd erupted with one huge throaty shout of stupefied loyalty. The crazed love in the air was so surreal that Michael felt utterly cut off from any human element in the scene. He was not angry. He was not afraid, only filled with a sort of remote wonder.

The Prophet waved his hands like a conductor, until they were all chanting, screaming, howling solely for the sake of making noise. Through the howling Michael could hear Ishmail speaking— softly, intimately, as if he whispered directly into each person's ear alone.

"I don't care what you've done, or who you are. What are you trying to hide from me? Is it illegal, immoral, degraded, depraved, deprived, aging, or fattening? I don't care. You've got to get it out. Let all the darkness out so the light can come in. It doesn't matter if you want to kill or lust or gratify your sinful hunger. You've got to choose. Is this God's playground or Satan's? You'll never find out until you do it, do it all. Do it now!"

In his detached mood, Michael remembered that moment—how long ago?—when Yousef had pointed down at the wadi below them and said there should be one place where God and the devil can fight it out alone. Now Ishmail had expanded it to the world.

Michael looked around. Some people were chanting ecstatically, some were crying, some had fallen to their knees in rapture. People tore off their clothes and reached for each other, clutching and ripping.

Ten feet away he saw swirls of violence, as the crowd fell upon its members and bludgeoned or stabbed or kicked. He heard a child screaming, a high thin note that seemed to go on and on. The desire to hurt someone now was in everyone's mind—hatred had won the race for being the first urge to purge.

I've got to get out of here! Michael shook himself from his daze, but half a dozen hands were grabbing him already. Enraged faces shot venom at him from staring eyes. He writhed, trying to escape the grasp of fingers digging into his arm, his shoulders, his neck. He shouted out in an animal scream to startle them, but for every hand that released him, two took its place. Adrenaline must have kicked in, because without thinking he swung his fist and smashed the two faces nearest to him. Blood shot from one man's nose; he squealed and let go, falling backward. The sight of blood momentarily shocked the others, who loosed their hold long enough for Michael to twist and lunge through the pack of bodies in his immediate vicinity.

Nobody ran after him—they were content to vent their hatred on the next random victim. A hole in the crowd allowed Michael to run another twenty feet. He could see a corner just ahead where 42nd Street ran east. Lowering his head, he bulled his way in that direction, praying that the mob would thin out. He knew it wouldn't, but he had no other choice.

Behind him the sound of Ishmail's voice was fading as the flatbed moved on. Michael paid no attention. He felt his head butt against a solid body; it was a heavy-set man whose mass made Michael lurch backward. He stood up, bracing himself for an onslaught.

Nothing happened.

The heavy-set man had his fists in the air, ready to fight, but his eyes darted around in confusion. "Come on out and face me!" he shouted. Two other belligerents, taking his cue, pulled in next to him. Michael was hunched over not five feet away, and yet they all swept the vicinity with their angry eyes, missing him entirely.

Whatever made him invisible, Michael took advantage of it. He bolted straight at the small group and plunged through them. Aimless hands grabbed at his shirt when they felt him strike up against their bodies, but he easily made it past. The same was true for the next clot of people he met, and the next. Rounding the corner, he kept running east until he hit Fifth Avenue. The crazed atmosphere didn't extend that far. Michael felt safe enough to slow to a walk while he regained his senses.

For some strange reason, despite the horrific scene he had barely escaped, he felt a thrilling sense of power, almost as strong as when he had sent the message through the derelict at the Dumpster. This wasn't the real world. It didn't control him through random events and forces beyond his control. No, this was a game—the game—that the thirty-six had been playing for centuries. He didn't yet know what all the rules were, but he'd figured out more than a little.

Number one: Things changed as he changed.

Number two: Evil is blind, which makes it afraid.

Number three: If he wasn't afraid, he could stay in the game.

From the very first moment when Michael had

dashed recklessly into the devastated village, not even caring whether an unknown plague would get him, he had been out of control. His whole stance of not being afraid had been a desperate attempt to hide how afraid he really was. Not just of all the things reasonable people think they should fear—he had been aware deep down that fear ruled everything. It was the mask that kept him from seeing his own power.

And that power was staggering. It could make a world, just by the ordinary act of thinking and wishing and living. Solomon had told him that—they all had—but he had to rip the shield of fear away before he could really feel it.

Total exhilaration swept over him. He hardly noticed that the wind had picked up, or that the dark cloud cover was dipping lower, like an engulfing fog. Suddenly a woman, thrown off balance by a powerful gust of wind, fell against him.

"I'm sorry, I didn't mean to—" The woman stopped in the middle of her apology, looking around in bafflement. Like the others, she couldn't see him. Another gust began to blow away the packages she had dropped on the ground. Wailing, the woman made a grab for them and moved down the street. Michael turned and watched; he saw a dozen other passersby throw up their hands as the wind, like an insistent hand, pushed them off balance. In half a minute it was a howling gale, and the whole street was awash with garbage from tipped-over trash cans, flying plastic bags, and newspapers whipping like tumbleweeds into the street.

Ishmail was responding.

Michael wasn't surprised that his unearthly twin knew when to make the next move, but the swiftness of his strike threw him off guard. From nowhere a cloud of dust rose; as it swept down Fifth Avenue, traffic came to a halt. Unwary cars were smashing into each other, but within seconds the storm was so dense that no vehicles could be seen.

Michael ducked for shelter into the deep alcove in front of an apartment building. One at a time other pedestrians joined him. Most were fashionably dressed; some tried to open umbrellas that the wind instantly turned inside out before snatching them away. No one made an effort to look unperturbed— the unnatural way that the wind had swept out of the sky provoked fear, even in the fashionable.

No one saw him. Michael took care to slide away if a body came too close. He wondered why this shifting scene, as it became darker and more menacing, had made him turn invisible. Was it a weapon he could use or a curse placed by Ishmail so that he would become a man of nothing, an urban ghost free to raid the best restaurants for food, the best hotels for a room, but otherwise to cease to exist?

The wind howled louder, as if to leave no uncertainty about what was going to happen. Michael decided not to fight. He launched himself back onto the sidewalk and let the gale throw him down the street like one of the tumbling black umbrellas that would never find home again.

Nothing changed for five days.

The storm was unprecedented, sweeping in from the Atlantic as far inland as Ohio, as well as down the entire coast. The usual explanations about shifting jet streams and global warming were not invoked. Without actually using the words "wrath of God," everyone knew the source of the immense sweeps of lightning that disrupted power everywhere, and the chaotic atmospheric disturbances that wiped out all communications. People huddled in the cold dark and waited for Ishmail to get over his tantrum.

When the storm lifted and the sun came back out, a few dreamlike touches were discovered. In the clearing skies the light seemed dim, and with the naked eye huge black blotches were evident on the face of the sun. They looked cancerous, every day swelling or merging with each other to form new shapeless tumors. The dark cloud bank never fully dissipated but hung offshore like a hired thug waiting for orders.

Most peculiar of all, however, was the silence of Ishmail. His face didn't reappear on television. He made no public addresses and issued no statements. If was as if he'd had his say, and now it was up to the world to react. The worst of the violence had ebbed in the storm, but the social fabric couldn't be knit back together. It only unraveled further.

Michael wandered the streets, having discarded the idea of leaving the city. He still wore his invisible cloak, so what did it matter where he went? His sense of confidence had been shaken momentarily, but so far hadn't deserted him. He wasn't afraid or hopeless. The knowledge that this wasn't a real world made him see everything with equal compassion, but also equal distrust. As Rakhel had told him long ago, this was as real as anything so unreal could be.

The streets, once people had the nerve to return to them, were filled with the shell-shocked. The "Purge the urge" campaign continued with less hysteria. Walking down the avenues, Michael saw constant looting. The air was filled with the sirens of police cars that would always be too late on the scene. Doormen became vigilantes, displaying their rifles to open sight if anyone came close to a prestigious building. Michael tried to find shelter early every night, since the rapes started early; murder was a matter for broad daylight.

Worry set in on the seventh day. Nothing was coming to him. He walked and walked, waiting to be shown the next move he should make, but there was only a blank. No inspiration, no urge to act, no message washing up from the faraway place where Rakhel and Solomon lived. He was a kind of Robinson Crusoe stranded alone on a desert island with five million people who didn't know he was there. The possibility that he would turn into a ghost began to become real.

To cheer himself up, he spent the seventh night in the presidential suite at the Waldorf, in a huge walnut poster bed presumably once occupied by TR, FDR, and JFK before the Arabs could afford it. Since no one saw him, he couldn't order from room service, so he swiped caviar and Dom Perignon from the cold lockup off the kitchen and waited for the chefs to turn their heads so he could grab a roast chicken and some steamed asparagus. It made a comforting meal that a ghost couldn't eat. He woke up the next morning with the kind of depression that could turn, if he wasn't careful, into panicky despair.

He sat up, half-wishing that hell wold break out again, when he saw her. A girl, perhaps fourteen or fifteen, stood in the middle of the room. Her back was to him, and she had the champagne bottle tilted up, drinking the dregs he'd left behind.

She was humming softly to herself. Michael sat up and threw the covers aside. A flying corner hit the wine glass on the bedside table, and it broke on the marble floor. The girl stopped and looked over her shoulder. Her eyes met Michael's with total unconcern.

"Hey," Michael said.

The girl looked closer now, her attention on him. She walked closer to the bed, saying nothing. When she was a foot away, staring into his eyes with calm assurance, they both realized at the same time what was going on.

"Stop!" Michael shouted.

But she was off like lightning, bolting across the bedroom. Michael jumped to his feet. He'd fallen asleep in his clothes, so all he had to do was pull on his sneakers over bare feet. By that time, however, the girl was across the living room, heading for the open door.

"Come back here!" Michael called out. "Don't make me chase you."

She had no intention of stopping. By the time Michael had made it to the door and out into the hall, she was dashing around the corner to the elevator bank. He had the advantage now, since it took time for an elevator to make it to the fiftieth floor.

He ran down the hall, but she was ahead of him. The elevator buttons weren't pushed; the stairwell door was just swinging shut. Michael lunged against it just as he heard the click of a lock. Unlike every other door in the hotel, this one could be made secure; this one could be made secure to protect the President.

Damn!

He had no choice but to pound the buttons and wait for the elevator. It took a few moments to arrive; they felt like an hour. Fortunately the car was empty. The girl wouldn't have the nerve to try the elevator herself, so he might have time to get down to the lobby before she could run down.

No luck. As the car descended, Michael realized that she probably knew the hotel fairly well, and there were several other shafts for the service elevators. When he jumped out at Peacock Alley on the ground floor, he knew she was ahead of him. He ran for the Lexington Avenue entrance, because it was the farthest away and the least used. If she was a smart girl, she wouldn't run for the nearest, most public exit.

Ten yards out the door, he knew he was right. The girl had made it to the next corner, still running, but now she was held up by a red light and heavy traffic, most of it police cars.

"Stop, I need to talk to you!" Michael shouted. She turned and hesitated. It was obvious that he could see her, and that she could see him. But no one else could. She had counted on that when she raided his room. What would the only invisible person in New York do when she realized that there was another?

She bolted. Going against the light she plunged into the traffic. Weaving through the lanes slowed her down, and Michael made up half the distance between them. She turned left on the sidewalk and headed uptown. It was a bad decision—she should have stayed in the street. After colliding with two pedestrians who hadn't seen her coming—naturally—the girl was barely two steps ahead of Michael.

He tackled her just before 52nd Street.

"Let go, let go, or I'll scream for a cop!" She writhed like a fish in his arms, a fish that could bite.

It took a while before he was able to pin her shoulders to the ground.

"Listen to me, just listen," he said strongly. "Either we can lie here in the middle of the sidewalk until people start tripping over us, or we can go peacefully and talk about this."

"There's nothing to talk about," she hissed, struggling harder.

"Stop panicking, I'm a doctor," said Michael. The sheer absurdity of this remark caught them both off guard. The girl almost burst out laughing.

"Is there a lot of call for invisible doctors?" she said.

"If I was an invisible lawyer you could sue me for assault." Michael felt her stop thrashing underneath him. "Okay, that was an ice-breaker," he said as calmly as he could. "If I let you up, will you be reasonable?"

The girl nodded and he let her up. "Liar!" he shouted as she dashed away again, this time having the smarts to run into the street. It was another couple of blocks before he pinned her down again.

"That wasn't nice," he said. "Are you an invisible juvenile delinquent?"

"Me? You should talk. Like you pay for everything—*not*!"

This time when he let her up, after minimal negotiations, she didn't run away. He held out his hand. "I'm Michael."

She didn't take it. "Char," she said sullenly. "It's pronounced like *shark*, but it's short for Charlene. What do you want?"

"Nothing, nothing from you, at least. But it's clear we're in the same boat. Doesn't that make us natural allies?" Char regarded this proposition doubtfully. "You can stay mad," said Michael, "but we seem to share the same taste in accommodations. Aren't we likely to run into each other again?"

"It's a big city, remember?" Char's hostility was just a formality by now, a habit acquired from too many days trying to survive. Michael decided to proceed on that assumption.

"I get the feeling you've been out here for a while. Maybe even before nobody could see you?"

Char shook her head. "Just a week."

"A week can be a long time. And a rough, scary time."

She could have resisted a little longer, but his sympathy was too obvious. "And you?" she asked.

"The same. I've been on the street about a week, too. But I might have a clue about what's going on, if you want to listen."

Curiosity, or the need to stop being alone, got the better of her. They walked uptown, mostly staying in the street, while Michael filled her in on the outline of his story. He left out most of what had preceded the chapter in New York, leaving it that he had been transferred from a foreign posting. Even so, the telling took a long time, and they were in the mid-eighties before he was through. He asked her about her story.

"You really want to know? C'mon."

She led him toward the river on one of the tree-shaded side streets that preserve the last illusion that New York is a placid refuge. They stopped in front of a well-kept old brownstone.

"Yours?" Michael asked.

Char nodded. "I don't come back here. You may not have noticed, but they can't hear you, either." She kept her eyes averted from the front door. "It started just like that. One day I was normal, and the next I had melted, only nobody came to mop up the puddle."

"You freaked?"

"Big-time. I knocked over stuff, and when my mom started looking around as if she was going crazy, I grabbed at her clothes. She screamed and ran out of the house." Char stopped, emotion welling in her. Michael realized that the family hadn't returned. He looked again at the New England shutters and the lace curtains behind them, the brass door knocker and the potted geraniums, now knocked over by the wind and withering.

"Let's go," he said softly. "It's not healthy for you here."

"As opposed to where else?"

"Just come on."

Stolen food from the best places tastes extraordinarily good. They crouched in the corner of the Oak Room at the Plaza, underneath the shelter of a piano. There was still a lingering swank in the room, but the hotel guests looked nervous. They dined in small, separate groups and talked in undertones. The piano was a safe hiding place. Michael assumed nobody would want to dance or hear Cole Porter that evening.

"How's your food?" he said.

"Okay. Is this really guinea hen? What's that?" Char asked, licking her fingers.

"It's like fried chicken if you own a corporation," said Michael. The remains of a feast were scattered around them. It was peculiar that nobody noticed the plates and glasses, but the hushed waiters had their hands full maintaining the illusion of order, given how much fear lingered beneath the surface.

"Can I have some of your wine?" asked Char.

"Of course not."

"Like it's going to stunt my growth," she pouted. "I could steal better in five minutes."

"Not and stay with me." Whether she took this as a threat or a promise, Char grew quiet. She was mulling something over. Michael wondered if it had to do with Ishmail; she didn't seem to connect her predicament to him.

"Are you trying to figure things out? I don't think you can," he said. "We need to concentrate our energies on getting out."

"Of the city?"

He shook his head. "It's more complicated than that. I don't want to give you false hope, but your family isn't really lost—they've just left you behind."

"I already know that," Char said. "You're rubbing it in."

"No, I mean they left you behind to go to another world. This all feels real, but it isn't. It's an image, a version of things that is sticking to us. Or we're sticking to it. Either way, we should be able to find an exit. It's a matter of finding enough power to do it."

Char began to get up. "Thanks for sharing that."

"Where are you going?"

"Someplace where I can be invisible without having to be crazy at the same time."

He pulled her back down beside him. "Listen to yourself. Invisible? There's no explanation for that, it's absurd. You're trying to live with it as if a sane person could. Like it or not, the rules have changed."

"Yeah, they've changed for you and me, but what about everybody else?"

"You think everybody else feels normal? Look around this room. These people are on the brink of insanity, too, only their way of dealing with it is to pretend. They're going through the motions of eating out at a fancy restaurant, taking their cars back to the suburbs, maybe even going to work—as if any of that matters. They're more stuck than we are."

"Don't try to make me feel like we're the lucky ones," said Char.

"All right, I won't, but it just might be that we're not alone. Have you thought of that?"

She shook her head. "I've barely had time to get used to you. I was sure that I was the only one."

"There you go. So what are the chances that you would ever find me by accident? Not very big. I think there's a plan behind all this, or at least a hidden mystery that we're meant to solve. It's not random."

She looked doubtful. "Okay, let's hope you're right." She looked away for a moment, and when she looked back her eyes weren't those of a girl going on sixteen but one going on ten. "You think this is the only way I'll get back to my folks?"

Michael put his hand on her shoulder. "Your folks aren't really gone. On some level you're still with them, only right now your mind is telling you that you're alone and no one can see you." Her eyes widened, as if she harbored new doubts about his sanity. "Just try to go with it," Michael said. "I told you it was complicated."

CHAPTER TEN

BROADCAST NEWS

S usan.

It was the third day with Char on the street when he spotted her. She was just coming out of a store on Madison, clutching two shopping bags. He stopped short, staring to make sure it wasn't a mistake. But no, it was some version of his Susan. She wore a nubby sweater and dark slacks with a long cashmere coat over them. Whatever life she was leading, it had the trappings of prosperity.

"Wait a second," Michael said to keep Char from crossing the street.

Susan hadn't noticed him yet. She had paused just past the revolving brass door of the store to look at the sky. It was as clear as the day before, but the sun was still scarred by the black spots. Worry creases appeared on Susan's brow.

"You know her?" Char asked curiously, following Michael's gaze. Their search for other "invisibles" had been fruitless so far.

Michael looked uncertain. "Yeah, I know her. But this is the first scenario where she might not know me."

"What does *scenario* mean?"

"Never mind. You wait here." Michael had decided to risk going up to her. Despite the cold, his palms began to sweat. He didn't know which would be worse, if Susan would be able to see him or not. He covered the distance between them in a few seconds. By now her back was turned; she was searching for a cab or driver of some sort.

"Susan?"

There was the briefest pause, then she turned in his direction. A wave of relief swept over him. "We need to go someplace where we can talk, all right? I think I can explain this."

She said nothing for a moment. "Taxi!" she called out, raising her hand. She would have bumped into him, rushing to catch the cab that screeched to a halt at the curb, if he hadn't jumped out of the way. He chased her, running by her side.

"Susan, it's me! It's Michael—look over here." Intent on not missing her cab, Susan pulled open the door and threw her bags in.

"I need to go downtown," she said to the driver. He looked irritated. "You shoulda walked over a block," he grumbled. "I gotta circle around now."

"Doesn't matter," Susan said, beginning to get into the back seat. Michael couldn't let her do that. Impulsively he grabbed her coat sleeve.

"Susan, just listen. Give me some sign." But she only looked puzzled, pulling her coat closer and slamming the door. The cab rolled off into traffic, and Michael watched it go.

"You could've jumped in with her. Of course, I would have killed you if you did." Char had walked up behind him.

"She couldn't see me, but she might have heard me, just a little," Michael mumbled glumly. He

·thought he had detected the faintest expression of recognition on her face. "Maybe there's a way to tune in, only you have to pay attention."

"You think you caught her attention?"

"Maybe."

"Dreamer."

In a weaker moment Michael might have lost his temper, but he didn't feel threatened or defeated by what had happened. "Look, I believe what I said about none of this being random. What you just saw was important. I've made contact; now we just have to follow it up."

Char looked skeptical. "You call that contact? She got away, she didn't notice you, and you have no idea where she lives. Contact like that is a big help."

"I never thought I'd say· this, but have you ever heard of respecting your elders?" Michael said irritably.

"I'm not sure—what was their first CD?" Char shot back. A second later she relented. "Sorry, I can see you're down. Maybe you're right. She might be our best lead, if you think so."

Michael didn't bother to accept this quasi-apology. He was already walking in the direction of downtown. Char ran to catch up. "Have you got some sort of plan? Where are we going?"

"I don't think 'where' matters. We don't have a map, and we don't have any expectations. So I figure all we have to do is put ourselves in front of the next thing that needs to happen."

"Like standing in the street to see if a truck hits us?" asked Char.

"Right. How does that sound?"

"Cool." Michael looked over at her—she was one

fourteen-year-old who was entirely capable of self-parody.

The cab shot down Park Avenue, hitting enough potholes to throw Susan around in the back seat like a sack of potatoes.

"You don't have to speed like this," she said. "It's not like we're late for the end of the world."

"Promise?" said the cabbie. He accelerated to the next light and slammed on the brake when it turned red.

Susan leaned back in resignation. It was a strange day in a stranger week. She had stopped watching the news. Everyone thought that was a peculiar thing to do; when had the news ever been so wonderful and so unpredictable? That was during the "Miracle Months." Now the air of menace had turned everything around; she didn't know a person who had ventured out on the streets during the storm, and few who thought it was safe now to leave the main avenues.

But her friends were right about her strange behavior. She'd known them all for ten years, ever since she had moved to Manhattan to work for the network, and yet there were times lately when Susan looked at all of them like strangers, or cardboard cutouts propped up against the wall to keep alive the illusion that people existed. In those moments she felt like a shell herself.

"You said Franklin Street?" the cabbie asked, breaking into her reverie.

"What? Yes, good enough."

He glanced at her in the mirror with puzzlement. In fact Susan couldn't remember where she had told him to go. Didn't she want to go home? For just an instant the panicky thought came to her that she didn't have a home. No, that was wrong. Franklin Street was where she'd have lunch, then she could go home later. She didn't have to think about the address now.

Ten minutes later she was paying the cabbie and looking around. Franklin Street was a good street for eating downtown, and she had her pick of places. One of the renovated taverns with an old steel ceiling and sawdust on the floor—yes, she liked that. It made her feel real, although that was a weird thing to think. She walked into the Pig and Whistle, which despite its corporate cuteness did reside in one of the old warehouses that once lined the block.

The waitress put her in a booth, and she ordered a beer and bratwurst. It wasn't the kind of food she ever chose, but the words had come out of her mouth automatically, almost as if someone else were speaking. It was a feeling Susan had been getting used to. She had the vague impression that she wasn't herself, but that wasn't necessarily new. Her mind had wispy patches of gray confusion in it that prevented her from looking too deep. She couldn't remember an old self, which was just as good as not having a self to lose. Whatever happened now, this minute, seemed to be the only reality she could relate to.

The food came, and she began to eat. This, too, she did automatically, without enthusiasm. Now she realized what was wrong. She'd taken an hour for lunch, promising Nigel to be back at the studio for the rehearsal of the five o'clock news. There wasn't time to go this far downtown. What was she thinking?

"Miss, miss." She waved her hand. "I need the

check." She was clear now about what was happening. God knows where she had been for an hour, but she was back. Susan reached for the last of the beer, but her hand missed the glass, which tilted and skittered off the table, crashing to the floor.

"Are you all right?"

Susan looked up at the waitress, who was standing over her with the check. "Did any of that glass hit you? I'll just clean it up. No big deal."

Susan nodded silently. Was she all right? The thing was, she hadn't even touched the glass, but it had moved and fallen. She started to stand up, but a hand was holding her back—a man's hand. Susan felt like crying out, then thought better of it. A man was sitting in the booth opposite her, and he looked as anxious as anyone she had ever seen.

"Please, just give me a moment," the man pleaded. She sat back down, a blank look on her face. "Do you know me?" he asked.

"No. Should I?" she said.

He looked even more anxious, but there was excitement in his face, too. "No, maybe not. It's just so amazing that you can even see me."

"What? See you?" Susan was confused. "Did we have an appointment?"

"Not exactly."

The man fell silent, as if searching for words that wouldn't come. He almost had tears in his eyes, and even though Susan would have assumed he was a crank, someone she'd better call the manager to handle, she unexpectedly felt sympathy for him. "Look, if I can help . . ." she said.

At that moment there was a stir at the other end of the tavern. Susan and the man opposite her both looked around. Customers at the bar had jumped to their feet. The barkeep was throwing off his apron and wiping his hand on a towel as he rushed toward the door.

"This is unbelievable," he said, his voice all but shaking. "We never thought we'd have the honor."

"Lucky you." Ishmail walked past all of them, looking around the bar. It was dark inside, and his eyes squinted. The astonished barkeep checked an impulse to say another word. Outside on the street he could see a long stretch limo and two police motorcycles.

Ishmail headed toward the back, his gaze fixed ahead. One of the customers had a fit of whiskey courage. "Welcome back, sir. You've been gone," he mumbled idiotically. Ishmail put him in his place with a glance, then walked directly over to Susan's booth.

"Yes?" she said. He was standing at her elbow, a gratifying smile on his face.

"Darling, did you forget?" said Ishmail. His smile became indulgent, as if dealing with a new bride or a slow child. "I scheduled our appointment with the chief of staff at two. We've got to hurry." He held his hand out for her.

"Don't listen to him," the man across from her said, his voice desperate. Feeling dazed, Susan looked at him again. "You can't listen to him. This is a trick."

For some reason Ishmail didn't hear this. He still stood there, waiting for her to get up.

"I've got to go," Susan said weakly.

"No, you don't," the man said. "I'm Michael. You know me, you can see me. I found you down here, and I'm going to take you away."

Susan shook her head as Ishmail leaned closer.

"Who are you talking to, darling?" he asked.

"Him." She pointed across the booth, and Ishmail followed her gesture, his eyes alert and sharp. Only now there was no one to see. The man called Michael had jumped up and was backing away.

Ishmail started talking to the empty place he had vacated. "I didn't think you were up to much, not at first. But you're getting better at this."

"Better than you think," said Michael from ten feet behind him. Ishmail didn't turn around until he saw where Susan's eyes went.

"Oh, so we're dodging around a little, are we?" he taunted, looking around. "It's not going to work. I don't need to see you anymore, you understand?"

Michael said nothing, watching as Ishmail took Susan by the arm. "Come on, we're going home. We can skip that appointment," the Prophet said. There was no chance she would resist. She might be able to see Michael, but her ability to define her own story had been captured and taken away from her long ago. Ishmail led her toward the door.

"Listen, if you can still hear me, where can I find you?" Michael asked, trailing by her side. He could see that she had the last shred of focus left.

"Nigel. I work at the studio with Nigel," she mumbled, but her awareness was fading quickly now. She stopped focusing on the spot where Michael actually was, looking instead a few inches in the wrong direction.

"You don't see anyone, do you, darling?" Ishmail asked with a mocking grin.

"No." Susan looked at her husband, all thoughts of her network news job, her friends, her past, and her old self from ten minutes ago vanishing like smoke. She wasn't sorry to see them go. They hadn't felt all that real, either.

All at once it started to snow, right there in the tavern. The flakes came from nowhere, and they fell with the fury of a blizzard. Susan stared blankly, not even caring what was going on, but Ishmail laughed out loud.

"My move!" he shouted. He was looking at the floor, already covered with half an inch of snow. A line of footprints could be seen; they were running fast for the door.

"No, no," the Prophet said. The front door slammed shut, as if blown by the wind. The footprints ran up to it, and invisible hands struggled with the doorknob.

"Locked," said Ishmail. "You'll have to do better than that." Letting go of Susan's arm, he started walking steadily toward the last place where the footprints had stopped. More footprints now began heading off to the left, then right, then back away.

"Confused?" Ishmail taunted. The blizzard increased in force, and the paralyzed onlookers, huddling in fear by the bar, could vaguely make out a man's shape as the snow settled onto invisible shoulders and a head. The head barely swung out of reach as the Prophet advanced and took a vicious swing with his fist.

"No!" called Susan from behind him.

Ishmail didn't turn around. "Why not, darling? What could this creature mean to you?" He swung again, this time wildly, because the snowy ghost had shaken off the telltale flakes from his body and disappeared. Ishmail grinned and followed the footprints. This time they headed away for ten feet and then suddenly ended. For a moment the Prophet waited, but no new prints appeared in the inch of snow on the floor.

He scowled and walked over to the last mark, swinging at empty air. This distraction only took a moment before he realized what had happened. Overhead a low light fixture was swinging back and forth; behind him the footprints continued on top of the bar, running rapidly toward the back of the tavern.

"No, you don't!" Ishmail cried. But it was too late. Susan felt a brush of air against her cheek, and the next moment the plate-glass window behind her smashed. The footprints had jumped onto a booth; that was the last anyone saw. Ishmail grabbed her arm and pulled her away. He seemed put out but not angry. A game was a game.

She decided not to mention that the strange man who left tracks in the snow had become visible, just for a split second, when he was about to leap through the window. He looked at her with sad, imploring eyes. Her heart had missed a beat. On the other hand, it could have been her imagination.

Char was waiting for him on the street. He ran up looking excited and damp, brushing off the shoulders of his parka. "Success?" she asked.

"Success. I got her to pay attention, and she definitely saw me. We talked." Looking over his shoulder, Michael pulled Char away from the scene quickly. "That's his limo. Better not tempt fate."

She had only a vague notion of what he was talking about, but she followed. "Are we going to take her with us?"

"That's a very good question," said Michael. "I'm not sure I know the answer."

"That's not promising," said Char. "You said she was part of the equation."

"I did say that, and I believe it. But she doesn't know anything other than what he's feeding her. She's like the rest of them—only not entirely."

"Because she saw you?" asked Char.

"That's just one clue. The other is that he's so anxious to keep an eye on her. That's been true since the first day. I don't know if he's using her to get close to me, or something else. It's part of the game."

"That's what you're calling it now?"

"For want of a better term." Michael slowed down as they rounded the corner and headed down Spring Street. He had had a fright in the tavern, but the fact that he had eluded Ishmail made him elated. It showed that he had some moves of his own; he wasn't up against a superman who was just toying with him. Something serious was afoot, and Ishmail was taking it seriously too.

At that moment a black woman pushing a stroller bumped into Char. "My fault," she said. "I wasn't lookin'. You all right, sugar?"

An hour earlier, this would have been an astounding event, and as it was, Char yelped. The black woman looked up from her baby. "Don' tell me I hurt you?" she said.

"No." Char shook her head.

A second black woman walked out of a store and approached. "I couldn't resist goin' in there, Betty. They had the most—" She stopped short. "Are you talkin' to somebody?"

"Huh?" The first woman looked at her friend. "Of course I am. I had a little accident with this girl here."

"Maybe you been drinkin' too much formula," her friend said. "It's normal to be peculiar when you has a baby, but you're pushin' it."

"Listen to me, lady, we need to have you come with us," Char said excitedly.

"What, go with you and that man over there?" the woman said. "No way."

"Now who are you talkin' to?" her friend demanded.

The woman was getting hot. "Let me be! Can't you see these people?" In total exasperation she began to walk away. Char kept up with her on one side and her friend on the other.

"No one sees us but you," Char pleaded.

"I'm beginning to get that," the woman said. "You're figmenting my imagination, so just get along with you."

Her friend was irate now. "Who are you tellin' to go away? I'm takin' you straight to the hospital unless you quit weirdin' me out."

"Don't listen to her," Char implored. She turned back toward Michael, who had hung back watching. "Can't you help me here?"

He shook his head. "When you're doing such a bang-up job?"

At this point chaos saw its chance. The first woman yelled, "Get outta my face, both of you!" while her friend, deciding that the baby was unsafe with a lunatic mother, tried to grab the baby carriage from her hands. She bumped into Char, almost falling down, which set her screaming, "Oh, my God!" like a demon possessed, which was what she thought in fact was happening.

Michael rushed in just as the two friends, now former friends, started swinging with their handbags. The whole situation was bizarre and amusing at the same time, but he managed to pull Char into the nearest open door. They stood behind the racks of a dress shop, peering out the front window as the two women continued their battle royal.

"What did you do that for?" Char demanded. "You should've helped me. We've been looking for days for someone like that."

Michael shook his head. "Call it a hunch. We're better off this way, by ourselves."

"Why? Yesterday you said—"

Michael pointed around the store, where several customers were pawing through the racks, paying no notice to him and the girl. "See, nothing's really changed. Most people, ninety-nine out of a hundred, can't see us."

"But somebody just did. Isn't that important?"

"Yeah, it is. Let's get out of here. We can finish this outside." He pushed the unconvinced Char out the door, back onto the sidewalk. The two women, who were now tugging at both ends of a screaming baby, paid no attention.

Half a block later Michael said, "You know what it's like not to fit in?"

"I have a pretty damn good idea," Char said crossly.

"Well, nobody fits in perfectly, ever. Everyone has a feeling of not belonging. If that feeling is strong enough, you actually stop fitting in. You might turn into a loner or a dissident, or else a madman or a genius. Some of these extreme people who don't fit in we call saints, but some are psychopaths. That's true in the normal world, and it's true here."

"So shouldn't we round up everybody who doesn't fit?"

"It would take forever, and we don't even know who we'd get. We could wind up with crazies and malcontents—just because you're a misfit doesn't mean you don't belong here."

"Great, that clears everything up."

"I know it's confusing, I know." Michael paused to think. "You see, we only need to gather a very small set of people, the ones who are like us."

His mind was forming something like a plan, but it was very slow in coming. As they walked, he started looking around more carefully. "See that man over there, the one with the dog? He glanced at us for a split second. I hadn't noticed that before, but I think there's a lot more like him." Michael was right. In the next few blocks a small sprinkling of passersby either looked their way or seemed to acknowledge their presence, if only by swerving slightly on the sidewalk to avoid a collision. No one made full eye contact, but now they knew they weren't just ghosts.

"This is really strange," Char said.

"Right, it's like being real to some people, half-real to others, and totally unreal to almost everybody else. But it's our way out."

"It is?"

"Yeah, because this is like competing movies. Everyone at first seemed to accept Ishmail's movie, just as they accept normal reality without a question. They don't know a big secret: There is no normal reality. All kinds of worlds are always competing around us—which means we can choose which movie to be in. It's our own movie, in fact, a script we're always writing, if only we knew it."

"You sound like you know what to do next," Char said, visibly impressed.

"Almost. We have to see a man about the end of the world."

With a little maneuvering they shanghaied a cab by slipping past an older woman as she slowly exited. It was going uptown, and Michael waited silently until they came to a red light in the mid-fifties.

"Come on," he said, jerking open the door and pulling Char out. The cabbie's head whipped around, but they didn't stop to check how much he'd noticed. The closest network building was on Sixth, which they made in five minutes; then it was another ten to slip past security—now armed after the rioting and the storms—and onto an express elevator which opened onto the national news floor.

Michael looked around. The floor was divided into two major sections. All along the left was the control room, staffed by directors and technicians at banks of monitors. They were visible behind plate glass; this was the national feed for network news—looking through the control room, one could see the set, now empty, from which the broadcasts came. On the right side of the floor were offices for the floor producers and managing executives.

"Char, I need you to do something for me," said Michael. "When I give you the signal, open the door and walk into that control room, and don't come out until I tell you to."

"Okay, but do I do anything?" she asked.

"Yeah, push every button in sight, and keep pushing for as long as you can."

"What for? What if somebody sees me?"

"I don't think anyone's going to. No one's noticed us so far. Anyway, this is a high-pressure place. If somebody was a misfit, they'd have been out of here already."

Char nodded, excited by the prospect of creating havoc, if not totally reassured about her safety. She placed herself beside the control room door. Michael walked the line of producers' offices until he found the one he wanted. He turned and held up his hand. "Remember, if someone gets too close to catching you," he said, "run for the elevator—I'll find you outside. Let's go."

He gave the signal. Char burst through the door and immediately headed for the big monitor board where the national feed came from. She started punching buttons as fast as she could reach them. At first nothing happened. Michael could see quizzical heads turning as the technicians noticed haywire readings on their boards. Ten seconds later, she hit pay dirt. The monitors began to go dark, switch to old stock footage, and roll crazily through looped commercials. The plate glass muffled the sound of a dozen directors shouting through their head mikes. A minute later the room was bedlam as Char, warming up to her work, jumped onto a main console and began stamping on one rank of controls after another. She looked up and grinned at Michael through the glass.

At that moment the other side of the floor erupted in loud confusion. Fifty phones rang at once as producers and assistants streamed out of their offices. "Get in there! I don't care what you have to do!" . . . "Jerry, kill the feed—don't think, just do what I goddamn say!" . . . "I just saw a two-million-dollar account get erased." . . . "Jesus!"

Michael paused long enough to make sure that no one had spotted Char, then he swung open the door marked with Nigel's name. It was a huge executive producer's office, and in the middle Nigel was on his feet, shrieking into two telephones at once. "I don't goddamn care how it started, get the effin' feed going in thirty seconds or I'm grinding your ass into hamburger."

"Hello, Nigel," Michael said. "Did I come at a bad time?"

Nigel's eyes were already starting out of his head with apoplectic rage; now they found another centimeter to bulge. "Blimey!" he whispered hoarsely.

"I know you're the captain of any crisis," said Michael, "but you might want to hang up and talk to me, eh?"

Turning pale, Nigel slammed down the receivers and slumped into his chair. "What are you doing here?" he asked suspiciously.

"Ah-ah, naughty," Michael reproved. "Take your finger off the alarm button, and put your hands on top of the desk."

Nigel scowled and complied, his manner growing cooler as his eyes narrowed. "I don't take this as a friendly visit," he said.

Michael walked the length of the plush gray carpet and sat on the edge of a sleek leather ottoman amidst a "conversationally" placed group of furniture. "Why so startled? Did you get assurances that I'd been eliminated, or is your faith in him so unshakable that you thought he could take care of anything?"

Suddenly there was a loud pounding on the door. Nigel opened his mouth, then paused, staring nervously at Michael.

"You can tell them to go away. I've locked the door anyway, so security isn't going to bail you out for a while, not with this mess on their hands," Michael said.

Nigel punched a button on his intercom and asked not to be disturbed for any reason.

"Good," said Michael. "If you think it's surprising that I showed up here, I'm just as surprised that you can see me. I'm supposed to be a ghost, courtesy of your boss."

"Ghosts generally aren't insane," Nigel said sourly, containing his nerves.

"And messiahs aren't supposed to be this fickle. You hitched your wagon to a star, and now he's sort of shooting all over the place. Tricky," Michael said.

"He can do what he wants," said Nigel curtly.

"Oh, but isn't that the problem? If he can do anything he wants, maybe the next thing he'll do is get rid of you—on a whim. That's got to be a scary thought."

Nigel had set his face into a stony mask, deciding to say nothing. Michael got up and walked closer.

"You're pretty self-motivated, we both know that," he said. "So it would be perfectly in character for you to make some contingency plans. Am I getting warm?" Nigel looked away, scowling deeper. "What did you have in mind?" Michael continued. "I'm sure you stole enough money to bribe an army. But if you thought about escaping on a private jet in the middle of the night, that fantasy didn't last long. This is his world; he's got rat detectors in every corner. So there's nowhere to run. Of course, another five minutes of this hellacious scramble on the nation's airways, and you'll need somewhere to run."

Nigel's eyes widened. "You're doing this!" he almost shouted, rising to his feet.

"Calm down. We're talking about you, and you have to pay attention. I don't know what your parachute out of here was going to be—maybe you've arrived at the stage of considering a faked suicide or a convenient murder—but your thinking has been too crude. You see, he knows you're not fully on board anymore, just as he knows I'm here this minute."

Nigel couldn't tell whether he was being bluffed or not, but his face went gray with terror.

"He's turned into a monster," he whispered. "You've got to help me."

"I am helping you," Michael said, softening the threat in his voice. "This scramble I've arranged is the best I can do to distract him. Now we come to part B: What to do about the savior who won't go away?"

"I don't think he can be killed," Nigel said—his voice was conspiratorial but still very frightened.

"Agreed. Even if he could be killed, it would turn out to be temporary. In case you haven't noticed, his kind can shift scenes anytime they want. They have their ways of jumping through time and eluding any trap we might devise."

Nigel looked startled. "What do you mean by 'they'? There's more than one of him?"

"In a way. You could say that any one of us has the potential to be like him. This is about making people believe your version of reality. That's his power, and he's very convincing at using it."

There was more pounding at the door now, and angry male voices could be heard shouting muffled orders on the other side. Nigel jumped up like prey in the sights of its predator.

"They're coming in," he croaked. "What are we going to do?"

"You'll be surprised," said Michael dryly. At that

moment there was a blast of gunfire. The *bing!* of bullets against metal stung their ears as the doorknob was blown off. Three high-security policemen forced their way in, guns leveled at Nigel from behind their shields.

"It's him! He held me hostage!" Nigel shrieked.

The cops moved in, not lowering their weapons. "Where is he?" the lead officer demanded.

Nigel pointed to where Michael stood, six feet to the officer's left. "Right there, get him! What's stopping you?"

The officer raised the bulletproof visor on his helmet. "What are you talking about?"

"Put your guns down, for God's sake," Nigel exclaimed.

The lead officer barked an order. "If that's better, sir, can you tell us what's going on here? Why were you locked in?"

"You idiots, because he—" Seeing the suspicious disbelief in their eyes, Nigel stopped. "You're wasting your time here. There's mass chaos on the network lines. Why aren't you looking after that?" He was beginning to resume a shred of his authority. The lead officer continued to stare hard at him.

"We emptied the control room of all personnel, but it's not doing much good. We got orders that the sabotage is being controlled remotely," he said.

"So you thought it came from in here? That's crazy!" Nigel shouted.

The policeman in line behind the lead man had been checking the room out. "I don't see anything like the kind of equipment he'd need, Lieutenant. If it's him, he'd have to be giving orders to a confederate outside the building."

"Is that true, sir?" the lead officer asked in a stony tone.

"No, of course not." Nigel was deeply agitated now, looking desperately back and forth between the policeman and Michael.

"Keep looking at me, sir, if you don't mind," the officer said. "We're going to put a man in front of your office here for protective custody. That means you shouldn't leave until I give you permission."

Nigel could hardly find words. "You're arresting me?"

"It's just security, sir. We'll be back."

"But who gave you this kind of authority?" Nigel protested.

"Who do you think?" Michael interrupted. Nigel's head swiveled in his direction, amazed that no one could hear him. The three cops left the room silently. After the door was shut, one could hear a heavy object, probably a desk, being shoved into place on the other side.

Nigel sank his head into his hands, repeating, "My God, my God," in a weak moan.

"I told you I was surprised you could see me," Michael said. "It's your best feature, actually."

"Shut up," Nigel snapped. "He's going to kill us."

Michael walked over and crouched down so that he could look Nigel in the eye. "Believe me, I can save you."

"How? I don't think the insanity defense works too well this week."

"I like that. Gallows humor is your next-best quality. Listen, Nigel, as powerful as Ishmail is, he can't control those who renounce him. That's why you could see me—you were already a defector, only you were trying to hide it."

"And I was jolly successful, wasn't I, judging by those cops bursting in?" Nigel remarked bitterly.

"Forget your own hide for just a second, okay?" Michael insisted. "The fact is, if we can find enough of us who don't fit in, we might be able to outmaneuver him. That's our only chance. You can't hide anymore; you're going to have to come with me."

Nigel pointed at the door. "How do we get through that?"

"Fairy dust. You didn't happen to steal some of that while you were at it, did you?"

The game of wreck-the-network was going well. Char danced her way from coast to coast, and the havoc she was wreaking caught the country off guard. Cities were primed for panic by the Prophet's recent rampages.

"Hippity hop, hippity hop." She'd forgotten exactly how to play hopscotch—not that she had the right numbered squares—so she had to content herself with pretending to be a bunny. It didn't take much to trigger mass exodus from many urban areas, along with a garnish of looting and street crime.

Char caught scenes of outbreak whenever she randomly hit a button that brought in the local news crews rushing from emergency to emergency in Los Angeles, Miami, or wherever. An eerie silence prevailed in the control room after it was evacuated and sealed off. When Char saw the SWAT team enter in full battle armor, she was afraid that they might seal off the door.

"That's enough good for one day," she said. "Time to egress."

She carefully inched the door open when she thought no one was looking and slipped onto the main studio floor. The area was too crowded; she couldn't get past the milling people unless she hugged the wall, and even then her progress was slow. Michael had told her to take the elevator and meet him outside—she wondered if the police might not have shut down the elevators, though.

Char glanced back at the door Michael had gone through; it worried her that two cops had barricaded it with an overturned metal desk and were now standing guard.

He'll kill me, but I'm gonna stay, she thought.

Suddenly the scene changed abruptly. As if at the snap of a finger, the room grew quiet, and people stopped shuffling nervously. They turned their eyes toward Nigel's door, which now was unobstructed. Char had been watching, and the two SWAT cops didn't move the desk away. It simply wasn't there anymore. No one seem disturbed by this.

A second later Nigel emerged from his office. Char took a sharp breath, because Michael was with him.

"I have an announcement to make," Nigel said, clearing his throat. He seemed nervous, but as he spoke, his confidence steadily returned. "I believe we can attribute this recent blackout, which lasted— how long did it last, engineer?"

A uniformed technician stepped forward with a walkie-talkie at her ear. "Best information I can get is thirty seconds, sir."

"Right," said Nigel. "An East Coast electrical failure of approximately half a minute resulted in brief dead air. Am I correct in assuming that it didn't spread throughout the country?"

The man with the walkie-talkie nodded. "No major disruptions east of the Hudson."

A few heads swiveled toward the control room. All the monitors were tuned to regular programming, and the directors were all in place.

"Very good," said Nigel. "I'd like to thank security for checking on us, but we seem to have survived the storm." He gestured toward two uniformed guards; no outside police were present in the room.

"What's going on?" Char said, confused. No one nearby looked her way. Michael lifted a finger to his lips. She must have gotten through to Nigel, however, because his glance darted nervously at her.

"As long as we happen to be gathered here," Nigel said, raising his voice, "I have another important announcement. It comes directly from that extraordinary person I am honored to call a friend."

There was a buzz in the room. As Nigel kept speaking, Michael wove through the crowd. "Time to go," he said to Char. "We're on a tight schedule. You did great, by the way." He took her arm and led her toward the elevators.

"What do you mean? It doesn't seem I did anything—it's all been wiped out," she protested.

"No, it was perfect," said Michael, pressing the buttons. "I had to take a chance that I could get Nigel around to our side. Then it was easy to start planting my version of things."

"I don't really get that, but okay. So what's he saying now?" asked Char. She looked back over her shoulder.

"At noon tomorrow, before a mass audience tuning in from all four corners of the world," Nigel was saying, "we will see the most stupendous spiritual feat in human history. If anyone accuses us of hype, tell them to hold still and wait. Oh, and commercial rates will triple for the hour preceding and afterwards."

The elevator doors had opened, and they stepped inside. "What's he talking about?" Char wanted to know. "If Ishmail's who he appears to be, he's going to get down here in two seconds and murder that guy."

"No, I don't think so," said Michael as the elevator started its descent.

"Why not?"

"Because I'm going to throw myself in front of a moving freight train."

"Really? And what am I going to do, hold your jacket?"

"No, you're going to be dialing for rabbis."

CHAPTER ELEVEN

ASCENSION

S he felt utterly empty.

Susan didn't understand why that should be. She had a perfect life, a perfect job—administrator of a major metropolitan museum—a perfect husband. That she could still feel this way frightened her. It was as if she wasn't in control of her life, and Susan had always prided herself on her self-control.

Count your blessings. Ishmail has given you everything you ever wanted, everything money can buy.

The thoughts in her head were like piped-in propaganda. Susan frowned, feeling the first sparks of a migraine. She picked up the sterling silver hairbrush from the dressing table and began brushing out her hair. *One, two, three . . .* She hadn't counted the strokes since her mother did it for her as a child, but now she regressed, hoping it would make her calmer.

Through the French windows of her dressing room she could look down into the street. It was quiet; her husband had diverted the traffic for her sake. Thoughtful.

The emptiness began to form an impulse, a struggling memory that was all her emptiness could feel. She wasn't always sure what this lack was, but she knew it was there, even when there were no words to describe it. *You have everything.* Do I have love? The propaganda voice laughed. Hadn't Ishmail told her she did? *Seven, eight, nine.* Maybe that wasn't the missing key—she couldn't be sure.

Susan shook her head, staring at her reflection in the mirror. Joy, faith, hope—those keys were also misplaced, and locked compartments remained. Her husband had said that the only things that mattered were things you could see and touch and taste. Real things, not phantom states of mind, invented by the disadvantaged to excuse their losses. Love was a convenient alliance, joy was a reaction to novelty, faith kept fools in their place. If she wasn't happy with all of this, she needed to face reality.

She was used to acting like Ishmail's idea of a human being. Still, her mind could not bridge that gap, that peculiar void inside her. She put her hand to her head, feeling the migraine stamp it with spiked heels.

Someone was banging at the door.

Susan looked worried. Her husband was working in his study. It was urgent that he not be disturbed. She went over to the window and peered out. There was a man in the street banging on the door. His light brown hair gleamed in the light from the street lamp. She pulled her head back in and drew the heavy curtains. But the pounding grew louder and more insistent. No one ever did that, or if they tried, they would never do it twice. No, she shouldn't even consider such things.

"Come out here! Come out and fight!" The lunatic's shouting seemed to penetrate through the walls. Susan quickly pulled on her robe. She didn't care if the man downstairs was a lunatic—she had to make him stop.

Before Ishmail noticed.

The door opened in Michael's face. Susan stared at him in startled surprise. She was dressed for bed, wearing a flowing, movie-glamorous nightgown and peignoir. Her hair stood around her head in a golden aureole; she looked like a pretty doll, unfeeling and compliant. He wasn't even certain this was the same woman he'd had to abandon in the diner.

"Do you know me now?" he asked. "I'm Michael. I said I'd come back for you."

"What?" The sheer disbelief in her voice was almost enough to make him doubt himself.

"Let me in. You know me." She bit her lip nervously, looking over her shoulder, but after a moment she reluctantly stepped aside. The house had the lifeless overmanicured look of a museum, a place where life was preserved, not where it was lived. The foyer was two stories high, lined with suits of armor and moth-eaten tapestries, which made it seem even more like a dead husk.

"You don't have to say anything," Michael said in a low voice. "You don't have to believe in me, Susan. I know how you feel right now. I can see it in your eyes." She was just waiting to die, hoping it wouldn't hurt too much. Other than that, there was only the tiredness that is the aftermath of long fear.

At the end of the hallway there were a set of double doors that opened into the library. Michael followed her into a massive baronial chamber where a roaring fire leaped in the fireplace.

"Is he gone?" Michael asked. Susan's face cleared, and she nodded—Michael had the uneasy feeling that this was true only because he'd just said it was.

"Can I tell him you called?" said Susan dully.

"No," Michael said. "I think you'd better not. In fact I think you'd better come with me now, and we'll find some safe place for you."

"Why? I'm already safe," Susan said. She still didn't seem frightened of this stranger, only curious. Michael's instincts told him this might be some subtle trap. If he frightened her, would something unpredictable happen?

"Look around," Michael said gently. "You're living in a perfect world here, but the past changes from moment to moment, doesn't it? You can't remember when you met your husband, or when he proposed, or even what your wedding was like—but that can't be helped. Everybody's got to make a few sacrifices, don't they?"

"Please," Susan pleaded, the first trace of doubt showing in her eyes.

"Maybe you think you're still in charge of your life, but he's been playing on deeper fears. You're afraid that you're not good enough or strong enough. You're afraid of the future and the randomness of things that could hurt you. Everyone's got these fears, but it doesn't work to give him your power. You've got to write your own story, whether you're afraid or not."

He could see in her eyes that she recognized something in his words—perhaps it was the echo of Yousef's plea, the one she had ignored. She looked around nervously. "My husband, I should—"

Michael risked taking her by the shoulders. "Don't think about him. It's a sham. Just look out the window." He pointed to a waiting taxi at the curb. "Don't pack. Just go with me. I'm not going to use any kind of force; you can ask the driver to let you off anywhere or to take you back here."

"What are you trying to prove?" asked Susan, perplexed.

"I want to pit my version of things against his. Surely you're a free woman, you can leave this house whenever you wish, right? Let's see how he reacts to one little ride, okay?"

Michael knew that more than his coaxing had to work. He hadn't tried to convince Nigel but had simply guided a different reality around him, pulling the Englishman out of Ishmail's influence. But he wasn't going to manipulate Susan. She had to make the choices that would affect her whole future life. If she wanted to stay here, she'd have to say so, and then he could cross the next bridge. Did he even have the power to undo what Ishmail had made?

"All right," said Susan. "I know you're wrong. My husband doesn't hold me prisoner. He won't care if I go out." She turned to go back upstairs.

"Wait," said Michael. "We're only going to be gone fifteen minutes. You don't have to tell anyone."

She paused, a look of troubled uncertainty on her face. Finally, she followed him outside.

The taxi was still there. Its headlights cut through the fog that was curling in from the ends of the street. The driver, one of the countless immigrant Nigerians who took up the job, got out to open the door. Michael stood on the steps with Susan. She was trembling.

"I'm cold," she said. "I need my coat."

"You've made it this far," Michael urged. "You don't know how big a step this is." He imagined that some curtains had parted upstairs and someone was looking down. But he ignored the prickles on the back of his head. "Keep going."

Something inside her gained resolve. Without another excuse she walked down the steps and got into the cab.

"Where we goin'?" the cabbie asked Michael. He got back into the driver's seat, and suddenly Michael didn't like that grin.

"Wait, Susan. Open the door." Instead of walking over to his side, Michael tried to open her door. It was locked. At that moment the cab screeched away.

Someone is always listening.

"Come back!" The cab was accelerating but had to slow down to take the first corner at the end of the block. Michael ran after it.

"Susan, make him stop!"

It was useless to shout. He knew that a man couldn't outrun an automobile, but he had entered a continuum in which there were no limits—he took personal responsibility for the fact that there were no limits—and he ran after the speeding taxi, keeping his eyes fixed on it as he gained ground.

In a moment he was right with it, still running but as if watching himself in an action movie where speed is thrilling beyond any need to obey the laws of nature. He could dimly see Susan's face through the glass but not the expression on it. She was looking the other way. He grabbed the rear handle and wrenched at it, but the door was locked.

Look at me!

Michael banged on the glass with his free hand, running alongside the speeding vehicle. "Susan! Open the door!"

He could see no other cars or buildings now, so thick was the mist. The only way to gauge the taxi's speed was by the howl of the engine and the laboring of his body as he ran. Now the taxi speeded up, veering from side to side to throw him off. Michael was jerked back and forth, slamming hard against the side of the taxi. It hurt more than a dream should, but then the whole notion that he could be hanging on was absurd—this was a contest of wills, not physics.

There had to be some way to stop the car. Michael dug in his heels. The ground beneath his feet gave like hot tar as his shoes sank into it. Impossibly, the taxi slewed toward him, and Michael could feel the tiny pinging vibrations through the metal as the door hinges began to buckle. The taxi's engine whined. Its wheels spun against the asphalt as it was dragged to a stop. The howling engine gagged and fell silent—the taxi was only an inert piece of metal now, not a runaway demon. Michael collapsed against it, panting with effort.

The fog began to thin, and all around him he could see the brownstones of Gramercy Park. It was the same place where they had started. They hadn't gone anywhere, despite the fact that his shirt was soaked with sweat and his body totally exhausted.

Each time reality was set aside this way it could not help but disturb him. He knew that Ishmail had been counting on that. Michael looked down at his hand, still clutching the handle, and pulled open the door. With a tearing, squeaking sound the whole door popped free. He dropped it and flexed his cramped fingers.

"You can come out now." He looked inside the passenger compartment; Susan was there, shaken but unharmed. There was no driver up front.

"Where did he go?" Susan asked. She sounded jittery, tearful.

"It doesn't matter. I told you your husband would react," Michael said. "Why do you think he wanted to do this to you, or me, or both of us?"

She was stepping out now, looking astonished at where they had ended up. She said nothing.

"I can give you an answer," Michael went on. "He doesn't need a rational reason. He simply manipulates for the sake of manipulation. You don't matter to him; neither do I. He's being carried forward by sheer momentum—this is the power he can wield, so he simply does. If he ever had a cause, for good or bad, it was lost a long time ago."

She was listening carefully, uncertain what to do or say. Michael said, "You don't even know if you went on a ride or if there was a driver in the first place. I don't think that's the kind of thing you should be forced to live with—and it's happening on a grand scale, not just to you. So let's go."

He held his hand out, and after a brief hesitation, she took it. In the darkness he could see a faint smile play over her face.

"You're a very slippery creature," she said. "But here we are."

Michael tried to draw back, but her hand held him in a vise. Their clasp was caught in the beam of the taxi's headlights. Michael's hand looked normal, but hers was translucent, and inside its pink flesh he was horrified to see that the bones were moving, tightening like claws over him.

"Don't struggle; it'll only get worse," said Susan.

Michael gasped with pain. "Why are you pulling this, Ishmail? I thought even you had standards for cheap tricks."

The Susan-creature's voice changed, faintly disclosing the ironic tone of the Prophet's. "No tricks. It's just time you got your next lesson. You've become convinced that I deal in dreams and mirages. But how does this feel?" He squeezed harder, and Michael nearly passed out, groaning from the pain that shot through his fingers and wrist.

"See? It's as real as it gets. You've been quibbling too much, friend. You want to have layers of real reality and unreal reality; you want to rule your dreams and play the victim when you're awake. That's typical. Your grudge against me is emotional, childish. You know what you really hate?"

"No, why don't you tell me?" Michael said defiantly. But his worst nightmare, that he had no power against the Prophet's will, was coming true. And if he couldn't stop the Prophet, no one could. He reached deep inside himself for the strength to go on. The words he needed came to him. "Tell me what I feel."

"You can't stand the idea of being here. You're too good for the real world, and yet you've convinced yourself that you're also helpless to change anything. So what happens? You leave a power vacuum, and somebody naturally comes in to fill it. That's me. My only crime is that I'm the only real person you've ever met. I take control. I exert power. I play with all the toys you left behind, and it's not my fault that you want them back."

At the point where Michael's fingers might have cracked, Ishmail let go. He stood back, regarding the man who was bent over before him, doing everything not to show his fear and pain. "So, what do you say?" Ishmail asked.

"To what?" Michael moaned.

"That." Ishmail was pointing to the door of his house. A second Susan had appeared there. She was looking toward them but without seeing.

"She expects you home any minute. You're late, and she tends to worry," said Ishmail. "Don't you think you should go to her?"

The other Susan stood there, searching up and down the street. Her expression was worried, but more than that, he could see that she wasn't the pawn of someone else. It was really her, as close to the woman he'd known as anyone could be—he could feel it.

"Go to hell," Michael said. "She's a shell, and I'll turn into one if I deal with you."

"You're wrong there," Ishmail corrected. "You keep trying to decide what's real and what's not. They've infected you, these new friends of yours. You want to know the truth? Everything's real, and nothing's real enough. Accept it."

"So why do I have to be tortured by you?"

"I think you know why. I'm like your tar baby. You find me sticky, you won't let go. Maybe you love me. Millions do. Yet you keep blaming me for holding on to you. It's just the other way around. I'm the one showing you the way out—take it."

Michael felt the pain withdrawing from his hand—he assumed the Prophet was causing that, too, as part of his incentive program. Despite his rage and fear, Michael had enough clear reasoning to take in Ishmail's message—and it was hard to contradict. Who had become obsessed about the real and the unreal? Who had taken on an evil double to fulfill some deep, stubborn fantasy? Who was driven by fear of his own weakness?

"But you'll still be out here, won't you?" Michael asked.

"Who cares?" Ishmail shot back quickly. "All you have to do is walk through that door, and you'll have everything back. How much easier can it get?"

"You mean, how much harder, don't you?" Michael looked toward the door. Susan was framed in the light that shone from inside the house. Across that threshold lay certainty, and sanity, and everything else he desperately wanted. Love. Absolution.

"Michael?" Susan called, and there was a note of the old acerbic affection in her voice. "For God's sake, what are you doing out there in the cold? Come on in the house."

"I can't," he said, and his yearning was as much for Ishmail's sake as for his own.

Nothing changed for a second. Susan should have stepped back in from the cold, or at least made a move. But she held her place like a professional actor on cue, or like a prop. Did it matter?

"What do you get out of this?" Michael asked. "You seem to be offering me a deal, but why?"

"I want to live in a world that proves, everywhere I look, that I'm right. You can't conceive of where I've been and what I've experienced. I've even been to heaven, and they didn't throw me out. I left, telling them to call me if they ever want new management. You can't imagine how boring angels are—they can't even talk, they just smile. I've had enough. I just want the peace I can make for myself," said Ishmail.

Michael faced him. "Too bad you can't have it. Because you know that you're lying. You'll never make peace. Whatever you create gets spoiled. You think I'm stuck on you? It's just the opposite. I'm the kind of misfit who won't go away, me and many others. We sniff you out every time. It must be infuriating. You get things going exactly like you want, you weave a picture that absolutely millions buy into, and then, like the smallest speck on a new blue suit, there's this irritating blemish. Why won't it go away? No matter what you do, there's always a catch."

"You're stepping on dangerous ground," Ishmail warned. Michael looked over the Prophet's shoulder. The other Susan had disappeared; the door to the house was shut.

"You've reeled the bait back in," Michael remarked. "But you had to, didn't you? It's all hollow."

"I can kill you, don't forget that," Ishmail said. "I don't need to see you for that." His light irony had given way to menace. There was a crackling in the sky, and suddenly a bolt of the killing light that had devastated Wadi ar Ratqah and Jerusalem slid out of the sky. Michael felt the hair stand up on the back of his neck. His nose prickled and his mouth went dry; there was a sensation of weight and resistance, as if he were drowning in dry water.

"If you think pain is convincing," said Ishmail, "you've forgotten about dying. It's such a laugh. You all pray, 'Oh, God, I don't want to die.' But you do, you know. You can't kick the habit."

It was hard to resist the panic Michael's body felt at the sight of the light, which wavered in a searching pattern, as if sniffing him out. He found himself breathing hard; a weight was crushing his chest. "You think you can force me to die?" he struggled to say. "Allow me."

Using every ounce of effort, Michael took a heavy

step toward the shaft of blue-white radiance, then another. It stopped searching for him and seemed content to wait. He wasn't looking back at Ishmail now. Ahead the burning light was scorching the grass edging the sidewalk.

"No, don't!" He knew without looking that it was Susan's voice. She was beside him now, deep distress in her face. "He let me go, you've won. All we have to do is get out of here. Don't do this!"

Michael shook his head. The light was five feet ahead of him now; he could feel his legs rebelling, wanting to run from what would happen to his flesh. Susan took his arm and tried to whirl him around.

"Look, Michael, he's gone. You called his bluff, and he had no choice."

For the second time Michael said, "And what do you get out of this?"

"You're being cruel. I love you, I want you to save yourself. Isn't that what you just said to me?"

"I don't know, were you there? Are you anywhere?"

Pushing her aside, he took the last step into the light. Before his foot touched it, he heard Susan wail with pain and loss. His ears were filled with the same humming sound he'd heard at the Western Wall. He stepped fully in, letting the radiance cover his body. . . .

Now he knew how they felt, all those people who had been enticed in. The feeling of coolness against his skin began as a soothing touch, then it seemed to penetrate, and his body absorbed its liquid, flowing luminousness. Delicious, fragrant light, comforting light full of words and memories. Caressing, longing, remote, remembering, intense, forgiving, nourishing, flexible, all-knowing light, the light of every promise that there was peace after conflict, sleep after struggle, paradise after pain. Now he could feel it all, just as they had.

The change didn't start for a while. Michael allowed himself to laugh and dance. Looking beyond the circle of blue-white, he couldn't see either Ishmail or Susan. An exalting selfishness overtook him. *It's all for me.* In that one phrase was the most wonderful thing of all—he deserved all of this beauty and richness. No one could enter with him, which meant no one could defile it. Only then did the faintest shadow fall over his mind. He looked away, wanting the delirious feeling never to end. But the shadow dogged his thought.

All for you? You don't deserve it. You're not ready.

Yes, I am, he thought anxiously. But the light knew better. The instant the shadow appeared, he felt different. The cooling radiance started to get warm, and deep inside he felt a new energy rising. It held guilt and sorrow, and all the painful things that the light was supposed to destroy. Only it didn't. It was like an X-ray of his soul. He saw himself in the guise of a thousand sinners; he saw his own violence and the hatred he felt against enemies who would hurt him. The shadow moved into formless blobs, like the black spots that had appeared on the sun. There was burning in him now, both in and out. He began to sweat.

Now is when they die.

The horrible pain wouldn't stop rising. He saw how much he didn't deserve heavenly bliss, how ignorantly he had thrown his fists or guns or spears into the violent dance. The torture he had been running from all his life lived within. His own voice judged against him and would never forgive.

Michael had the impulse to pray, or at least cry out with the anguish he had been hiding for so long. What did it matter? Maybe the light came from God, and he was meant to perish like the others.

"I found him, Michael—look!"

With blurred eyes he could see Char. She was standing at the edge of the light. Someone else was there, someone much harder to make out. Michael reached his hand toward her.

Pull me out.

"Well, the old sayings still apply: No good deed goes unpunished." Char's voice sounded very knowing, undisturbed by concern. "It's much harder to save the good than the evil. What can you do?"

Stop laughing at me! Get me out!

He never found out if his panic would have been the last stroke that killed him. His final glimpse of Char was strange—her smile hung in the air like the Cheshire cat's, then slowly the other one, the cloudy figure next to her, began to merge with her body. A strong arm reached into the light and pulled him free. Michael lay on the ground, still sweating, waiting for the inner torment to wane.

A bearded face leaned over him curiously. "What if I told you that you're still in my study room? That would be a joke, *nu*?"

Solomon?

"Yeah," Michael gasped. "Quite a joke."

"Don't worry, you're not ready for that. But you asked me for a rabbi. We assumed that was another message. As it happens, I was already the rabbi. How lucky is that, I'm asking you?"

Michael was almost able to sit up; Solomon helped him. "You mean that runaway girl was a disguise?" Michael said, just coming out of his daze. "She almost cried when she took me to her empty house. Why did you make me go through this?"

"You wanted us to intervene. Well, we can only do one thing besides watch—we can make someone wake up a little faster, just a little. You were ready, so we came."

"So that's it? Once I wake up, all I do after that is watch?" Solomon nodded. "What if that's not good enough?" Michael challenged. "Hasn't anyone ever changed the rules?"

"No, never."

Michael looked around. The killing light was gone, and so was the city block and the houses on it. "Wait, wait. I'm not going where you want me to go. Not yet."

Solomon frowned. "What do you mean?"

"This is the way to nowhere."

"You prefer unreality?"

"As a matter of fact . . ." Michael could stand up on his own now. "I'm not ready to leave. He's convinced too many people, he's made a mockery of miracles and healing. You say you help wake people up? He's the anesthesia that keeps them asleep. But there's got to be more of us he hasn't convinced. He's in his own invented hell, and he knows it. He'll never find the Light again. If that's not Satan, all the ingredients are in the fridge and the cookbook's open."

Solomon nodded. "I can't deny it, but—"

"No," said Michael. "I don't care what you're going to say. I've set a trap for him, and he's about to fall into it."

"What trap?"

"Wouldn't you like to wait and see?"

The old rabbi looked doubtful. "Are you going to disappoint me by doing too much good again?"

"Absolutely. Or are you egging me on?" asked Michael.

Solomon shrugged. "I'm old, but I know the only trap that you could possibly set for him."

"Right." Michael grinned. "We're going to sell him a cheap ticket out of hell."

They soared over the Hudson half a mile south of the bridge, then turned in a circle toward Newark. The helicopter made loud *thwap*ping noises, even back in the luxury passenger compartment.

"Why are we doing this? Tell me again."

"It's expected, and besides, it could be the biggest event ever." Nigel almost had to shout to be heard. "We can always turn back."

The Prophet waved a dismissive hand. "No, it's all right. But I don't like to be stage-managed. Do you understand?"

"Yes, sir," Nigel said contritely. He sat back, hoping they wouldn't have to talk anymore. The tension in the compartment was thick. It wasn't beyond Ishmail to crush him in some exceedingly unpleasant way.

Below them was a brown-green stretch of the Jersey meadows, looking surprisingly rural for a place in sight of the city. The helicopter pilot said something inaudible over the crackling intercom from the front cabin.

"I don't care where you set it down, just do it," Ishmail grumbled. He never did anything against his will, and Nigel knew that when the broadcast went out to the nation promising a stupendous event, the Prophet could have retaliated in force. It didn't happen. In some way that Nigel couldn't understand, the plan Michael had set into motion was rolling forward, as if everyone were taking their place according to an invisible script, or stepping into a web of unseen design.

Only it was still too early to say who was the spider and who the fly.

They touched down on the edge of the open space and stepped out of the craft. A black limo was waiting. Without a word Ishmail got in and slumped in the back seat. Nigel knew not to sit anywhere near him; he settled into one of the facing jump seats. They started off toward the far end of the field, some quarter of a mile away.

"I don't remember when this was planned," Ishmail said.

Nigel sent up a silent prayer, not so much for his soul as his skin. "We had orders to build a makeshift stadium just for this event."

"Whose orders?" The Prophet sounded suddenly suspicious.

"Presumably yours," said Nigel smoothly. Michael had told him it would come to this. He had said that liars are the easiest people to lie to, if you could keep your face on. Nigel thought his face was going to collapse into gray putty any minute.

Ishmail said nothing—a good sign, at least compared to killing Nigel with a red-hot poker or whatever he did to express irritation. (It was dawning on Nigel that he had an inescapable tabloid imagination.) They rode in silence for a moment, bumping along the dirt track that wound around the edge of the brown-green space.

Michael had told him what to say next. "People need to see signs. They're mostly simple, and unless you show them your divinity in some form they can recognize, you'll lose them eventually."

"What?" Ishmail said, scowling.

"I'm just talking about possibilities," Nigel explained nervously. "Even Christ showed who He was at Pentecost."

"You mean the Transfiguration, idiot. Don't tell me about things I could have stopped. It's irritating."

"Anyway, it's your own words I'm repeating, as best as I can."

This was the biggest lie yet. The Prophet seemed uncertain, the first sign Nigel had ever had that his power might not be absolute. Not that one sign did much good—who was there to really oppose him? Acting on faith wasn't Nigel's strong suit.

When the tinted rear window rolled down, Nigel looked out. What he saw was astounding: As he'd predicted, a full-scale stadium stage had been erected in the middle of the meadow, complete with massive speakers and an immense picture of Ishmail. Over it in two-story letters the workmen were finishing off the final touches of a billboard: ASCENSION. The last N was being hauled into place with a winch.

Ishmail looked impressed. "You saw to the details yourself?" he asked.

Nigel, who hadn't lifted a finger and could hardly believe what he saw, nodded. A crowd had already formed, huddling in groups around portable heaters. The weather was crisp and clear, warm for late November; the ground was hard but free of snow.

As they looked around, Ishmail became more comfortable. He approached the stage and mounted the steps. Several microphone stands were scattered in a wide arch from the center of the dais. Otherwise the wide wooden space was bare.

"I don't need mikes, you know that," said Ishmail. He barely moved his lips, but from forty feet away, standing at the bottom of the steps, the sound in Nigel's ear was so loud he almost cried out. Seeing his discomfort, the Prophet faintly smiled. "You've done well," he said. "I've had something like this in mind for a long time. So it doesn't matter that you've been lying to me all day. I work in mysterious ways."

"Where would you like me to be?" asked Nigel. "The camera crews will be arriving any minute." He knew that Ishmail despised trivial questions; he glared at Nigel and turned his back. So Michael had been right about that, too. He'd told Nigel to sneak into the middle of the technical crews, and then steal a truck and run anywhere he could. This was the only contingency against failure. Nigel didn't care—he would be quite happy to vote with his feet.

An hour later he had vanished. The swelling crowd had reached a size no one could count. Bodies stretched far beyond the quarter-mile field, and however packed in they were, a constant stream of new arrivals flowed in and got absorbed. Banks of cameras lined the edge of the stage, and enormous floodlights lit every corner—these were needed because the sun had begun to dim by the moment, filled with new, larger black spots.

Ishmail stood to one side out of sight behind a screen, looking upward with satisfaction. The effect of the dark sun added to the mystery of the event. He reminded himself that he was a master of improvisation.

"Ready, sir."

He walked into view with total assurance, letting the roar of humanity wash over him. It had become his life now, accepting the adulation of millions, and if he couldn't get what he wanted, this was second-best. What he really wanted was God's apology for creating such ignorance and blindness in the world. An Almighty didn't have to allow evil to exist; He could have abolished death and made people loving and aware.

Ishmail, like all of them, was the victim of divine incompetence. At least he had the power to deal with it.

"My children," he intoned. He was using the trick of projecting his voice so that he seemed to be speaking confidentially in every ear. The frenzied shouts that had greeted him dwindled away.

"We come to a new stage. I meditated long on this day, wondering where to take you. I haven't done enough for you. True, I have calmed the tempest and the sea. I have brought peace among men. I have fed you, bathed you, loved you. Has anybody ever loved you more?"

There was no shouting in response, only a moaning, whimpering sound, as if the assembled multitude were begging for salvation.

"I came unto you because you are lost and abandoned. You are huddled on a chunk of rock tumbling through the cold void, and nobody cares. You wanted to be special, to be the chosen ones? You never had a chance."

Ishmail began dancing back and forth on the edge of the stage, only a few feet from the first row of people, who didn't dare reach out to touch. His face was glowing with excitement; his skin sparkled with sweat.

"I know now who is with me, and who is not. Today I will give you proof, because not everyone will leave this place. Some will ascend with me, others will be destroyed. Is that what you want?"

Stunned, the crowd milled in fear, but they were too packed together to escape. Cries of, "Yes, yes!" arose here and there.

"Then give me your power. Surrender yourselves to me, and I will use you to ascend to my Father and beg for your lives. Are you ready to do that? Do you need more proof? Then behold, I will take the first of you now."

He reached down, and yet no one could believe that he was beckoning them on stage, not at first. Then as he kept saying, "Come to me, come," they realized he was being literal. A handful of the bravest climbed up next to him on stage. As each arrived, Ishmail touched their heads with his healing hand. Its effect was immediate. The people cried out ecstatically and raised up their arms in paroxysms of joy. This sight encouraged others, and a second, larger wave moved forward.

"Feel my presence! This is my judgment!" Ishmail shouted.

He touched the next few worshipers, but this time something new and terrible happened. They cried out, too, but it was a cry of extreme pain, and then they collapsed motionless on the stage.

"I am loving, but I am fierce," said Ishmail. "This is the lesson you were brought here to learn."

Seeing what could happen, the closest newcomers tried to back away, but behind them thousands more were pushing to get near the Prophet. They screamed and begged, they crawled toward the stage on the ground. As they arrived, he dealt out their fates indiscriminately. A mother might writhe in joyous abandon, not noticing that her child had fallen down dead. The bodies quickly disappeared under the next surge.

"I summon you to love divine!"

The Prophet flung his arms up into the air. The black sun seemed to expand, to fill half the sky.

"What about you? What about you?" a new voice said. It was coming from one of the microphones on stage. Ishmail jerked his head around, wondering who would dare to interrupt him.

"Be quiet, this is a time for my presence," Ishmail said. He rushed forward with more energy, "saving" two or three people with each touch, sweeping down a row of them like a scythe through ripe wheat.

"I will not be quiet. You have summoned divine love, and I am here."

Seeing no source for this voice, the people on stage looked around in confusion. Ishmail grew angry.

"Who are you?" he shouted.

"Am I not the Father you summoned? I am well pleased with you, Ishmail. It is time you ascended."

"No!"

The Prophet's scream was so adamant that it swept the crowd like a shock wave. The forward surge of bodies came to a halt.

"What do you mean, my son? Is not your promise fulfilled?" the voice asked. Ishmail whirled around, knowing immediately that it was Michael, but unable to see him.

"You are not divine love," Ishmail shouted. "This is an impostor, a demon. Leave us, I command it!"

The crowd stirred uneasily. A moment of silence

followed, and everyone wondered if they were about to witness an exorcism or a battle.

"You see?" said Ishmail confidently to the nearest worshipers.

"No, they do not see," the disembodied voice interrupted. "I cannot leave. I love you too much."

Ishmail rushed to the closest microphones and knocked them over. A screeching noise made the crowd cringe and hold their ears. "Get out!" he screamed.

"Don't be afraid, my son. You have done enough. Your mission is fulfilled."

The voice seemed to emanate from behind the Prophet, who turned to find it. He swiped at the air with his hands, killing a few unfortunate bystanders. But there were too many people on stage; the voice could be anywhere among them.

"Let your Prophet go," the voice said. "Join me. Let him have his reward."

"I don't need a reward!" Ishmail shouted. But the mob, recovering from its hushed awe, began to believe the divine voice.

"Ascend . . . take the love . . . go!" As the voices mounted, Ishmail stared around himself venomously. Were they mocking him? Had they found the courage to turn on him, or was this their worship?

"Do not think of me," he said in a calmer, more controlled voice. "I ask for nothing."

"You do not need to ask. We give you your reward freely, of our own," the divine voice replied. Then a few of the nearest people parted, and Michael stepped forward. He tapped Ishmail on the shoulder, and he spun around.

"This is a sweet moment," Michael whispered in his ear. "Enjoy it."

Ishmail lunged, but Michael had stepped aside too quickly. His voice echoed from every speaker in the amphitheater above the sound of screams and shouts.

"People! Divine love doesn't show up in our lives like rain. It must be sought and won. The journey to joy is difficult, but it is possible. Believe me. How could love ever be found without such as Ishmail? Has he saved you? Give him your voices." Michael could begin to hear the crowd's support swell to a roar. "More!" he shouted. "Who has saved you?"

"Prophet, Prophet!"

As he received the full impact of the hysteria that he had called love, Ishmail became enraged. "Save them?" he jeered in a hoarse whisper to Michael. "They're fools. No one is going to do anything for them. They just want me. What's the alternative? Some lemon-fresh, enzyme-activated messiah, salvation in a pill, holy grace in a handy spray?"

"There is more to us than that," Michael said in the Prophet's ear. These words were broadcast to the crowd; he didn't have Ishmail's trick of turning his voice on and off. Michael summoned all the power he could find for the last act.

"He tells you he wants your power so he can save you. But if you have that power, why give it to him? Use it yourselves! He's lied to you, tricked you—look at the wreckage of his blessings. Does that look like love to you?"

There was no longer any trick of seeming to be the voice of God. Michael spoke directly from his soul.

"Do you want to see him go to heaven? Do you? Then let's send him," Michael shouted over the babble of the crowd. "Do you think he deserves to go?"

The crowd below didn't know how to respond. Some cried, "Yes," and some, "No." A few, who could see him, shouted for Michael to get off the stage. Others merely booed.

"I do. I think he should go to heaven, and I'm going to help him get there. I think he deserves it. I love what you were, Ishmail. I love what you could be. But you never really healed me. Now I'm asking you."

Michael held out his hand, stepping forward. He knew for the first time that he could be seen, wanted to be seen, by the Prophet.

Ishmail recoiled. "Stay away from me!"

"Come, Prophet," Michael coaxed. "It's time to make good on all those promises."

The black sun had dwindled and sparks of fire seemed to spray from the corona, each one brighter than the sun itself, each one a messenger. The sound of the wind sweetened, transforming itself into a chord, a choir, the sound of a thousand perfect voices singing as one.

"No!" Ishmail said. He closed his eyes tightly, covering his ears.

Tears came to Michael's eyes at the beauty in the sky. It wasn't happening because of his will, yet he felt merged with the will that made it happen. "What are you waiting for? This is what you said you wanted. Go," he whispered to Ishmail.

The crowd began to chant: "*Go, go, go . . .*"

The Prophet started to rise into the air, struggling in some invisible grasp. The merciless indifference of the television cameras, trained on him from four platforms around the rim of the stadium, showed everyone on Earth his face—it wasn't beatific.

"You're all afraid!" he shouted at the crowd.

"Give me your fear! Give me something I can use!"

Down below, the men and women encircled the stage, waiting. Above, Ishmail screamed silently and struggled in the arms of the angels, being pulled farther and farther into the sky until he could barely be seen.

"Go home," Michael said into the microphone. "Forget him. He used you, but the only reason you let him is because you thought you were abandoned. I know, I was one of you. But a truth was pulled from my despair. We are all God, a God with a million faces."

He tore off the microphone and tossed it away, then looked down at the ground, and the circle of men and women. Only one place was still empty.

"What took you so long?" Rakhel said, holding out her hand.

"Air traffic. It was unbelievable," said Michael, climbing down from the stage and taking it. The circle was complete.

Far above, the Prophet was a tiny dark speck, wreathed in angels—or were they a trick, the only illusion the thirty-six ever allowed themselves to perform? He ascended into the irresistible light that was pure to others and torment for him. The light was mirrored in the souls of the thirty-six, whoever they were.

Slowly it faded. Clouds gathered, and it began to rain, gently washing the scars of the Earth.

The stadium was almost empty.

Michael blinked, feeling as if he'd awakened from a long deep sleep. He gazed into the faces of those who stood beside him; then, slowly, they released each other's hands and began to walk away.

"Where are they going?" Michael asked Rakhel.

"Back to their lives. What? You think this is a full-time job with benefits?" Rakhel grumbled.

Suddenly all the Lamed Vov could be seen in their incredible diversity: black, white, young, old, male, female. And all of them looked upon him with love. Each was suffused with a blue-white radiance; each held within his or her hands a glorious blue-white lotus. Perfection. The human soul. The true image of the mind of God. And as Michael accepted this, the only reality behind all the masks and all the lifetimes of wearing masks, he felt something for the first time—he was one link in the eternal quest journeying toward the Light. In faith and hope Michael felt that certainty enter into him, changing him in the way that a child changes to become a man.

"You're catching flies," Rakhel remarked. He must have been gaping. The spell broke, and the ones walking away were people again.

"Are you a perfect thirty-six again with him gone?" asked Michael. "Or are you still interviewing?"

Rakhel waggled her finger. "We'll be in touch. Or maybe not. Who knows?"

She turned away and began walking slowly toward one of the exits in the rain. After a few steps she stopped and rummaged in her bag for a plastic rain hat, which she tied over her hair. In his mind, Michael heard something she'd said to him once. "Battle, murder, sudden death—Your mind cast everything in terms you understood. It's always been you who shaped the world, not him."

Now he accepted the truth. The running fight, the Prophet's attacks on him, the destruction in Jerusalem—he had expected horrors, and so they had been granted to him.

"It's no one's fault," Rakhel turned and said. "*Fault* means there's an 'us' and a 'them,' but there never was. There's just an everyone. There's no wrong way, Michael. It all leads to the right place in the end. As for what you did, I can't complain. A little strenuous, maybe a lot gaudy, but you'll learn."

"So we won?"

"We always win. The universe is made of Light. Nothing is made of anything else—eventually this is seen, and then all the troubles end."

She laughed, an old woman's earthy cackle. "But until it does, oy! Who would give up the drama? Not you."

"Does anyone ever give it up?" Michael asked. She laughed much louder.

Solomon had called them *watchers*, but it was an inadequate term, and Michael had misunderstood it. To say they were watchers implied that there were two things: the watcher and what was watched. But that wasn't true. There was only manifestation endlessly contemplating Herself in the silver mirror of Her creation. To watch was to be. That was what they did. They lived, each one of them, the best life they could, and as they did, the universe discovered itself in the mirror. In doing what they did, the Lamed Vov were the watching itself.

Nothing more.

Nothing less.

"Well, now," Rakhel said. "Let's see if there's another rabbit hole around here. I'm restless."

The rain stopped, and the sun began to peek through the clouds once more, gleaming on the clean pools of rainwater and the newly washed ground.

"Hey, Michael, chappie," Nigel called. "You

planning to stand out here in this cornfield all day?"

Michael turned around. The limousine, black and gleaming, was still sitting there, parked beside the ASCENSION sign that was tattered from the rain. Nigel was standing beside the car, shaking the uniform cap abandoned by the fleeing chauffeur.

"Just this once," he said, bowing his head.

"Okay, just this once, I accept," said Michael. The passenger door opened.

"Where is he?" Susan said. "Oh, good. I thought we'd lost you. This driver has very strange ideas how to get to the airport. Come on, we've got a plane to catch."

He climbed in, deciding this once to accept an unsolvable mystery as well. Wherever she had been, she was back.

"Well, no more messiahs and no more plagues from the sky. I feel pretty good," he said.

Susan looked puzzled. "Has it ever occurred to you that maybe you have a God complex?"

"No. Only God has time to play God," Michael said. "I was thinking out loud."

"So, where have you been?" she said. "I needed you."

"Not more than I needed you," Michael replied. "Where are we going?"

"Wherever our fancy takes us. Isn't that what we decided?" Susan smiled. Her eyes seemed to know something she wasn't revealing.

"I can hardly wait to get there," Michael said, and took her hand.